Rise of an Oligarch
The Way It Is: Book One

CARLITO SOFER & NIK KRASNO

NEPLOKHO PUBLISHING

LONDON

First published in Great Britain in 2014

By Neplokho Publishing

A CIP catalogue record of this book is available from the British Library.

ISBN 978-0-9930827-1-9

This is a work of fiction. Names, characters, businesses, organisations, countries, places, events and incidents either are the product of the authors' imagination or are used fictitiously. Any resemblance to actual persons, living or dead, corporations, organisations, entities, events, or locations is entirely coincidental. This book contains sexual themes, violence, objectionable language and behaviour. If you are UNDERAGE, easily offended, unable to discern the difference between fiction and reality, dislike the use of profanity, are uptight, or righteous to the point where reading this book may pose danger to your immortal soul, then you should immediately cease reading any further. The authors accept no responsibility for any thoughts you may form after reading this book. *Caveat emptor.*

To our wives, families and the benevolent people of Ukraine

1 Bullet in the Head

The impact whipped the head backwards, hurling the body to the ground. A man stood over the now motionless figure, waving his gun and looking in all directions, while the pretty blonde screamed in terror. The shooter squinted through the telescopic sight and studied where the bullet hit the target. Blood trickled from a wound just above the fallen man's right eye.

Commission number 27 was complete. He now had four minutes to disappear without a trace. He disassembled the Dragunov, checked that he'd pocketed his cigarette butts and water bottle, and exited the apartment. The client would be very happy.

Tel Aviv, 2013

As dawn approached, the first rays broke through the heavens, streaking the sky with purple and orange ribbons. A faint flickering of lights speckled the horizon, like fireflies fleeing the coming day, as the city began to wake from its slumber. Soon the sun would rise, and the cool breeze that blew from the northwest would carry the early morning scents of shakshouka, rugelach and morning pastries across the flat plains to the medical facility.

Reached via an unmarked turning off Highway 6 that swept around a vast orchard planted specifically to prevent prying eyes, the private hospital catered only for the wealthiest, most powerful clientele. Usually, at this unholy hour, the building was silent. The private rooms and patient areas lay in relative darkness, the staff areas dimmed to a soft blue hue and a small crew of essential staff saw to the patients' needs.

But today was different. The building blazed with light and buzzed like a beehive with excitement and anticipation. Doctors and nurses rushed about in all directions, barking orders to subordinates in readiness for the arrival of the air ambulance.

At first the patient's identity was kept secret, but once the medical records started to arrive, some of which surprisingly bore his name, the rumours began spreading at once, filling the hospital with an equal mixture of excitement and disbelief. Everyone had an opinion - some were joyful of his critical condition, while others were excited to get a closer look at such a celebrity and wished him well.

Two nurses stood outside the entrance smoking cigarettes, making no attempt to conceal their anger and hatred.

"I knew he would end up like this. They always do," one of the nurses spat disdainfully.

"If the rumour is true, I hope he dies before he reaches the hospital. I wouldn't want to make any effort to save that mafioso."

A passing doctor overheard the conversation and stopped in his tracks.

"Why is that, Nurse?" he asked. "So what if he extorted most of his wealth abroad? He's done nothing wrong here in Israel. Do you know that our new surgery wing was constructed solely from his generous donations? We must do everything we can to help him whether we like him or not."

The nurses looked at the doctor with disinterest, took a puff on their Marlboro's, and shrugged.

"The cars are here!" a porter shouted, and the nurses turned to watch a convoy of vehicles pull up by the entrance.

A melee of doctors, hospital managers and security people surrounded the vehicles and escorted the visitors inside.

The nurses studied the scene with little excitement as the scrum of people passed by and entered the hospital. The chain-smoking nurse, a dowdy-looking woman approaching middle age, lit another cigarette with the one she'd just finished.

"Did you see that Russian whore? She's going to inherit billions; can you believe it? She'll probably waste it all on clothes and jewellery, the slut."

She turned to a fresh group of nurses who had joined her for a smoke.

"Don't be envious, Dana," another nurse said. "Did you catch a glimpse of that tall dark guy in a white shirt?"

"I didn't see a ring on his finger. You might try your luck with him. I'm sure you won't need to work night shifts in the hospital ever again."

Dana turned red, while the other nurses burst out laughing. They needed to relieve the feeling of agitation somehow.

"Where is the patient?" a young nurse asked. "Who are those people?"

"Oh Irit, you're so naive. They're the bodyguards and associates, checking out everything before our superstar arrives," Dana sneered.

***

"REVA 101, this is Ben Gurion. Maintain altitude till marker two, approach is clear to runway two, copy that?"

"Copy that."

"Parking spot twenty is secured, proceed immediately after landing. Ambulance is on site. Repeat...Ambulance is on site."

"Copy that, tower. Turning at marker two. Beginning approach."

The pilot landed thirty minutes ahead of schedule thanks to a generous tailwind that carried the plane across the Mediterranean Sea to Israel. The pilot smiled to himself - he had earned a $10,000 bonus for the early arrival, as promised before the flight by the man dressed awkwardly in the tieless black suit which failed to conceal his broad shoulders and bulging muscles.

The crew speculated that the man looked like a Russian gangster from a Hollywood movie and he helped compound the perception by not speaking with anyone the entire flight. Instead, he sat alongside the patient, looking menacing.

A private air ambulance costs tens of thousands of dollars, so whoever used their services was unlikely to be a teacher or a farmer. The promised bonus was the norm for rich Russian clients; and the norm included not asking too many questions.

As the plane taxied towards the private gate, Arthur, the Russian muscle in the black suit, fired up his mobile and muttered the only words anyone on the plane would hear.

"We've landed."

The phone went back in his pocket, and he returned to his strong, silent-type act.

Arthur stepped out of the airplane's doors into the humid Tel Aviv air. He had visited Israel many times before and recognised the familiar scents of the summer Mediterranean climate.

Within minutes the patient was secured in the helicopter which took off immediately, carrying Arthur and the patient to the hospital. The patient was unconscious but stable, covered in tubes and wires filling him with oxygen and fluids and monitoring his vital signs.

"Make sure we reach hospital quickly," Arthur said to the helicopter pilot in thick Russian-accented English. "And you make sure he lives," he ordered the doctor.

The doctor looked at Arthur, nodded quickly, and returned his attention to the screens.

***

Masha, the woman referred to as a 'Russian whore' waited in what was laughably described as the VIP Waiting Room. It had two brown leather sofas, two arm chairs, and a round white table with some magazines. There was a flat screen TV on the wall and water and coffee machines in the corner. It was a proper coffee machine, not one that makes brown water called 'coffee' from a mix of powders. The room wasn't too fancy, but it was quiet and its soft lighting was much more hospitable than the bright neon lights that doused the hospital's other areas.

Masha was in her mid-thirties. She wore tight dark-blue jeans, a light-blue blouse, a white jacket, and clutched a small Louis Vuitton handbag tightly in her lap. She was in best designers from top to bottom. The matching rock-sized diamonds in her earrings and ring could be seen from outer space.

Her eyes were puffed and red from crying, lack of sleep and stress. It was obvious that she was a fit, gorgeous woman even when she was on what seemed to be the verge of a nervous breakdown. Nevertheless, her lustrous blonde mane and make-up were perfect and her outfit, shoes and accessories were effortlessly matched and wouldn't be out of place on the cover of Vogue.

Sat opposite Masha was Boris, a man in his early-sixties, balding, red-faced, above average height with a small belly. He wore khaki trousers, a black polo shirt and a heavy gold necklace around his thick neck. In contrast to Masha, he sat expressionless, focusing all his attention on his smartphone.

Pacing between the two was David, an elegant forty-something with a tan that hinted at some Middle Eastern blood in his family. He alternated between pacing the room back and forth like a caged tiger and trying to comfort Masha.

"Mashenka," David quietly said to Masha as he sat down beside her, "his condition is stable. It has been fourteen hours and he has survived the flight here. These doctors are the best in the world; nobody is better than Doctor Rosen. Our champion will come through this. He always does. It will take more than this to take him down. I promise you, he'll be fine."

Masha didn't avert her gaze from the floor. Boris looked up from his phone for a second to study this interaction, and then returned his attention back to the screen. He was pleased that David had taken upon himself the job of comforting Masha. While trying to appear empathetic, his mind was racing, calculating the situation's immediate practical implications. It didn't look too promising. The deal in Belarus was in danger of falling apart, and he suspected that within the week a battle for control of the business would commence.

Boris didn't expect his friend to recover. With a bullet in the brain it didn't matter which doctor treated you and how much he's paid, the chances of survival were still slim. He'd been amazed when the message came through that the patient had arrived in Tel Aviv still breathing.

Boris was surprised that he felt even a hint of sadness for his friend's condition, and not only because of the threat to the business. He believed that he had lost the capacity to have such feelings a long time ago. This kid had played a major part in his life for the past twenty years. Their relationship wasn't always smooth - in fact they often argued and disagreed, but Boris knew that were it not for this young man, he would probably be just another grey, alcoholic, retired manager.

"David, speak with Arthur. Where are they?" Masha said, interrupting Boris' thoughts.

"Mashenka, don't go crazy. It has been only ten minutes since they've landed."

"Please," Masha persisted.

David saw the overwhelming sadness in Masha's eyes and relented. He hit the speed dial button and called Arthur.

"He said they'll be here in around ten minutes," he reported after he'd returned the phone to his pocket. "No change in his condition."

With Masha temporarily placated, David sat back in the chair and tried to relax. He looked over at Boris and realised he was surfing the internet on his smartphone.

"*Probably looking at porn sites*," he thought, suppressing a smile. At least it might help Boris think clearly. Everyone needed Boris to have a clear mind. Soon, they would need to make some difficult decisions.

Masha returned to staring at the floor, desperately trying to push the assassination attempt to the back of her mind. It was futile - the scene played in a loop no matter how much she tried to suppress it.

Everything happened so quickly, and yet haunted Masha's mind like a slow-motion replay. One minute he was kissing her on her cheek, smiling at her with his blue eyes sparkling. The next second his head yanked backwards as his body flew onto the sidewalk.

Within seconds Boris grabbed her from behind, and pushed her into the bulletproof Rolls Royce. Gun in hand, David towered over her husband, protecting him while desperately looking around for the shooter.

The next thing she remembered was driving to the local hospital escorted by police cars and motorcycles. Boris was talking to her but she couldn't hear a word he was saying. Oh my god, they shot her husband. The bastards.

After a consultation with the medics they decided to fly her husband to Israel. The doctors there are the best for treating bullet wounds - people get shot in Israel frequently. That was the best chance of saving him.

Now, sat at another hospital in Israel, the enormity of events was finally sinking in. She was worried about her husband, about their two young children and about herself. And yet, she knew she had to remain strong as her husband would expect nothing less. She couldn't break down, not now, not here. As always, she had to look her best. People were watching. People were always watching.

***

The helicopter roared as it touched down on the helipad. Instantly an assortment of medical staff surrounded it, detaching and reattaching vital lines and drips. Masha, David and Boris heard the helicopter approach and sprinted out of the waiting room but by the time they reached the roof the patient was already on his way to the operating theatre.

"I'm here, darling!" Masha cried as she tried to join the throng of white coats. A doctor blocked her path and said with a practised sympathetic smile, "I'm sorry, madam, medical personnel only. Please, return to the waiting room and when we have any news, I'll come and find you straight away."

Masha, Boris and David hesitated, unsure of what to do. They stood there, lost.

"Stay in the waiting room, try to relax," the doctor continued. "There isn't anything you can do right now. Save your energy for later, you'll need it," he advised them before rushing off to join his colleagues.

"Arthur!" Boris called out, seeing him at the back of the group of doctors.

Arthur jogged over and reported in.

"The journey was okay," he informed everyone. "I'll guard the operating room."

And with those few words he left to watch over his master.

"It's good that we have Arthur keeping an eye on security," David offered.

"Indeed. Soon the news will find its way to everyone. Business associates, business rivals, the media and probably even Mossad will arrive to sniff around. What a fucking mess," Boris added some words of wisdom, shaking his head.

"I wish they'd just leave us alone," Masha whispered almost to herself.

David overheard the comment and studied Masha closely. She was struggling to maintain her composure and appeared to be on the brink of losing control. He carefully placed his arm around her shoulders and pulled Masha's trembling body close to his.

"I'm afraid an attempt on the life of your husband is headline news," David sympathised. "We'll do our best to keep the parasites at arm's length."

"I'll make sure of it," agreed Boris. "Media interest is inevitable, but we must contain as much information as possible."

***

The operation lasted for five hours and was a mixed success. The good news was that the bleeding was under control and the patient had survived. The bad news was that the bullet remained in his brain.

Doctor Rosen explained the situation to the impatient bunch nervously waiting in his private office.

"I was able to stabilise the patient. However, removing the bullet was too risky. His body suffered severe trauma in the last twenty four hours. He must remain in intensive care with life-support for at least two or three days to recover and get stronger. After that we'll reassess and decide on the next steps."

"Thanks doctor, we appreciate your efforts," David told Doctor Rosen in Hebrew. "Make sure he gets through this and we'll make sure that your efforts are properly rewarded."

Doctor Rosen nodded; he knew just how lucrative such business could be.

The group left the office and returned to the waiting room to decide a plan of action. Tanya, the personal assistant, was tasked with liaising with the medical staff and any visitors or information-seekers. An attractive long-legged brunette in her early thirties, she would be much better at the job than the unrefined Arthur.

The rest of the party departed after spending long hours at the hospital, leaving Arthur and Tanya strict instructions to check in every half hour regardless of whether there was any news to report or not.

Before they could leave, Arthur's phone rang; he spoke a couple of short, stilted sentences and then hung up.

"Sasha and mama arrived," he informed the others.

"Good...He'll need his mother and brother when he wakes," Masha said, trying to sound positive.

"Come...we should go now," Boris encouraged. "Arthur: you should return to guard the theatre. Don't forget to check in with me regularly."

Arthur nodded, no discernible expression on his face, and walked away.

Arthur had a hard shell, but inside, well, he was harder still. He made his living protecting or taking lives, the choice dependent on whether those who paid for his services asked him to be an assassin or a bodyguard. He was completely loyal to his boss, but didn't have any warm feelings toward him. Warm feelings were something that he erased from his life a long time ago. The only thing he felt now was a lust for revenge.

Despite Arthur making enquiries with several contacts, no information about the assassination attempt had been received yet. Arthur despised that this had happened on his watch, even if he wasn't present at that moment. It was his job to protect; that's why he was paid. He had failed, and now all he wanted was to make the attackers suffer before he ended their lives.

For now, however, his boss was laying still, a bullet stuck in his brain and his blue eyes shut.

2 Shattered Lives

I couldn't open my eyes. I wasn't dead. They say 'I think therefore I am,' so since I was thinking I assumed I was. It was like watching a movie of fragments of my life. Some were vivid and coherent. Some were blurred and maybe even false, as certain events seemed strangely distorted. But I wasn't at a cinema, I was weightlessly floating in darkness and the pictures were shown around me, each time at a different place. My earliest childhood memories were scarce and seemed so distant.

Kiev, 1977
Despite the freezing weather, Kiev was magnificently covered by a white powdery layer of snow. As the sun was shining, the whole city beamed in rays of light. Father and I were walking hand in hand and it seemed like a stroll in winter wonderland. We then entered an office in a grey building for "an important meeting during which I should behave my best," as my father put it.

"This is my youngest son, Misha, or officially, Mikhail Vorotavich," my father said proudly.

"Year of birth, parents' names and place of residence?" the man behind the desk asked.

"Year of birth 1973, parents Leon and Golda Vorotavich, residence: Kiev, Ukraine."

"Who is that, papa?" I asked my father, pointing at the gigantic portrait of an old man in military uniform. His shirt was decorated with so many stars and medals, they covered half of his chest. Surely, a brave war hero who won many battles.

My father coughed uneasily. Smiling nervously, he said, "Misha, don't be silly, you know who that is. That's Leonid Illych Brezhnev, the General Secretary of the Central Committee of the Communist Party and our father and dear leader."

I remember being confused by such a long title and wondering how I could have two fathers. As I continued studying the painting, music started playing outside the room, echoing through the corridors.

"Stand, Misha!" my father commanded, grabbing my arm and forcing me to my feet.

"Be glorious, our free motherland,
A reliable stronghold of people's friendship!
The Party of Lenin, the strength of the people,
Lead us to the triumph of Communism!"

When the interview was over, my father thanked the kindergarten officer and we quickly left. We carefully walked home through the icy streets under the falling snow, father wearing his big brown sable fur cap. He explained, his breath a thin-white smoke, "The song we'd heard was our national anthem and whoever shows disrespect could end up being severely punished. You have to be careful, Misha."

I could sense his anger and was sure that I would barely escape being deprived of all my toys, as this was the most serious punishment I could imagine.

Nobody was too tender with kids in those years. Spanking children with a belt was customary. It was the country that mattered above everything else.

I remember the teacher telling us that Ukraine was part of the Soviet Union, alongside Russia. "The Soviet Union is the largest and most glorious empire that the world has ever seen," the teacher lectured. "We're all proud comrades. We're all like brothers. We're so lucky to be part of the greatest nation that has ever existed. We love our country and our country loves us like a mother loves her children."

***

I grew up in communist Ukraine. My family was part of the Jewish minority within the Ukrainian minority, within the Soviet empire. We were second class comrades. It was like in George Orwell's Animal Farm: *"All animals are equal, but some are more equal than others."*

My father was the deputy chief of the Ukrainian branch of a state-owned construction trust. It was probably the highest position to which a Jew, who wasn't a member of the communist party, could reach.

The position demanded, beyond the official job of administrating state-owned properties, doing favours to senior members of the communist party. When the deputy chairman of Kiev's communist party needed to renovate his dacha he knew that all he needed to do was to call my father and everything would be arranged without delay.

If the chief controller of the people's economy decided that he needed to build an extension to his house, he had my father's home phone number to circumvent a shortage of bricks in Kiev. One call, and surprisingly, the lack of bricks wouldn't apply to the people's controller. Abracadabra - for him, bricks could be pulled out of thin air.

The favours were probably reciprocal. We were relatively privileged and lived well in a nice spacious apartment. I had my own room, as did my older brother Alexander - or Sasha - who was two years older than me. We didn't miss out on anything and lived a fairly comfortable life. We felt secure. My father's position at work was solid, or at least we thought that it was.

When I was five years old, my father began to teach me to read Russian, believing it would be more beneficial than Ukrainian. For a long time I couldn't grasp it - I was only five, after all - and he would get upset with me, slamming his fists on the table. But thankfully, one day the pieces of the puzzle somehow fell together and the strange symbols in front of me began forming words I could understand.

The reasoning behind my reading lessons became apparent when I was six years old, and my parents took me for a meeting with the headmaster of what would be my new school. Because I could already read, the headmaster decided I should skip the first grade and go straight to the second one. So not only was I the youngest and smallest child in class, but everyone was familiar with the school but me. I was an outsider. I was thrown into deep water and had to quickly learn how to swim or sink.

There was only one other Jewish kid in class, his name was Yuri Malinovsky. Soon, Yuri would become my best friend.

***

The school was a long, dark, four-storey building and very intimidating in comparison with the small and cosy kindergarten surrounded by a big yard which was green in summer and covered with snow in winter. We used to get so excited when the first snow fell. We built snowmen and had snowball fights. Kindergarten was all about playing and singing, while school was all about studying and discipline.

The school's overall atmosphere of violence and oppression was depressing. The teachers were strict and gloomy and many children were brutal. Misbehaviour was severely punished, sometimes physically.

The only bright spot was the automatic soda machine. You insert a coin, press a button and poof; the machine fills a glass - if it wasn't stolen by a drunkard for vodka. This was nothing short of a technological wonder - watching the machine working was more enjoyable than drinking the beverage.

We started each morning with *politinformation* - an update on contemporary external and internal events. Frequently its emphasis was on all the bad things about America: unemployment, poverty, unfair exploitation of proletariat, racial segregation, and so on. People were treated as slaves by immoral capitalist magnates. They were focused only on money-making, without any respect to fellow citizens or the country. The American leaders were corrupt; America was just a dreadful place. After hearing all that it was perfectly clear that the proletarian revolution in America was imminent.

How much I regretted then that I was sent straight to the second grade. Being the youngest, smallest and Jewish, I was an obvious target for bigger kids to bully me relentlessly. The head bully was a heavy-weight kid named Igor, who was at least a foot taller than me. He used to call me names, harass me regularly, and steal the sandwich that my mother had prepared for my lunch. I hated that guy, but he looked so enormous to me that I didn't dare to confront him. I just made sure to spit a few times into my sandwich before he came to demand his tribute.

One day, Igor approached me. My memory of his sweaty face and palms, the smell from the spots under his arm pits when he strangled me, and his ugly sadistic smile, which I would rather forget, is all too vivid. He had been stealing my lunch for a whole week, but I was too embarrassed to say anything to my parents or the teachers and was really hungry and angry. I was on the verge of exploding.

I could've probably asked Sasha to intervene and he would surely have taken care of Igor. However, our father had always taught us to handle things ourselves: "If I'm not for myself, who will be for me?" I didn't want everyone to think that I was a cry-baby, asking my big brother to defend me, so I had to deal with the situation somehow.

"Zhid, give me your sandwich or I'll punch you in your ugly Jewish face," Igor growled with an expression full of hate.

My shackles rose immediately I heard the word zhid, which was a derogatory term in Russian, meaning something like *dirty Jew*.

Instead of giving Igor my sandwich, I pushed him. The fury caused by him calling me zhid surpassed any fear. He didn't budge by much though; it was like pushing against a wall. He was shocked that I had dared touch him and studied me with an evil look. He came towards me, probably to do as he had often promised - to punch the Jew out of me. Before he could hit me, I lunged forwards and punched him first.

"How's that for a sandwich?" I screamed as menacingly as possible.

I was probably influenced by a Soviet propaganda book about Dynamo Kiev footballers that I was reading at the time. The book was a true story set in 1942 in Nazi-occupied Kiev, when the Dynamo team dared to win a football match against a Nazi Wehrmacht team despite the threat that they would be executed if they won. They were fearless.

Igor beat the shit out of me. Damn, it hurt. After finishing slamming his fist into my face and banging my head on the floor he threatened, "I'll kill you, you stinking little prick. Hitler should have sent you all dirty Jews to Babi Yar and finished the job. Next time I tell you something, do as you're told or it will be the last time you do anything."

I was afraid that he would do as threatened, so I told my mother that I was sick and stayed home for a week. When my mother wasn't looking, I put the thermometer above my hot tea, making it look like I had a fever. I was scared shitless to go back to school.

When my father saw my face covered with bruises, he whispered quietly so my mother wouldn't hear, "I hope the other guy looks worse. Remember Misha; if you're going to fight make sure you win."

When I did return to school, Igor came to greet me, smiling ominously like Josef Mengele, when he tortured Jews in Auschwitz.

"The little Jewish boy is back. No more hiding behind mama's skirt at home. You wait and see. You're dead. Suka blyad."

As Igor and his friends sniggered at me, I punched him in the face as hard as I could. It wasn't because I was brave, it was purely because I was afraid that he was going to kill me and I didn't know what else to do. I couldn't stay home forever and I couldn't tell my mother that I had fallen down the stairs on my face again to explain why it was all black and blue. You can get away with such a lie only once.

Now, I just stood there, expecting Igor to really finish me. This was it; this was going to be my end. To my surprise, Igor just turned around and walked away and never came near me again. Bullies don't take beating well. In fact, all the bullies left me alone from that day onwards.

I learned that the best way to fight violence was with violence. Eye for an eye beats turning the other cheek every time. Bullies bully easy targets, not those who fight back. Never again was I impressed by physical superiority after that. Big balls count for more than big muscles.

***

One hot spring day during the break between classes I debated with Yuri whether the quickest way to move from one class to another was through the corridors or through the windows. Feeling a bit mischievous, I demonstrated to Yuri the window route by climbing onto the ledge and shuffling to the next room. Unfortunately a teacher saw some kids in the yard looking up, cheering on my silly prank.

"Mikhail Vorotavich! Stop that immediately," the teacher yelled. "If you fall down I'm going to beat you up with my stick until you won't be able to walk ever again."

It was a miracle that I didn't fall and break my neck. The teacher rushed to the classroom, grabbed my ear and took me to the headmaster, who summoned my father.

The headmaster wanted to expel me for reckless behaviour and negatively influencing other children.

"What your son has done is very serious. He risked his life, and he gave a bad example to the other pupils. I don't think he can keep attending our school," he told my father who looked like he was going to burst a blood vessel.

Luckily though, he was able somehow to *convince* the headmaster to give me another chance. Back then I didn't understand what was in the envelope that my father placed on the desk between them.

"I'm sure we can work something out," my father said, almost whispering. "My son is a good boy. He didn't mean any harm. Please, give him another chance and I'll show you my gratitude."

The headmaster nodded as he took the envelope and quickly made it disappear into a drawer in his desk.

"I suppose kids are kids," he replied with a chuckle. "All kids must get a proper education to be able to contribute to the state. Fine. Giving your son another chance is my duty as a good citizen and an educator."

I wanted to ask what just happened, but instinctively decided against it. Later in life I realised that when you want someone to do something, an envelope is the best method of persuasion. Even the head of an educational institution for young children wasn't unlike every other public official in Ukraine. Bribery was an important tool to comprehend from an early age. The headmaster got cash and made the right decision. I stayed at school.

Although my father was calm, I knew a severe punishment would inevitably follow. On the way back home, we stopped near one of the cistern trailers that sold kvass. On hot days people entering and exiting the nearby Metro station were eager customers. My father asked for a small glass for me and half a litre for himself, paying the seller eight kopeks. While we were drinking, my father pointed to the Olympic bear decorating the cistern. It was *Misha*, the mascot of the upcoming Moscow Olympics of 1980.

"Misha, because of your irresponsible behaviour, I've decided not to take you to the opening ceremony of the Olympics at Respublikanskiy stadium. You need to learn to be careful. You cannot behave stupidly, especially if people see you."

Although all the main events were to be held in Moscow, some Olympic football games were hosted in Kiev, so Kiev would have its own opening ceremony. Not going to the games was a real disaster for me. My dream was shattered, but deservedly so. I knew my father was as stubborn as a mule, and once he decided something he wouldn't change his mind. I wasn't angry with him, I was angry with myself for being so stupid. I'd learned a valuable lesson: mistakes have consequences.

***

Because of my father's position, we lived a fairly decent life. However, our fortunes turned sour at the beginning of the 1980s. The Communist Party initiated a wave of cleansing, removing unreliable individuals from managerial ranks. They needed a scapegoat in the construction trust, and for an unknown reason my father was singled out.

It started as it usually does with anonymous complaints that my father told jokes about the communist party, listened to Israeli radio and spread Zionist ideas. That was blasphemy in the regime's eyes.

Using such ammunition, the KGB could hand out a ten year sentence of correctional works in a diamond mine in Siberia. Rarely did anyone return after serving such a sentence. One of the mottos of the KGB was: *give us a person and we'll find the offence he committed.*

Regrettably, if the KGB had singled you out, the court trial would be just a farce, as a KGB's indictment was tantamount to a conviction. All those party bosses who my father had helped over the years, denied that they had even known him once they heard that the KGB was involved. Everyone was scared of the KGB and did anything to avoid its attention.

I didn't really know whether my father was anti-communist or even a true Zionist. I was too young to understand these things. But even if he was, he hardly deserved what was coming.

It was true that my father was active in the Jewish community. He used to cherish Jewish traditions, tried to speak some Yiddish at home and often hosted Jewish bohemia in our apartment. Friends used to gather in our living room, drink vodka, talk and sing. One of my father's friends usually brought an acoustic guitar and played as everyone sang enthusiastically. My parents sent me to bed, but I used to stay awake and listen to them from my bedroom until the small hours of the morning.

> "Blooming pears and apples all around her
> With the morning mists beneath her feet
> Walked Katyusha slowly by the river
> On the rocky riverbank so steep.
> She was walking, she was softly singing
> Of her silver eagle of the steppe
> Of the one for whom her heart was beating
> Of the one whose letters she was keeping."

But my father didn't do much more than that. It was very hard to leave the country and almost impossible to emigrate. So he was just talking and singing about Zion and Israel, rather than doing anything about it. He wasn't going to fight the communist regime and risk losing his comfortable job. He wasn't going to risk imprisonment in Siberia like many refuseniks. However, it didn't matter what he did or didn't do - he was doomed once he was chosen as a sacrifice for the communist party's needs.

One evening when I was almost nine years old, we heard a loud knock on our front door as we were all sitting at the kitchen table eating dinner.

"Police. Open up!"

My parents exchanged a silent, worried look. My father sharply exhaled, stood up and went to open the door. Three uniformed men barged into our house, almost knocking my father down as they swung the door open. After stepping backwards and gaining his balance, my father tried to ask them what they wanted, but one of them just forcefully tossed him to the floor.

"You know very well what we want, Zionist spy."

A policeman picked him up, pushed his face into the wall and handcuffed his hands behind his back. They searched our apartment, apparently knowing in advance what they wanted to take. They took our radio, some of the letters addressed to my father, especially those from abroad, and a few manuscripts of young Jewish writers that they drafted by themselves and gave to my father to read. They threw our possessions on the floor and broke everything that was in their way. Our apartment looked like it was hit by a tornado.

While being handcuffed, my father looked at Sasha and gasped, "Sasha, take care of your mama and Misha until I return home. Don't worry about me."

And to my weeping mother he said, trying to steady his trembling voice as much as he could, "Don't cry, Goldushka. It will be alright. I didn't do anything wrong."

I saw one of the policemen, certain that nobody was watching, place some green papers inside one of the books that they'd singled out to take. His colleague invited two of our neighbours to sign search protocols as witnesses. As they showed our neighbours their findings, the policeman dropped the book, as if accidentally, and all the green papers fell out onto the floor.

I shouted, "I saw you stashing the green papers inside the book."

"Shut up," they barked at me.

"I saw it, I saw it, I saw it," I yelled. But nobody seemed to pay attention. My father was blamed for something he didn't do.

"Look, this traitor has more than three hundred dollars here!"

The policeman took a long coercive look at the neighbours, while holding the green dollars in his hand and nodding his head meaningfully. The neighbours probably believed me, but they knew that not signing the protocols would be bad for them. With trembling hands, they took the official papers and signed. Possession of foreign currency implied a breach of currency regulations. This was a serious criminal offense that could easily be interpreted as remuneration for espionage services by a foreign intelligence agency.

"Filthy Jewish traitor!" the policeman spat at my father.

My father tried to protest, but it was pointless.

"Shut up," the two men yelled as they pushed him out of the apartment.

Before disappearing, my father whispered to me, "Poka, Misha! Be a good boy."

At the time, I didn't know that these short words were my last memory of my proud father, as I saw him being dragged like a dog on a leash, pale and shaking. My mother was crying. Sasha was crying. This was the single time in my life I saw him crying. I wasn't crying - I was too furious to shed any tears.

Something was terribly wrong. I was certain that it was some kind of a misunderstanding. Surely my father would return home in a couple of days. It didn't make any sense that the country that loved us like a mother would take my father away.

He was accused of plotting against the communist regime and sent to a correction facility in Siberia. We used to get letters from him for a couple of years, and my mother kept them like Katyusha in the song. One day these suddenly stopped. An official state letter arrived instead, with the red hammer and sickle on its letterhead, informing us that my father had perished with pneumonia.

Our little happy family was shattered the day my father was taken away. The country, the authorities, the KGB, the police and all the other pretend law enforcement agencies became my number one enemies. Those who were supposed to protect us, betrayed us and took my father away. The fuckheads.

After my father was prosecuted, our apartment in Kiev's centre was confiscated and we were relocated to a small flat on the outskirts of the city. Our big apartment belonged to the construction trust, not to us. In communist Ukraine nobody owned their house. We were simply informed that by such and such date we needed to take ourselves and our belongings and move elsewhere.

Poverty became our reality. No more ice cream, cinema or toys. My mother's answer to anything I asked was, "We don't have money for that, Mishenka," as she tried to suppress her tears. The colour of my childhood turned grey - the grey buildings, the grey filthy snow after the first day if falls, and the grey, sullen face of my mother.

I shared one small room with Sasha, while my mother slept in the living room. We lived on the third floor, with no lift, in a large concrete state-built house with over eighty identical grey flats. All my and Sasha's clothes were hand-me-downs from a couple of sympathetic neighbours. Their children were older than us and their grandfather had been killed in Stalin's time for alleged treason. They felt that our fate was somehow similar to theirs so they felt sorry for us. I hated that people felt sorry for us. It was such a desperate feeling.

My mother had to sell most of our belongings to cover our daily needs, yet still we were always short of cash to buy basic stuff, even food. Most of our old furniture was too big to fit our modest new apartment, so my mother sold them. At night I would hear her sobbing gently, and many times I would cry too, silently so that Sasha wouldn't hear.

I remembered how not so long ago I sat in a different room in a different house, listening to the sounds of singing and laughter at my father's Jewish bohemian gatherings. How had things changed so dramatically? It was too much for a nine year old to understand.

My mother started taking extra shifts at the textile factory, as well as an additional job of delivering mail and newspapers on weekends. Sasha and I eagerly helped her, dividing the distribution area between us. She always seemed tired and miserable. It was as if she'd aged by a decade since my father had gone. I promised to myself that one day I would make enough money so my mother wouldn't need to work at all. Ever.

***

It was 1986, and I was thirteen years old when Ukraine hit the world news headlines when a reactor at the Chernobyl nuclear power station exploded, sending a radioactive plume across Europe. Common Ukrainian citizens didn't know about the incident for over two weeks because State Television and Radio didn't report anything. Complete silence. But nothing of that magnitude could be covered up indefinitely, and soon rumours and conspiracy theories went wild.

We tried to intercept the Voice of America or other foreign radio broadcasts in Russian, but as always these transmissions were constantly jammed by the KGB. Others fished for information from anyone who might be even remotely connected to the events in Chernobyl. At first, the rumour was that there was a fire at Chernobyl and a single person had perished. Nothing too extreme.

A few days passed and a whole range of alternative versions spread, all alleged to be a hundred percent accurate. Some stated knowingly that while scientists were testing some new super weapon, it had exploded, completely erasing from the face of the earth a fifty square kilometre area. Others took a different angle, saying it was a heroic defence effort against a new American super weapon, which despite being deflected had left the same fifty square kilometre area completely barren.

The most bizarre story was that our military had battled Martian aliens at Chernobyl, like in H. G. Wells' *War of the Worlds*, and our brave army had won.

The scariest story was actually pretty close to the truth, claiming that there had been a tremendous radiation leak and that we were all going to die. That is unless we drank twenty droplets of iodine a few times each day. Some terrified believers died of a self-inflicted fatal dose.

Aliens, weapons or just a radiation leak, our mother chose the cautious approach, telling Sasha and me to stay at home and to get our homework from schoolmates.

As she left for work she issued a final warning, "If anyone leaves the apartment while I'm gone, you're going to regret it for the rest of your life."

That was a huge disappointment, since we'd planned on watching the workers demonstration parade on the first of May - International Worker's Day, a big holiday in communist USSR. But after such a threat, we knew that our mother was serious.

The demonstration actually took place as if nothing had happened. For allowing people out on the streets under a radioactive airborne contamination any Western government would've been sacked and someone would've been prosecuted. In the USSR, however, it was perfectly normal. The preservation and cultivation of the ideology were much more important than the life and health of the people who were serving the Soviet Union.

Over time we would learn of the desperate efforts to contain the damaged reactor within a huge concrete sarcophagus. Many fire-fighters and armed forces personnel died of radiation sickness. Nobody cared to warn them about the dangerous consequences of the exposure to lethal levels of radiation. Using their hands and shovels, in many instances without adequate protection suits, they cleared radioactive debris and dropped lead into the reactor. Good men who served in the military were sent to die. It made you wonder why anyone would want to serve in the army. The politburo had never hesitated to use citizens and soldiers alike as human shields against Nazis, radiation or any other threat.

Finally, weeks after the whole world knew about the Chernobyl disaster, we were given details of the accident. By that time, polluted radioactive water had already leaked into the rivers and water supply, so informing us about the severity of the problem was too little, too late. Everyone was exposed and many people would die of cancer years later. For months we looked for mutated fish with three eyes in the Dnieper River. We wondered whether we would glow in the dark and our children would have seven fingers in each hand.

My mother decided to send Sasha and me to live with her sister in Leningrad in the north west of Russia, far away from the radioactive danger. We were more than happy to spend the entire summer with our cousin Tolik, who was older than Sasha and about to be recruited by the Soviet army. Tolik came to meet us at the train station.

"Hello cousins. It's good to have reinforcements coming," he greeted us jokingly. "Welcome to Russia. Welcome to the city that never sleeps. We're going to have the best summer ever."

It turned out that he wasn't exaggerating.

The trip to Leningrad would turn the boy into a man. I fell in love with Northern Palmyra, as poets called it, while spending the summer there. Although Kiev always remained my favourite city, Leningrad firmly took second place.

June in Leningrad is a magical time as the sun never really sets. The Beliye Nochi - or White Nights bath the city in their luminous brilliance as winter finally eases its grip and

Leningrad stirs from its hibernation. The view of the sun kissing the horizon above the Gulf of Finland is astonishing.

One such night Sasha, Tolik and I were hanging around Nevski Prospekt - Leningrad's main avenue, and started chatting to three Latvian girls. Being inexperienced with the opposite sex, I stood behind my brother and cousin and let them work their charms on the two older, sixteen year old girls, while the obviously younger girl sidled up next to me, bringing an instant blush to my cheeks. The group slowly ambled away with me and the girl tagging along at the rear.

"What is your name, boy?"

"Err...Misha...My name is Misha."

"Misha...that's a nice name. And where are you from, Misha?"

"I'm from Ukraine. Kiev," I answered proudly. "And...err...what's your name?" I added shyly.

"I'm Jelena. We come from Riga," she said, gesturing to her two companions who were laughing and joking with Sasha and Tolik.

"I don't really know where that is," I replied truthfully. "But if the girls are all like you there, I wouldn't mind visiting it someday."

"Ha ha, you're a little charmer, Misha," Jelena laughed. "Look, there are steps down to the river. Let's take a look," she said and took my hand in hers.

I let Jelena drag me towards the steps, casting a glance back at Sasha and Tolik, who were oblivious to me and my new friend.

We found an isolated spot under a bridge and sat side by side with our feet dangling just above the river. Feeling light-headed from the magical atmosphere and the excitement that she not only wanted to be there with me, but also was two years older than me, I kissed Jelena quickly on her lips. I moved my head back to observe her reaction, expecting her to push me in to the water and run away. Instead, she kissed me back.

Her lips were wet and her skin was so soft. She smelled so fresh. We kissed and hugged as my heart raced. My hand slipped underneath her shirt, feeling her firm young breast. Instead of slapping me and moving my hand away, she allowed me to feel her warm body, although an attempt to reach her lower parts was brushed away. I got so excited and aroused I thought I was about to explode.

"Not here, Misha," she said, noticing the bulge in my trousers.

I blushed, embarrassed by my obvious excitement.

"Don't worry, Misha, it's nice you feel this way," Jelena whispered huskily whilst rubbing my erection.

"Maybe I can help..." she said softly, and began unbuttoning my trousers.

I thought I would explode before she even freed me, but I managed to last three or four strokes before I came. It was the best feeling I'd had so far in my young life. Jelena giggled and kissed me gently.

"Come; we should find our friends," Jelena ordered, and took my hand again. We walked in silence, holding hands, back to where we'd first met. Thankfully Sasha, Tolik and the girls were waiting for us.

"Ah, the young lovers return!" Tolik teased, instantly bringing a new flush of embarrassment to my cheeks.

"We were just talking," I protested, but the raised eyebrows hinted that Tolik and Sasha didn't believe me.

"Don't worry, Misha," Sasha said as he looked at the giggling girls. "There's nothing to be embarrassed by spending time with such beauties."

Our group said our goodbyes, with promises to meet up again. Jelena kissed me one more time and then the girls left, never to be seen again.

Instead of celebrating my bar mitzvah as every thirteen year old Jewish boy turning into a man, I lost my virginity. Well, technically I didn't - a hand-job doesn't really count, but still I felt like a man and it was better than any celebration.

The White Nights last only a few weeks, marking the annual tourist high season. We didn't want to miss any of them, so most evenings were spent pursuing girls and spending Tolik's modest savings buying alcohol. For a boy who'd rarely seen anything of life outside of Kiev, it would be a summer vacation I would remember as one of the best of my whole life.

When the summer was over, it was straight back to the gloomy reality of life in Kiev.

***

When Sasha reached the eighth grade he finished with full-time education. He moved to a professional technical school to combine paid work with various training courses. In socialist Ukraine no child labour was allowed, so this was the only way for him to bring money home.

Sasha tried his hardest to replace our father, and his efforts to contribute to the family finances were greatly appreciated. I'd always looked up to my older brother and desperately wished to follow suit and help out the family. But Sasha and my mother didn't share my enthusiasm.

"Don't be stupid, Misha. I promised papa I'd take care of mama and you. You're the smart one in the family, little brother. Go to school and become a famous engineer or a doctor, so you can take care of mama when we're older."

"But I want to earn money and help you and mama. I'm old enough to work. I'm not a child anymore," I protested.

"No, little brother. Studying is your job. Stop arguing and do as you're told."

With those words, my immediate future was set in place. I would do as Sasha ordered and excel at my studies. Becoming an engineer or a doctor was never a dream, but I had to contribute to the family. If studying was my job, then I had to do it well.

I soon discovered that excelling at school wasn't only about being smart at studying hard, it was also about being smart at manipulating the system. In Soviet Ukraine you learned quickly that playing the system was the only way to get ahead in life.

When I was fifteen, I sat an important physics exam. Yuri and I were walking home after school and comparing our answers, and to my horror I discovered that I had made a stupid mistake on one of the questions.

It was my own fault - I'd been distracted by Olga, who was tall, thin, and blonde with blue eyes. My hormones were running wild and during the exam I spent more time daydreaming about what I wanted to physically do to Olga than concentrating on the physics questions.

I was determined to correct my mistake at all costs, so I sneaked into the teacher's office during a break between classes, found my paper, corrected the mistake and put the paper back into the pile. As I was about to leave, the teacher entered.

"What are you doing in my room, Mikhail Vorotavich?"

My heart was jumping out of my chest and I had to think fast. Luckily, I had noticed an ad for a physics contest on the school board the day before. Trying to keep a calm expression and a steady voice, I composed my reply.

"I...err...I was looking for you to ask whether I could have your sponsorship for applying to the national physics contest for high school children."

The teacher looked at me through narrowed eyes, and I thought there was no way he'd believe such an obvious lie. My knees were trembling.

"Well, Misha. That depends on how good your score is when I mark your exam. We shall see."

I thanked him and quickly left the office. I thought that I had barely escaped from being thrown out of school. This time my father wasn't there to bail me out by paying the headmaster to give me another chance.

A few days later the exam results were in, and I scored a perfect mark. The teacher was very impressed by my score and proudly agreed to sponsor me, not only because of the grade but also because I had the confidence to ask for his sponsorship. I won third place in the contest, but was disappointed that the prize was a series of physics books. Cash was more useful, so I sold the books for a few rubles.

So, I was rewarded for cheating, not for studying hard. A good life lesson.

***

Although we'd moved to another part of town after my father was sent away, I stayed at my school in the centre of Kiev. The commute was long - a fifteen minute walk to the Metro, forty five minute underground journey, and another twenty minute walk from the Metro station to school. Every day I passed our former apartment, spat on the ground and cursed the KGB, the authorities and the damn USSR that left me fatherless.

The only thing that I was ashamed of was that I was the poorest kid in class. I tried to conceal it as much as I could. Anything that my classmates had and I didn't, I just explained that I didn't like it or didn't need it. But deep inside, of course, I wanted the same things as everyone else, like a new school uniform each year or sausage sandwiches for the lunch break. My mother could afford only veggie sandwiches, as meat was too expensive for us.

"Don't expect things to just work out for you. If you want something, you need to put in the effort to achieve it. And if you do something, make sure that you take the time to do it properly," my father used to say. I had to do something, both for myself and my family. I had to earn money somehow.

Most of my classmates didn't have such worries. They were the children of Ukraine's elite - senior members of the communist party, high ranked army officers and distinguished state officials. Most of them didn't give a shit about studies and grades; they knew that their parents would take care of their careers. The boys would join their father's organisation and the girls, depending on their looks and family standing, would marry a man from a similar social class. They would focus on having children and looking pretty.

Some, however, were afraid to take bad grades home, as violent punishments were common. As I was always short of cash, I used my brainpower to make some money by helping my schoolmates with their exams, earning a reputation of being smart and one ruble for my troubles.

Next to our school was a small eatery - a foul place that served horrid-looking meat dumplings with sour cream. It was mostly haunted by drunkards, who came to check whether vodka supplies were already delivered, so that they could alleviate the effects of their hangover by getting drunk again. I looked completely out of place there, but I didn't care. The dingy bistro, rarely visited by teachers or anyone other than the local boozers, was a perfect base for my little enterprise.

Students got out during their test by saying that they needed to go to the toilet. They sneaked to the eatery with parts of their exam paper for me to solve. I answered the questions and gave the paper back to them when they had to go to the toilet again later on. Diarrhoea soon became a common ailment at our school. The worried parents even insisted on calling the sanitary services to enquire what was wrong.

At that time, when an engineer's monthly salary was around eighty rubles, one ruble was a considerable amount. It was a high-risk endeavour though, with very serious consequences. If any wrong ears had heard about my small business, I would've been severely punished. Not only because I was helping students to cheat in their exams, but also because any kind of entrepreneurial behaviour was considered capitalist influence and alien ideology. As preaching communist philosophy was a sin in America, running a profitable private business was a sin in the USSR. This was the bullshit that the communists fed us for decades.

Once, I tried to give five rubles to my mother when we went to a bread shop. She lacked two rubles to buy a cake after spending an hour standing in the long queue. She didn't refuse to take my money, but she beat me when we returned home. She was certain that I couldn't have earned so much money by valid or legal means. Well, she was right. I didn't push it and preferred not to explain my little scheme to her.

I saved half of the money that I earned and spent the other half on luxury goods, such as books, vodka, and cigarettes imported from Bulgaria. In the USSR there was almost nothing from the United States or other capitalist countries - no American movies, no Levi's jeans, no Marlboro cigarettes. Nothing. So Rodopi cigarettes from

Bulgaria were as foreign and exotic as we could imagine back then.

***

I graduated from high school when I was seventeen. Even though I spent the least amount of time attending classes, spending most of my time on the streets, I graduated second in class, thanks to my photographic memory. The top pupil was the son of two scientists and based on his pale skin and large, oversized glasses, he probably spent all his time studying. Usually I would see second place as failure, but I was content with my achievements at school.

At the school's graduation party, we spent all our efforts chatting up the girls from other classes since our class wasn't blessed with many pretty girls, except for Olga. We tried our best to get the girls drunk, hoping that alcohol could get us a little action. But it didn't. Alcohol wasn't a stranger to these girls. It neither lubricated our way into their hearts nor their panties.

After lucking out, we decided to go to one of my classmates' house and drink until dawn. We raided the vodka from his parents' cupboard. While many homes lacked bread, everyone had vodka - a staple in Ukrainian households. We spent the night talking about girls, football and the university entrance exams. Teenagers in Ukraine had the same interests as teenagers in the rest of the world. Getting drunk, getting laid and sports are universal activities for all teen boys.

We liked our country but we hated communism in its distorted Soviet form. We had a dream that Ukraine declared war on America just to surrender the next day to be annexed to the United States. During the Cold War America was the enemy of the communists, and as my enemy's enemy is my friend, we were on America's side.

I learned many lessons during my high-school days: the value of friendship, never snitching on your friends, the state is the enemy and manipulating it is a virtue not a sin, and if something is prohibited it means you just need to pay to make it allowed. But most importantly, and never forget it, the key to survival is to fly below the radar, unnoticed. Once noticed, you're doomed. The state and your enemies would hunt you down.

I didn't know it but Ukraine was on the verge of a revolution. The end of the USSR was nigh. It would be the end of life as I knew it.

3 The Meeting

Tel Aviv, 2013

Three days had passed since the operation. The patient was stable and his life wasn't in immediate danger, but all tests confirmed he was in a coma. Doctor Rosen couldn't say whether he was going to wake up in a month, a year or ever again. It was unclear whether he had suffered permanent brain damage. Was he the same man inside the motionless body?

The initial shock had subsided and the enquiring calls from all over the world were answered. Now it was time to make pressing decisions. Boris invited the Group's senior managers from Kiev, Moscow, Tel Aviv, Geneva, Sao Paulo, Luanda and Singapore to an urgent council meeting. To accommodate everyone, David rented a lavish villa in Herzliya Pituach, one of the wealthiest neighbourhoods in Israel, conveniently not far away from the Group's Israeli headquarters.

The villa's main advantages were its high stone wall, its secluded location and its proximity to the sea. Arthur split the security detail so the majority could guard the villa, leaving six men to patrol the sea in three separate speed boats. As a final precaution, a luxury yacht was moored at the marina in case Arthur recommended holding a maritime meeting rather than onshore. Arthur always had a backup plan and an escape route.

In keeping with Arthur's usual strategy, the location for the rendezvous was determined at the last minute. All the senior managers gathered in one place would be too tempting a target for the Group's enemies. Each person and vehicle would be checked when entering and exiting the grounds. Visitors were asked to remove batteries from their mobile phones to minimise the possibility for remote recording of conversations and GPS monitoring. The Group was under threat and Arthur didn't take any avoidable risks.

About a dozen black Mercedes and BMWs arrived. One by one the managers entered the villa and gathered in its spacious living room. The bodyguards and drivers waited outside, smoking and chatting with those they knew. Others stood straight-backed and silent, observing everything from behind dark sunglasses.

As the guests made themselves comfortable, David casually wandered over to Boris.

"Look at this place. Walls, armed guards, patrol boats in the sea. We didn't take such measures even when I was in the military. This isn't real. It looks like the base of a villain from a Bond movie."

"I know what you mean, but this is Arthur's setup and after the shooting, who can be surprised at such a show?"

"You're right, of course. It just brings home what we have accomplished, and what we stand to lose."

"Defeat isn't an option, David," Boris whispered softly. "We have all worked too long and hard to capitulate without a fight."

A waiter entered the room and handed out the customary shots of vodka. Boris cleared his throat, raised his glass and proclaimed, "*Na zdorovya!* To the health of the boss!"

The rest of the men raised their drink and chorused, "*Na zdorovya!* To the health of the boss," and emptied their glasses in a single gulp. The gathering knew better than to leave a single precious drop. Communal vodka drinking was a holy ritual.

"Gentlemen," Boris continued, "if you would join me at the table, we have some business to discuss."

The group handed their glasses back to the waiter, and with formalities out of the way they each took a seat at the table. With everyone settled, Boris started the meeting.

"Thank you all for arriving on such a short notice. You have all visited the hospital, so you're acutely aware of the situation. Except for praying for a speedy recovery, there isn't much more to say about that."

Boris paused and looked up to study the faces of his colleagues.

"I assure you that the order and control of the Group remain solid. Everyone should keep calm and focus on the immediate objectives. We have a successful business and we owe it to ourselves to preserve it. You should all prepare for the possibility of hostile actions by competing groups that will likely try to use the situation to their advantage. We can't show any sign of weakness. Together we stand strong. Together we are invincible."

The speech was met with silence. David shuffled nervously in his seat alongside Boris. Usually, the boss would head such a meeting and it wasn't uncommon for a rousing speech to be followed by applause. He was the only one who had the full picture of all operations across the Group in his head. He remembered every small detail of every project across all the different businesses. His people admired him.

Boris and David had to quickly learn everything. The boss had a talent not only to manage but also to lead. He knew how to engage and motivate people. He asked for everyone's opinion, but he knew how to make the tough decisions. He wasn't afraid to roll the dice and take risks. He had balls the size of a football.

Everyone was concerned about the project in Belarus. The Group was bidding to construct the Belarus segment of a new seven hundred kilometre highway between Moscow and Minsk, and it was one of the largest projects the Group had undertaken so far. It was high profile and potentially massively profitable. The project's code name was *Highway to Heaven*, and Boris was intent on ensuring that it wouldn't end up as a highway to hell.

***

Arthur secured a private room at the medical facility to remain close by. He constantly analysed the sequence of events in his mind. He had been in Kremenchuk, some three hundred kilometres south east of Kiev, when the assassination attempt happened. His mobile had rung, with David's name displayed on the screen. A feeling of foreboding had swept over him at the time, as it was fairly unusual for David to call. Years of security work had given Arthur an acute sixth sense, and as he hit the answer button he already knew something serious had happened.

"David. What's up?"

"He's been shot. He's not dead, but it's bad. Really bad. Wrap up your business and get back here as soon as possible. We may be under attack."

Within just a few minutes, Arthur had jumped into his car and raced back to Kiev. His mind flooded with ideas of who could be brave - or stupid - enough to attempt to assassinate his boss.

The first priority was to uncover who was behind it. He couldn't leave the investigation in the hands of the Ukrainian police, which was both incompetent and untrustworthy and possibly in the pockets of the perpetrators. Whoever was courageous enough to sanction the hit must have some serious backing.

While he was driving, Arthur called Andrei Topolski, the Group's chief security officer in Moscow. Since the assassination attempt was made in Kiev, representing a failure of the Group's local security personnel, someone impartial from another location was needed to conduct the investigation. Arthur's attention could then be focused on protecting the boss. The phone was answered by a cold, monotone voice.

"Yes."

"Andrei, this is Arthur."

"Hello Arthur. I've already heard about the assassination attempt. I'm guessing your call is related to the incident."

Arthur frowned. It was less than two hours since the shooting, and Andrei was already aware of the situation. In one way it was good to know he was on top of things, but on the other hand it showed that nothing that happened in Kiev could be kept secret for long.

"Andrei, go down to Kiev to investigate the shooting. I want to know who's accountable for this. I want answers and I want them yesterday. First off; figure out from where the marksman took the shot and whether any traces were left behind," he commanded.

"Leave it to me," replied Andrei. "Rest assured, we'll find the fuckers and take care of them."

"Good. Don't waste anyone before we question them. I want to know who sent the shooter and why. Get together whatever you need and get to Kiev on the first flight tomorrow morning. No point coming now as it will be dark soon. My man will be waiting for you."

"Okay. We'll keep alive whoever we catch so you can personally blow their brains out. I'll keep in touch," Andrei answered, and killed the connection.

Arthur chucked the mobile into the centre console and looked at the speedometer in frustration, wishing the roads would allow a faster drive. Arthur knew that Andrei would use both the formal channels of the security services and police and the informal channels of his connections to get leads. There was no doubt in Arthur's mind that Andrei would come up with names within a few days. But Arthur's experience told him there was a possibility that knowing who was responsible may be even more unsettling.

They had to quickly discover who was behind the assassination attempt and whether they were going to try something else. The list of potential culprits was virtually endless. It could've been business rivals from Ukraine, Russia, Belarus or a dozen other countries. It could've been the secret services of any of those countries and a dozen more. The Group's closet was full of skeletons. And it was a big closet.

After driving for four hours, Arthur arrived at the hospital in Kiev. David, Boris and Masha were all there waiting, and Boris wasted no time informing Arthur of his plan. The boss was alive but the bullet remained in his brain, so he, David and Masha had decided to fly him to Israel with Arthur escorting him for protection.

Arthur had spent the car journey wracking his brain for an answer. Nothing stood out just yet, except for a bad feeling about Denis Filatov, a so-called friend and associate, who had asked for Arthur to be sent to Kremenchuk two days before the shooting. Arthur rarely left his boss' side unless absolutely necessary, and then the one time that he did, an attempt was made on his life. This was no coincidence. Whoever did it knew that Arthur wasn't going to be around.

The one detail that was clear already was that this was no amateur setup. The shooting required planning and precise intelligence. Snipers need to prepare, find a position and know where and when the target would appear. This was a professionally conducted operation with the stench of the KGB or something similar all over it. Before jumping to any conclusions, Arthur needed facts. The truth would surface. It always did.

"These sons of whores aren't going to stop until they achieve whatever they're after," thought Arthur. "What bloody mess have you got yourself into this time, boss?"

4 The USSR is Dead, Long Live Ukraine

Before 1991 the people in the USSR were living on another planet, isolated from the West behind the Iron Curtain. And then in 1989 the Berlin Wall fell, and within two years the USSR dissolved. Mikhail Gorbachev, the reformist, or the best CIA spy as some argue, swayed the Soviet empire enough to be broken-up by the republics' leaders in the aftermath of a failed military coup by hardliners. Ukraine, freed from the grip of the USSR, started a turbulent journey from a communist republic to a supposedly democratic, free-market economy. The winds of change were felt everywhere.

Kiev, 1991

With my regular schooldays over, I started studying civil engineering at the Institute of Higher Education in Kiev. It wasn't because I wanted to study, and I certainly didn't want to become an engineer. Planning roads and buildings had never been a dream of mine, but there were several good reasons for pursuing that career.

Every Jewish mother expects her son to become a lawyer, a doctor or at least an engineer - you basically have three choices. Unfortunately, being Jewish in Ukraine meant that I would probably need Gorbachev's personal recommendation to the rector of the Law School if I was to have any chance of being admitted there.

There was also nothing appealing in becoming a doctor, working long hours in Ukraine's underfunded and decrepit public healthcare system. Saving people's lives or contributing to society was never a strong enough motivation for me, so medicine was never really a choice of mine either. By a process of elimination, this left me with engineering - in my mind, the best choice from a bad bunch.

There were more pragmatic reasons to go to university. University students weren't drafted to the military, and I didn't have the slightest desire to join Ukraine's armed forces.

Another reason was that university students were paid stipends. Although it wasn't much, a small monthly allowance was better than nothing. You go to university, you study a bit and then get some money. This appeared to be a very nice arrangement.

And finally, and most importantly, this is what Sasha expected me to do. I couldn't disappoint him after he had done so much for our family over the years, supporting my mother and me. He had sacrificed his education so I could have mine, so I had to do what I had to do.

At least I knew that I could get into university with my good high-school grades without the need to bribe anyone or use personal connections. You rarely got anything based on merits.

Once again I was one of the youngest students in class. Most students were from the small towns outside Kiev, were four or five years older than me and entering university after finishing their military service. Regrettably, there were only a small number of girls studying with us - engineering wasn't very attractive to attractive women.

Since I was fresh out of high school I had a fresh mind, unspoiled by serving years in the mind-numbing armed forces. I was far better than most other students in subjects that required intensive studying, especially mathematics. This, and being one of a handful of students from the big city, earned me respect from my fellow students.

As Ukraine was newly independent, business entrepreneurship - a new concept in the previously communist country - was blossoming. But the government was in turmoil, leaving a fertile ground for gangsters and racketeering groups, extracting protection from the new businesses. The businesses had to join a protection racket, known as *krysha* - a roof in Russian. Usually, the protectors protected their clients from nobody but the protectors themselves.

Many young athletes joined the gangs instead of aspiring to gold medals in the Olympics. You could easily discern the kind of sport they did by their body shape and injuries. Well-built with a broken nose - a boxer. Broad shoulders with torn ears - a wrestler. Enormous muscles with little to no brain - a bodybuilder. Short with broad shoulders and a quadratic head - a weightlifter.

The few of my schoolmates who spoke decent English were engaged in illicit trade with tourists, selling soviet souvenirs, like babushkas, samovars, military hats, watches and belts. Through my connections I had a constant supply of western clothes my friends had obtained from Brit or German tourists.

I remember proudly showing off my Adidas Torsion sneakers, which were relatively fresh on the market even in Germany, with a matching black Adidas sport suit. I felt exceptionally elegant wearing the latest fashions from Western Europe, adopting mostly a sport style, just as any good racketeer would.

Soon enough I was able to establish quite a reputation with the *dembels*, or military veterans, who lived in the institution's dormitories where most students stayed. If you knew where to look and had the right connections, you could buy anything at campus, from clothes and trainers to weapons and drugs.

One of my mates from high school, Shurik, who was studying road planning, suggested that we play *preferans* with our neighbours. Preferans is a popular card game throughout Eastern Europe that requires three or four players and can be played for money, as was often done by students at the institute. I agreed, and Shurik led the way to one of the dorms on a different floor to ours. He knocked lightly on the door, which was opened by a mean-looking man I would soon learn was named Gigo.

At first sight, it was clear that it was necessary to be cautious around this guy. His broken nose was an indication of his favourite sport, his head was as big as a punching bag, and when he spoke, his thick accent confirmed my observations. A Georgian boxer.

We organised a game and played while drinking beer and vodka. The course of the game, which requires considerable thinking and planning ahead, together with the alcoholic socialising, allowed me to get to know Gigo better. It was obvious that he was a bit slow-witted and savage, and it would be better to have him as a friend, rather than an enemy. I didn't drink too much so I could keep my wits about me. Shurik kept our glasses topped up as I joined the game as the fourth player. It was too easy - I counted the cards and won. Gigo was a bad loser and didn't take his loss well.

"Pah! You have the luck of the devil," Gigo declared, looking threateningly at me. "I need a piss."

Gigo staggered off and I waited a few seconds before going after him.

"Gigo... wait a sec, man."

I caught up with him before he disappeared behind the toilet's door.

"I only really play for fun. You don't need to pay me, my friend. Only do me a favour and collect the money from the other players for me. I'll gladly relieve those peasants of a few coins and share some with you."

Judging from Gigo's furious behaviour, it was unlikely he would've paid me anyway. This way I hoped I could get him on my side and use his threatening look for my own benefit. Gigo stopped dead and looked at me quizzically. For a brief moment I wondered if I'd made a bad decision, but then Gigo smiled, showing his gold teeth.

"Okay, let me piss first."

I returned to the others, who'd opened another bottle of vodka. Gigo sauntered in as the glasses were filled.

"Yes...a toast to our victor," he said, grabbing a glass. "To Misha."

"To Misha," the group chorused.

"And don't forget to pay the man," Gigo added aggressively. "I get upset when my friend is upset."

There were a few nervous laughs, but before the other players left, they made a point of counting out their losses in front of Gigo.

I stayed behind and helped Gigo finish the bottle. An idea was hatched to set up a nice hustling scheme. Gigo would find a couple of students, and I would join the game as a fourth hand, pretending that Gigo and I didn't know each other. The plan was to lose small amounts as bait then later on switch to using marked cards on the higher stakes. These hands would be fixed so that Gigo won, and the students and I would owe him money. Eventually Gigo would declare, "The game's over. Now the three of you pay me my cash."

A few days later we put our plan to action, and the scene played out just as I'd predicted. When the time of the game expired and the pot reached a decent size, Gigo won the hand and demanded his winnings.

When I protested saying, "I want to continue playing to have a chance of winning my money back," Gigo threatened me.

"Pay now or I'll shove a bottle of vodka up your ass and break your arms. You won't be able stop shitting from your enlarged arsehole and have no arms to wipe your bum."

I immediately paid him. Following my example, the other students paid up without further complaints.

***

I was impressed with Gigo's natural extortion capabilities and keeping with the spirit of the time, I was looking to expand our entrepreneurial activities. We started extracting protection money from the *lokh* students - lokh being Russian slang describing a sucker.

We began coercing the lokhs into paying us monthly fees for protection. I did the talking and ruthless Gigo did the threatening. I had a natural talent for acting. Gigo had a natural talent for looking frightening.

Our normal pitch was, "You have a nice business. All the gangs roaming the streets; it's terrible. The bastards have no respect to honourable business owners like yourself. The country isn't what it used to be," I said while shaking my head, making tut-tuts of disapproval and taking a long, deep sigh.

"It would be a shame if something happened to your business. You know that the policemen don't care; they work with the damn hooligans. But don't you worry, we're here to help you. For a monthly fee we'll ensure that you and your business and your family are safe. You wouldn't want someone like Gigo here to do something nasty to your daughter/wife/girlfriend/mama. Believe us; it's going to cost us more than you."

Racketeering didn't feel satisfying. I didn't enjoy it and I didn't like doing it, but I had to make a living somehow. I became a bully like Igor from my first school. It was easy money but nothing to be proud of. Decency and business were bad companions.

One of our *clients* was a student named Vlad who ran a video store next to the university. To prove him our worthiness and to ensure that he had enough money to pay us, we helped him collect debts from customers who didn't pay on time. What we didn't realise was that the video store was in the territory of a violent racketeering gang. One day we went to Vlad and demanded our monthly payment, but he shrugged his shoulders and protested.

"I've already paid protection to another gang. Their leader, Nazar, threatened me that if I didn't pay he would burn down the store and kick my ass."

Vlad actually expected us to intervene on his behalf against Nazar.

"I'm paying you protection, so protect me. Nazar will hurt me. Please help."

We weren't a real racketeering gang; we were just trying to act like one. Gigo, being an ex-boxer and not the sharpest tool in the box, told Vlad we would sort it out.

"You don't worry, Vlad. We take care of you."

"Thank you, I hear that Nazar is vicious."

"Let us worry about Nazar," Gigo said in a soothing voice. "Now you pay us."

Poor Vlad didn't have enough cash to pay us since the other gang had already taken his money. I told Gigo to beat him, but not too rough. Vlad, who was two years older than me, started crying and begging for mercy like a little girl. I felt sorry for him. The decent people I knew were just about surviving, while the crooks and manipulators were much better off. And I needed to be better off.

Gigo took his promise to Vlad seriously. We left Vlad in tears and walked back to campus.

"We must go to the other gang and make sure they stop fucking with our clients. You and I go now to talk with this Nazar. He cannot take money from our clients."

"Gigo, are you fucking crazy? Did you forget? We don't really have a gang, it's just the two of us," I reminded him.

If it was up to me, we would've quit the racketeering business altogether and moved to a less complicated enterprise. However, soon I found out that it wasn't that easy to get out once you were in.

A couple of days later, as I was leaving the institute, counting my profits from another successful preferans game, five guys jumped out of a shabby Lada and walked towards me.

A vicious looking thug blocked my path while his gorilla-looking friends surrounded me. He had a scar on the left side of his face which ran all the way from his forehead to the side of his mouth, giving him a lopsided grin when he spoke.

"Privet, student. Nazar sends his regards. Our friend Vlad tells us you've been collecting from our area for quite some time."

I had to think fast.

"Listen, smart guy," I replied with as much confidence as I could muster. "You can tell Nazar that if he has any financial demands he can present them to Zhigan. This is his area and we collect for him."

"Bullshit."

"That's his car over there," I said, pointing to a BMW parked nearby. We stared at each other for five long seconds. I knew there were only two options he was considering: either kill me right away or get instructions from his boss and then kill me. As my stare was unwavering, he probably decided that I wasn't bullshitting. He gave me a dismissive look, spat on the ground, turned around and jumped back in the car.

I almost shat myself. Zhigan was a notorious racketeer. I'd never met him and didn't have any wish to do so. This incident proved once again that wits and guts were superior to muscles and physical force. My quick thinking and control over my nerves drove those suckers away.

I knew it wouldn't take long before Nazar found out that I had nothing to do with Zhigan. Moreover, Zhigan would be furious if he found out that someone he didn't know was using his name for backup. I was in deep shit. When I met up with Gigo I told him about the incident.

"I know what you must do, Misha," Gigo told me, nodding sagely. "You must go pay Nazar a visit before he finds out what happened and that we have nothing to do with Zhigan. You must settle things with him."

"You're joking, he'll kill us!"

"This is business, my friend. The institute is our territory. Students are our clients. We must protect our territory," Gigo preached.

Gigo poured a couple of glasses of vodka and sparked up the joint he'd been rolling when I'd found him.

"Relax, Misha. We'll sort it out."

You should probably hold off making big decisions when you're drunk and stoned, because a few shots and puffs later I agreed with Gigo's stupid plan. As the Jewish Talmud teaches, "If someone comes to kill you, get up and kill him first."

We wobbled, stoned and drunk to the headquarters of Nazar's gang in an old industrial park of abandoned garages and storage warehouses close to the Dnieper River. As soon as we entered the compound, Nazar and his crew appeared from nowhere, surrounded us and blocked the exit.

Meeting Nazar was a shock. Because of his reputation, I'd expected him to be a huge, imposing figure. Instead, he was shorter than me. He had black hair swept back from his forehead, a stupid looking beard that only grew below his lower lip, and a lazy eye. He did look sinister, but physically he wasn't that impressive. I thought that in a one on one fight, I would stand a chance, but unfortunately that wasn't the ratio.

"Who the fuck are you and what the fuck do you want?" he hissed. I couldn't tell where the hell he was looking as each of his googly eyes was looking in a different direction.

"Nazar, we're here to clear up the unfortunate misunderstanding about the video store," I replied as calmly as possible. "We want to make it up to you so no bad blood runs between us." I was trying to use short words, not to confuse him.

"The video store? Ah, yes...so you're the two fools who mess with my business."

He looked at Gigo with one of his eyes and said, "And you must be the famous Gigo. I thought that you were taller."

"Did the thinking bit hurt?" Gigo sneered. "Do we sort this out or not?"

I hadn't seen Gigo that intoxicated before. I realised that his judgement was way out of focus and he would drive us straight into a brutal confrontation. I shivered. Here I was trying to find a peaceful resolution, and Gigo decided to act like...Gigo.

"How many motherfuckers do you have with you, Nazar? Six. Why don't you bring six more to make it fair," Gigo went on, obviously stoned out of his mind. Gigo was never clever with words and this wasn't the time to be a smart ass.

Nazar nodded his head and three guys jumped us from behind. The next thing I remember is lying in a heap with a thug forcing me to look at Gigo. Poor Gigo looked like he'd put up a decent fight, but had eventually been overwhelmed. Two men with bloody faces held him down, while another pinned his hand on a wooden block.

"You see what happens when you fuck with my business," Nazar was saying to the bloody mess that was my friend.

Nazar pulled a meat cleaver from behind his back and waved it in Gigo's face.

"I arrange for you a discount in manicure," he screamed and chopped off Gigo's middle finger. I then understood why Nazar was the leader of his gang; he was a ruthless son of a bitch.

Gigo was yelling, I was yelling. Nazar, yelling like a mad dog, picked up the amputated finger and tossed it to the side. A large, ugly rat came out of a broken water pipe, grabbed the finger and scurried away with its prize.

Nazar pointed the cleaver at me and shouted, "Now it's your turn, you little fucking ball sucker. I'm going to chop off your dick and force it down your fingerless friend's throat."

I felt that I was going to throw up. But before I had a chance to do so, everything went black. I was knocked out, unconscious.

A voice entered my dream-like state.

"Misha...Misha...come on," the voice urged.

I awoke to find Gigo's battered face looming over me. My mouth felt salty with blood.

"Come, Misha. We should leave now."

"What? What's going on? Where..."

"Nazar has gone, but they'll be back soon. Come on."

Dizzy, I noticed that Gigo was holding his bleeding finger. I quickly removed one of my shoelaces and wrapped it as a tourniquet around the bloody stump.

Together we staggered back to campus in a terrible state. I needed thirty two stitches and my left arm was broken. Gigo lost his finger and it wasn't going to grow back. But we were lucky; apparently, just after I passed out, one of Nazar's gang came running into the compound and told him that a rival gang was in the area, and everyone left to confront the intruders, giving us an opportunity to escape. I reached for my dick and thankfully it was still there. The last thing I needed was another circumcision.

The relief was only temporary. Nazar would be looking to kill me.

***

The economic conditions in young independent Ukraine were tough. The country entered a deep recession, pushing people to escape in alcoholic and narcotic virtual realities. Everything was consumed to get high. Radiator liquid, medical spirit, au-de-cologne, glue steam, codeine, ephedrine. Anything with psychoactive effects. If you could swallow, smoke, snort, inject or stick it up your butt and it got you high, someone in Ukraine would've tried it.

Vodka was my choice of a drug. We either bought vodka or used its homemade substitute. The vodka that we distilled was cheap, awful shit, but who cared about the taste after a couple of shots?

Many students replenished the stock of the ingredients - wheat, rye, barely, corn and potatoes - from their home villages, and chemistry students provided basic lab equipment. We had a splendid little brewery running at the dorms, ensuring we avoided producing fatal amounts of methanol, a by-product of homemade alcohol - so don't try it at home.

I had nothing against smoking weed or against smokers. Some of my best friends were more often stoned than sober. I enjoyed smoking marijuana, but I liked vodka better. Weed makes you think more and vodka makes you think less. I was thinking all the time so I liked the smoothing effects of vodka, giving my mind some well-deserved time off.

The weed smokers were a fertile ground for making extra money. Gigo had a Georgian cousin - one of countless cousins, who was a dealer of marijuana and hash. The dealing was done under the cover of an apricot stand at Kiev's central market. I used to buy from Gigo's cousin in bulk, cut the pack to small plastic bags and sell them to students.

Ukrainian weed smokers were always looking for ways to make the smoking more economical. Rolling paper wasn't cheap, so smokers emptied cigarettes and used them instead, after removing the filter so the good stuff wouldn't be filtered down. The cigarette's tobacco was mixed with the marijuana so it lasted longer.

Another way to increase the smoking's efficiency was the parovoz, literally meaning locomotive in Russian. With a parovoz, one weed smoker exhaled into the mouth of another smoker so the smoke could be recycled and used again. This was Ukrainian efficiency and high-tech industrialisation at its best.

I stayed away from heavy drug users. The main reason was that local gangsters controlled all the dealing of heavy drugs, such as codeine, ephedrine and morphine.

Messing with drug barons or stepping into their territory could mean serious trouble, like finding yourself at the bottom of the Dnieper River with cement shoes around your feet. Dealing light drugs to fellow students could've been done unnoticed. As I've learnt over the years, flying below the radar was a key for safely reaching old age.

Dealing drugs, of course, was officially illegal. However, while it was a serious offence, its illegality was only a small nuisance and a big business opportunity. If a policeman caught you dealing drugs, an envelope might solve the problem. But if another drug lord caught you dealing drugs, an envelope would solve nothing. He would take the envelope and still shoot you if you were lucky, or torture you and then shoot you, if you were unlucky. You were better off with a policeman than with a hard-core drug dealer.

Another aspect that provided safety to small drug pushers was that nobody was likely to snitch to the police. The police was the enemy. Snitching was a serious crime in gangster rules, which were predominant in comparison with state laws. The penalty for snitching was physical punishment - broken limbs or death. The students knew that if they were to snitch to the militsiya, they would need prosthetic knees, and with the poor healthcare system in Ukraine you were better off avoiding its services.

***

While my Jewish mother always taught me to complain, I had no reasons to do so. Overall, between my protection business, light drug dealing, card hustling, the monthly university stipends and fees from helping students in their exams, I was doing quite well for a seventeen year old university student, boasting a nice business diversification.

I wasn't ashamed of my economic position anymore. From the outcast among my schoolmates, I became almost rich in comparison with most of my fellow students. That felt good! Nobody dared to ignore me at university, and many admired me.

After a few months at the institute, I was able to move out of the dorms and rent a small one-bedroom apartment. It was well equipped with a video cassette recorder and a colour television.

The Godfather movie was my favourite. I felt an affinity with the character of Michael Corleone. He, like me, was inherently moral but was pushed into a life of crime by necessity. Michael had to do what he did to protect and provide for his family. I had to do what I did to stop living like a poor, worthless Jewish boy.

My apartment soon became a mecca for small student parties. I entertained my guests with vodka, smoke and the latest movies and music. This made me extremely popular with the ladies, and provided a comfortable place to keep a low profile under Nazar's radar.

During the break between semesters, students were sent to a labour camp in the countryside. I probably could've escaped this pointless activity by buying a certificate from any doctor, but, since it offered some time off and a good hideout from Nazar, I actually embarked on it enthusiastically. It wasn't like I really intended to work there anyway.

I thought that it was a crime against humanity to send us to the fields in the middle of the rainy, freezing, intolerable November weather. While I didn't expect a limousine to take us to the countryside, seeing what looked like a World War II truck waiting for us fell below even my modest expectations. It was roofless, so we were exposed to the cold downpour for the entire journey. Our vodka supplies started to vanish immediately, as we passed the bottles around, attempting to warm up.

Drinking vodka on a truck wasn't the wisest idea. Since the truck hardly had springs and shock absorbers, the ride felt like taming a mustang. The first few students vomited right inside the truck. After another fellow did it next to me, I warned the rest that I would personally throw the next one to do so out of the truck. The threat was heeded and the next round of pukes was delivered outside, by bending over the truck's sides.

We were heading southbound on the Kiev-Odessa highway. However, approximately thirty kilometres away from Kiev the truck turned left on to a dirt road that had been washed away by recent heavy rains. The famous saying ascribed to Gogol, that Russia has two troubles - idiots and roads - was still actual.

After the third time that we had to push and pull the stuck lorry out of the mud, the driver suggested that we might continue on foot.

"Laddies. You're too heavy a load. It's only one kilometre left, so you'll be in the labour camp in no time, if you walk instead of struggling with this truck in a swamp."

He had a point, so we disembarked, looking forward to reaching some dry, warm shelter soon. After walking an hour and without seeing any sign of a settlement on the horizon, it became clear that the driver's distance estimate was - how to say it mildly - a little bit fucking inaccurate.

After walking for three hours, we started to smell the cows' shit. Civilization was near! After another half an hour the stench became unbearable. I was sure that now it wasn't a dirt road anymore - we were treading on a shit road.

Soon we found further evidence of humanoids: the drunken kolkhozniks staggering, lying and moaning along the road.

It was the middle of the working day when we arrived; nevertheless it seemed that the entire grown-up populace of the village was drunk out of their skulls. No wonder there was an acute shortage of workforce for harvesting.

Seeing this decadence, we had no intention of putting our shoulders to the wheel instead of our drunken comrades. Most of us pretended as if we were diligently harvesting beets during the day, while we spent the evenings partying wildly.

The first evening at the camp I saw a familiar face: Olga, the girl from my high school. I immediately noticed that she had her horse-like teeth fixed. Dentists in Ukraine didn't have braces, so I didn't know how they were fixed. But I didn't care. She looked even better than before. I had to have her.

As I was a slum dog, not spoiled by luxurious living conditions, the Spartan environment of the camp wasn't much of a nuisance. Olga, on the other hand, was the daughter of a prominent communist party boss, brought up in central Kiev. The princess was on the verge of a psychiatric meltdown once she'd realised where she was. When she saw me, she smiled and walked over.

"Oh, Misha. I'm so glad to see you here. It's lovely to see a familiar face."

Olga hadn't looked at me twice during high school since I had no money and I was basically just another poor Jewish boy. Now that I'd managed to make some money, which was obvious to anyone from my foreign outfit, Olga somehow found me more attractive.

Like a good and caring friend, I invited her to hang out. Nothing was better than a damsel in distress for a knight in shining armour to make his move.

"It's nice to see you too, Olga. You look nice. Very nice," I said, trying to act cool and aloof.

Olga smiled shyly and played with her hair, rolling it around her finger. It was obvious we didn't have much to talk about, so I decided not to waste any time.

"How about going to my room to catch up? I have some music and a bottle. That's the only entertainment here. No dance clubs or cafes. Only mooing cows and mooing locals. They might play an accordion or balalaika around here, but we shouldn't expect more than that. What do you say?"

Olga smiled, looked around at the scruffy students, and agreed to go with me to my room. After listening to a mix of underground Russian and English music, and emptying a bottle of vodka, Olga and I were soon making out.

I started to undress her as we were passionately kissing and feeling each other.

Olga panted breathlessly, "We shouldn't do anything," while helping me to undress her.

"Don't worry, we won't do anything," I replied, and continued removing her clothes.

She pulled her pants off and started to rub against me. I lay on top of her and plunged into her wet tight pussy.

"Oh my god, yes, yes. Oh Misha, stop, stop. Oh my god, yes, yes."

She was panting and moaning, while saying in a hoarse voice, "Stop, stop, we should stop," but wrapping her legs around me, not letting me withdraw out of her even if I wanted to.

I could hardly talk, but whispered, "Don't worry, relax, we aren't doing anything."

When I'd finished, Olga slipped out of the bed, got dressed and headed for the door.

I whispered drowsily, "What about a good night kiss?"

She came back, kissed me on my cheek and left the room. Did I feel satisfaction conquering the hottest girl from high-school? Not really. I knew it was my new reputation and vodka, rather than my charm that had enabled me to bed Olga.

Next morning I discovered that all my sheets were covered with blood. The shagging did start a bit strange, as I felt as if I was breaking through a barrier. Was she a virgin? I didn't have any other explanation. It wasn't her period for sure. I really felt pity for the poor girl to lose her virginity in such a brisk and unromantic manner. It was supposed to be special experience for her. To spend it drunk with a drunk and indifferent guy like me seemed a waste.

Since no change of sheets was envisaged throughout our sojourn in the kolkhoz, I had to pay five rubles to a camp's commandant to get a clean set. I couldn't sleep in sheets covered in Olga's blood.

I expected to feel the same bliss and satisfaction as I had years ago in Leningrad with the girl from Riga. Instead, what I felt was emptiness and an unsatisfactory anti-climax. Conquering Olga felt like reaching the peak of Mount Everest only to find a flag already stuck there. In Olga's case I was the first one, but I was irritated that an occasion I'd had so many wet dreams about went so mundanely and literally filthy.

I lost my entire libido for her. When Olga sidled up to me the next evening, I made it clear our encounter the night before was a one-off. To my surprise, she shrugged and walked away. Released from her mama's tight supervision in Kiev and overcoming her initial shock, she seemed to have shed her inhibitions overnight. She ambled over to a table full of male students and spent the evening drinking and flirting outrageously. Later, I glanced over and saw her making out with another student on a bench in front of everyone. Maybe it was for my benefit, but I didn't care. Olga was a turned page for me. I think that I was key in liberating her, showing her that girls should have fun too.

As for me, I learnt a lesson that love follows money. I recalled that episode often, each time I heard the Red Hot Chili Peppers song *Breaking the Girl*, released two years later.

"*Twisting and turning, your feelings are burning, you're breaking the girl.*"

***

Around this time, my mother increasingly spoke about leaving Ukraine and immigrating to Israel. The looming repercussions from my misunderstanding with Nazar and his gang were a strong enough reason for me to think about going with her. Every time I thought about Nazar I instinctively covered my groin with my hand. Staying in Kiev was dangerous. Maybe it was time for a change of scenery. Maybe it was time to change my place and change my luck.

5 History Repeated

The forces that were behind the glorious Soviet empire, working quietly in the shadows, were still pulling the strings behind the scenes.

The man who was once known as the Puppet Master watched the news with what was his closest version of a grin. As Russian TV, carefully censored and peppered with necessary intonations, reported on the latest police crackdown on striking factory workers in Ukraine, he raised his glass of vodka and downed it in a single gulp. All that was needed was a single spark to ignite the country into flames. Ukraine was drifting ever-closer to the European Union and it needed steering in the right direction.

Chisinau, 2013

The four men sat around an oval table in a room filled with cigarette smoke. They hadn't been together for nearly a quarter of a century, but they'd never lost contact with each other. Together, they had witnessed the world hanging on the brink of a nuclear war in 1962 after the Bay of Pigs Invasion and the Cuban Missile Crisis. They served as high ranking officers in Afghanistan in the early 1980s, and they'd seen their proud empire's dissolution in 1991 after the failure of a coup d'état that they secretly supported.

The reunion was held on neutral ground, in Chisinau, the capital of Moldova. Official papers would say they each were there for the anniversary celebrations of Moldova's liberation from Nazi-Romanian occupation. Discretion was paramount; the last thing that they wanted was for the press to sniff around and report that the gathering had ever happened.

They all dressed in ceremonial military uniforms, with an iron ring on the index finger of their right hands. It bore the Soviet Union's hammer and sickle, alongside three stars. Each star represented one of the three republics in the iron union: Russia, Ukraine and Belarus - the three original republics that founded the USSR in 1922. This was a token of their loyalty, worn only at internal, secretive forums.

The Minister of Defence of Russia, a man now in his seventies, poured vodka for everyone. After they emptied their glasses, he stood, put his hands on the table and started the meeting.

"Well comrades, it has been a long time since I had the pleasure of seeing you all. After so many years, I doubted we would ever meet like this again."

The three men sat around the table nodded in agreement.

"When I received the coded message, I must admit my old heart skipped a beat. The fact that you're all here is pleasing to an old general. I'm sure that you, like me, have had enough with being reduced to insignificancy by the Americans and Chinese. Even small countries, which feared us for years, like Poland and the Czech Republic, behave insolently. They have joined the European Union and NATO!" The minister's voice rose almost to a shout as he spat the words out.

"They avail their territories for NATO bases while NATO remains our enemy, no matter what false appeasing palaver they spout. There are idiots who try to drive a wedge between our fraternal nations and push towards other European countries. Make no mistake, EU is NATO, you shouldn't have doubts about that. It cannot continue. The contingencies we arranged for so many years ago are still in place. Current events dictate we take action. Comrades...it is time to return to the glory of the East Slavic Empire."

He slammed his fist on the table and glared at his three colleagues who all nodded wisely, obviously sharing the minister's displeasure at recent events.

"I tell you now that you all have my personal assurance that if you help your countries to cooperate, Russia won't forget. Russia will remember those who stood by its side. The Soviet Union will remember its heroes. Now, the time has come to reinstate and reunite our common Motherland and rectify the mistakes of 1991."

The Minister of Defence of Ukraine and the Minister of Defence of Belarus nodded in agreement.

The Russian minister continued, "There are some who will do whatever it takes to impede us. We need to stop them at all cost. We cannot order our secret security forces to intercept them since we cannot risk our plans leaking. We can count only on a small circle of loyal officers to take care of things."

The minister sat down and allowed his speech to sink in. Eventually the Belarusian stood.

"Comrades, I would like to say that I too was pleasantly surprised when I received the message to meet you all. I too have activated my part of the arrangement. My president knows nothing, but even if he did, he would hardly oppose the plan. We'll easily persuade him to delay our enemies. You can count on our cooperation. Russia can count on its Belarusian brothers."

After a short pause to ensure that the Belarusian minister had finished, it was the turn of the Ukrainian minister to stand.

"I'll do my part as discussed through proxies, although the situation in Ukraine is more complicated."

"Complicated?" the fourth man, who had barely spoken till now enquired.

"This rotten demo-*crazy*," he distorted the word in disdain, "has penetrated even the army ranks. This makes everything more problematic, but I have a crew that I can count on. Russia can count on its Ukrainian brothers." He added before sitting once again.

Silence fell in the room. The three ministers looked to the fourth man, waiting for his input. He was in his late-seventies, with a full head of snowy white hair and his upper lip and chin covered with a thick white beard. While he wasn't young, his stern gaze emanated physical strength and power.

He bent forward slightly and extinguished his cigarette in an ashtray. Leaning back in his chair, and without standing, finally he stated his position.

"Comrades, your loyalty won't go unnoticed. We need to act smartly because we cannot win in an open conflict. The world isn't what it used to be. We need to act behind the scenes, deep in the shadows. It's good that you're all eager to fulfil the promise we made so long ago. Let me fill you in on what has already been done and what is now required from each of us."

He paused while lighting another cigarette with a silver Russian replica of a zippo emblazoned with the emblem of the KGB - a broadsword superimposed on a shield background, red star with the hammer and sickle, and the words *КГБ СССР*. He briefed the ministers, covering each detail of the plot that he expected them to implement in the near future. He ensured that everyone clearly understood their role and responsibilities.

"I have done my bit at this stage. You still need to take care of yours. You need to take care of those who can thwart our plans or come close enough to assembling the pieces of the puzzle and figure out our strategy. We cannot take any risks."

The three ministers listened to the fourth man with awe. Now they understood the bigger picture. Some recent events that they didn't deem connected were presented to them as woven into a grandiose master plan. It was reassuring to know that the plan had already been initiated and the reason for the meeting was merely to discuss the personal responsibilities of the three ministers. The men listened carefully as the old man laid out what was expected of them. Despite having no political office, and having retired long ago, the white-haired man was definitely in charge.

Once, in a different life, he had been their superior. Men spoke of his ruthlessness and brilliance with a mixture of fear and admiration. Some doubted his very existence, as his name and position were kept secret, but those who knew him, referred to him as the *Puppet Master.*

6 The Land of Milk and Honey

Hate crimes and anti-Semitism in Ukraine weren't uncommon. The frequency of violent incidents against Jews rose rapidly after the fall of the Soviet regime and the weakening of the security services' control as neo-Nazi, skinhead and extreme national groups all crawled out of the woodwork now that the intolerant communist regime had gone.

Kiev, 1992

One Friday night as we sat around the dinner table, my mother told Sasha and me of her intentions to leave Ukraine.

"I've decided I want to move to Israel. Life here doesn't get any easier. In Israel, Jews can live proudly. Since they took your papa away we have nothing. Nothing at all! Gornisht. It's time for us to make Aliyah and return to the Promised Land."

"But mama, I have a wife and baby son and a stable job," Sasha interrupted. "Yulia won't want to move to a distant country where people speak a foreign language. Mama...I can't go with you."

"We should be together, Sasha. Mishenka...talk some sense into your brother," she ordered.

I felt between a rock and a hard place. I hadn't had time to formulate my own opinion, let alone try to convince my stubborn brother to commit one way or another.

"I have a good job," Sasha reiterated before I could say anything. "Yulia is pregnant again and I don't want her to give birth in a foreign country where we don't speak the language. Perhaps we'll join you in a couple of years when the baby grows up and I save some more money. That's the best I can do, mama."

"Oy vey, Sashenka," mama said sadly. "It's my entire fault. I'm glad your papa doesn't hear that his eldest son is afraid to live in Zion."

Yuri, my best friend from school, had made Aliyah in 1991, and I'd received several letters extolling the virtues of Israel. He told me that the food was good, the girls were pretty, the beaches were beautiful, and the weather was fantastic. It didn't even snow in winter. It wasn't grey.

With Sasha adamant he would stay, I decided to go with my mother. Not because of Zionism or ideology, but rather because the bleak future prospects of the crumbling Soviet Union seemed pale relative to the bright prospects of a new adventure in a faraway land.

Another incentive to get away from Kiev was Nazar. Word on the street was that he was still looking to kill me and I was living on borrowed time. It was wise to try my fortunes somewhere else.

If I was leaving for good, I wanted to make sure that I had some capital on me to start a decent life abroad. Without anything to hold her back, my mother made her arrangements and left for Israel within a month. I would join her shortly, as soon as I'd found a way of getting my money out of Ukraine.

***

Since there were no direct flights from Ukraine to Israel, I had to take a train to Bucharest, the capital of Romania, and fly from there. I'd managed to save twenty thousand US dollars during my time at the Institute of Higher Education from my various enterprises. At the time, emigrants were allowed neither to leave any property behind nor take anything across the border beyond personal belongings of limited value. These restrictions were insignificant to me as I'd learnt from a tender age that when the state disallowed something it just meant that you needed to pay the right people to allow it. So, I devised a plan.

Sasha somehow managed to arrange for me a private audience with Ukraine's deputy chief of customs, Vladimir Samsonov. Never expecting anything good from the authorities, and having limited experience with Soviet bureaucrats, I didn't quite know what to expect when I arrived at his office's shabby reception room. The old and dirty chairs were arranged with their backs to the dingy grey walls, underneath a set of windows that looked like they hadn't seen a decent clean for years. "*What a welcoming and hospitable place*," I thought to myself.

I was a bit nervous and had an urge to go to the toilet. The toilet's door was locked, so I politely asked the secretary for the key. She could've been good-looking were she not so haughty, unfriendly and bitchy.

Looking at me with contempt, like something a cat dragged from a garbage bin, she reluctantly handed me the key stating, "Keep it clean, yes? Don't you make a mess in there, yes?" As if the toilet was clean; it even lacked toilet paper.

Finishing my business in the toilet, I handed the key back to Miss Pleasant, and sat in one of the musty chairs. Vladimir made me wait for over half an hour, doubtlessly on purpose to demonstrate his seniority. Everything was designed to belittle the visitor.

I knew that I had to bribe Vladimir. I'd never bribed anyone before so I was a bit edgy. I'd done all kinds of stuff which could easily be categorised as felonies under the Ukrainian criminal code, but here I felt totally exposed. If

Vladimir wanted to turn me in, he could make one phone call and that would be my end.

Finally, the secretary's phone rang. She picked it up, nodded, and told me, "Deputy Chief Samsonov will see you now."

Crossing the threshold into Vladimir's office was like moving into another dimension. The opulent interior was a drastic contrast to the dilapidated reception area. Most of the spacious office was occupied by a massive table that could easily seat thirty people. At the other end stood an elegant mahogany table at which was sat Vladimir Samsonov.

He made no effort to raise his head from whatever he was pretending to read. He was dressed up in a perfectly ironed, olive green uniform decorated with medals, with gold leaves on the collar and a hat too wide for his head. He appeared to be in his late fifties, although men in his position were usually younger than that.

Years later I learned that most of these offices had a backdoor room. In these hidden spaces big bosses were shagging their female subordinates, and their secretaries arranged generous meals for special guests. The real, intimate business was done there, accompanied by vodka, which was always kept in a small fridge. I, of course, wasn't special. Vladimir didn't honour me by inviting me to his special compartment and he didn't even offer me tap water as refreshment. I was nobody.

After several minutes had passed, Vladimir finally looked up from his notes. He peered over the top of his glasses, studied me closely, and then gestured to the seat in front of him. I assumed a business like countenance and sat before him.

"So," he said in a bored voice. "What can I do for you?"

I took a deep breath and attempted to keep a steady voice.

"Thank you for seeing me, Deputy Chief Samsonov. I'll soon be leaving for Israel and it's important for me to take a few family heirlooms."

"I see," Samsonov said with disinterest. "And what heirlooms are these?"

"Nothing expensive, sir. Simply some old Hebrew books and my great-grandmother's silver necklace. I'm hoping that you could arrange a green channel for me so that the customs officials don't search my belongings. I would be happy to make a donation to the country for its understanding and generosity."

To make it sound more credible I showed him an old silver necklace I had bought for a couple of rubles at the market in Kiev. Obviously the whole story was a lie; I didn't have any old books and I didn't even want to take the worthless necklace. What was important for me was to not be searched, so I could smuggle my cash.

Vladimir knew the rules of the game much better than me. He'd agreed to meet me because he anticipated a donation. As he studied the worthless necklace, I could sense the figures being multiplied and added in his brain, expecting to see the dollar signs in his eyes. Eventually he sat back and made a great show of stroking his chin, before his face broke into a friendly smile.

"Don't you worry, friend. If you pay me three thousand dollars as a contribution for the country, I'll phone the border straight away and give the order to comrade Constantin Sabo, chief of customs at Chop, to escort you personally through the border. I'll even make sure that my colleagues on the Romanian side let you pass as well. You'll be treated like a little prince. Yes, you will my friend."

I was eager to finish this unpleasant conversation, so I readily agreed to the terms. I excused myself, went out to the reception room, counted the cash out of Madam Bitchy's nosy sight, returned and handed Vladimir his fee without bargaining. Non-bargaining was to my detriment, as I was soon to find out.

I thanked Vladimir, quickly left his office, as his bitch Cerberus ignored my farewell, and headed straight to the train station with my backpack, one suitcase and seventeen thousand dollars. I found my carriage and settled down for the journey to Chop, the border crossing into Romania.

After the night spent crossing the plains, next morning the scenery on the way to Chop turned into a mountainous landscape of endless forests, fields and small villages dotted with ancient houses that looked like they hadn't been painted for centuries. I spotted farmers working the fields with antique machinery, and tractors that resembled tanks from the First World War. The countryside looked desperately poor, as the system had already started to crumble, together with the rest of the regime.

At the Chop border crossing a customs inspector told me that Chief Constantin Sabo wanted to see me. I had paid dearly for a VIP treatment and now the time had come to consummate the service. The inspector kindly offered to keep an eye on my luggage so it wouldn't be left unattended. That was exactly what I'd expected, so I presumed that everything was progressing as planned.

I was led to an office and offered a seat in front of Chief Sabo. To my surprise, my luggage appeared seconds later and was placed on the table between us.

"So, comrade. Shall we see what you're carrying across my border?" the chief said once the inspector had left the office.

"There's no need, sir. Deputy Chief Samsonov has personally cleared my passage to Romania," I replied, conscious of my shaky voice.

"That may be true, comrade, but I'm responsible for everything that passes through this border. Now...open the case and the backpack."

There was no point in protesting further. I unzipped the case and the backpack and emptied the contents onto the table.

"Ahh, what's this?" Sabo said in mock surprise, greedily eying the bundle of notes.

"Sir, I have clearance..."

"Enough! Listen, kid; if you continue to protest, I'll simply write protocol about your attempted smuggling of dollars. If you're lucky, then maybe you'll be able to leave Ukraine in five or six years' time under an amnesty decree. Deputy Chief Samsonov called me and told me that you may have something interesting with you, so there is no point spouting his name."

Silly me. When I didn't protest paying the three grand, that fucker Samsonov knew I must have more.

"It was very naive to expect Deputy Chief Samsonov wouldn't take advantage of your situation. I don't take pleasure from doing this, but I have no other choice. If I don't execute his instructions I'm going to lose my job and perhaps a couple of teeth. I'm really sorry, kid."

Sorry or not, he took all my money.

I swore that I would take my revenge against Vladimir. I believed Constantin that it wasn't his initiative and he was just following orders. I left the office in a daze and headed back to my compartment in the train. How could I start a new life with no money? Stupidly I had no contingencies, no backup plan. I'd thrown all my eggs in a single basket by trusting Vladimir Samsonov. I wouldn't forget his treachery.

Many years later, all it took for me was to make one phone call to force Vladimir to run. My people tracking him last spotted him planning to cross on foot the narrow strip of the border of Russia with Norway. I imagined Vladimir walking through snowy woods, hunting reindeers and running away from bears and wolves, his path illuminated at night by the aurora borealis. I hoped his filthy flesh sated one of the noble animals. But I'm jumping ahead.

Back in Chop, I climbed to the upper bed of the compartment, turned my face to the wall and for the first time in years, I wept. All the toughness of a racketeer and extortionist gave way to the bitter tears of a kid.

Very soon, we were at the Romanian checkpoint, where the scenario was repeated. The customs officials ordered everyone off the train and systematically stripped us of anything of worth. When they came to my possessions they were annoyed that their Ukrainian colleagues had left them nothing to steal. I didn't even have a pack of cigarettes to confiscate.

"Those Ukrainian pigs leave us nothing?" they complained. I shrugged my shoulders and raised my hands, sharing their frustration.

Eventually, I would arrive in Israel empty-handed and poor, with just the clothes that I was wearing, a worthless Pushkin book that nobody wanted to take away from me and little else. Even my new Adidas sneakers didn't make it across the border as they were taken by the Romanians, who claimed I was smuggling them. So, from the Romanian border onwards I travelled barefoot until I was waiting for my plane at Bucharest Airport, and a sympathetic elderly couple offered me a pair of sandals for the flight to Israel. Once again I received second-hand footwear like a miserable beggar. I hated being poor.

***

Israel was so different than Ukraine. The mixture of yellow sand dunes, scrubs and white apartment buildings seen from the plane and applause of passengers as we landed. The repeated questioning at the border crossing by uniformed men and women, seen everywhere. The hot, humid and sweaty climate under the blazing sun. The sense of urgency, tension and impatience of the mix of diverse people. Welcome to the land of milk and honey!

The 1990s saw a massive wave of Jews leave the Soviet Union when Mikhail Gorbachev's liberal government opened the borders as part of *perestroika* and finally eased restrictions on travel abroad. In a relatively short period of time, over one million Jews arrived in Israel, making up about 20% of the Israeli population.

Clearly, the influx of Russians changed Israel's demographics. Some areas became a *Little Russia*, where Russian was more commonly spoken than Hebrew. Local grocery stores stocked Russian newspapers, dark, heavy rye breads and cheap vodka.

At the young age of nineteen, I was still inexperienced. I had big expectations of what life would be like in my new country, and I certainly wasn't prepared for the somewhat hostile welcome of the local Israelis. The impression was that we, the Russian immigrants, weren't much more than a nuisance. In Soviet Ukraine I was a filthy Jew, here in Israel I was a filthy Russian. I was an outcast everywhere!

Nobody was waiting for us or greeted us with open arms, except perhaps for the employers who soon realised that a cheap and experienced labour force was arriving. Generally, the immigrants didn't speak Hebrew or English, so Russian doctors, engineers and scientists had to work in factories or take demeaning jobs like cleaning to make a basic living.

According to the law, all Jews making Aliyah are immediately entitled to Israeli citizenship, provided that they demonstrate that they are Jewish or at least one of their parents or grandparents is.

When the time came to enrol for a modest allowance payable by the state to new immigrants I went for an interview at the Ministry of Absorption. The officer who interviewed me had a twitch in his eye, causing his left eye to wink uncontrollably every minute or so. Coming to Israel from Ukraine, I wasn't sure about the local habits. Do you need to pay anything to state officers, or bribe them, to get an allowance as was the custom in Ukraine?

I sat in the office as the officer went through my papers. The man looked up at me and winked.

"Sure. I get the hint, sir. I'm new here so you need to tell me how much."

The officer's winking went into overdrive.

"I'm sorry?" he replied. "How much what?"

"How much I need to contribute."

"Contribute to what?"

"You winked at me. It's a sign that I need to pay you. No?"

The officer smiled awkwardly and shook his head.

"No, I didn't wink. This is Israel, not Russia. We're not criminals here. You don't need to pay anything," he said while winking at me again, leaving me confused.

The officer had difficulties transcribing my name into Hebrew, so I decided that this was an opportunity to start a clean sheet and make my name more Israeli. When in Israel, do as the Israelis do.

Misha became Moshe, which was close enough. The choice of surname was more difficult, but after a few minute thought, I decided to change my surname to Shaarim - the Hebrew translation for Vorotavich, meaning gates. The officer accepted my choice and signed the papers with a friendly wink.

Moshe Shaarim was born that day. Perhaps, unlike Misha Vorotavich, Moshe Shaarim would be a law-abiding citizen.

The positive side of being nineteen years old is that you can cope well with crises and the challenges that life throws at you. The drive of youth, the physical strength, the optimism and the sense of adventure, as well as naivety and stupidity, help overcome the daily hardships. Youth is both blessed and cursed at the same time.

I was lucky since my English was quite good, and generally excellent compared to that of most of my fellow Russian immigrants. Soon I discovered that speaking English was far better than twisting my tongue trying to speak basic Hebrew with a heavy Russian accent. The advantage of speaking English was felt almost everywhere, from the reaction of ordinary people on the street to the reaction of girls when I chatted to them.

The superiority of English was absolute. It was funny and insulting at the same time to see how ladies got really excited when I introduced myself as a tourist from the Netherlands and really contemptuous when I introduced myself as a new immigrant from the Soviet Union. The Dutch tourist was appealing while the Russian immigrant was appalling.

After a few months in Israel, hanging out with an American friend, I learned how to speak English with a decent American accent. Misha underwent yet another transformation into Michael. Michael Gates. I was a human chameleon, changing my colours to blend with the surroundings. For Russians I was Misha, for Israelis I was Moshe and for Anglo-Saxons, I was Michael.

I used to date girls for months, saying that I was an immigrant from New York.

"I came to visit Israel from Greenwich Village, New York City and stayed because I just love it here. This place is so awesome. The weather, the food, the people and especially the beautiful women, like yourself."

In Israel most people speak some English, but far from a level to be able to discern the accent of another English speaker. They didn't notice the deceit and liked and accepted me. However, once I turned back to being Russian all the fondness quickly disappeared. It was like in the Cinderella story. When the clock struck midnight I turned from Prince Charming Michael to dirty poor Misha dressed in rags.

Well, it wasn't the first time that girls liked me for the façade and not for who I really was. It wouldn't be the last time either.

***

When I arrived to Israel I was sent to a school run by the Israel Defence Force. The fenced compound was in Jaffa, a little south of Tel Aviv. It included a few long wooden buildings surrounding a large square filled with white gravel. In the middle of the square the Israeli flag flew from the top of a white flagpole. On one side of the compound there was a yard with eucalyptus trees and a few wooden tables to which benches were attached from both sides; a perfect place for a picnic.

The school - or *ulpan* - provided us with food and basic accommodation while we combined Hebrew studies with working in military supply storage bases. We worked together with immigrants and other volunteers, the majority of whom were Americans in their fifties. I never really believed the Soviet propaganda machine's depiction of America, so I wasn't surprised that the Americans weren't ruthless people, trying to squeeze every last cent from others. They were actually quite nice, but seemed too open and naive at times.

The contrast in attitudes between the middle-aged Americans and the Russians was amazing. The Americans arrived in Israel full of patriotism and Zionism. They aspired to contribute and went about their work diligently, however elementary it was - whether it was folding shirts or sweeping the floor. They just got on with things with typical American enthusiasm. Everything was *awesome* to them.

The Russians, in contrast, used to leave the military base at night with contraband stuffed in their pockets. They stole anything: underpants, soaps, t-shirts, socks and whatever they could put their hands on in the military storage. The Americans came from a capitalist country of excessive wealth, while the Russians came from a poor communist country where shortages of basic items were normal. The survival instinct of the Russians was to steal since they lacked means to buy much for themselves and their families.

The ulpan was fun. I met many Jewish youngsters from around the world, although as always I was the youngest of the bunch.

There I met my first Israeli girlfriend - one of our soldier-teachers. For my eye, accustomed to Slavic girls in Ukraine, Rachel was more exotic than good looking. Her tanned skin, coal black curls, impressive fit body and Middle Eastern facial features immediately caught my attention. Although the military uniform wasn't the best outfit to compliment the girl's body, I couldn't have possibly ignored a handsome pair of gravity-defying firm breasts, clearly protruding from underneath an ugly olive green military shirt.

She was Israeli-born, but her ancestors were from a once prosperous Jewish community in Yemen.

Although I enjoyed the ulpan and tried to have as much fun as possible, the endless rules and regulations were hard to abide by, and Rachel certainly helped ease the stress.

The youngest American at the ulpan was a guy named Roger. We formed a close friendship pretty early on as he was always the first person to agree to skip classes and have some fun. He was a laid-back Californian stoner who was in Israel primarily to please his parents and ensure his trust fund wasn't pulled. He never had any intentions of being studious in any way. He was a good wingman because of his good looks and dirty-blond hair, and before long we were hanging out and planning for our next great escape.

We spent a lot of time together because Rachel helped with Hebrew lessons on the side and wasn't always free when I had some spare time. Unfortunately, Roger and I were as bad as each other, and the last straw for the administrators at the ulpan was when we snuck out one night and went to a free Latin party at Tel Aviv old seaport. As was usual, our intentions were good; we planned on getting back to base before the morning roll call. But before we knew it, we were dancing and drinking all night with some gorgeous students from Tel Aviv University. Potential shag on the sea shore with a pretty girl whose name I think was Ruth, was more appealing than the walk back to the ulpan.

When we finally staggered in at ten a.m. we were frogmarched straight to the chief. Like naughty schoolboys, we were told to wait outside his office until he was ready to see us. The fact that we were still drunk probably didn't help our case when we tried to talk him into letting us stay.

"We wanted to better understand the culture of the Israelis so we can integrate into society better. If we don't socialise and mingle with them how will we get to know them and learn their language? The party was an excellent assimilation opportunity," I explained to the chief, who wasn't that much older than us.

"This isn't the first time your name had been mentioned to me, Shaarim. I don't believe you value your place here and think it would be best for everyone if you left."

"Hey, come on, dude, it's not that big a deal," Roger interrupted. "How about you cut Michael some slack. He's fresh off the boat and still acclimatising."

The chief waved away Roger's protests.

"We have had too many complaints already, and the Major has ordered a crackdown on this behaviour."

"Fair enough, he'll behave from now on, I'll guarantee it," Roger said, trying to placate the chief.

"Sure, letting the cat guard the cream."

It was pointless though; the decision had already been made, and Roger was on the shit-list too. After a five minute lecture on how we were surrounded by enemies who wanted us wiped off the map, and the ulpan was there to teach us discipline and instil pride in the Israeli nation blah blah blah...we were both expelled.

And that was the end of that as well as of my relationship with Rachel, who didn't want to see me anymore once she spotted some lip gloss on my face when I bumped into her as Roger and I left the chief's office. It seemed that wherever I went trouble followed closely behind.

***

Now I was faced with a dilemma. My mother lived nearly a hundred kilometres north of Tel Aviv and I had no money to get there. Yuri, my friend, had left Israel shortly before I arrived to join his uncle's real estate business in the Czech

Republic, so I couldn't borrow money from him even if I wanted to. Without too many choices, Roger and I stayed in Tel Aviv and slept on the beach, using Roger's large array of T-shirts as blankets.

After a few weeks of living rough we rented a room in a youth hostel, with promises of paying our rent out of our next imaginary pay packet. The hostel was in a rundown area near to the beach and was filled with hookers at night and drunkards during the day. I felt at home as it reminded me of Kiev. I had to make a living somehow, so I took a job in a carpet factory, working twelve hour night shifts.

In the mornings about twenty Russian girls started their shift. I often stayed after finishing my shift to chat with them. In the evenings before going to work I went out with some of the girls. So, the job provided both money and pleasure. Combining business and pleasure was a principle that I've kept ever since. You live once and you should make the best out of it.

I worked with a thirty-something guy named Hizgil, who was a Mountain Jew from Chechnya. Physically, he was the strongest person that I'd ever met. The sewing machines were loaded with huge drums of cotton each weighing well over seventy kilos. Hizgil would lift a drum over his head and hold it with one arm while standing on one leg. He should've gone to work in the circus.

He told me stories about his tough childhood in Chechnya, and compared to some of his tales, my own childhood in Kiev was relatively comfortable. He was a true tough guy, and he came from tough people.

He also told me that he was still a virgin and horny as hell. During coffee or smoking breaks I used to recount my adventures with the girls and this usually got him really excited. Often he used to run to the toilet after we talked to take care of his urges. I decided to help the guy and convinced one of the Russian girls in the factory to take him out. She relieved him of his virginity and probably applauded his exploding passion that he had been accumulating for years. I was happy to see that he didn't make her explode.

I would never forget his final words after regaling me with a story of violence and treachery, "Don't ever betray a Chechen. He'll cut off your testicles and feed them to his goats. Chechens are like elephants, they never forget."

***

When I turned twenty I received a letter from the Israel Defence Force. It was time for me to be drafted to the service.

Since military service wasn't part of my plans I needed a counter plan. Many men went to see the military psychiatrist, making up stories to avoid conscription due to mental illness. One popular story was about a guy who goes to see the army psychiatrist, reverses his trousers' pockets inside out, pulls out his dick and tells the psychiatrist, "I'm an elephant."

But that wasn't my style. I had another option. It was time to once again go to university to postpone conscription. Because Ukrainian universities weren't recognised as reliable academic institutions by Israel, perhaps because you could buy an academic degree, I needed to enrol in a pre-university preparatory programme.

I got a place in Tel Aviv University's dormitories while I studied for the entrance exams. Once again, I didn't need to invest much time or effort in the studies since what I had learned in Kiev's Institute of Higher Education was more than enough to place me as one of the best students. I had plenty of time for other activities, which included finding a job to support myself.

My fluent English and blonde hair helped me land a job as a pool boy in one of the luxurious hotels on Tel Aviv beach. I was able to hit on American tourists for whom I was exotic. For Americans to date a Russian communist was like for an angel to date a demon. Sweet forbidden love. For American women, Misha from Russia was more attractive than Michael from New York. Or maybe shagging anyone foreign or unusual was just a part of their vacation itinerary. However, money was still insufficient working at the pool and being a gigolo was a step too far, even for me.

I had to find an additional source of income, preferably not an extra job. The cold truth of the universe that you can't live decently off normal work had already ingrained itself on me.

Not too far away from the university is one of the wealthiest neighbourhoods in Israel; Ramat Aviv. The spoiled rich teenagers used to come to the preparatory programme, searching for students to help them with their high school exams. While disguising myself as them and taking their actual exam was too risky, I offered the same arrangement I had back in Kiev.

I sat at a café across the street from the dorms, and the kids excused themselves from the exam and sneaked questions to me. Later on they would blame an upset stomach, excuse themselves again, and collect the answers. Diarrhoea epidemic all over again. The rich kids paid generously for my discreet services. While I intended to live a crime-free life in Israel, legitimate money was too tight and illegitimate money was too easy, and tempting. What else could I do?

***

Armed with decent grades both in the preparatory programme and the exams, it was time to properly go to university. The two most prestigious university study subjects in Israel were the same as back in Ukraine: medicine and law. Jewish mothers always pushed their children to study these subjects. Being a doctor wasn't appealing so I chose law. Knowing the legal system would always be helpful, in particular to those who want to find loopholes and bend the rules. If you don't know it how can you bend it?

I was admitted to the most sought after university in Israel, the Law School of Tel Aviv, with all the top young Israeli students. Since I was one of a small number of students who hadn't completed military service, once again I was the youngest in the group.

For the first semester I took the studies seriously. In the second semester a big student strike broke out over tuition fees and there was no school for two months. We paraded on the streets shouting in front of the policemen, "If we don't study we'll become policemen." Had we disrespectfully shouted that in front of policemen in Kiev they would've thrown us into jail and broken some of our bones on the way in. I never went back to sit in classes after the strike ended.

After taking the first set of exams I realised that they weren't too difficult and I easily attained a passing grade. I managed to fulfil my academic obligations without attending the lectures as I always had a few helpful friends who signed my name at classes. For assignments, we would meet at the cafeteria just before class, borrow a couple of papers and rewrite ours in a few minutes. Copying from a few different papers concealed any traces of plagiarism and was sufficient to get a passing grade. Law school allowed me to pursue an academic degree without attending university in person. I spent far more time sitting in the cafeteria, playing cards with my friends than visiting lectures.

I managed to save enough money from my 'tutoring service' to buy a ticket to visit Ukraine. While I enjoyed my time in Israel, I missed home. I was eager to see Sasha and my old friends. I was twenty one, and the trip to Ukraine would change my life.

Misha Vorotavich was about to be reborn.

7 Needle in a Haystack

Kiev, 2013

Andrei Topolski accepted the new assignment from Arthur with a great deal of enthusiasm. He had been working as the chief security officer of the Group's Moscow trade house for almost seven years, although it wasn't what he considered to be work even if his huge salary hinted otherwise. To Andrei it was more like retirement.

The main focus of the Group's activities was elsewhere, so Andrei's responsibilities were relatively limited. He was charged with conducting background checks on new employees to ensure that no suspicious characters penetrated the Group, he spied and reported on the local managers and made random verification checks on transactions, making sure the kickbacks weren't their prime stimuli. And he drank vodka from time to time with Moscow's police and tax chiefs to keep appraised of any gossip.

After being the Head of Moscow's Criminal Investigation Department in the militsiya during Soviet times, the work in the Group was boring and uneventful. In his old role, he had confronted the most vicious gang leaders as they drifted to Moscow, where most of the wealth was concentrated. Nowadays, he was ashamed of his pensioner's position. He missed his old glory days.

The investigation into the assassination attempt was a challenge, reminding him of his glorious past. He knew he'd be a bit rusty, but he was certain he hadn't lost his hound's instincts. During the flight to Kiev he studied what little information he had. He scribbled notes in his notebook, as he had done his whole working life, using code names for people and places so that anyone who saw the collection of scribbles wouldn't have a clue what he was writing. The plane started its descent, and soon Andrei was standing in the arrivals area at Kiev's Boryspil International Airport.

"Andrei?" a voice called out from the throng of people hanging around the exit.

"Yes, I'm Andrei. Who sent you to meet me?" Andrei asked, cautious of being intercepted by someone who wanted to keep the assassination attempt quiet.

"Arthur sent me; my name is Petro," the man answered.

"Good. Then let's go."

Petro led Andrei to a battered old VW and opened the passenger door for him.

"Arthur thinks it's best that your presence here doesn't attract unwanted attention. None of the Group's local security was filled in on your arrival. I belong to Arthur's *inner circle*," Petro emphasised the last two words.

"Smart thinking," Andrei observed, being sure now that Petro was a former officer in the SBU - the Security Service of Ukraine. "Let the scums who did this think they're safe."

"So where do you want to go?"

"I think I should start at the Parus Business Centre and study the scene where the boss was shot."

"No problem. Anything I can do to help?"

Andrei thought for a moment, and then fished out his notebook and scanned the pages.

"Actually, there is," he said as he placed the notes back into his pocket. "I hope soon to have the list of all mobile phones that were operational within a one hundred metre radius from Parus one hour before through one hour after the assault. I want you to go over the list and establish the identity of every owner that'll be missing on the list."

"Surely, there will be thousands of entries! Parus is dead centre of Kiev!"

"Arthur told me to use as much manpower as necessary. I appreciate it will take time and money to gather such information, but do whatever it takes. I don't intend leaving one iota of evidence open to speculation."

Andrei was under no illusions. There was no way that the marksman himself had a mobile phone on him as every communication the assailant needed would've been done well before or after the job. But his accomplices, if any, or his client's representatives might well have been on the ground to validate the result.

Petro steered the VW into an underground parking garage and walked with Andrei to the place where the boss was shot. Andrei stood completely still, his eyes darting from building to building, window to window. A small stain on the pavement, hastily cleaned but still evident, showed where he had fallen. Andrei re-enacted the walk from the main entrance, stepped over the faint mark, and stood where he calculated the boss would've been when the shot was taken.

"Petro; stand here, exactly where the boss was shot. I want to evaluate all possible angles."

Petro stood on the spot, and Andrei studied the various angles and positions where the shot may have come from.

"Okay...the boss was shot just twelve meters from the exit to the North West from Parus. Thus, the building itself prevented any possible shot coming from the opposite South East direction. The shot couldn't have been taken from Parus, as the boss was too close to the building."

"I see that," Petro agreed, nodding in approval.

"There are no high rise buildings in any other direction apart from Shovkovichna Street," Andrei remarked, pointing at the multi-storey residential buildings leading from Lipki district up to Parus. "This limits the location to just three buildings from their fifth floor upward."

Petro followed Andrei's line of sight.

"That was very swift, my friend. I think you've done this before."

"Once or twice," Andrei lied.

"If you look at the roofs, you'll see they aren't a reasonable option because of their cone shape. The shooter would have limited space, and the apartments in the buildings higher up the slope of Shovkovichna Street overlook the position. That leaves the apartments themselves."

"You think the shot came from within an apartment in one of those three buildings?"

"Yes. That means we have..." Andrei counted to himself, "...maybe two hundred apartments to check."

"Only two hundred? Judging from the number of windows there are many more apartments than that."

"I disagree. The lower windows would only be suitable if the shooter could guarantee no trucks or whatever blocking the line of sight. A professional wouldn't take such chances. No; fifth floor upwards is what we must concentrate on."

Andrei studied the probable trajectory for a couple more minutes, all the while scribbling furiously in his notebook.

"So, Petro, when was the meeting here arranged?"

"Err... I believe it was only a week before."

"Okay. I want to know who rented or was trying to rent apartments in the buildings suitable for the sniper's mission during that week. I'll contact Boris and get all the details of the meeting. You should assemble a team of five people from your so-called inner circle right away. Ensure you have at least two females among them. Question estate agents, residents, concierges, neighbours, dog walkers, dogs, squirrels, drunks, beggars, anyone. Find out about all the rent deals done between the first and ninth of August in those three buildings," he said, pointing at the buildings in Shovkovichna Street.

"I'll get on it immediately."

"Now, I don't want to invoke a strong resonance, so use an indirect rather than a straightforward approach. Present yourself as a newly relocated senior manager of any company having headquarters in Parus, coming in from Kharkov with an urgent need for an apartment for you and your family."

Petro, realising that the list of instructions was getting longer, pulled out a notebook and started taking notes.

"Send out some ladies to hang out in the nearest park to chat with young mums with baby carriages, as if checking the surroundings of an apartment before moving in. Those are usually bored and gossipy types, so they might know which apartments were empty and occupied recently. Other than that, I trust your own imagination."

"Okay Andrei, I've got that."

"That's all we can do for now. You go, Petro, start organising straight away."

"Yes sir, I'll report back to you when everything is in place," Petro replied with a respectful nod.

After dismissing Petro, Andrei called Yaroslav Pilipchuk, an SBU deputy chief, to schedule a dinner with him. Andrei knew Yaroslav wouldn't be too pleased to receive the call unsolicited, but Andrei didn't have time for rituals and reverences.

The receptionist finally connected Andrei after he resorted to a veiled threat if she didn't comply. Years in the security business had taught Andrei how to circumvent bureaucratic niceties. Finally the connection was made.

"Yaroslav, I came from Moscow just to have a word with you for a few minutes. We must meet today, sorry for such a short notice. I'll owe you one."

Andrei knew that Yaroslav couldn't just plainly refuse helping one of the Group's security chiefs. Andrei was sure that the boss wasn't stingy with Yaroslav, so he'd happily arrange for the list of mobile phone numbers and the identities of their owners, where they were known.

With a meeting with Yaroslav agreed, Andrei then called Aleksey Nifontov, a former SBU major who now worked for the Ministry of Communication, supervising cellular operators. Each time when either Aleksey was in Moscow or Andrei was in Kiev, they didn't miss an opportunity to drink a shot of vodka or two together and help each other to arrange presents for their wives upon returning home.

Andrei hoped that with Aleksey's influence on cellular operators he could arrange the data he needed maybe even quicker than through the SBU. Andrei didn't care who delivered first, the faster the better. In forty minutes Aleksey joined him in the Arena bar opposite Bessarabsky market for a shot of midday vodka.

"So you see the urgency required for this investigation," Andrei explained, after laying out his needs.

"Leave it with me, Andrei. I'll get all the numbers of all the mobile phones. I'll do it for you, my friend, and next time I'm in Moscow you'll invite me to the best brothel in town. I know you have connections to get the numbers from police or SBU, but you need not bother. No way will those imbecile wankers do it quicker than me."

"Thank you my friend, your help will be remembered."

Andrei felt like Sherlock Holmes, solving the mysteries one by one. Satisfied he had done all he could at that point, and still having time before meeting Yaroslav, Andrei called Oxana, his young Kiev mistress, hoping to catch her at home.

Damn, he had missed this kind of action for years. He felt elated. Oxana wouldn't regret for a minute hosting him in such an energetic mood. He was horny like a Duracell bunny on Viagra.

"Oxana won't be able to walk tomorrow," he thought to himself grinning. "Screw me, I must abandon this pseudo-retirement. Some action makes me feel twenty years younger."

8 There's No Place like Home

Kiev, 1994

When the plane started its descent I was startled by the sight of the dark city below, with only a few dim lights visible in a city of three million inhabitants. It reminded me the stories from World War II of blackouts when people turned off the lights upon the approach of German Luftwaffe bombers. Kiev was eerily dark. Electricity supplies were undoubtedly cut at night to save costs.

The plane landed and armed with my brand new Israeli passport, I joined the queue for non-Ukrainian visitors. I passed through customs and immigration without a hitch, and walked through to step on Ukrainian soil once again. I was home, and it felt good. I closed my eyes and breathed in the scent of my homeland - oh how different it was to Tel Aviv! I must have looked like a nitwit, standing there in the arrivals area with my eyes closed and a stupid grin on my face. My moment of peace was soon interrupted.

"Misha! Misha!"

I opened my eyes and there was Sasha running towards me.

"Misha!" he said again and shrouded me in a bear hug.

"Oh little brother...it's so good to see you."

"It's good seeing you too," I gasped as the air was squeezed from my lungs.

We exchanged the customary three kisses on the cheeks
- left, right, left, and patted each other on the back like good
Ukrainians.

"Yulia and the children cannot wait. Come...I have a
car outside," he exclaimed while yanking my suitcase from my
hand and leading me towards the exit to the car park.

"You still have the old Volga we bought you?"

"Ah...patience brother; you'll soon see," Sasha replied
cryptically.

We entered the short term parking and I followed
behind Sasha as he slalomed through the rows of cars.

"How do you like this beauty?" he asked, patting the
hood of an old Volvo.

Maybe it wasn't a fancy car in Western Europe, but it
was mightily impressive for a twenty three year old public
servant in Kiev.

"Nice," I nodded. "You have done well for yourself," I
replied truthfully.

"Get in then, Misha, or the children will be asleep
before we get home."

As we drove to his house, Sasha said, "You need to
come back to Kiev, little brother. I can fix you with good job
at my company. We can send money to mama every month
to take care of her. You have nothing in Israel. Nothing,
gornisht. You can have good life here. A very good life;
believe me."

A couple of years earlier my mother told me exactly the
same words about Kiev and asked me to go with her to Israel.
Now Sasha was telling me that I had nothing in Israel and
asked me to come back to Kiev. The sad thing was that they
were both right.

Sasha drove through the centre of Kiev on the way to
his house. It wasn't too late, around ten in the evening, but
the big city's streets were almost empty, with hardly any cars

or pedestrians. I didn't notice a single smile during the forty five minute drive. The overall atmosphere was sombre. People seemed poor and unhappy.

Most of the street lights were off. Those that were on used low wattage bulbs emitting faint lights. Even the central roads were in a terrible condition with broad and unattended holes and cracks in their asphalt layer. The feeling was of neglect and disrepair.

"The city looks miserable, Sasha," I told my brother. "It doesn't strike me as a place where you can have a good life."

"It's deceptive. As papa always used to say: don't judge a book by its cover."

"I always say judge the book and its cover."

"Stop being philosophical and listen, Misha. You need to look beneath the surface. Most people aren't doing well; that's true. But if you know how to play the system here the opportunities are limitless. Give it a chance and I'll teach you how you can make lots of money without working too hard. You'll see; you can have a good life here. There's no place like home."

Indeed, Sasha did appear to have a good life. The Volvo turned off the highway and Sasha drove through what looked like a fairly affluent area of the Kiev suburbs. Eventually he pulled into a driveway in front of a spacious, well-maintained three-bedroom house. Yulia heard us approach and ran from the door to greet us. She had a broad smile and her eyes sparkled with happiness. Once the hugs were out of the way, Sasha grabbed my suitcase from the boot of the Volvo, and we went inside. I could see why Yulia was happy: the house was spacious, well-decorated and well-equipped with modern furnishings.

The children had already fallen asleep, so we all sat at the kitchen table and caught up. Yulia was particularly animated, gushing about the new home, the well-equipped kitchen that was stocked with a variety of foods, and that Sasha earned enough so that she could stay home with the kids. It was a huge contrast to how we all used to live before I left Kiev.

Soon after I had left for Israel, with a reference from my father's old colleague, Sasha landed a job in the housing department of the construction corporation where my father used to work, administering state-owned residential properties.

When people needed to repair or renovate their home they needed the corporation to send workers. When people needed an allocation of an apartment or to relocate they needed the corporation's approval and apartments. State construction almost ground to a halt when the economy entered recession so there was a dire shortage of properties.

People had two options for advancing in the queue. The first option was obvious: you waited. And waited, and waited until you forgot what you were waiting for. The second option was the bread and butter for corporation managers: you bribed your way up the list. Democracy or not, some things never change.

With the right oil in its wheels the bureaucratic machine can work surprisingly fast. That was where Sasha could use his position to make some extra cash.

So Sasha accepted envelopes to help people. He knew that he couldn't drive a Volvo around the city if his boss wasn't getting a piece of the pie, so he proved his loyalty by sharing contributions. Employees who proved their loyalty were likely not only to keep their job, but also to be promoted.

When Sasha's boss, Sergei, left his post to become deputy mayor he took care of loyal Sasha. Sasha became the head of the department that was responsible for selling assets designated for privatisation.

As part of the privatisation process many residents of Kiev were given apartments for a symbolic price. Most preferred to cash in quickly on their property and buy cheaper apartments in the city's outskirts. To my surprise, the few hundred dollars that I'd brought with me from Israel represented a small fortune, and I could afford to buy a modest apartment in a good location. It happens to a country in recession with the value of its currency dropping through the floor.

The huge business opportunity was obvious. The real estate market in Kiev was undergoing a revolution after years of communism. Now, properties could be privately owned!

I decided to accept Sasha's offer and join his company. I asked around and found out that Nazar and his brigade had been wiped out by a competing gang, but Nazar himself had escaped and disappeared. I was certain that he would surface again, but I was glad that he wasn't around now. With the threat of Nazar out of the way, I thought that staying in Kiev was the way to go.

I was back!

**

The one thing that nagged me was that I still had unfinished business in Israel - law school. I'd discontinued my higher education once before in Kiev, and this time I wanted to see it through. As always, where there's a will, there's a way. All that was required was a bit of creativity.

Amazingly, I was able to progress with my law degree remotely, although officially it wasn't a long distance course. I achieved this with a little help from one of my friends.

On the first day at university, I was wandering the faculty's corridors, looking for the lecture hall for the first class on *Fundamentals of Law*. Soon I lost my way among the hundreds of students rushing in all directions. I spotted a man walking along with the course's book in his hand. He stood out among the throng of students because he seemed to be gliding along, completely unflustered and oblivious to the chaos around him.

I approached him, smiled and asked, "Hey, I see that this is your first day too, isn't it? My name is Shaarim, Moshe Shaarim. Nice to meet you. Do you know where the lecture hall is?"

He returned the smile.

"I have no idea. But hey; let's look for it together. I'm David. David Zabbana."

"Nice to meet you," I said, offering my hand.

"Privet, drug. Kak dela?"

I was stunned.

"I said, 'hi friend, how are you?'"

"I...I know. I just wouldn't have guessed you spoke Russian."

"I know many things," David said without a hint of cockiness. "My mother is Russian."

It was fraternal love at first sight.

David and I soon started to hang out together. We went to parties, hunted girls and experimented with illegal substances. These experiences can get people really close. We became good friends, so when I returned to Kiev, David agreed to help take care of my academic obligations in Israel. He signed my name in lectures' attendance sheets and kept me informed of academic duties. He rewrote some of his papers and handed them in as mine. Once, he even received a higher mark on a rewritten paper in *Family Law*, one of the most complicated subjects, as it was "short and to the point" as indicated by the professor. All I needed to do is come once a year to sit the exams. David couldn't do that for me.

I figured that one day I would be able to repay him for his kindness and willingness to help me without asking for anything in return.

***

Having my academic affairs taken care of in Israel, I could focus on doing business in Kiev. After six months of 'training' in the construction corporation, and thanks to my basic understanding of legal principles and civil engineering, and even bigger thanks to my boss-brother, I was promoted to the position of deputy head of the housing department.

I was allocated a small office with a desk, a phone and a small cupboard. It didn't have any windows, but at least it had a door. I bought myself two suits, one blue and one black, and a sleek, James Bond briefcase with a brushed-aluminium finish. Every morning I walked from my apartment to work in the large, long office building. I'd become a Ukrainian bureaucrat.

But I was a nice bureaucrat. I genuinely tried to give clients a good feeling and some hope, even though it was impossible to help everyone as our resources were limited. Nice attitude and service with a smile, though, didn't get in the way of making money.

I had 'no smoking' and 'I don't take bribes' signs on the desk in my small office. When people came to see me with an interesting request, I put down the *no smoking* sign and suggested to the person to have a smoke. The hint was well understood. If I bent the 'no smoking' rule, then the 'I don't take bribes' rule was flexible as well.

I discovered that some people were actually interested in construction services, whether for building a dacha or renovating their apartment. Our company was poorly budgeted, so delays in our official construction schedule were pretty frequent and the builders' salary arrears were stretched to a few months. So, why not let them earn a bit for themselves and for me?

Sasha explained to me the secrets of the operation. "Not all the budgeted materials are necessary to be used in construction. There are many ways to write them off and sell them or use them privately."

"But what about official papers?" I asked, knowing the probable answer already.

"The paperwork sometimes gets logged in the wrong file, and unfortunately, we dispose of old papers fairly regularly. It's an unfortunate scenario that has led to many invoices perishing before they were scrutinised properly. We really should update our filing system!" Sasha added, trying to suppress a smile, "But don't worry, if the potatoes get hot, I've a seasoned arsonist as a friend who will burn our archives."

Since I had to be present at the office, I paid an old school friend, Seva, to work for me at the sites. I used the corporation's construction materials that we didn't actually use and paid the skilled and experienced corporation's workers to get the job done, using the corporation's equipment, under Seva's supervision. And I paid everyone from the bribes that I collected as the corporation's employee.

Everyone was happy. The customers got the construction completed without waiting years in queues. The workers got paid on time without any arrears. And I was making some money.

Nobody was hurt because we embezzled corporation resources. If anything, I helped the corporation deliver a high-quality service on schedule to satisfied customers. I should've received an employee of the month award. At least this was how I looked at it.

***

I decided it was time to celebrate and show my appreciation. I organised a party for forty people at a posh restaurant, inviting Sasha, Sergei, Seva, and some of my colleagues and old friends from school. Vodka flowed like water; there were live musicians, singers and half-naked dancers to entertain the guests as they sat through the finest dishes served in Kiev that evening. The entire event cost me less than two hundred dollars, including a generous gratuity to the restaurant's owner. It was unbelievable. I realised then that with not too much money I could buy half the country.

As the evening wound down, and guests started to say their goodbyes, those who could still walk continued on to one of Kiev's exclusive night clubs. The clubs were exclusively aimed at the rich, so if you weren't dressed well and smelled of money, the bouncers wouldn't let you in. The flashy atmosphere inside the club contrasted massively with the gloomy reality outside. Everything was shiny. The lighting was bright and colourful, everyone was smiling, drinking, snorting and dancing. Beautiful women, who were on par with top Western models, were throwing themselves at the men, who by their very presence were likely to be extremely wealthy. I agreed to foot the bill for those of us that were left, and the party carried on through the night.

I don't remember how the evening ended, but I woke up with a luscious girl in my bed. I gave her some money for a taxi and she disappeared. What could be better than that?

I later found five used condoms lying around my apartment. I was sorry that I didn't remember the night before, and in particular what I'd snorted or dropped to make me into such a sex machine. That was the scenario that I preferred to imagine instead of the possibility that I had wasted one condom after another trying to pull them on to my flaccid penis, unable to erect properly because of excessive drinking. Then the thought hit me that all the condoms might not be mine, and that maybe I'd staged an orgy at my apartment! Oh god, I hoped not - especially with my brother in the same room!

Having some money made it really easy with the ladies. Because of Ukraine's poor economic conditions, exposing girls to the good life attracted them in droves.

A few months after I'd settled down in Kiev, and once the money started rolling in, I splashed out on a BMW. Any night I was bored I could just cruise into town and collect girls: sometimes a single chick and sometimes a group of birds together and take them for a spin. I would park up somewhere nice, open a bottle or two of champagne, and before I took them back, a shag or an orgy was almost guaranteed. They say power is an aphrodisiac, and it's true.

Two years before I'd been sleeping on the beach in Tel Aviv, and now I was splashing money, driving a cool car and shagging gorgeous women. I'd tasted the good life and its taste was exhilaratingly sweet.

***

Life was good, but it can always be better. Newly independent Ukraine had the potential to become an emerging economy because of its diverse industrial capacity, fertile soil and strategic location between Russia and Western Europe. I was certain that Ukraine would soon attract western investments once the country stabilised. If we could build up a portfolio of properties and land, once the big investors started snooping around Kiev, we would be in a prime position to cash in. It would take a lot of time, money and clever manipulation of corporation resources, but with me and Sasha at the helm, it was a plan worth pursuing.

In business, timing and luck are huge factors in deciding whether a venture is successful or not. As if to prove that point, shortly after Sasha and I had decided to expand our business, I received a call from my old childhood friend Yuri. The call would push our expansion plans into overdrive.

The day after I took the call from Yuri, there was a BBQ at Sasha's dacha. When the opportunity arose, I took Sasha to a garden arbour and told him what Yuri had relayed to me.

"You remember my old friend Yuri?"

"Malinovsky?"

"Yes. Well I had a conversation with him yesterday that might benefit our business."

"Okay, I'm listening."

"Well, you know I missed him by a few weeks in Tel Aviv? That was because he moved to the Czech Republic to work for his uncle's real estate business."

Sasha shifted in his seat, leaning forward and steepling his fingers.

"He told me that after the Czechs broke from Soviet influence, his uncle's company did pretty much what we're planning on doing now. They made huge amounts of cash and a lot of contacts."

"Very interesting news, little brother. And he wants to share knowledge with us?" Sasha asked, his interest rising.

"Better than that. He has gone back to Israel now and started his own business connecting wealthy businessmen and developers with properties in the old Eastern Bloc. He has the investors if we have the properties."

Sasha smiled. I knew he would be pleased with my news and he didn't disappoint.

"Well then; if that's true, and Yuri's people want to invest in Ukraine, then we should start collecting every available plot we can lay our hands on. It's time to make some serious money, little brother."

"Indeed it is."

***

With a new venture in its infancy, and the potential of making large sums of money, I wanted some familiar faces around me. One of the first things I did over the following days was to re-establish my connection with Gigo, my Georgian business partner from the Institute of Higher Education in Kiev. His brain wasn't his strongest attribute, but he was strong, fearless and loyal and that was what we needed.

We started small, but after a few months we targeted a block of land in Kiev's centre. We sent Gigo and his friends to convince the owners to sell us their privately-owned lots or pass to us the usage rights where that was the legal status. When Gigo returned he had all the papers signed, granting us legal rights over the whole block.

"It looks like everything went smoothly, old friend." I congratulated Gigo.

"It was easy. Your proposal was generous enough for everyone, except one fool who didn't like the opening offer."

"And you talked him around?" I asked, knowing that Gigo's debating skills weren't his trademark.

"Of course! I told him I wasn't going to burn his apartment, and I wasn't going to hurt him or his wife. I said I would take their two children when they returned from school. I would tie their son to a tree in the forest and rape the daughter so the son could watch. And then I would shoot her in the legs and leave them both to die in forest, but not before I cut off the thumbs of the son."

"I can see how that might help him reconsider his options," I mused aloud.

"That's not all," continued Gigo. "I let him picture the charming scene in his head for a few seconds, then I whispered in his ear that I'm worse than Stalin - my guru and compatriot. After that, he agreed to sign the papers," Gigo finished, with a victorious smile, showing his gold teeth.

"Well done, Gigo," I answered with a smile that didn't reach my eyes. "I'm glad that he agreed and you didn't need to execute your threat."

I didn't ask Gigo whether he was serious or not about his intimidation. Something about his excitement implied that he would've preferred that the seller had tested his seriousness before agreeing. I was afraid to know the answer. I was also happy that Gigo was on my side.

With the block of land legally ours, I called Yuri with the good news. Within days, Yuri had several offers from foreign investors, and we sold it to a company that planned to construct the first shopping mall in Ukraine.

***

Fuelled with the spirit of entrepreneurship I always kept an open mind to business opportunities. This is what capitalism is all about.

When I was studying at Tel Aviv University I befriended a Colombian guy, Juan. He told me that his uncle in Colombia was a drug baron who produced top quality cocaine. I never believed him, since all his stories were distorted by heavy drug consumption. His connection with reality was questionable.

When visiting Israel to sit my end of year exams at law school, I was smoking weed with Juan. We were both lying on the beds opposite each other in Juan's room at the dorms unable to move as we were stoned senseless.

Juan was crushed on his bed, joint in his hand, looking at the ceiling. Too stoned, I heard his hoarse voice as if from a distance, "Misha, hombre, mi tio, Carlos, está buscando maneras de enviar sus productos a Europa."

"Juan, speak Hebrew. I don't speak fucking Spanish. You're smoking too much strong shit."

"Sorry, man. Man, my uncle, Carlos, is looking for ways to ship his produce to Europe. The US o'fucking A, the main target market for my uncle, declared another war against the Colombian drug cartels. Fuckers, man. They do this shit all the time. They ain't leaving the people in peace to smoke weed, man. This is making business difficult. So Carlos is looking for new business venues across the big Atlantic pond. You keep saying you do some business in Europe, man, so maybe you should have a word with Carlos. Man."

I moved slowly from lying to sitting on the bed.

"First, pass me the joint."

After taking a long puff, I said drowsily, "Second, sure, put me in contact with Carlos. I might have a solution for him."

Two weeks later, I met Carlos in London. Surprisingly enough he was indeed flesh and blood. He was a professional drug dealer, an expert on every intoxicating substance. After hanging out with him for two days, during which we were higher than the Empire State Building, I reached the enlightenment that Colombians had a similar mentality to that of Russians. They live every day as if there is no tomorrow. Probably because for many, there wouldn't be.

Then, it was down to business. We sat in two Chesterfields, deep-buttoned leather couches in a private English gentlemen's club. We smoked Cuban cigars and sipped twenty-one year old El Dorado rum. Carlos wore a white linen shirt, Panama hat and white silk scarf. He couldn't have looked more Latin even if he tried.

"Come on my young gringo friend," Carlos said. "You told me that you had a programa for bringing my produce to Europa. Let's hear it."

I laid out my plan, "Ukraine is a large country, bordering Russia to its east, and to its west countries that share borders with Western Europe, such as Poland, Slovakia, Hungary and Romania. The port of Odessa on Ukraine's Black Sea coast is the largest Ukrainian seaport. Thousands of ships dock at the port every year, including ships from South America. Cocaine can be hidden within cargoes, inside anything from industrial furnaces to excavated pineapples. The custom inspectors at the port, like every official across Ukraine, are notoriously open to bribes to get cargoes through. Once the drugs are inside Ukraine, the shipments can then be transported to its western borders. The border custom officials can be paid to look the other way and from there the drugs can be trafficked into Western Europe."

Carlos listened intently, the fingers of one hand lightly pressed against those of the other hand, forming a church steeple cross.

"I have the connections with the customs personnel at the seaport and the western border. I can arrange for the officials in Romania to skip checking our trucks. From Romania all Western Europe is open. I can organise for transporting the cargo from the ship to anywhere in Western Europe. All you need to do, Carlos, is to put the cargo on a ship going from Colombia to Odessa. I'll take care of the rest. This is so fucking easy."

"Si, si," Carlos said, nodding. "Your programa could work. We can try one small shipment of coca to test it. If it goes well, this could be the beginning of a muy bello friendship."

Carlos seemed impressed with my plan. Within three weeks we received the first cocaine shipment. Most of it was transported to the western border and into Romania. The plan was executed seamlessly.

My old friend Constantin Sabo, the customs inspector who took my cash when I made Aliyah to Israel, was happy to be paid and to close his eyes when the drugs were transported into Romania. He was downright surprised to see me after three years. He was delighted to receive the Pushkin book, which he once allowed me to pass through the border, as a personal gift. His happiness wasn't because of the book's beautiful verses, but rather because of the ten hundred dollar bills hidden inside.

We sold a small amount of coke locally in Kiev to selected clients as a favour. The market in Kiev for expensive drugs was immature since users lacked money to buy cocaine and heroin. However, my growing wealthy business circle and some relatively affluent business owners were appreciated receiving high-quality Colombian coke. It wasn't mixed with soda, baking powder or rat poison. It was pure, good shit. I made money and friends.

My foray into drug trafficking ended earlier than expected when Carlos was shot dead. The word was that the CIA took him out as part of a covert fight against the Colombian cartels. This rumour prevented me from attending his funeral in Bogota, as it was suspected it would be closely watched by DEA agents.

While I was upset that Carlos died, I was somewhat relieved that this business was terminated for me. Semi-illegal business, such as purchasing properties with the help of bribery and coercion, was one thing. Fully illegal business, such as heavy drug smuggling, was another thing altogether. I didn't want to get too much involved in a business that could connect me with the most wanted criminals in the world and the secret services of powerful countries. I tested the water and found it too hot for my liking.

Keeping a low profile was still one of my guiding principles.

This was an unsatisfying experience. But as the famous British philosophers Sir Mick Jagger and Keith Richards said, "I can't get no satisfaction. 'Cause I try and I try and I try and I try." So, I kept trying.

***

We were making money that was sufficient to classify us as affluent or perhaps even rich. I was able to leave my small apartment and buy a nice studio flat in the centre of Kiev. I didn't want to flash my wealth too much, since on paper I was a modest bureaucrat with a public service salary. However, for the first time I could afford much more than a decent living. Nevertheless, as always, I fancied more.

After a while I quit the job at Sasha's company, but not before I siphoned what I needed: the best workers, sufficient stock of construction materials, tools and even some heavy machinery such as cranes and bulldozers. Sasha was able to channel the properties that we wanted to buy. I was responsible for raising capital, mainly through Yuri; buying titles, convincing people to sell titles - sometimes with Gigo's help - and selling blocks of property to developers and buyers.

As I wasn't a public servant any longer, I wasn't so concerned about hiding my wealth. Rapidly climbing up the property ladder, I moved out of my small studio apartment to a 250 square metre penthouse that I had constructed by purchasing and converting six apartments on the highest floor of a historical building that was located within walking distance from the main street of Kreschatik. It had magnificent views of the city, the Dnieper River, Saint Sophia Cathedral and the Motherland Monument.

Gigo was building his small private security service, which enabled him to extort protection from businesses, as he had strived to do from our university's time. We had money to pay for more thugs to join his force and he effectively created a mini Georgian army in Kiev. Georgians were a minority in Ukraine and they were happy to find a welcoming home in our organisation. They were strong, tough and cruel when they needed to be.

I had to look, relentlessly as always, for the next big opportunity. I didn't have to look for long. What drove me on was to always dream bigger.

9 No Turning Back

Kiev, 2013

Andrei was having lunch with Oxana at a fancy restaurant. Screwing her at her apartment wasn't enough to keep her satisfied. Since he wasn't such a frequent guest in Kiev she wanted more of his company, although Andrei had serious doubts that he was the only one she was dating. He also had to buy her presents and take her out once in a while. Showing her a good time was well rewarded in the bedroom. The happier she was, the happier she made him.

His mobile rang and vibrated, nearly falling off the table. It was Petro.

"This is work, Oxana, I'll be back soon."

He stood up and stepped outside to the noisy street, while answering the phone.

"Yes, Petro, any news?"

"Well, we talked with estate agents working on the apartments in those buildings. Three apartments were rented for a short time period just around the time we're focusing on." Petro tried to sound neutral and not to mention specific details in case someone was listening.

"We talked with the landlords, and one of the apartments remained vacant during the entire time, although rent was prepaid and no one asked for a refund. Nobody seemed to actually live there."

"Okay. Go on"

"We've contacted the cleaning lady through the building's maintenance company. She said that the apartment was clean when the renting period was over. But she can swear that someone has moved the kitchen table and left it next to the window. Guess what this window overlooks?"

"The Business Centre," Andrei replied, feeling the exhilaration of a piece of the puzzle falling into place. "Do we know who rented the apartment?"

"That's where it gets tricky. The apartment was rented by a company incorporated in Lichtenstein. We couldn't identify the shareholders yet. The entire deal was done through e-mail exchange and they asked for the key to be left under the rug by the apartment's door. Well, it happens this way sometimes, not too unusual. So I put out some feelers to try to find out more information and, guess what, this company didn't do any business anywhere, ever. It's not even used as a holding for some subsidiaries. It might have been incorporated just to rent this apartment. This is a classic modus operandi of the three letter services and rather typical instrument to leave no footprints. That's what they do to cover up their tracks."

Andrei knew very well which letters Petro meant. These were either FSB - Russia's Federal Security Service, the successor agency of the KGB, or SBU.

"Yes, that's right. So this could be those organisations. There are plenty of guys who were trained and learned their ways. What else do you have for me, Petro?"

"Nothing more right now."

"Good job, Petro. Make one more effort in this context. There are individuals acting on behalf of these entities. Somebody wrote e-mails and somebody also collected the key from under the rug. Try to follow who these might be. Also, rent that apartment for a couple of days, but not in your name. And meet me there, I want to have a look around to see whether any other hints were left behind."

Andrei didn't expect to find anything. Those who did it were professionals, who leave places clean after they leave. Andrei didn't like the direction to which the investigation was leading. Clearly, they were dealing here with someone organised. Someone powerful. Maybe even a sovereign-sponsored hit which is many times worse than a private one. They were treading on thin ice and their lives were in danger.

But, there was no turning back now, was there?

10 Dreaming Big

Kiev, 1996

Our operation in Kiev continued to flourish so much that within a couple of years I'd accumulated a few million dollars and was looking to diversify the business.

Venturing into high-risk, high-reward businesses seemed like the right move. As they say no guts, no glory; no pain, no gain. I was young, business opportunities were abundant, and I was happy to roll the dice and take the risks. I felt like I was in a card game. If it's your day, then you're almost unbeatable. And these definitely were my days.

In the past all I'd wanted was to secure a better future for my family. Now I saw how I could actually achieve it. Our real estate business was relatively low risk by Ukrainian standards, with every policeman and public official corruptible, the immediate legal risks to the business were negligible. But I already knew the business had a glass ceiling. We were making money, the pace was even, but we couldn't earn much quicker than we were doing already.

I recognised that the real opportunity at the time was in the energy sector. The privatisation drive in Russia and Ukraine enabled entrepreneurs to buy stakes in previously state-owned oil, gas and mineral companies. These were Russia and Ukraine's crown jewels. Now, they were offered at literally fire sale prices. I needed the cash and connections with the right people at the government to get a deal done and get my hands on a lucrative asset. Wealth and government were interconnected in Ukraine. Money could buy political decisions.

The emerging deal involved Anton Lozinski, the First Deputy Minister of Energy and Coal Industry of Ukraine. He was in his middle thirties, short, with a round, large belly. I was wondering when was the last time that he actually saw his dick without a mirror.

Sasha and I sold Anton a charming apartment in a central area in Kiev. Anton, who was a happily married man, housed his mistress in the flat. This was a common practice for senior men. Not having a mistress was considered strange and raised rumours about sexual preferences.

While handing him the keys of the deluxe, renovated apartment I told Anton, "In such a cosy nest that you've acquired, just five minutes' walk from your office, I'm sure that you'll visit your mistress more often."

"Yes, of course!" Anton enthused. "With more frequent visits, I hope I can keep up with her; her sexual appetite is incredible."

"Well maybe I can help you to keep up," I said, handing Anton a generous bag of pure Colombian coke.

Anton's eyes lit up and he quickly pocketed the drugs.

"This will help me to suppress my piggish appetite," he declared. "Coke is the best cure for obesity. And now I can fuck my mistress all night long. I lose two whole kilos in a single such session."

When he offered to pay for the coke I was surprised, as most officials never offered to pay for anything.

"Forget it, Anton; keep your money. This one is on me, my friend. Friends don't pay each other for pleasure. Consider it a small bonus for buying the apartment. We're always glad to provide something good for your diet. Who knows, maybe in a few months you end up as thin as a movie star?"

I knew that the day would come when Anton could be handy. He valued my discretion on his recreational preferences and we developed a relationship of mutual trust. Every couple of weeks I would pop round to his apartment and hand him some coke, neck a couple of vodkas and then leave. After one such visit, I decided it was time to reveal my plan.

"Before I go, I want to tell you that I'm looking to purchase a stake in a company in the energy sector. Please let me know if you hear of anything interesting. I'm sure that it can be beneficial for both of us and for the country."

Anton smiled at my words, and I wondered if I'd revealed my hand too soon. But his reply was a pleasant one.

"It's funny that you mention it, Misha. A state-owned company that produces natural gas is going on sale through a tender. If that interests you, then I'll keep you in the loop. The privatisation is important for the country and we need to find serious bidders like you to participate in the tender."

"Please do that, Anton, such a deal is definitely of interest to me," I answered seriously, although inside I was screaming with delight.

With the First Deputy Minister on my side I would know the bids in advance and guarantee my tender was accepted. While in theory the bids were supposed to be undisclosed to rival bidders for the tender to be competitive, the fact was that in Ukraine every lucrative tender was rigged. As Albert Einstein's saying goes, if the facts do not match the theory, change the facts.

I organised a syndicate of three investors. Two were Yuri's connections from Israel, and the third was my newly incorporated company, called *Neplokho Holdings* - neplokho meaning not bad in Russian. We incorporated a subsidiary for the deal, calling it Neplokho Energy, whose three shareholders were the two Israeli investors and Neplokho

Holdings. I didn't know it back then, but this was the birth of the mighty Neplokho Group.

Anton disclosed to me the competing bids in the tender. We tendered our bid, which was just one thousand dollars above the next highest bid, and unsurprisingly, we won. Luckily for us, the criteria focused on price, ignoring the various bidders' experience and other factors that were inconvenient for us. Anton got his share of the deal. Everyone was happy and I was the joint-owner of a 51% stake in Azov Oil & Gas Company.

As a new member of the supervisory board of the company, I flew east to its headquarters in Donetsk to have a look at my new acquisition. Escorted by Anton, I was greeted by Boris Uralski, the company's chief executive officer. He was already an industry veteran at the age of forty three, which was young for managing such a large company. When I entered the company's office building Boris was waiting in the lobby.

"Welcome Mr Vorotavich," he said, shaking my hand firmly while smiling warmly.

"It's a pleasure to meet you, Boris," I replied.

"The pleasure is mine. The board is looking forward to working with you."

Boris didn't mention my young age or inexperience in the energy industry. He personally greeted me at the lobby, and his body language was open and confident. Either he really meant what he said or he was a good politician. After he introduced me to the company's executives, we went to his office and raised a glass of vodka to our health and the company's success. I had a good feeling about him.

Normally I would put my own man in charge of the company, but Boris was Anton's man and surprisingly enough he did a great job, managing to keep most of the company's assets following the turmoil in Ukraine and the privatisation process.

His official objective was to run the company as efficiently as possible to create shareholder value. His unofficial objective was to primarily funnel revenues into our private pockets. I didn't want to share the profit with an insignificant minority shareholder - the state still holding a 49% stake.

Another significant advantage of having Boris on board was his connections with senior, powerful figures in the government. During his time as the CEO of Azov Oil & Gas, he'd established solid relationships with officials as he was running one of the largest companies in Ukraine.

Since Boris was older than me, the state officials took him seriously. They didn't consider him a young, inexperienced kid, as some of them would've perceived me. After they got to know me, however, and in particular after I paid them for their extracurricular services, they would soon change their minds about me. But until they had done so, it was helpful to have Boris around.

Ukraine's own production of natural gas covered only about a quarter of its domestic demand. However, we weren't interested in selling domestically since the price was regulated. Boris, using his connections, managed to get us a quota for unregulated sales abroad for half of our production. Even Anton, who had tried to help with his own connections, was surprised by the positive result that Boris achieved. Boris demonstrated his true value to the company. Over the years he would become my right-hand man.

***

As I was constantly seeking new business ventures and projects for Neplokho Holdings, and our business was expanding rapidly, I needed to recruit help with managing the Group. David Zabbana, my good friend from law school, was an obvious candidate.

After finishing his military service in the Israel Defence Force, David completed his law degree, as well as a degree in business administration. David was smart and energetic, and a reliable friend I could trust. I also felt that I owed him a favour since he helped me finish my law degree when I returned to Kiev.

David's mother was Russian and his father Romanian. But his look had nothing European or Slavic in it - a mystery. I told him that he should run a DNA test to confirm the identity of his real father. His answer was always, "Go fuck yourself."

David knew how to get by and bend the rules. We called it a kombinator in Hebrew - a person who knows how to pull some tricks to manipulate the system or to find on the fly solutions for problems. That and his command of Russian made him perfect for doing business in Ukraine.

I called David and tried to entice him into working with me.

"Listen, David. Why don't you come to work with me here in Kiev? Except for your parents, you have nothing in Israel. Nothing! What's the worst that can happen? I'll pay for your flights - first class, and put you in a nice hotel with an endless supply of drugs and women. You've never seen prettier and easier women in your life; believe me. Come here for a month, try it out and if you don't like it, you can go back. Worst case scenario is it would be a nice, free vacation before you become a lawyer, slaving for twelve hours every day. At least you would have some unforgettable memories to sweeten your boring, grey routine. Come on, you deserve it. What do you say?"

After putting it like that, it was an offer he couldn't refuse, so the next day David Zabbana flew to Kiev.

***

Since we always kept an open mind, extraordinary opportunities soon presented themselves. One noteworthy project involved a new regulation concerning veterinary vaccinations of domestic animals such as cattle, pigs and sheep.

Anton, who after our successful dealings considered me as a reliable and discreet business partner, introduced me to his friend Roman, the head of the State Veterinary and Phytosanitary Service of Ukraine. David had arrived in Kiev that morning, so as a way of introducing him to the manner in which business was conducted in Ukraine, I took him with me to the meeting at a traditional Ukrainian restaurant to meet Roman and discuss his brilliant scheme. After introductions, and the customary vodka shots, it was time to talk business.

"The process is simple," Roman began. "We pass a new regulation requiring mandatory vaccination of domestic animals. Unfortunately there's no proof whatsoever of the vaccine's effectiveness. But we purchase falsified academic research papers from real scientists to highlight the immediate need for the vaccine and the real danger of not using it. We then produce it and everyone must buy it. We create the demand and the product from absolutely nothing. By the time the regulation is enacted, the logistics for its implementation should be in place. There will be a certain amount of investment involved, and that's where you come in. Anton has informed me that you could be the perfect partner for this operation."

"So we pay set up costs and purchase the scientific papers, the vaccination law is passed, and our company is guaranteed to win the tender?"

"Of course. It is a simple plan, but potentially lucrative."

David had been a silent companion, but now he leant forward and said, "I don't like the word potentially; it hints at the possibility of losing money."

Roman seemed a little put out at the statement, but forced a smile before he replied.

"Anton has informed me that you're serious people. I wouldn't insult you by proposing something that will lose money. I have some draft numbers I can give you that set out our projections. I'll leave them with you, if you like."

"That would be preferable," David answered.

"Then I believe everything is covered," I announced, bringing the meeting to a close.

I was happy that David had jumped straight into his new role, so I let him take the figures from Roman to study at his own volition. David was still green in Ukraine and didn't know that potentially meant guaranteed when arranged properly. But I didn't want to spoil the plot for him. He'd learn.

Using Roman's connections, the dodgy research and our money, we were able to *persuade* the Office of Agrarian Policy and Food of Ukraine to enforce the mandatory vaccination of all domestic animals across Ukraine, with our newly formed subsidiary, Neplokho Pharmaceuticals, charged with supplying the vaccine.

The wholesale cost of each vaccine was minimal as it was purchased from a Chinese manufacturer. The placebo vaccine was sold to each farm with a margin that was enough to cover the payments to the Minister of Agrarian Policy and Food of Ukraine, our friend Roman and a finder's fee to

Anton for the introduction, as well as to generate a sizeable profit for Neplokho Pharmaceuticals.

Morally, David and I didn't like this project. We basically stole millions from the people of Ukraine who paid the vaccine's full price for a service that was completely unnecessary. It was similar to the protection business, just in a different wrapping. After years of living in poverty I felt for the poor farmers. However, I got over it. It was just business, nothing personal.

It was more difficult for David to come to terms with the scheme.

"I'm a lawyer, not a thief," David protested. "This is like Robin Hood in reverse; we steal from the poor and give to the rich."

"Most lawyers are thieves, David. Don't be naive."

"Okay, lawyers bend the rules here and there. Lawyers lie when it's in the best interests of their clients. And yes, lawyers sometimes behave unethically when it's in their best interests. But this, Misha, this is a fraud, theft, embezzlement, bribery, forgery and a dozen more criminal felonies. Misha, this isn't right. It isn't right I'm telling you. I'm not sure I want anything to do with it."

"It's your choice, David. I won't force you to do anything you aren't comfortable with. But if you leave, then the deal will still go through with or without you."

"But if I go back to Israel, what am I going to do? Being a lawyer sucks. You work like a slave and the senior partners get all the glory. You get to spend all day going over every little fucking sentence in a contract that nobody wants to read. Being a junior lawyer in a law firm is for losers. Over here it's like the money just waits to be collected. People here are suckers. Screw it."

"Then what's your problem?" I asked. "You either quit and return to Israel, or stay and make a lot of money."

"You make it sound so straightforward, my friend."

"There are too many complications in life already. Your choice is a simple one."

***

To help David decide whether to stay or go, I took him out that night, to hit Kiev's top clubs. He didn't like the dodgy dealings in Ukraine, but I was sure that he'd like the local beauties. David's exotic, almost Persian look was going to attract the ladies like moths to a flame. Over a few drinks at a trendy bar, he soon noticed that the Ukrainian girls were simply gorgeous, while the men were mainly ugly, in both soul and appearance.

"I can't believe how beautiful the girls are in here!" David said incredulously. "Did you hire all the best hookers to hang around, to sway my decision?"

"David...how could you offend me like that? I wouldn't do such a thing," I replied, feigning shock.

"I'm not so sure."

"Seriously, my friend; this is just a normal gathering of normal girls. Factory worker or shop-girl by day: sexy huntress by night."

"And what are they hunting?" David asked, intrigued by the statement.

I leaned in closer, beckoning David to mirror my movement.

"Come closer."

"What? What is it they hunt?"

I cupped my hand and whispered in David's ear.

"They hunt cock. Money-smelling cocks. You idiot, they're the same as the girls in such clubs in Tel Aviv. The only difference is that here they're easy. They don't play games. They want to hang around money, fuck, snort coke and have expensive things bought for them by fools like you and me."

"Well...I kind of knew that."

"We're just lucky here that the girls are exceptionally beautiful, and easily impressed by a small show of generosity."

David leaned back into his chair, smiling and shaking his head. I watched as he drained his vodka, and then studied the girls standing around, hoping to be noticed.

"You know what?" he finally said when his curiosity had been satisfied.

"What's that, my friend?"

"Kiev girls are pretty fucking hot," he said, with a wink.

I took a bag of powder from my pocket and poured a pile out on to the table.

"What, here in the open? Just in front of everyone," David asked, looking around nervously.

"Don't worry. The police aren't allowed in this club. And even if they were, they would probably sell you some shit. Calm down!"

I looked at David, who grinned back at me. I divided the mound into a series of lines using a credit card, pulled a bill from my wallet, and snorted a long, fat line of coke.

"Damn that's good," I gushed, wiping my runny nose with the back of my hand. "That's Colombian shit, my friend. Enjoy!" I said, offering David the hundred dollar bill.

"It would be rude not to," he said, before hoovering up his line in double-quick time.

"Buy one of these girls a drink," I stated matter-of-factly, "and later on you'll be snorting coke off her sexy tummy while her friend blows you."

"I can think of worse ways of ending an evening," he joked.

"A man needs to relax in the way he enjoys most of all. You and I... we cannot change the world. That's the way it is. If you cannot beat them, why not join them? Work with me, David, and I'll make you rich beyond your wildest dreams. I promise. Are you ready to do what it takes?"

"I was born ready," answered David, with his face red and the veins on his forehead bulging as if they were about to explode.

"Well then, let's drink to that," I said as we raised our glasses and drunk the ice cold vodka.

"So, you are with me?"

"For my sins...yes, I'm with you."

"We're going to be the fucking kings of Kiev!"

***

When I went to bed, alone, after the night with David, the effects of the cocaine slowly left my system. My thoughts turned darker as I started to come down. I couldn't fall asleep as my body was full of energy. I felt my heart beating hard, feeling each heartbeat in my head like a drum.

All kinds of incessant questions wracked my brain. Was David right? Are we pieces of shit? What's the point of all this? Have I just brainwashed my best friend? Am I going to die tonight from an overdose? What is mama going to think when they find my rotting body after a week? If my papa could see me now he would die of shame.

I woke up with a hangover, feeling my head buzzing. My ears rang constantly. I went to the toilet, threw up, ate a breakfast without any real appetite, and decided that fuck it, the project would go on.

***

In line with tradition, we didn't pay any taxes on real profits. Taxes aren't for the rich.

My accountant, whose nickname was *The Bookkeeper*, was a very tall, skinny, pale man with large black-rimmed glasses and thin blonde hair. He looked more like a mantis than a man. He was the Picasso of creative accounting. He didn't care about generally accepted accounting principles, laws or regulations. They were purely an inconvenience, getting in the way. All he cared about was money, and how to make his clients happy. He cooked the books and our tax bill was inconsequential.

With or without taxes, the true profits were channelled to our offshore accounts through our brokerage firm in Switzerland, Neplokho Brokerage Services. The firm's task was to contract all the export produce of Azov Oil & Gas Company at cost price and sell it at real price to European clients, thus accumulating all the profits in Switzerland. We hardly made any money in Ukraine and didn't have any profits for which taxes were due.

David, who was now a fixture in the company, was still trying to master the local nuances of business.

"Why, with such loopholes in the tax enforcement, do you even bother to pay tax at all?" he asked, after I'd explained our tax shenanigans.

"It's because of another Ukrainian peculiarity. According to the law it's perfectly fine to declare losses. However, if you declare losses, in practice, the local tax inspectors are instructed to refuse to accept tax returns reflecting such losses. 'You don't earn money, close the business' they would say, and 'you spoil our statistics.' I could just coerce them through my connections, but I don't want to be a black sheep. So I've instructed my accountants to pay a symbolic corporate tax, thus keeping us in line with all the other sheep. You can piss in the swimming pool, but don't do it from the top diving board. We don't want to attract attention."

"Ha ha, I can see how that might be noticed," David sniggered, picturing the scene in his head.

"If you keep your head down and don't interest anybody, the tax authorities leave you alone, and the secret services won't sniff around. The police won't waste any effort to inspect you, no matter what you do."

"That's good to hear."

"However," I warned, "if you hit the headlines and flash some money, then suddenly the tax authorities are all over you. Not so much to collect taxes, but rather to ensure that you pay them to leave you alone. If you attract such attention, then the chances are that your competitors or enemies have likely paid the taxmen to give you some trouble. Nothing here is incidental."

"You and your Ukrainian peculiarities," David said. "I'll never understand this place."

"Yes, you will. Give it a couple of years and we'll make you more Ukrainian than borscht. By the way, if you ever feel nostalgic for law and justice, let me know. I'll buy you a position as a Supreme Court judge. You'll see what justice means here from the inside, and I might benefit from having such a distinguished colleague in the courts."

"I'm not sure I'd want to get involved with what you consider to be *law* in this country."

"I understand. We have our own distinctive way of dealing with legal complications here."

"So who is the Group's main legal counsel?"

"There isn't one."

"How is that possible?" David asked, surprised by the revelation.

"I'll try to explain. You see, contracts are usually just a hand shake. The sanctions for breaching them may vary from a bullet in the head to a car bomb."

"With such sanctions, it isn't surprising that parties usually abide meticulously to the contract," David said understandingly.

"Exactly. You don't hear about shots and explosions very frequently, huh? You see; here a lawyer's work is a total frustration. They're just writing clerks, nothing more than that. It doesn't matter how well the contract is drafted or what advice they give. If nobody intends to go to court to protect their rights then what's the point of having a lawyer? The only advice they follow here is which ammunition to use," I explained.

***

I had never been a religious man, but often I would pray at the local synagogue. The holy place gave me an opportunity to disengage from reality for a couple of hours and focus on nothing but praying and chatting with the other men. It felt safe, pure and spiritual, and gave me the one real chance to relax away from my hectic lifestyle.

It also meant I could engage with the rest of the Jewish community, who felt much the same as I did. The dwindling number of Jews who were left in Kiev needed to feel part of a community, members of the tribe, and so the synagogue was our tribal meeting place.

Another reason to go to synagogue was that most of the rabbis had strong ties with overseas orthodox Jewish lobby organisations. Generous donations to the synagogue were often rewarded by valuable connections with prominent Jewish businessmen who were engaged in the fields in which I was interested. The rabbis' global network was surprisingly wide and powerful. Surely, god was on their side. A sufficient donation could even buy a miracle or two.

As I was praying, minding my own business, Boris came in. He wasn't Jewish so I assumed that it was something urgent. He seemed tense. Once he spotted me, he came near and whispered into my ear, "Come outside, Misha. We need to talk."

We stepped outside to a balcony, and took a seat in the sheltered area to avoid the heavy rainfall.

"What is so urgent that you have to disturb my prayers?"

Boris finished lighting a cigarette, took a big puff, and exhaled hastily.

"I've been informed that Vova Bondarenko, director at Neplokho Pharmaceuticals, has left the company and joined Zhivotnyye Vaccination Services, our main competitor. Our informer reported that yesterday he was personally introduced to the senior management at Zhivotnyye by the new minister."

This wasn't good news, as Zhivotnyye Vaccination Services was the baby of the new Minister of Agriculture, appointed in lieu of our recently-sacked partner. Legally the company was owned by his brother through an offshore shell company.

"That isn't good news, Boris."

"Vova, the son of a bitch, disclosed to them details of the tender that Neplokho Pharmaceuticals won half a year ago. He took with him sensitive materials, proving that scientific research corroborating our vaccine's efficiency is dodgy. It's a complete disaster."

"If it gets out, then yes; it will be bad for us."

"It'll be all over the news if his new boss decides to leverage this info. We're dead. What do you want us to do? We probably need to leave the country."

I didn't think that the impotence of our vaccine was a state secret. We were strong and our former partners in the Ministry of Agriculture were involved enough to quell any complaint, prosecutor's office investigation or other nasty accusations that those damn farmers might throw our way. But now, they might have proof against us rather than just allegations. This was much more serious.

Vova was simply a traitor. I gave him a good job with a good salary and he spat in my face. He was too greedy. He stole incriminating documents from us and probably handed them to our competitors. There was only one thing to do with a traitor.

"Stop panicking and relax. Go find Gigo and tell him to get a trusted guy and find Vova right now. I'm sure the son of a prostitute thinks we don't know shit yet, so we may surprise him. Take him to the abandoned storage depot next to the Dnieper. I'll meet you there."

"Okay, Misha, I'll get right on it."

"And make sure Gigo knows how important this is. He doesn't need details; just make sure he knows not to rest till that traitor is found."

Boris nodded and took off immediately. I went back into the synagogue to finish praying. I knew what I had to do, and praying seemed appropriate. I recited a Kaddish, a prayer that mourners recite after the death of a close relative.

"O God, full of mercy, who dwells on high, grant proper rest on the wings of the divine presence for the soul of the deceased.

May his resting place be in the Garden of Eden. May the master of mercy shelter him in the shelter of His wings for eternity; and may He bind his soul in the bond of life.

God is his heritage and may he repose in peace on his resting place.

Now let us respond: Amen."

I spent several hours waiting at the synagogue, till eventually a call came from Boris. Feeling the vibration in my pocket, I stepped out so not to desecrate the holy place on Shabbat.

"That thing we discussed," he said, sounding like a Hollywood Wiseguy. "It's done."

"Good. I'll be there shortly."

I pocketed the cell phone and closed my eyes. I knew what was coming and I needed a couple of minutes to prepare myself.

"*Okay, Vova. Let's see how happy you would be with your new job,*" I thought as I headed for my car.

I arrived to the abandoned industrial site, which was the same place where Nazar had nearly killed Gigo and me a few years before. Gigo, Boris, Revaz, who was Gigo's guy, and Vova were waiting for me in a large empty warehouse. The rain still fell heavily, beating a staccato drum beat on the metal roof as I entered the warehouse. Above the immense noise of the rainfall, I could already hear Vova screaming for mercy.

"Mr Vorotavich. Please. I can explain. I didn't m…"

"Keep your mouth shut, traitor," I spat with disdain. "Nobody saw you take him?" I asked Gigo.

"Nobody see, boss. We bundled him out the rear entrance of his building and threw him into the boot."

"Okay."

I now looked at Vova for the first time. He had a black eye, several abrasions on his face, and a piss stain on his trousers.

"Please...Mr Vorotavich...I..."

"I said keep your mouth shut," I shouted.

Vova hung his head and started crying, but I felt no pity for him. He had betrayed me, and there had been no reason to do so.

"Gigo, Revaz...hold this son of a bitch on his knees and keep him quiet. Gigo: give me your gun."

Revaz covered Vova's mouth with a heavy duty masking tape. His protests and begging stopped as he resigned himself to his fate. He stared at me with his eyes almost bulging out of their sockets, trembling with fear and shaking his head. I was trembling too, hoping nobody noticed.

"Cover his eyes too," I demanded.

I slowly screwed a silencer onto the firearm, focusing all my attention on the gun in my hand, ignoring the others. I then held it up, and pointed it at Vova's forehead.

"You're a fucking traitor. After I gave your life some meaning, did you think that I wouldn't touch you because the new minister extended you his helping hand? Your new master will come to me soon, after realising that he cannot substitute my operation with his. You made the wrong choice, Vova. You know the punishment for traitors. God have mercy on your fucking soul."

Vova started wriggling, but Gigo and Revaz held him in place. I placed the silencer against Vova's forehead and pulled the trigger. His head yanked backwards and a small ribbon of blood trickled from the wound. Gigo and Revaz stepped away, letting his body fall back to the ground. I stood over the body and took one last look at the traitor before delivering a double-tap. I handed the gun back to Gigo and wiped blood splatter from my forehead with the back of my hand.

"Wipe it off, remove the silencer, then put the gun in his hand and dump the body of this shithead next to the Dnieper."

"Next to the river? Is that wise, *boss?*" Boris asked, calling me boss pointedly.

"I want the body to be found. I don't think anyone will betray us again. Spread a rumour that he started to work for a competitor just before he died. This needs to look like a suicide but the people that matter need to understand that it wasn't."

"As you wish, boss."

"Good job, you two," I directed at Gigo and Revaz. "There will be a bonus in your next wage."

Gigo and Revaz smiled, and then nodded deferentially. Respect for the boss was prerequisite in this business, and I'd proved myself worthy of their loyalty.

"Thank you, boss. Good job," Gigo growled.

I left the others to deal with the body, and drove home. On the way I started shaking as the adrenaline left my body, so I pulled over when I saw a real shithole of a bar, went in, and ordered a bottle of vodka. I drank three shots in a row to calm my nerves.

I felt like Michael Corleone in The Godfather, when he killed Virgil Sollozzo and the corrupt Police Captain McCluskey because Sollozzo had attempted to kill Vito Corleone, Michael's father and the capo di tutti capi: the Corleone family's Godfather. It was Michael's first brush with the family business. He had never killed before but he stepped up and murdered two men who threatened his family. A man has got to do what a man has got to do. There would be no turning back for Michael after the killings.

The police investigation was completed within a week, with the conclusion that it was a suicide. So what if the suicide note contained a few typical misspellings of Georgian among the Russian, and Vova wasn't even Georgian? The man was clearly a magician as he was able to shoot himself three times in the head before perishing and going to hell.

The documentation that Vova stole never surfaced. Either Vova didn't have a chance to pass it on or the people who received it understood that they didn't want to mess with me. Those who needed to know who killed Vova, knew it was me. The message was loud and clear.

It had been the hardest thing that I'd had to do in my life, but it was necessary to protect my business, my friends and my family. I had to do it myself since I was the boss, and in my mind the boss should be both judge and executioner. Only wimps ask their people to do such things for them. I had executed a man. However, in Vova's case I never regretted that I did. If his move had succeeded, it would've been my corpse fished out from the river, as I had no illusions about what the new minister was capable of doing to take over my share of the market. As the Americans would say, this was pre-emptive retaliation.

I'd proven to myself that I had the guts to deal with such situations. I felt that I could defy ministers and government officials and come out with the upper hand. I felt that I had what it took. I was the capo di tutti capi, the boss of all bosses.

On that rainy day, the oligarch was born.

11 Boris

Kiev, 2013

With the boss helplessly lying in a coma, stable but with no signs of waking any time soon, Boris flew back to Kiev to take care of things and see how the investigation was proceeding. Arthur would keep an eye on Masha and the children, and if there were any developments, it was just a short hop across the Med if he was needed in Tel Aviv.

Boris reclined in the comfy first class seat and closed his eyes. His mind drifted back to when Anton Lozinski first introduced Misha to him. It felt like centuries ago. Boris was a respected and powerful manager of a state company with solid ministerial backing. He had prolific connections and promising career prospects, either as a manager or a politician, if he decided to join the ministry. It took him years, but he managed to master all the secrets and politics of moving up the hierarchy, primarily by licking the balls of his superiors and playing the perfect tyrant with subordinates.

It had taken time to develop some respect towards Anton, who as deputy minister was his superior, albeit almost ten years younger in age. And then one day, he had called Boris and told him that the day after he was going to introduce him to Mikhail Vorotavich, the future owner of the factory and soon to be the new boss.

Boris was speechless for a few long seconds. But soon, he came to his senses and said that he was looking forward to the meeting.

After the introductions and meeting the other board members, Boris invited Anton and the new boss for a meal. As the lunch unfolded he gradually warmed to Mikhail. He was surprised that the young man seemed to quickly grasp all the nuances of the business. Clearly, he wasn't some stupid spoiled rich brat. Boris understood that this kid was a self-made millionaire who started from nothing. Boris admired that. At the end of the meal, Misha told Boris to stay behind with him when Anton left.

"Thank you, Boris. I would like to spend some more time with you to better understand the business."

"That's fine, Mikhail. I'll be happy to share with you all the secrets of running a factory. Sometimes you need more than managerial skills."

"That's good. But please, call me Misha."

From just an hour spent together, Boris managed to discern that the young man was going places, and he could join the ride if he so wished. Something about Misha made Boris inclined to bet on the boy. And damn, was he right! Yes, the kid lacked connections. And yes, he didn't have the finesse of those who grew up in the old system. But his audacity and killer instinct compensated for all those minor shortcomings.

Boris wasn't considering his retirement even though he was nearing the age. He never married and didn't have children. Working kept him going and he was afraid that once he retired he would get bored, sick and die. He didn't have any real hobbies, apart from drinking alcohol, spending hours in the sauna and having sex with prostitutes. So what would he do without his work? Go fishing?

Siding with Misha turned out to be a great decision, and before long Boris was reaping the rewards of their close relationship, with a flash new car, a luxury apartment, and a hot young girlfriend to keep him warm on the nights he wasn't shagging prostitutes in a VIP room of one of Kiev's swankiest nightclubs.

Boris wasn't young anymore, and his heavy drinking left black holes in his recollection of what happened the night he met his latest girlfriend. Mixing alcohol with the pills that he was taking for reducing his cholesterol and blood pressure had a toxic effect. But he could give up neither the pills nor the alcohol.

He remembered waking up with an extreme hangover, looking around and noticing the flowers near his bed. He took the flowers out of the vase and drained the water in a single gulp. After quenching his initial thirst, he staggered to the kitchen where he was surprised to see a strange girl drinking coffee, wearing his button-down shirt. The girl looked up from a newspaper and smiled.

"Good morning, lover, although from your look this morning would be good for you only in the afternoon," she said smiling. "Do you want a cup of coffee?"

Still dumbstruck, Boris just nodded. He watched the girl pour a fresh cup for him, and tried desperately to piece together what had happened the night before, but the memory wouldn't come to him.

"Yesterday was nice, very nice. You're like a cuddly bear, Boris. A cuddly, naughty sex-machine bear," the girl said as she handed Boris the steaming cup.

"Err…thank you…err," Boris managed to stutter.

"It's Natalia."

"I'm sorry?"

The girl smiled at Boris.

"You're trying to remember my name, aren't you? I'm not surprised your memory is cloudy. You were pretty out of it last night," Natalia said, taking a seat at the breakfast bar.

So, this was Natalia. She was just there, in Boris' apartment, wearing nothing more than his shirt. Not even panties. Boris studied her carefully as she sipped at the hot coffee. Her blonde hair, blue eyes, young body and silky long legs were spectacular. And her face! She was stunningly beautiful.

As Boris couldn't remember whether they'd had sex already, he didn't want to leave this particular issue undecided. It was a good opportunity to satisfy his morning libido, which was amplified by a peek at the girl's neatly trimmed pussy, just visible under his shirt. A good method of fighting a hangover was some intense sexual activity. He casually bent Natalia over the bar and took her from behind right there in the kitchen, without saying a word.

Since that morning Natalia had stayed with him.

Boris grew up in the old world of communist USSR. The new world, capitalist Ukraine, required a completely different set of skills and a completely different mind-set. Boris considered himself lucky that Misha believed in him and gave him the opportunity to adapt to the new world. Only those who were able to adapt to capitalism would be successful. Misha was one of the new breed, young enough and ambitious enough to adapt.

Some of the skills that worked under communism were still useful under the Ukrainian distorted version of capitalism. Under communism you had to work the system to get anything or anywhere. If you just followed the rules, you got nowhere. These same skills were necessary under capitalism too, if you wanted to make exceptional amounts of money.

Boris knew how to do it and he had old-school friends in strategic positions. The old Soviet comrades took care of each other since they appreciated the mutual benefits of doing so. They were their brothers' keepers. You do for me and I do for you. Manus manum lavat, as the Romans defined it centuries ago. He thought that Misha and he made a good team, complementing each other's skills perfectly.

But now Misha was lying in a hospital bed, hanging between life and death. Boris wished him to wake up. It would be boring without him.

12 Aim High

Kiev, 1997

The combination of the massive privatisations in Ukraine and having Boris on board brought a new set of incomparable business opportunities. Being the right person at the right time had never been truer. The right person was Boris with his connections, and the right time was now when the state was selling assets at bargain prices.

All I needed was the money and the appetite to take a risk. They say that most failures aren't of those who aim high and miss but of those who aim low and hit the target. I aimed high. Always high. The target this time was Ukraine's lucrative metal industry.

Metal production, especially the iron and steel industry, is the dominant heavy industry in Ukraine. Ukraine is the world's eighth largest producer and the third largest exporter of iron and steel. After Ukraine's independence, the privatisation wave that swept the country didn't pass over iron ore mining companies and iron and steel mills. They were all up for sale.

Under communism everything was planned ahead. Now, under the free market, the factories had to compete and find suppliers and customers. They needed to adapt to the new world, but adapting takes time. Turmoil and privatisation led to opportunities.

The funny thing was that the metal factories were gigantic, employing tens of thousands and sometimes over one hundred thousand workers. However, out of all those employees there wasn't a single salesman who knew how to sell what they manufactured. There was just no need for salespersons under communism. For the archaic Soviet management teams at these factories, to organise new supply chains and organise export deals, was virtually impossible.

Boris was well connected with senior people in the government and the State Property Fund of Ukraine, which was responsible for the privatisation. As a fellow manager of an energy company, he had close relationships with the managers of some of the largest metal factories. We decided to target Lugansk Steel, in the east of the country in the Lugansk District.

We obtained insider information that the factory, which employed seventy thousand workers, had a privatisation plan in place. According to the plan the suppliers of the factory would get 10% of its shares, the employees would get 10%; 40% would be offered to large institutional investors through a tender and 40% would remain under state control. We needed to get 51% to achieve complete control over the factory.

The privatisation plan aimed to offer a sufficiently large stake in the company to attract a strategic investor capable of financing the factory's modernisation. It also aimed to leave the state on par with the investor, so it kept partial control over the factory because of its strategic importance to the Ukrainian economy as a major employer. We, however, had a plan to counter the privatisation plan.

To buy 40% of the shares that were offered via a tender we needed to borrow some capital. My group didn't have enough money for such a large investment and anyway I didn't want to risk the Group's funds. Ukrainian banks weren't an option as lenders, since interest rates were in double digit figures. I expected to realise a return on the investment within two to three years so this option wasn't economical as interest payments would be too demanding. Bringing financing from abroad was almost unheard of at that time, with no foreign institution wanting to lend money to Ukrainian corporations.

Miraculously or not, David kept nagging us for three months with incessant demands for documents, collaterals, due diligences and other bullshit that I couldn't stand. However, he managed to bring us a seventy million US dollar credit line from Oldman Sucks, the renowned American investment bank. This was unprecedented.

The guys at Oldman were smarter than those in any other investment bank because when they smelled money they were like sharks smelling blood - they wanted a piece of the action. I didn't trust them, but we needed them, or more precisely we needed their money.

We issued convertible debt against the loan since Oldman wanted the option to convert some of the loan to equity. This was great as it was a sign of confidence in the deal. David somehow convinced or bullshitted the bankers that we were good to repay their loan.

David was learning quickly.

The simple part of the deal was incorporating Neplokho Metal, which bid and won the tender. This gave us 40% of the shares. We needed another 10% and a bit. To get the 10% that was distributed to employees we had to pull some rabbits out of the hat.

To start our plan in motion, Boris arranged a meeting with Stepan, the manager of Lugansk Steel. Stepan was a tall, once physically strong man in his late forties, who was unable to deal with the ever changing reality around him. His way of coping, like many of his countrymen, was to bury his head in a bottle of vodka at every opportunity.

Boris somehow convinced Stepan, with a small monetary incentive and a promise to keep him employed after we took over his factory, to delay paying the salaries of the workers. The withholding of salaries would commence a few months before the workers would receive their shares.

To convince Stepan to play ball, Boris invited him to a resort in the woods where he could begin the softening up process. A driver went back and forth to the city, constantly supplying fresh girls, drinks, food, a live music band and whatever else was necessary. On his way back, the driver transported empty bottles, clothes stained with vomit, food, spunk and other hints of what was happening in the resort. Boris paid for everything, so Stepan wasn't holding back on his indulgences.

Boris and Stepan drank whisky and vodka for five days straight, fighting morning hangovers with some beers. As respectful and conservative senior managers they adhered to the classic ritual of drinking in the entrance room to the band's accompaniment, sweating in the steam room, shagging in the washing room and drinking again in the entrance room.

Thankfully, the effort wasn't a futile exercise, because Stepan finally agreed to our proposal. Poor Boris had to sacrifice his body for the greater good. I promised him a fat bonus if we took over the factory, and an all-expenses paid stay at the Truskavets mineral water resort to take care of his liver.

On the day that the workers received their shares we hired a few minibuses to drive through the neighbourhoods and villages in which they lived. They were literally starving after not receiving their salaries for the previous few months. We offered them cash and a bottle of vodka for their share certificates, and they gladly parted with their shares. We had a notary on each minibus to affect the sale on the spot.

After three days of going through neighbourhoods and villages, we collected 9.5% of the shares for peanuts, and a few crates of vodka. The workers didn't know what the value of a share certificate was and were happy to get some cash to buy food. They were too starved to ask questions.

Eventually, we collected almost 50% of the shares, but needed another 1% to pass the 51% hurdle and achieve complete control. It required some creativity and this is something that I had no shortage of.

To achieve a majority stake, I bought some debt from the factory's creditors. After their repayment was artificially defaulted, again with Stepan's help, we initiated a bankruptcy procedure. I wasn't afraid that the court would liquidate the factory, as no one was insane enough to send seventy thousand angry workers on to the street, so the court didn't have a choice but to agree with my reorganisation plan. It provided for issuance of additional 20% stock against my modest investment availing some cash to the factory to remain solvent. I even paid the judge to order a write-off on some real debt to the non-influential creditors that couldn't fight back.

It cost me over a hundred million dollars to purchase a 40% stake at the tender. It cost me less than ten million to get another 20% and write-off debt on the way.

We arranged for Oldman Sucks to convert some of its convertible bonds to shares as well, as the bank wanted in as a shareholder. In return, some of our loan was written-off and we gained a powerful strategic partner.

At this stage I started to admit to myself that I was corrupt too and not just simply adapting to the corruption around me. There was no denying it anymore. At a meeting with David, I shared my unease.

"We're corrupt, aren't we? After everything we studied at law school about ethics, we aren't any better than all the other low-lives here."

"That may be true, but who can blame us? You have two choices. You can be honest and not do business here or you can be corrupt and make money. There isn't a third choice."

"Yes, I guess you're right," I answered. "At least we're good corrupt people. We're modernising the factory and helping its employees to keep their jobs. They should thank us."

Once again, everyone involved was happy, except for those creditors whose debt was erased. Eventually, I thought, I would raise the salaries of employees or at least pay them on time and thus sweeten for them the past few months of hardship. I was corrupt, but I was also decent.

After all the dust settled, I decided to keep Stepan on the payroll with a formal position of a director. We made his job purely nominal, as my own man, who was appointed as his deputy was to actually run the business. Although just a middle-age drunkard, Stepan saved me a fortune by playing along with our plan. Having been the manager of a factory that was of national importance for fifteen years, it meant that everyone in the region knew him and he knew everyone, from the police and security services to the biggest mafioso. Now, Stepan had enough money for a jacuzzi every day, filled with vodka instead of water.

***

As a side kick of overtaking Lugansk Steel, we acquired a variety of assets without any business orientation or clear connection with the factory. It came with a sanatorium on the shores of the Black Sea in Crimea, a hospital, a cinema and most interestingly, a football team - Metallurg Lugansk.

It was in the First Ukrainian league, just under Premier. While it wasn't as popular as the Premier league team that represented Lugansk, it did have its devoted fan base. It was an underdog, and I liked underdogs.

As I was a fervent Dynamo Kiev supporter, I didn't immediately warm to the idea of sponsoring a Lugansk football club. However, I couldn't simply throw it away or disband it. This would turn seventy thousand heavy industry workers against me, as football and vodka were their main passions in life. Against such a number of angry hard core, steel factory workers even Gigo with all his thugs couldn't prevail.

I decided to keep the club and see whether I could improve its positioning in the league and its finances. I suspected that the manager of the club and probably some of the players found a way to monetise the sport. Our team sometimes strangely lost games to supposedly inferior rivals. Own goals, goalkeeper's silly mistakes, such as bird watching during attacks by the rivals, and players intentionally hitting other players and getting stupid red cards, were some of the ways we lost matches. Someone was making money from gambling on fixed games.

While I didn't have high hopes for the club, I didn't like what was happening. I assembled the entire club's personnel in an auditorium. I took Gigo and the head of Lugansk Steel labour union with me and told the guys, "You see Gigo here. If I see that someone is throwing one more game, you won't need to deal with me. You won't need to deal with Gigo, either. But we'll tell all the workers at Lugansk Steel that you're throwing games. You'll need to deal with seventy thousand angry workers. And we'll pay the police not to intervene when they decide to show you what justice means for people who throw games of their beloved team."

The union chief slammed his fist on the table to demonstrate the union's preferred way of tackling such situations. Silence fell in the room after I finished with my little motivational speech. It was possible to hear the mice squeaking in the boiler room at the corner of the auditorium. Hell, it was possible to hear a mouse farting.

"Now you bastards better start winning games and make your mamas and me proud," I carried on. "I saw you play and you're not bad. If you finish the season without relegation I promise that each one will get a thousand dollars and the best scorer will marry my daughter."

They were so dumb or dumbfounded that no one even smiled.

"That was a joke; I don't have a daughter," I continued. Some smiles finally appeared, although most were still unsure whether smiling was appropriate. This was a tough crowd.

"But seriously, the best scorer will get a brand new BMW. If you manage to finish top three, I promise I'll distribute one hundred thousand dollars among those who deserve it."

Once I showed them the stick, it was time to show them a carrot so they actually made an effort. I knew that the money was safe with me since there was no way for the team to finish in the top three. Spending a few tens of thousands seemed a small price to pay to make seventy thousand workers happy.

A roaring: "Misha! Misha!" filled the room. Perhaps all these guys needed was someone to motivate them. It felt good to be loved by the crowd. Perhaps I should've been a football player, a rock star or a politician.

No more games were ever fixed again. The club won some and lost some but it wasn't relegated to the Second league.

Football, however, as drugs, gambling and other sticky stuff, rarely lets you off the hook. As the years passed, I found myself deeper and deeper involved in this sport.

13 The Dark Continent

Luanda, 1997

It was impossible to grow big in any business without protection from the SBU. My contact, Colonel Ivanenko, who was receiving a monthly fat envelope from me, urged me to consider helping to revive Ukrainian military exports to Africa and other third world countries through my connections abroad.

Ukraine is a big military force in Europe, second only to Russia in military strength. At the same time, Ukrainians are the fifth largest consumers of alcohol in the world. A nation of drunks controls one of the most powerful armies in the world. At least Ukraine had given up its nuclear weapons in 1996, removing the risk of an intoxicated general stumbling onto the red button.

Ukraine had a huge, cutting edge military industry with massive stores of sellable equipment. It included anything from rifles and machine guns to heavy artillery, tanks, airplanes, electronic warfare equipment, missiles, war ships, anti-aircraft weaponry, radars, communication systems and virtually everything to equip a modern army.

I met the colonel, who was in his mid-fifties and always wore a black suit and dark sunglasses, at our usual meeting place at a high-market Ukrainian restaurant in Kiev, owned by my old friend Seva. He ordered the same food every time we met: cabbage soup followed by meat grilled on a skewer with potatoes, a couple of beers to wash it all down, and a glass of vodka at the end of the meal. He always told me the same joke.

"Patient sees his doctor and complains that he suffers from insomnia, nervous breakdown and depression. Doctor says: Take this medicine for insomnia, this one for nervous breakdown and this one for depression. So patient asks the doctor: Do you have anything else besides vodka?"

I always laughed politely. Say one thing about the colonel, he was consistent. Or perhaps he was suffering from a mild Alzheimer's disease.

He claimed: "Colonel Ivanenko's bosses are in charge of all military exports. Both the State Export Control Committee and the State Special Export Company have a monopoly on official military exports. They're staffed primarily with SBU officers. Without authorisation of the committee, no military or dual-use merchandise can be sold legally. Colonel Ivanenko can get the authorisation to export anything. Colonel Ivanenko can even get an authorisation to sell nukes to Saddam Hussein, had Ukraine not given them up under fucking Budapest memorandum."

He paused to emphasise the point and let me have a chance to admire what he just said. I was aware of the huge amount of contraband arms smuggled out of Ukraine, but that applied mainly to small items like firearms, ammunition, handheld rockets and spare parts. I already knew that if you wanted to sell a warship or a radar system, it would be practically impossible to smuggle them out of the country. Overall, the proposition sounded like a serious offer from a serious man. Perhaps a loony, but nevertheless a serious man.

"You find the buyers," he continued, "Colonel Ivanenko arranges authorisation, supply and transportation. You then collect the payment and transfer to Swiss bank account as per Colonel Ivanenko's instructions, minus your commission of course. You understand?"

"I understand," I answered. I understood that the guy was a fucking psychopath, referring to himself in the third person. "Let me check what I can do and get back to you."

With the Soviet Union's collapse, Ukraine lost its direct military ties with most African nations. The seasoned diplomats and Soviet foreign military intelligence officers, who had connections with decision makers in third world countries, were inherited by Russia. Ukraine still didn't know how to connect with African nations. An intermediary was needed. And I was a perfect intermediary.

David had an Israeli friend, Joshua, from his days in the military. He was involved in the defence business and natural resources trade primarily in Africa.

My plan was to use Joshua's help to reinstate Ukraine as a substantial military exporter in some of the African countries. I knew that the Russians were still strongly present on the continent and they wouldn't be happy with competition from Ukraine. I hoped that Joshua's connections led to levels high enough with the clients to surpass the Russian resistance.

Being a middleman in arms deals meant being strong at both ends, convincing both buyer and seller that they needed your indispensable services. Nobody liked to pay the middleman unless the deal couldn't be done without him. In many ways, doing business in Africa was similar to doing business in Ukraine. Officials' personal incentives were the major part of the normal course of business. While the weather and the people were vastly different, we should've felt right at home doing business in the Dark Continent. Many high-ranking officers in several African countries had studied in the former Soviet Union and spoke Russian, making communications easy.

David contacted Joshua and arranged a meeting for us, and as expected, Joshua jumped at the chance of doing business together. He introduced me to several officials in the ministries of defence of a few African countries, with all meetings conveniently taking place in Geneva. Pretty soon, we agreed the terms of our "friendship and cooperation" under which any arms deal I brokered would kick back to the officials between 30% and 50% of the proceeds. Not so different from the Ukrainian style of doing business.

I felt that I was all set on the buyers' end. The buyers had no direct connection with the sellers and I was the one who was paying them back their share. Now, I needed to sort out the sellers' end, the Ukrainian side. I had to have the SBU pigs in the loop, but I certainly didn't want them to pocket the majority of the profit. I paid them a huge monthly salary anyway and the African side had already pushed down my profit margin.

Besides, as the SBU were the Ukrainian successor of the KGB, I wasn't too fond of this organisation, although my childhood's anger and hatred became less acute over the years. I neither forgot nor forgave what the KGB did to my father.

The SBU was just the interface. It didn't have anything sellable, except maybe for information. Those who had arms for sale were the military and the defence industry, not the SBU. I wanted to bypass the blood-sucking leeches. I'd defied ministers already; I thought that I could defy the SBU as well.

I needed a direct connection with the military, which could sell existing arms' stock, and the defence industry, which could manufacture new arms. I needed to have first-hand prices and not those inflated three-fold by SBU supervisors. I was sure that once they'd asked me in, they wouldn't risk throwing me out and thus jeopardising the orders for the arms and disappointing formidable opponents, such as the military and defence industry chiefs. I was walking on eggshells and had to tread carefully.

Through Boris, I had my connections with Ukrainian government officials. They introduced me, for a small fee, to General Milkovenko, as well as a few directors of arms manufacturing plants.

At the beginning I thought that my job would be easy. First, agree astronomical prices with the buyers. Since the buyers' representatives were paid back a good chunk of it, there was no conflict of interests. Second, get the lowest possible quotes from the Ukrainian sellers for the merchandise, whether in stock from the military, or to be produced to order from the plant. A chunk of the proceeds would go to the SBU, so Colonel Ivanenko and his associates wouldn't be too pissed off that I was working directly with the suppliers.

Of course, I had to take care of the appropriate payments in Ukraine, to ensure that the agreed merchandise left Ukraine at all. I didn't need to manufacture anything, buy the inventory or pay for insurance. I was the perfect middleman who took his cut when the money and merchandise exchanged hands between the parties.

What a perfect plan. What could possibly go wrong?

Well, almost everything. All the pre-payments were made to the factory on our first radar deal, which should've brought me a fifteen million dollar net profit. The supply time was nearing, but then the client's inspection team reported to its superiors that the radars were far from ready. The Africans called me and they weren't happy.

"No radar on time we eat your left leg. No radar at all, we eat both your legs."

I didn't think that they were using metaphors, but seriously threatening me with cannibalism.

As my contacts in Africa were getting agitated, I urgently sent my own inspection team to the factory. I was furious to find out that most of the prepayment had been blown by the factory, which was in dire financial straits, to cover salary arrears and other pressing debts. That was what they claimed anyway. I wouldn't be surprised if a large part of it was stolen by the factory's management. Some essential radar parts hadn't even been ordered from third party manufacturers, as the plant had run out of money.

It was a huge setback. Both the deal and my reputation were in serious danger, as well as my legs. There was no other choice but to bridge the financing from my pocket and to send my people to literally live at the plant to make sure that the radar was completed without further delays. On top of that, I couldn't escape penalties on late delivery. My profit from the deal was wiped out and I didn't even break even. I had to pay two million dollars to compensate the Africans.

But it was valuable lesson, because now I understood how the business worked. To make a deal happen, I couldn't just wait for each party to perform its contractual obligations. Trusting the Ukrainians or the Africans to just fulfil their roles had been a mistake. I needed to have an active hand in each stage of the deal, keeping tight control over the payments so they wouldn't be stolen or wasted. I had to have my own people ensuring that every stage of each transaction progressed according to schedule. And I had to have levers in place to pressure parties to do their parts in the agreed way. Once I learned how to operate in this industry, and I built my reputation, the deals started to flow.

On certain occasions, if my Israeli partner, Joshua, was strong enough at the buyer's end, we made shit loads of money. We were able to squeeze the lowest price from the Ukrainian exporter, and then sold the goods to the buyer for five or six times more than their cost. We ensured that the quotes were never exchanged directly between the seller and the buyer. If direct contact was established, we had measures in place to prevent any direct or government to government sale. Slowly but surely we progressed in this closed market, where only a few can survive and succeed as intermediaries.

While it sounds simple after our initial hardships, it wasn't so. Arms dealing required a special attention to security, espionage and counter espionage activities of the countries involved. Different secret service agencies were carefully observing every step we made. Big brother was watching big time.

Ukraine, Russia, the United States, the United Kingdom, Israel and probably several other countries relentlessly follow every movement in the global arms trade business. I asked myself whether it was worth it. The risk was that once the agencies had their eyes on you they would never let you out of their sights. Nevertheless, the answer was clearly affirmative. We had prospects of nine digit deals and intended to leave a fat margin in our pockets. This area was so exciting. I wanted to feel like James Bond or a Lord of War.

Colonel Ivanenko's role in my business was almost symbolic. He grudgingly accepted pay-offs from me, but I was sure that he wasn't happy with how it all turned out. He probably planned to either replace me with a more loyal arms dealer or have a bigger chunk of the pie. I was paying him so he wouldn't kill the hen that laid the golden eggs. But as soon as he found a goose as replacement, the hen was going to the BBQ.

***

I wondered who in my immediate surrounding was an SBU agent. This was the first step towards acute paranoia. I was joining the club of high ranking officials, businessmen and the like. They all suffered from paranoia.

I couldn't afford the luxury of going to see a shrink due to a panic attack. What would my colleagues say if they found out that I was losing my marbles? But even if you had paranoia, and you knew it, it didn't mean that you weren't being followed. Did it?

That was why almost all delicate conversations were spoken in an Aesopian language of hints and allegories. Sometimes it was difficult to decipher what was agreed even for all participants. More than once I left meetings together with David and each one of us thought that the other understood everything. But often we didn't.

It was one thing to use known metaphors like "the motherland will not forget you" meaning "we will reward your services, if you deliver," to call a big boss "papa" and an insider in an organisation "advisor." But to conduct an entire conversation using only riddles and enigmas was a task for a Pentagon encoding unit, not for me.

Sometimes it was just too grotesque. I freaked out when we held one meeting in Geneva, following Joshua's introduction. David and I met with supposedly a representative of a serious African buyer from Zimbabwe. We rented at the last minute a private room in a hotel to reduce the risk of surveillance.

We met him at the hotel's lobby. Mr Mufasa introduced himself, and the three of us went to the room. He was short, wore a white hat, had thick round glasses and held a suitcase from crocodile leather. He searched our private room, gesturing us with his finger to be quiet. We sat down around a table.

Mr Mufasa started the discussion, "I understand that you're in the egg exporting business. Now, we don't eat chicken eggs. We need ostrich eggs. If the eagle sits on an empty nest the eggs won't hatch. So for the eagle to land, the eggs must be fertile." He paused looking at us, nodding knowingly.

"Do you mean these eggs?" I drew a bomb on a paper and showed it to him. He nodded.

While nodding he continued, "The snake in the garden is after the eggs. We need two mongooses to catch the snake before it reaches the eggs so the eagle can land safely. Otherwise the elephant will drink all the water." And so on, and so forth.

David and I didn't have a clue what he was talking about and what all these animals and their eggs had to do with anything. That was too much. I didn't want to know.

He was nuts or smoking something too strong. I excused myself, as if to make an urgent phone call. I never returned to the room. David caught up with me later. He said that I missed a lesson in zoology.

David observed, "Did you notice that we didn't drink anything with this guy? In every meeting we drink vodka or something else before we get down to business. Perhaps we didn't understand what he was saying since we were sober."

"I've been a drunk for many years. I assure you drunk or sober, we didn't understand because there was nothing to understand."

Was he a lunatic, was I a lunatic or were my lines of business attracting the lunatics?

***

One particularly good weapon buyer was Angola. Since 1975 it had been torn apart by a bloody civil war caused by a power struggle between two former liberation movements. They had fought the Portuguese for independence and now fought each other for power over liberated Angola. Tribalism was well-rooted in Africa. The borders that the Europeans had arbitrarily drawn on the map, sometimes using a ruler to get straight lines, ignored the true African nations.

The Angolan war also served as a surrogate battleground for the Cold War. Aligned with the two Cold War super-powers, one Angolan side in the civil war, the MPLA, was Marxist-Leninist and backed by the USSR, while the other side was the anti-communist UNITA, which was heavily backed by the United States. Putting ideology aside, what was important for me was the opportunity to make money.

We tailored a big transaction between the parties. Ukraine was going to supply the MPLA a full range of arsenal, including AK47 Kalashnikov assault rifles, RPGs, jeeps, trucks, armoured fighting vehicles, heavy artillery, anti-tank missiles, and plenty of ammunition. This time we focused on low-tech weapons that didn't require special training and maintenance. If the deal was successful we planned on a high-tech follow-up deal, including tanks and helicopters.

To assure the relevant people once again that their personal share was guaranteed and that they could wire us the first payment, Gigo and I flew to Luanda, Angola's capital. We wanted to personally shake on it and to be there to counter any last minute surprises, courtesy of the Russians.

As there were no direct flights from Kiev to Luanda, we flew with KLM via Amsterdam. The 14-hour flight in KLM's business class was pleasant and uneventful, which was a striking contrast to the welcome that we received when we landed on African soil.

As we lined up for the usual customs and immigration formalities, a local uniformed officer with two armed soldiers approached us and pulled us from the queue. For a split second I was worried that we'd been set up, and our hosts were about to make us disappear, probably at the behest of either the Russians or one of our other competitors. As my mind raced with what options we had to make a run for it, the officer spoke.

"Welcome, welcome Senor Boorootoveech. Pleasure to make your acquaintance, sir. My name is Joao de Cruz, at your service, sir. Please, please. Follow me. We get sir past security and straight to lovely hotel. Welcome to Angola, sir."

It was amusing how this massive guy, a full head taller than me, spoke like a little baby. A wave of relief flooded over me, and I noticed Gigo unclenched his fists. Good old Gigo; he was ready to take on armed security officers with his bare hands!

We followed Joao, and the two soldiers followed us. The airport's terminal was a grey cement building, with some bullet marks still evident on its wall. We entered the hall through a small side door. It was hot and humid with only a few squeaking old ceiling fans to lazily push the fetid air around.

The passport inspector sat behind a glass window, smoking a cigarette with an armed soldier standing behind him. Joao nodded to the man and he waved us through without bothering to look at our passports.

The terminal had no shops or sandwich kiosks. It only had three merchants with stools. All three seemed invalids, as one was missing a leg, another had an eye patch and the third one smiling, lacked half of his teeth. We left the terminal and were escorted to a black Mercedes. The driver wearing a smart uniform, white hat and gloves, hurried round to open the door for us.

"Welcome to Angola sir," he said, bowing deferentially.

The door shut behind us, and Joao got into the front passenger seat. The car pulled away, and Joao turned to address us.

"We take sir straight to lovely hotel. Sir can freshen up and then we take sir to lovely dinner. Please don't leave hotel before we come to get you. Not very safe for white sir. Please, please," Joao insisted.

When I entered the Mercedes I had felt an itch on my neck. I smacked it, looked at my hand, and saw it was covered with blood and the carcass of a fly as big as a flying cow. I wondered whether it was a tsetse fly and I was going to get the sleeping sickness.

"*Welcome to Africa! What a great start!*" I thought to myself. Let's hope this wasn't a bad sign.

The car soon entered the outer districts of the capital city. Luanda, which had once been a grand, modern city, was a real shithole, making Kiev appear to be a beautiful, modern, well-constructed city in comparison. After Angola's independence most of the Portuguese escaped the capital, leaving the unskilled local population to run the city and maintain its relatively well-developed infrastructure. This, together with the damages caused by the civil war, a huge influx of refugees and the ever-growing slums resulted in a slowly decaying, totally dysfunctional city.

It was terrible; the roads were destroyed, with just random patches of asphalt, sewage ran through the streets and rubbish was everywhere. Almost every building looked like it was on the verge of collapsing. Everything was neglected.

Joao turned and faced us once again.

"Please, please. If sir sleeps with beautiful local women, sir mustn't forget to use condom. Sir should use two condoms. Local women are beautiful but not very healthy. HIV all over the place. Please, please, sir remembers what Joao says and sir have wonderful time."

We arrived to the hotel, which was supposed to be five-star, the best that money can buy in Luanda. Not only was it dirty, but the paint was peeling, the carpet from the entrance to the check-in desk was sticky under our feet, and there was a terrible musty smell that seemed to follow us around. I swear I saw a mouse running across the lobby. When I told Gigo he said, "You're imagining. The snakes probably eat all the mice."

A porter in full western-style uniform took us up to our room, and the horror show was complete. We tipped the man and had a full inspection of our accommodation. It was awful - the beds were old and lumpy, and although the sheets and towels were clean, they were stained and threadbare. What on earth had we let ourselves in for?

We had a few hours until our business dinner, so we slept fully-clothed on top of the covers until Joao came to collect us later that evening.

The dinner was to be hosted by the Minister of Defence. As the minister was late, Joao kept assuring me that he would show up 'any moment soon.' Joshua had told me many stories about meeting African officials, and I wasn't surprised at the minister's tardiness. What would be considered unprofessional or rude in most of the business world was par for the course when dealing with African officials. The minister finally arrived forty five minutes late. An extraordinary level of punctuality in African terms.

The meal was served, and we ate a mix of fine Portuguese food and local dishes. The water-buffalo stew, crocodile dumplings and ostrich kebab were delicious, and I wondered whether these guys ate every animal they could hunt. The minister drank copious amounts of red wine for the duration of the meal, so much so that at the end of the evening Joao had to carry him to his car.

Joao returned to our table and told us it was time to leave, and he would escort us back to the hotel.

"I'm a little worried that we didn't discuss any business, Joao," I told our guide.

"Sir, do not worry. Minister likes you and your friend. He see you tomorrow and talk, okay sir?"

All my previous meetings with African officials had been held on neutral ground in Europe, so this was a new experience for me. I had pictured us staying in a luxury hotel, eating fine, European cuisine, and maybe being taken on a safari to see giraffes, elephants and lions in the wild. I mentioned the safari part to Joao, and he laughed.

"Not many animals now, sir. We have long war and we eat animal."

I was gutted. When I was a boy I had read a book about David Livingstone, the famous English explorer, and was looking forward to seeing some of Africa's magnificent beasts.

The next morning we met at the minister's office to finalise the details. The minister studied the paperwork and then smiled.

"Excellent, Senor Vorotavich," he finally said. "We have a deal."

At the end I had a SWIFT confirmation of the first instalment, for the magic number of twelve million dollars, indicating that the funds were on the way to my account, from which four million I was supposed to pay back to some unidentified Swiss account.

It was as simple as that. No scrutiny of fine print or anything else. As far as the Angolans were concerned, we had a deal, and if we veered from the agreement, we were dead.

Gigo and I politely refused the minister's offer to celebrate with some local girls, as well as the escort back to the hotel. It was just a short drive, so we took a car as all we wanted was to go to the hotel bar and drink. There wasn't anything else to do anyway.

On the way back, we stopped at a red traffic light. Two jeeps pulled up on either side of our car and armed uniformed men jumped out of the vehicles. Without saying anything to us, they broke our car's windows with the butts of their rifles and forced us out, pointing Kalashnikovs at our heads. My first thought was that the Russians were behind this, to take me out of the picture. I silently bade farewell to this world.

Hoping though that all they wanted to do was rob us, I took out my wallet and handed it to them together with my Breitling watch. After one of the soldiers took my belongings, I dropped on my knees and raised my hands over my head.

"Please, please. Take all our money and the car."

Gigo, unfortunately, hadn't learnt much about self-control over the years. Instead of following my example and quietly handing over his belongings he started to argue with the armed men. Since it was difficult to argue in Georgian or Russian with the Portuguese-speaking Angolans, Gigo augmented his point with a perfect right hook to the jaw of the muggers' leader.

The punch connected well, accompanied by the characteristic sound of a broken bone. Gigo's opponent went down unconscious. Gigo looked down at his adversary's falling body with satisfaction, but his success was short-lived. In Africa life isn't worth much. The muggers weren't interested in a fist fight and Gigo had only brought his fists to a gun fight.

From there, everything became slow-motion. Gigo looked at me with a huge smile spread across his face, his gold teeth sparkling, but the smile contorted to one of surprise, quickly followed by pain. The robbers opened fire with their AK47s and riddled Gigo with bullets. He fell to the ground and his body shook like he was performing a perverse dance. The firing stopped, and Gigo lay dead in front of me, blood pouring out of the multiple wounds and pooling around his body.

What a waste of life! Before I could react, they hit me on the head with the butt of a Kalashnikov, and I blacked out.

I woke up in hospital with Joao standing over me.

"Please, please. Sir must lay still. Joao told sir not to go out of hotel. It isn't safe. So sorry about sir's friend. Senor Geegoo was very brave. We found those who killed senor Geegoo and hurt sir. Here is sir's wallet and watch that they took. They won't take anyone's belongings ever again. They are now crocodile's food at the Zambezi River."

Despite Joao's childish language, I didn't doubt his words.

I was told that after they knocked me out, the robbers drove off leaving Gigo and me lying on the street. They weren't working for the Russians or anyone else; they were just local thieves who saw two westerners out alone and couldn't resist robbing us. What they didn't know was that we were under the protection of the Minister of Defence. Joao, who turned out to be the head of Angola's Ministry of Defence Special Operations Unit, was basically charged with enacting whatever the minister asked him to do, such as making the robbers disappear from the face of the earth.

Gigo was dead. Out of all the dangerous businesses that we'd been involved in over the years, he died in a stupid robbery. What a fucking waste.

Gigo was a true friend. Now, he was just a dead friend.

***

After recovering from my concussion, I headed back to Kiev. I needed to replace Gigo immediately, before the people who worked under him decided to offer their services to a competitor. Our businesses were expanding fast and we needed a professional security officer.

For a couple of years I had tried to persuade my cousin Tolik to join the organisation. Sasha and I didn't have many relatives, and so we had always been very close. After finishing his regular service as a paratrooper in the Russian army, I first asked him to join us, but he had volunteered for the Chechen campaign instead.

He was like an older brother to both of us, and we were devastated when we heard he had been killed fighting just outside Grozny. Losing Tolik was a serious blow, both emotionally and from a business perspective as we'd always presumed he would tire of being a soldier and come and join us. But he was the type of man who loved living on the edge, so such an end was inevitable.

The last time we saw him, he visited us in Kiev along with his army buddy, and Sasha and I made sure they had the best of leaves before they returned to the battlefield. Tolik's friend was Arthur Slotski. He served with Tolik in the paratroopers division during their regular service, before Arthur transferred to Spetsnaz, Russia's military Special Forces.

The last time I had seen Arthur was at Tolik's funeral. Now, I needed someone like him, the best friend of my cousin. Someone I could trust absolutely.

Currently a retiree, Arthur was a professional. He always dressed in a plain black suit, neatly pressed white shirt and polished shoes. To a casual observer he was probably middle-management or a clerk. How wrong first impressions can be.

When Arthur accompanied Tolik to Kiev we all went to a Sauna. Arthur's body was extremely muscular and covered with scars, at least two of which were from bullet wounds. He had a simple green tattoo with the emblem of the Russian paratroopers next to the symbol of his blood type. He never smiled and hardly spoke, even after a few shots of vodka, which didn't seem to affect him at all.

All it took was a couple of phone calls and a half hour's wait, and I got hold of Arthur's number. I called and asked him to meet with me in Kiev as I had a proposition for him. Arthur agreed to come, and I offered to put him up in a swanky Kiev hotel for a few days while I present my proposal to him.

He arrived in Kiev the next day and without massive persuasion on my part Arthur agreed to join us as the Group's chief security officer. For him, working for his deceased best mate's cousin was more important than money and I was sure Tolik had told him that our security needs were anything but dull.

14 Business or Pleasure

Kiev, 1997

After the unsettling events in Angola I needed to relax. One additional role that we had to do as part of the business with Africa was entertaining the envoys and officials who came to Kiev to inspect the goods and meet the suppliers. We became experts on traditional and less traditional Ukrainian hospitality.

I needed a good party to overcome the ordeals of Luanda. I needed to mix some business with pleasure. Following the Soviet Union's fall and the end of austere communist leisure, the former Soviet nations increasingly offered decadent and glamorous recreational options.

I had to arrange a top-class reception for the Minister of Defence of Uganda and his party when they visited us as part of the inspection of arms. Uganda was one of the main buyers of Ukrainian weapons and we intended to make the envoy feel very welcome. We wanted to show them what Ukrainian cordiality really meant and the perks enjoyed by those who were working with us. It had to be nothing short of completely blowing their minds.

David and I decided to organise our grandest event so far. We invited our business associates and others we wanted to keep happy, including politicians, public officials and military officers with whom maintaining a good relationship was important for business. Splashing money on them wasn't a waste, but an investment.

The party was planned exclusively for a hundred guests. Not too many and not too few. David rented a renovated sixty-metre long cruise liner on the Dnieper River. It turned out to be an excellent choice on his part because the crew was well trained in hosting such extravagant events and being on a ship ensured that nobody would bother us, and the guests could enjoy the scenery as we sailed down the river.

The menu featured the best food money could buy, with Beluga caviar and pizzas topped with Italian white truffles. The bar was stocked with Cristal and Dom Perignon champagne, as well as premium vodka. The final touch was that David arranged for two renowned chefs to fly in from Paris and Tokyo to cater for our guests.

The entertainment consisted of a hundred models, arranged by Gigo's cousin, Hardik. He managed a model agency and supplied us with his most beautiful girls. The models were on top of the hundred guests, so the ratio between men and women was one to one. I paid Hardik extra to show my respect and condolences for the recent premature loss of his cousin.

David organised four suites with Thai body massages with happy endings. He personally made sure that the masseuses weren't lady-boys, but authentic Thai supermodels. He also personally tested their massage skills and confirmed that the end was indeed, extremely happy.

The final piece of entertainment was the drugs. I made sure there was a decent supply of pure cocaine, as I knew that this was the only way to keep Kiev's police chief entertained. We arranged unlimited amounts of marijuana, pre-rolled into ready-made joints, and different pills in different colours. I was told that the pink ones made you love everyone and the blue ones made you feel that everyone loved you. I cherished late Carlos's mantra that ecstasy made you feel that you were among the gods, LSD made you feel like a god and cocaine made you feel that you were in charge of the gods. We had enough drugs on the ship to supply all of Amsterdam's narcotic needs for a month.

Food, tick. Drinks, tick. Sex, tick. Drugs, tick. What else could a man possibly need?

***

The guests were invited to board at four o'clock in the afternoon, with a proposed sailing time of six p.m. We wondered which local politicians would arrive and which would pass on the invite, too embarrassed to be seen at such an event. Based on our experience with the invitees we assumed that until ten or eleven o'clock the behaviour would be more or less civilised. After that the ship would look like Sodom and Gomorrah. And that was exactly how the evening transpired.

I decided I wouldn't greet the guests personally; David would take care of that. I arrived at the ship at around five o'clock, grabbed a bottle of vodka and a busty blonde and took her to one of the suites. We didn't speak much. I had nothing to say and she knew what she had to do. After relaxing in her company, and downing a few shots, I went out to mingle with the guests at around seven. The ship was at capacity and everyone seemed to be enjoying the party.

Before going to face the crowd I went to the upper deck balcony to enjoy the views. As the ship started sailing down the river, the scenery was beautiful. We passed the Hydropark, a renowned recreation river island that boasted beaches and countless cheap cafés, pubs, nightclubs and other lowlife entertainment. Spending a night in Hydropark without being poisoned by outdated meat shashlik, stabbed by drunken hooligans or sedated and duped by a prostitute was considered quite an achievement.

The party was just warming up, so I decided to finally join the action inside the main hall. I took a deep breath and went inside. The lower deck was full of round tables where dinner was served. Each table had a mix of male guests and female models, eating, chatting and laughing. Still behaving like gentlemen at these early hours, they were using their best charms on the ladies as if courtship was required to win them over. What a waste of energy! They were all prepaid to be won.

The middle deck had a dance floor and a bar. It wasn't filled yet since it was still early. To maintain the show of wealth we had hired a DJ from Ibiza to keep the party going until the last dancer collapsed. In a separate, smaller hall a live band was playing Ukrainian and Russian hit singles, gangster chansons and music for slow dances. I knew that some of the more elderly crowd would become nostalgic and melancholic once they were drunk, so it seemed like a good idea.

The upper deck had sofas and comfort zones around long tables on which piles of joints were ready-rolled. This area was designed to host the after party and give everyone a chance to relax and chill out. When the party moved to this stage, people could cool down and watch the sunrise over the city's buildings or wherever the hell we would be sailing. It would be fabulous.

When I went to the lower deck, the Vice Prime Minister of Ukraine, Vitaly Vasko, who was appointed to his position thanks to my influence, was the first one to raise a toast. Undoubtedly, Vitaly was charismatic and knew how to speak and hypnotise the audience. Personally, I thought that he was full of bullshit. Some people made entire careers on nothing but bullshit and Vitaly wasn't an exception.

He warmly greeted the delegates from Uganda, which pleased me as this was a bona fide government official greeting my African guests with respect, and so reinforcing their sense of importance. He finished his toast with a na zdorovya - to your health in Russian. The audience answered with a roaring na zdorovya and everyone emptied their drinks.

The second man to make a toast was Mike, an American guy who controlled the local grey drug market. His company basically sold without a prescription, medicine that wasn't manufactured by any well-known pharmaceutical company. He probably infringed several international patents, but as long as he was paying someone off, he would be safe to carry on with his business. Half-jokingly, I thought that if our animal vaccination went wrong, I could rebrand the vaccine for humans, picking any ailment that it supposedly treated, using Mike's network for its distribution.

I met Mike when he arrived in Kiev a couple of years before, following a Ukrainian girl who he thought had fallen for him, but she dumped him almost immediately when she discovered he wasn't filthy rich. Once he saw that there were thousands of pretty women in Kiev, he got over her quickly. I supplied Mike with his first capital and now he wanted to show his gratitude and loyalty. Speaking in Russian with a funny American accent, Mike wished me all the best. He was done in less than a minute to the relief of everyone. *Na zdorovya* and empty the drink.

After Mike, the order of the toasts became random. After a dozen *na zdorovyas* everything became a bit blurry. The deck was swinging around and not only because of the current.

Before I completely lost the ability to speak, it was time to take the party to the next level. I walked to the low stage and gently rapped my glass with a spoon to get everyone's attention.

"Ladies and gentlemen, thank you all for blessing us with your presence. We hold this party in your honour to thank each and every one of you for being true friends and partners. Nothing is better than being among friends like you," I said, while thinking that half of these gentlemen friends would sell me and their mother without a second thought and that all the ladies were hookers.

"I hope that you enjoyed the dinner. You're all welcome to come with me to the dance floor where we can really start the party. Na zdorovya!"

I raised my glass, everyone stood up, emptied their drinks, and we all went swaying to the middle deck. I walked over to the African contingent and personally escorted them to the disco.

The Ugandans seemed a bit shocked as we entered the dance floor, but soon got into the party's spirit. They were drinking and dancing, each with two girls on their arms. People started dancing on the tables and on the bar. People in their sixties were dancing with girls as if they were young students again.

I had been drinking constantly for a few hours and was starting to feel drunk, so I sneaked off to my suite and snorted two thick lines of cocaine to get my senses back together and to be able to continue drinking. The evening was still far from over and I had to function properly. Now, I had a fresher eye on the surroundings. The party was becoming unbridled, which meant that I could put all official stuff aside and start enjoying the debauchery.

The party moved into its next stage. The music changed from pop and American rock to the thrum of house and trance. It was interrupted from time to time by old Russian gangster songs heard from the adjacent dancing hall, as some drunken guests demanded an increase in the volume. At least, they didn't want to sing themselves, otherwise it would have been a total cacophony, like a drunken Russian karaoke.

Vitaly lurched towards me on very unsteady legs.

"Hey, Misha, very nice party. The girls are fabulous. What's with those drugs, though? I was told you have a whole deck full of drugs. This isn't right, you know. I don't like this shit. I personally don't care if someone does, but if the word leaks out that I took part in a drug festival, I'm dead."

Being drunk, he had lost much of his eloquence, but was still able to state clearly what he meant.

"Don't worry, Vitaly, I hate this stuff too," I lied reassuringly and covered it up with more lies. "The chief of police is here to verify that no credible source talks and that we have only legal surrogates served. I insisted on that. If some prostitute would mouth off, who would believe her, right?"

Vitaly smiled drunkenly, hugged me and staggered off to the direction of the Russian music hall.

People were dancing everywhere. As dawn was approaching, it was time for me to go to the upper deck to chill out. Up there, people were making out on the sofas, sometimes in trios. Everyone was drunk, drugged up or both. The entire hall was filled with sweet marijuana smoke which gave me a rush just by being there. People were smiling widely with fully dilated pupils. Some had their eyes closed, some were chatting and laughing. Everyone seemed to be enjoying the entertainment. I didn't think that my hospitality services were required anymore, so I decided to go out to the balcony to watch the sunrise peacefully.

When I headed outside, a gorgeous blonde stood in my way, holding two glasses of vodka in her hands. She was so beautiful with long flowing hair, legs that went on forever, and luscious full breasts. Her emerald green eyes hypnotised me. She must've been Aurora, the goddess of the dawn. I must've been ridiculously high, as I felt like Satyr, a lover of wine and women.

Oh, I was so fucking high that I felt that someone put my brain in a jar full of hot water. Anything I looked at seemed to be breathing and moving, full of life. I was hallucinating. I wasn't sure whether this woman was really beautiful or I thought that she was the most beautiful thing that I've ever seen in my life because I was so fucked up.

"Please, allow me to raise a toast with the most handsome man in this fine party," she said.

"I wish the complements were true," I answered. "I won't refuse another drink with such a beautiful lady. It's amazing that now the women hit on the men in Kiev. What next? You're going to pay for dinner?"

The blonde smiled.

"You don't remember me, do you? You did hit on me a year ago at a party that Hardik organised."

She was right; I didn't remember her. But, I really liked her. She wasn't taking herself too seriously, she wasn't taking me too seriously, and she had confidence and some chutzpah. She smelled really nice and fresh too.

At this stage I was on the verge of spinning out. I was becoming more drunk and fucked up with every passing minute. Along with the vodka, marijuana and cocaine, I had also swallowed a few pills over the course of the evening. From past experience I knew that I probably had another thirty minutes before I passed out, although losing a sense of time I wasn't sure whether these thirty minutes would take ten minutes or an hour.

Hardly able to speak, I asked her, "Why don't you come with me to my suite? The view there is fantastic."

"Oh, you're sweet, but I won't come with you to your room tonight since you won't respect me in the morning. But call me tomorrow and I'll let you invite me to dinner. Men still do pay for dinner, right?"

She slipped a note with her number into my shirt pocket, kissed me softly on my cheek, turned and walked away. I felt my cheek where she kissed me and gazed at her perfect ass. It was spectacular. I was chemically in love.

The last thing that I remembered from that night, before waking up alone in bed at noon the next day with a heavy hangover, was that she told me, "By the way, my name is Masha. Remember me."

I've never forgotten her. And she was real, not a phantom devised by my intoxicated imagination.□

15 Family

Tel Aviv, 2013

Masha didn't stop yelling at the household staff. She thought that they were taking too much time for preparing lunch. It showed that she was nervous. And she was also angry and upset with Misha's close friends. They mentioned an option to appoint a legal guardian for Misha. How did they dare? It meant they didn't believe in Misha's recovery anymore.

It had been five days of nerve wracking uncertainty since the operation. Although the doctors told her that Misha wasn't in immediate risk anymore, being stable and in a coma wasn't much different than being dead. On the contrary, the coma made it difficult for everyone because of the uncertainty. It was neither here nor there. Nobody knew whether he was going to ever wake up and if he did wake up whether he was going to be the same person. The extent of the damage to his brain was unknown. There was no closure.

"Misha's going to be just fine," she tried to persuade herself. "I'm going to have my husband back."

Misha and Masha could live almost anywhere in the world. They had houses in Kiev, London, Geneva and Tel Aviv. When Dima, their eldest son, was three years old, and Erica, their daughter, was born, Misha decided that the best place for them was Tel Aviv. It was important for him that the children would study in Hebrew and grow up among Jews in Israel. He didn't want them to experience anti-Semitism as he did when he was a kid.

The children grew up bilingual. They spoke Russian at home and Hebrew at school. They also learned English as a foreign language. Misha always said that languages were an asset for life.

Masha reminisced how she first saw Misha. It was in a private party in 1996. Misha was standing there, handsome and smelling of money. Masha walked up to him, planning to make a move. But he was drunk. Two other tall, beautiful girls were chatting with him, giggling and being very physical, touching him nonstop. She decided to back off. Masha knew her true value; she wasn't desperate. There would be another time, if that was destined to happen.

One year later another opportunity presented itself. It was in a party on a ship on the Dnieper River. She didn't believe that it was sixteen years ago. She had heard about Misha and came to the party to basically hit on him. He was a rising star in the business arena in Ukraine. He kept a low profile and didn't flash his wealth like the other young oligarchs. But Hardik, the model agency's owner who organised the party a year earlier, had told her that Misha was surely in the top ten. They were arrogant. He was modest. They dressed like clowns, flashed their money and behaved obnoxiously. He was elegant, charming and had a good sense of humour.

All night she kept a close eye on him from a safe distance, waiting for the time to strike. When Misha sneaked out from the crowd, she struck. It was perfect. He was drunk, alone and probably horny since he was looking at her as if she was a beauty queen. She made sure that she was looking her best and started a conversation as casually as she could master when you actually try to hit on someone. The rest, as they say, was history.

He called her the next day and took her to a dinner in a romantic restaurant. They sat on its terrace overlooking the city, talking and laughing. They then went to a night walk in the garden of Saint Sophia Cathedral. The garden is closed at night, but as Misha said, "This is a matter of finance." He was a perfect gentleman.

He swept Masha off her feet. She fell in love with him and with everything that he could offer her: security, stability, and anything that money could buy. She believed that he was loyal to her. Above all, he treated her with respect. He never hit her and never raised his voice, although she knew that he could be very different with others. She loved this about him above everything else. Perhaps even more than his money.

She wasn't a naive little girl. She knew that to get really rich in Ukraine unorthodox business practices were sometimes required, but she wasn't that curious about the specifics. Like an ostrich she buried her head deep in the sand. What you don't know cannot hurt you. He was her chance to fulfil all her dreams, and she wasn't going to risk it by asking too many questions. He didn't say much and she didn't ask.

Misha prepared Masha to the contingency that someday, someone could attempt to hurt him. She didn't know why and she didn't want to know - ignorance is bliss. Misha welcomed her discretion.

"Just promise me that you aren't a professional hitman," she pleaded jokingly.

"I promise. Professionals earn from what they do, while I'm doing it for free," he joked back.

Misha also fulfilled the role of a father figure filling the void of Masha being brought up just by her mother. Her mother told her that father vanished without a trace. There were no pictures of him, no letters, nothing that even suggested that he ever existed. It was like the earth swallowed him. She swore that one day she would look for him. But that day had never come. Her intuition was that she wouldn't like what she might discover.

And now Misha was gone as well.

***

The worst had happened. She was supposed to be prepared, but she couldn't come to terms with the situation. She was debating with herself how to explain the events to the children. They did know that papa had an operation and that he was now recovering at hospital. However, she didn't tell them the details and the background. How do you explain to small children that someone wanted their papa dead?

Dima seemed to accept the situation in a surprisingly calm way. It looked like he was more upset about cancelling the trip to Rome that was scheduled in two days' time. Little Erica seemed to be more upset than usual. She was crying frequently. But Masha was unsure whether this had anything to do with Misha's condition. Misha was travelling often, so not having him around wasn't supposed to be something unusual for the kids.

Lunch started on time. The atmosphere was tense. Masha and the children were sitting in their dining room on the sixteenth floor in one of the modern residential towers in Tel Aviv. Misha's brother and mother went to the hospital in the morning. Golda insisted going there every day to sit next to Misha's bed and read the newspapers to him.

"Misha hears me," Golda explained to Masha. "When he wakes up he needs to know what happened in the world. He's a big businessman and must keep track of what's going on. When he wakes up we'll all go to holiday in Switzerland. You, Misha and the children. Maybe Sasha and his family will join us, as well as your mother, Masha."

Masha envied Golda's optimism.

The view of the Mediterranean Sea from the penthouse's west all-glass wall was magnificent. Masha was gazing into the distance when Dima's voice interrupted her daydreaming.

"Mama. The children at school told me that papa is suffering from *assassination*. This is a long word. What does it mean?"

"Let it be, sweetheart. Your friends probably heard something from their parents and they don't know what to ask. Papa is recovering from an *operation* and I hope that soon he'll feel much better."

"What is an assassination?" Erica asked.

"Assassination is if somebody was trying to hurt papa," answered Masha. "But we don't know whether this has happened. I think that next week you'll stay home and study with Anastasia." Anastasia was the children's private tutor. "I don't want the children at school and kindergarten to ask you silly questions and bother you. Now finish your food if you want a pudding."

Not going to school and kindergarten for a few days sounded like a treat for the children. The questions ceased.

After lunch, Masha called Tanya to get an update from the hospital, but there was no news. "There isn't any change in his condition," Tanya reported. "If there is any news or developments I promise to call you immediately."

Masha looked far away at the horizon across the sea. Her sad face reflected in the window. It felt like years had passed since Misha was shot. She felt old and tired. She thought about the past as it helped block the awful reality of the present. The past was known, and filled with happy memories. It was the present that was concerning.

"Misha, wake up!"

16 A Perfect Storm

In 1997 a financial crisis hit South East Asia following the collapse of the Thai baht. Because of the crisis, the demand for oil and metals dropped. The drop in oil price hit Russia hard, leading to a political and economic meltdown. Foreign investors pulled out of Russia in a panic. In March 1998 Russian President Boris Yeltsin dismissed the Prime Minister and his entire cabinet. Crisis!

Kiev, 1998

That was when Yuri and our Israeli partners in Neplokho Energy started calling me almost every day with anxious questions and ideas. Yuri was my friend, so it was easy to calm him down.

"Except for immediate negative implications, I don't anticipate any long-run disasters in the energy sector," I explained. "We need to sit tight and wait for the storm to pass. The world still needs fuel to drive cars; this hasn't changed. And it won't change either. The price of oil will bounce back. Those who don't panic will make money. That's the way it always works. You'll see, Yuri. Trust me."

"Fine. I trust you, Misha. But it's difficult to keep our partners calm. They're nervous about the situation. They want out."

"Then it's up to you to convince them to keep their nerve. The crisis will pass, and those that blink first will be the ones regretting their impetuousness."

For our Israeli partners, Ukraine and Russia were one and the same. They were certain that we were heading for an economic Armageddon. So after a few attempts I didn't bother wasting my time on calls with them, just to be their shrink, reassuring them on a daily basis that everything was going to be alright. I kindly left this task for Yuri.

Things got worse as Russia entered a vicious circle. Revenues from its main exports of oil and metals were falling, so tax revenues were declining due to decreasing productivity and increasing unemployment. Russia couldn't borrow money through the capital markets since investors demanded ridiculously high interest rates on Russian government bonds to compensate them for the risk of lending to Russia. Russia had no other choice but to swallow its pride and ask for foreign aid. It received bailout funds from the International Monetary Fund and the World Bank to prop up its economy.

The Russian government failed to properly address the crisis, and about five billion dollars from the bailout aid were alleged to be stolen. Consequently, on 13 August 1998 the Russian stock, bond and currency markets completely collapsed. Inflation in 1998 surpassed 80%, the stock market was down 75% and Russia officially defaulted on its national debt. A real, full-blown financial crisis was in effect. A perfect storm.

Although I didn't foresee the magnitude of this crisis, I sensed the opportunity that it offered. Being inside the events, rather than seeing them reported by TV channels, I knew that nothing extreme was going on. People were panicking out of all proportion.

Our Israeli partners in Neplokho Energy, worried by world news reports, asked for an urgent conference call. When I took the call, the voice on the other end sounded on the verge of hysteria.

"We're losing all our investments. The economists here and in the United States say that this is the end of the Russian economy. The country is bankrupt. The value of our investment is plummeting. They're falling off a cliff. It's a disaster. We want out. Now! We want nothing to do with Russia. You gave us your personal pledge."

My answer was simple.

"I understand your worries, and I agree that it was a bit farfetched on my part to guarantee your investment, but I'll honour my commitment and buy your shares at their nominal price."

I paused to let my offer sink in, and then continued.

"I got you into this mess, and I'll get you out of it. I'm a man of my word, and if you so wish, we can do the transaction today. Personally, I think that the economists don't know what they're talking about. But what do I know. It's your choice. You'll get back your original investment."

I was certain that they were ready to sell the shares for any price, to save at least some of their money. However, Yuri had insisted that I offered them the principal back. That was anti-business, not to use their panic to achieve the best price. But my friend and partner's opinion was an important factor.

Yuri made the point that it was best to keep amicable relations with the investors since we may wish to partner with them again in the future. It was essential to maintain our reputation. I agreed with Yuri and bought his partners out for the same price as their original investment.

A few years later, the value of the shares that I bought in Neplokho Energy during the 1998 crisis for a few hundred million dollars reached several billion dollars. That's right; several billions. Every crisis is an opportunity if you just see the big picture.

As it always happens in life, when the shares skyrocketed, Yuri's partners weren't grateful anymore that I bought them out when everything was crumbling around. Instead they complained that I bought their share for a lentil soup, even accusing me of blowing the crisis out of proportion. Silly hypocrites!

17 Here comes Johnny

New Year was approaching, so I decided to take Boris, David, Sasha and a few select business partners and clients away from Ukraine's cold winter to somewhere nice and warm. We decided to go to the Maldives Islands in the Indian Ocean.

Most people who visit the Maldives stay in nice hotels and resorts, most of which are located on magnificent private islands, offering a luxurious, secluded vacation. We, however, wanted to experience the Maldives the way the mega rich and famous do. After all, while I was trying to avoid being famous I was certainly filthy rich.

I rented the Soneva Gili Resort exclusively for three days, which cost me one million dollars. I spent another two million to ensure that my fifty guests had everything that they ever dreamt of in terms of food, drink, drugs and women. To me, these were the four fundamental needs of every man. I wanted everyone to remember this as another unforgettable Misha Vorotavich party, competing with the one on the ship on the Dnieper. We were about to enter the new millennium - a good reason to celebrate.

I always believed that three days was a magic number for parties. I was sure that after partying for three days in non-stop decadent fashion, I wouldn't survive another day. The three days on the island were like a dream. As often happened at my events, people were having the time of their life. The place soon looked like the last days of Pompeii with people dancing on the beach, having sex everywhere, and taking drugs in the open. All social inhibitions and conventions were thrown aside. Some women spent the whole time naked, and unfortunately, so did a few of the men.

As I was mingling among the guests, David, probably for the first time during the evening released himself from a girl's embrace, and introduced me to John Wiseman, an MBA graduate of the prestigious Harvard Business School. John was an American Jewish boy who David met in Tel Aviv when John was there for a student exchange programme. He was twenty eight, two years older than me, and was about to be promoted to a more senior position in Oldman Sucks' headquarters in New York City.

David invited John to the Maldives since he thought that it would make sense to establish a closer relationship with our insider at the bank. John had played a pivotal role in the approval of Oldman Sucks' seventy million dollar loan for Lugansk Steel's purchase, so getting him closer to us could be advantageous.

Having an insider who can disclose information from behind the scenes can save a lot of money because he can tell you the price that you can realistically achieve. Like in poker, knowing your opponent's hand is a huge plus. When you deal with investment banks you can never know how they extract money from you. When you purchase a firm, and they represent the buyer, they depress the price to increase their fees. When you sell a company, and they represent you, they inflate the price to increase their fees. Hell, they do anything to increase their fees. This is basically legalised corruption.

John had short, straight brown hair. He wore a polo shirt tucked into his khaki shorts, a brown belt and brown leather boat shoes. His business casual, yuppie, nerdy style clearly marked him as the token American among us. He looked a bit startled with what was going on around him.

I took David aside and whispered to him, "Make sure that your friend is integrated into our humble celebration. If you cared to invite him at the first place, ensure that he's having a good time. I want him to see the attractiveness of cooperating with us."

With David on his tail, I was sure that John wouldn't miss much of the action on offer. He had to see that with us he could get any vice that a man wanted. This was the first step in shifting him to the dark side.

John was naive as most Americans I met seemed to be. But he knew finance, he wasn't afraid of taking risks, and he was eager to make money. I thought that I could use such a guy working for me as I was thinking to take over a bank in Ukraine or Russia when a good opportunity presented itself. We would need an in-house investment banker if we were to pull off such a coup. But now was not the time to discuss business, so we just exchanged pleasantries.

"Thank you for coming John," I said as I shook his hand. "Please, enjoy your time here and don't be shy, eh? Make yourself at home and take pleasure in the hospitality."

"Thank you sir, it's certainly very...different to what I'm used to."

"Have a drink, smoke a joint, dance with a pretty girl."

John smiled, thanked me once again, and wandered off to mingle with the other guests. A couple of hours later, I caught David's eye and gestured for him to join me.

"So how is our American friend enjoying the party?"

"He seems to enjoy what he's seeing. But he's a spectator, not a participant. No drugs, no women, just light beer. What is it with light beer? I don't get the point of having a beer with low alcohol."

"Ha ha, yes I know what you mean. Okay, David; you go back to your women. I'll have a word with him."

I invited John to join me. We settled on two plush striking white sofas on a balcony that overlooked the party. Around us chic drapes were billowing softly in the wind. The beautiful powdery white beach was in front of us, and the glass-like inky ocean stretched to the horizon with barely a ripple. Below us, beautiful women danced around the coconut trees and paddled naked by the shoreline and the lapping waves. The ambience was laid-back with a glam party vibe.

We were smoking Cuban cigars and drinking single-malt whiskey, which John didn't dare refuse, as we surveyed the scene.

"This is quite a view, don't you think?" I finally said to break the silence.

"It takes some beating, sir."

"That's why we work so hard. We work hard and play even harder. Sometimes I forget that."

"I'll drink to that."

"Listen, Johnny: I don't think you should continue working for Oldman Sucks any more. If you want to make real money, you should come and work with me in Kiev. Look around you." I gestured with my hand to the partying people around us.

"Do you think that you'll go to such parties while working for Oldman? I don't think so. You'll have fun with me. And I'll make you rich beyond your wildest dreams. Come work with me and you won't regret it."

I handed John my business card. "Think about it, but not for too long, and give me a call."

John took the card and studied it before placing it in his wallet.

"Thank you, sir," he replied. "I appreciate your offer. Let me think about it, I promise I'll get back to you very soon."

"Good. Please call me Michael," I replied.

***

A week later, John called me.

"I've been thinking about your offer, Mr Vorotavich and I'm very interested. But I need a written offer. If I'm going to quit Oldman Sucks just before getting a promotion and move to Kiev, I need to have assurances," he said.

"Johnny, please call me Michael," I reminded him. "I have a better assurance for you. I'm going to transfer to you an advance of two million dollars on your salary if you come over here. We'll open for you a Swiss bank account and transfer the money immediately. Nobody needs to know that you got this money. Is that a sufficient assurance for you?"

John didn't know yet that contracts and written offers didn't have much weight in Ukraine. Deals were based on mutual respect and fear.

The line went silent for a few seconds, and I knew I had him hooked.

"I guess I'll see you in a few days, Mr. Voro...Err...Michael," he finally said.

I immediately called David and told him the news.

"This is excellent. A corporate banker on the team will be most useful," David enthused.

"I'm glad that you're happy. You'll be guarantor for the two million dollars I'm about to transfer to him. He's your recommendation, after all."

"Fair enough," David said without a hint of protest. Losing two million dollars wouldn't have a huge impact on him. "He'll show up, I'm sure of that."

John arrived in Kiev a few days later and we made sure he felt welcome and warm. We gave him a nice two bedroom flat in the centre of Kiev within walking distance of the office, and a silver Mercedes with a driver on standby twenty four hours a day, seven days a week.

"You should just ask for whatever you need, including drugs and women. Everything will be delivered to your apartment. Everything will be prepaid. No questions asked. All you need to do is to tell your driver how you like your drugs and girls and how many you want."

You can't be more explicit than that.

John, however, wasn't accustomed to the warm and welcoming Eastern European hospitality. He was too shy or afraid to ask for any good vices. I told Boris that John hadn't accepted our offers of generosity, and Boris wasn't too impressed.

"It doesn't make any sense, Misha. He's young and single. Why wouldn't he want pretty Ukrainian girls? If he were married, I could buy it. Americans are sometimes funny about being loyal to their wives. I couldn't understand it, but I could buy it. This isn't natural. I'm telling you he's a virgin or a pederast."

"Oh Boris, you're so funny sometimes," I sniggered. "I think our American friend is just a little shy."

"Pah! It's pathetic. How we ever lost the Cold War is beyond me," Boris lamented.

***

While we were busy partying in the Maldives, and while most people were busy with holidays around New Year, we received the news that the president had replaced the Director of the Security Service of Kiev, sending the old one to another location. The old one was no other than Colonel

Ivanenko, who had given me my ticket into the defence business. However, we thought that we had some time to regroup, since Ukraine was virtually dead between first and tenth of January. Everyone was engaged in New Year's and then the Orthodox Christmas celebrations.

Colonel Ivanenko was on our payroll, representing our krysha. If our krysha couldn't protect us anymore, it was clear that we should expect a blow. We didn't know the new director and so we didn't contact him when he started his new position. We didn't properly pay our respect and didn't pay him for his trouble of keeping us secure.

When John arrived at the office on his first day, he opened the door to a scene taken from a Quentin Tarantino movie. Fifteen masked men were standing in the office wearing black from top to bottom, with bulletproof vests and machine guns. The computer servers were shut down, phones jammed and all the employees were lying on the floor, face down with their hands behind their heads.

John stood at the door, paralysed with fear. He was supposed to be greeted by lovely Svetlana, my personal assistant, but there he was, face to face with Captain Svetanov and his masked gunmen. The Captain approached John, pointed a machine gun at his face and barked at him in Russian to lie down on the floor. John didn't understand what the hell was going on and what the hell the crazy masked man was shouting at him. Luckily, his instinct was to drop everything and lie on the floor. He pissed himself, being sure it was an armed robbery.

"*Oy vey. I'm going to die. Oh, mother!*" was all John could think.

Lucky for him, two men forcefully picked him up, frisked him and found an American passport in his jacket. Since the security services preferred not to harass foreigners from Western Europe or America, unless there was a real reason, John was released after an hour. He went back to his flat, locked the door, and refused my calls.

The mask show was nothing more than the new Director of Security saying hello, informing us that there was a new sheriff in town, and giving us a push to come and pay our respects. I trusted that he was sane enough not to kill the golden goose. He knew well that we were paying good money to get along with the security agencies.

Nobody in the office was harmed, and the masked men left once they had conveyed their message. They took with them a number of computer servers, which was a little concerning, although I was certain that nothing too incriminating was on them. Anything that could be used against us, such as the spreadsheets with details of who received bribes and in what amounts or how much taxes we underpaid were kept well away from the office. I was sure that the new director was just collecting compromising materials on each and every person who had any kind of influence or financial clout, in case he ever needed leverage.

Colonel Ivanenko, although we paid him generously, admitted that he had a stash of info on us. The problem was that the most sensitive materials left the SBU archives together with departing senior officers who had collected them. While their substitutes engaged in collecting new materials, who knew when the old stuff might pop up?

I called John the next day, and finally he answered. His voice was shaky as I explained that the incident was nothing serious.

"These things don't happen often, John. Statistically you'll probably never see a violent act again in Ukraine."

"Fuck me, Michael. I thought they were going to kill us all!"

"No, no, it was just a show - a performance, if you like, or a ride in Disneyworld. I understand it would be unsettling for you, but that is how business can be sometimes."

"Not in fucking New York, it isn't!"

"Things are a little different here, Johnny. I understand you're shaken up a little. Have some vodka, get a whore to take your mind off things and have the day off. I'll come see you tomorrow some time, and we'll start afresh, okay?"

"Fine. I'll see you soon."

The mask show had been the first unsettling experience for John in Ukraine. It wouldn't be the last.

John was a nice Jewish boy, who grew up in Long Island, never experiencing violence in his life. The most violent activity in which he had ever been involved was probably playing squash. The move from safe America to crazy Kiev wasn't easy for him, and I'll give him his due; he didn't quit. He understood that it was his opportunity to make some serious money. Within a few days the incident seemed to have been forgotten.

Being a Harvard MBA, an ex-Oldman investment banker, and a Jewish American did mean that John was greedy. Only a few weeks had gone by when he came into my office and asked for a two million dollar loan. This was on top of the two millions that he had already received from me.

"Two million dollars? I'm glad to see that you feel much better after the little incident on your first day. You already got two millions. Why do you need another two?"

"Well, I need the extra money to buy a villa on Pechersk Hills. I think the area is awesome and I think it could be a great investment."

I was surprised by his lack of tact.

"Johnny, how quickly you've turned from a lender to a borrower. Amazing!"

I took him to my office's window, put my arm around his shoulder and pointed at the Ukrainian bank down the block.

"Now take a look at the bank opposite our office. You see, I have a non-competition agreement with them. They don't trade sunflower seeds, that I sell, and I, in return, don't give loans. However, I do pay salaries and bonuses. Show me that you're worth it and soon enough you'll have a villa on Pechersk Hills. You'll have ten villas if you want."

"I get it. I just thought it would be better to ask you."

"Now Johnny, you've already received two million dollars from me. So don't try to put your dick in my ass. And by the way, consult me first about any real estate offers you get. No villa in Kiev costs anything close to four million dollars. Whoever offered you the place at that price is taking advantage of you being a foreigner. Tell Arthur the name of the guy and he'll teach him a lesson. With that amount you can buy the entire Parliament compound."

"Okay, okay. I got the point. No problem; it was worth checking."

"*He has so much still to learn here*," I thought to myself.

18 Crimea

Crimea is a peninsula in the south of Ukraine located on the northern coast of the Black Sea. It was conquered numerous times throughout history by anyone who happened to be in the region. Finally, in 1954 it was gifted by Russia' Nikita Khrushchev to Ukrainian SSR for the 300 year anniversary of the countries' union. It had been a tourist destination for years. Stalin's favourite, where of all the places of the gigantic USSR he chose Yalta, a famous Crimean recreation town, to host Roosevelt and Churchill for the 1945 Yalta Conference.

Crimea, 2000
During a party in Kiev, when I was already ridiculously drunk I encountered a gorgeous girl. Without thinking too much about it I gave her my business card and told her, "Call me if you want to go to Crimea for a few days. We fly in my private jet, stay in the most beautiful hotel and have fun for a whole week. I pay for everything. We totally forget about the world. Only you, me, the sun and the sea."

Two days later, she called me. Who wouldn't take such an offer? We took my plane and flew to Crimea. We landed at Simferopol, Crimea's capital, and from there drove to Alupka, a beach resort.

The sun was shining bright, high above the rocky coast with the broad beach strip on one side, and the mountains on the other. When we drove along the beach road, the sight of elderly men with young women walking hand-in-hand on the beach always both entertained and repulsed me.

Since this "only you, me, the sun and the sea" drunk idea became boring after I conquered the girl, I thought that it would be great to get John down to join me in Crimea. Besides working, the kid had a rough time getting used to Kiev and he needed some fun.

He had been working long hours. The problem with Americans is that they don't know how to properly balance work and life. They work too hard and don't enjoy themselves. It was fine to work hard and play hard. Americans, however, didn't get the playing bit. If you didn't enjoy yourself you would get burned. I didn't want to see my investment in John burning up, so I decided that he must have some fun, even if I had to force him to do so.

Boris and I had a bet on who could coerce John to sleep with a prostitute first. I thought that this was a golden opportunity to treat him to Crimea's warm sun and set him up him with a local babe.

"Johnny, take the first plane and come to see me down in Crimea. Don't give me the bullshit that you're afraid of flying; I don't buy it. Bring with you your sunglasses and swim gear. We're going to have business meetings next to the pool. My driver will wait for you in the airport."

I really wanted John to have a relaxing time. But once again the circumstances overpowered my intentions.

John landed in Simferopol International Airport and my driver picked him up as planned. On the way to the resort, John asked the driver to stop at a shop since he wanted to buy a pack of Marlboros. Shortly after arriving to Kiev he started smoking for some reason. Smoking cigars was one thing, but smoking cigarettes? This was a nasty habit, which I had given up years ago.

John went into the shop and before he knew it, two Tartars approached him. Accustomed to tourists, they could sense a foreigner from a kilometre away. One pulled a gun and pointed it to his head, while the other took his wallet, watch and suit. They said nothing and he said nothing. The shopkeeper was nowhere to be found. They left him standing in the middle of the shop, in broad daylight, in his shorts and ran away. John didn't know what to do with himself.

When he arrived at his suite I had to calm him down. Again. After he smoked five cigarettes in a row and drank three shots of vodka, I attempted to persuade him, "These kind of incidents don't often occur in Ukraine."

On his first day at work he entered a room with fifteen armed men and now he had been robbed by two armed Tartars. Luck was not on John's side.

I told him, "Johnny, statistically this should've never happened to you. This is a once-in-a-million bad luck. Having been twice in armed situations a third time won't happen. Your anti-luck should now become super-luck. You should go and buy a lottery ticket."

John said, "Now I understand the meaning of the name Crimea. It's Crime with an 'a.' Goddamnit. What the fuck?"

***

The incident made me think whether I should retain this kid and whether he was some kind of lokh. Just two months before I almost had a fight with Boris since I had fired his nephew from the representative office of Neplokho Steel in Belarus. The nephew was duped and robbed by a local prostitute.

My main argument wasn't the incident itself, but rather the premise that led to it. If the rich guy that we made out of his nephew, paying him a ten grand monthly salary, needed a street prostitute in such a country where it was easier to shag than taking a shower, then he had a serious lack of judgement. In Minsk you go to the supermarket and come out with a lady wanting to fuck you. We couldn't rely on him as our representative abroad. Boris defended his nephew, naturally, but I was resolute.

Now I realised how hard it would be for John to get used to the surrounding reality or "globe Ukraine," as Ukrainians called their own country, referring to the drastic difference between Ukraine and the rest of the world. It was a different planet.

Were it not for the two million dollar advance, I would've probably fired John immediately. However, I decided to avail him a bit more time. If the two millions were a waste, then I was a lokh too. I hoped that I wasn't. While at that time these two millions were two of many others, as the saying that I liked goes, "to become really rich you need to love each dollar separately."

The twentieth century was over and a new millennium dawned on us. I already had more money than I ever dreamed that I would possibly have. I wondered what I should do in the new millennium. What new challenges should I tackle? Making another million or ten wasn't exciting anymore, although I didn't lose my financial appetite altogether.

What other goal could I pursue? I had been spending virtually all my life doing businesses that weren't helpful to society. I hadn't produced much, and whatever my plants produced was probably outweighed by polluting the environment in the process.

I hadn't discovered anything helpful. I hadn't contributed to any country. I hadn't done anything cultural. I had been focusing purely on making money. And most of my money was done in unethical and illegal ways.

So what other objective was worthwhile except being the best at what I did? Perhaps it was time to try something new, like politics.

Perhaps it was time to try to change the world.

19 David 007

Tel Aviv, 2013

The knock at the door startled David. He was gazing aimlessly at the television, watching the nine o'clock news in his living room when the sharp rapping alarmed him.

He opened the door and wasn't overly surprised to see agents Shimon and Avner looking back at him. He had been expecting Mossad to pay him a visit sooner, rather than later.

Soon after David left Israel and started working with Misha in 1997, Mossad made contact with him. The Israeli Institute for Intelligence and Special Operations, better known as the Mossad, was interested in the information that David, as an ex officer in the Israeli Defence Force, could supply. He was working with a rising star in the Ukrainian business arena, and Mikhail Vorotavich or Moshe Shaarim was an Israeli citizen, so Mossad wanted to keep a close eye on him. Mossad knew that Vorotavich was involved in arms dealings and that was enough to justify Israel's close scrutiny.

Most of Ukraine's military technologies and secrets were bought by foreign intelligence organisations for peanuts right after the fall of the USSR, so David wasn't required to perform any hazardous spying missions behind enemy lines, like breaking into any nuclear research institute and copying its blueprints. However, as Ukraine was one of the largest arms suppliers in the world, Mossad wanted to know where those arms were heading.

Ukraine had previously been in possession of a large arsenal of nukes and Mossad suspected that despite Ukraine's declaration that all nukes had been destroyed under a treaty with America and Russia, it was possible that some had been 'mislaid' by the government. They could well find their way into the hands of one of Israel's many enemies. Even if the nuclear weapons had been destroyed, Ukrainian scientists still had access to nuclear technology, which they could also sell.

David didn't want to cooperate with Mossad, but he didn't really have a choice. Mossad assured David that any information that he supplied would remain confidential. Misha's business interests wouldn't be hurt, unless of course they threatened the security of Israel or its close allies.

David's main concern was the Ukrainian Government, through the SBU or any number of other avenues, finding out about his arrangement with Mossad. The best case scenario was that they would indict him for espionage. This was a serious risk since the punishment was severe.

The worst case scenario was that the Ukrainian secret service wouldn't even allow David to appear alive before the court. They would squeeze out of him everything that he knew, and then they would kill him. Either way it was likely that he would disappear forever.

David knew that the relationship with Mossad went both ways. If he provided decent intelligence, he would also receive information that was useful. If the Mossad had intelligence on threats to David and Misha, David would be informed, unless, of course, revealing it wasn't in the best interests of Israel.

Shimon and Avner took a seat and refused to have coffee or water.

"David, we have come to warn you," Shimon went straight to the point; no small talk. "We believe that powerful people are responsible for the assassination attempt on

Shaarim. We don't have conclusive intelligence and what we do have, we cannot share with you at this stage. However, based on the way that it was done, probably using a powerful long-distance sniper rifle, and the precision of performance, we believe that professionals are behind it. They knew exactly where and when Shaarim was going to be at his meeting, and such operations require precise intelligence. We wouldn't be surprised if an insider within your group cooperates with them. We think that there's a mole, but we don't know who it is yet. You must take all precautions. Keep your eyes and ears wide open."

David listened intently. He already suspected that the attempted assassination was a high-level, professional operation. However, seeing Shimon concerned, and the suspicion of an insider cooperating with the assailants, made David even more anxious.

"What do you want me to do?" David asked.

It was Avner who answered, "It is fairly simple. One: share with us any information that you get. Two: keep yourself safe."

David sat with his head in his hands. He already suspected that something big was brewing, and forces that were outside the organisation's influence were targeting them. Nothing Mossad had told him was new, but endorsement by one of the best security services in the world was worrying. Would they go after Boris next? And then him? And is there a mole? Was there anyone he could trust?

"Okay," David finally said. "We have our own investigation running. As soon as I find out anything I'll keep you informed. Thanks for coming over."

Shimon and Avner left David's apartment.

Before David closed the door behind them, Shimon turned around and said, "Don't try to be a hero and do anything yourself. You're dealing with professional killers here. These cruel Russians will remove any obstacle without thinking twice. You have my mobile number. As soon as you discover something, call me. Don't hesitate. Take care, David."

David closed the door and returned to the sofa. He poured himself a large whiskey and stared into space.

"Who's behind this crap? Could this shit get any worse?"

20 You and I will Change the World

Kiev, 2001

At the beginning of the new century I felt invincible. Every business that I touched turned to gold. And most importantly, it seemed that luck was on my side. With good luck you don't really need anything else.

I was now approaching thirty. I felt experienced and clever, and with parliamentary elections approaching in Ukraine, I decided that it was time for me to go into politics.

One clear motivation was that as a politician I would have more power and more connections. Being a politician could be good for business. Instead of buying politicians I could be one.

Another reason was that I had some genuine aspirations to change the world. I believed that perhaps with enough money and political power I could help Ukraine to be a better country. I had no intentions to cease corruption, since it was highly profitable. However, I wanted to see more of the country's wealth actually go to its people.

It was almost a decade since independence, so perhaps it was time to start thinking about Ukraine's people. Maybe my destiny was to change the way it was. I wanted to make a difference and start building a legacy.

Deep inside, I knew that these aspirations were probably too noble for me. I would likely abuse my parliamentary powers for more mundane goals, such as making more money for myself. However, there was nothing wrong in feeling noble, especially if you were drinking something noble at the time you were thinking the noble thoughts and I was just pouring myself a third glass of delicious French cognac. Some of my worst and best decisions were a result of drinking alone.

When I settled in Israel I lost my Ukrainian citizenship. Unfortunately, I required the citizenship to run for parliament, so I arranged for it to be reinstated retroactively. Although the Ukrainian constitution didn't allow dual citizenship, nobody would know. I was Moshe Shaarim in my Israeli passport and Mikhail Vorotavich in my Ukrainian passport. Two completely different, unrelated persons. Who would find out?

Soon enough my new party was registered: The Ukrainian Liberal Party of Progress and Order. I didn't have pangs of remorse for plagiarising the motto of Brasil. I felt Ukraine needed it more at the moment.

I had no aspirations to compete with Ukraine's political leaders. At least, not yet; but I was convinced that I had a decent chance of winning more than twenty seats out of the four hundred and fifty in the Verkhovna Rada. I based my conviction on two factors that were critical for the success of every politician: money and bullshit.

I had plenty of money, and I could raise even more through my connections and business associates. Many of them would be interested to see me entering the Ukrainian parliament as the mutual business benefits were obvious.

As for bullshit, I had been practicing it all my life. I learned to look people in the eyes and lie like there was no tomorrow. I didn't like it, but it was nothing personal, only business. I didn't think that anyone in Ukraine and Russia became really rich without being economical with the truth on his way up. Bullshitting came to me as naturally as breathing.

I was in no doubt that I had all the skills that a politician needed.

To get into parliament I needed to convince a few million people to vote for my party's list. I could nicely supplement the vote by rigging some of the election's results, where possible, but rigging wasn't sufficient to gain the desired number of votes, especially since all influential opponents were rigging too. So there was no other choice but to organise a professional election campaign.

I hired a campaign manager, Vladimir Tischenko. This balding, middle-aged guy, with a thick ginger moustache was clearly both a sycophant and a sleazy character, but he was a seasoned expert in Ukrainian politics and possessed all the suitable credentials.

He told me, "You want to get into parliament? No problem. I get you into parliament. I know all the tricks in the book since I wrote the book. I can get a monkey into parliament if the monkey does what I tell it to do."

Vladimir organised advertising campaigns; events for Jewish voters, conferences for businessmen and road shows for the workers at factories across villages and small towns. My people toured the country for months.

And that was only the tip of the iceberg.

While it was challenging to swing votes from established parties at the national level, it was much easier to ensure that my candidates would win at the local constituencies. I nominated my old friend Anton Lozinski as one of my party's local candidates. Anton had lost a lot of weight but gained a lot of popularity after serving two years as the Minister of Energy and Coal Industry, acquiring the reputation of a reformist.

My other people were spread over the areas where I felt strong. While I was from Kiev, I decided to run in Lugansk, where as an owner of Lugansk Steel and its attached local football team I was insurmountable. Besides, I thought that I looked better on TV and appeared closer to the laymen with Lugansk in the background. Its industrial scenery, full of chimneys, smog and rattle of heavy machinery, looked far better than Kiev's posh environs.

At the local level, where we felt a powerful opposition, we used every dirty trick to eliminate competition. We intimidated and beat up rival candidates, and paid generously to others to concede their candidacy in our favour. We were well prepared for carousel voting, where our buses full of supporters would drive around on the election date, casting their votes multiple times.

The main policy of my political manifesto was an unequivocal change of Ukrainian external policy towards joining the European Union. This was something that I genuinely believed in, and the polls indicated it had strong support.

All the other political agendas were purely opportunistic. It was easy to make promises during the elections because I knew that as a politician I would never have to make good on any of my proposals since it wasn't an enforceable contract. Promises are cheap, delivery is costly.

We gave the men bottles of vodka and the women crates of food and promised that they wouldn't lack for either if they voted for us. We promised to invest millions in developing the rural areas, and millions in developing the cities. We promised more capitalism to businessmen and more socialism to workers. We promised higher minimum wage to employees and lower minimum wage to employers. We would've promised to put a Ukrainian donkey on Mars before the end of the century had it brought us votes. We promised, and promised and promised.

Pretty soon the elections turned nasty. All the dirty laundry that could've been discovered about me and my people was made public. Unlike Russia, where all the significant media was subdued to state control, the Ukrainian media was much more independent. Silly freedom of speech.

My Israeli citizenship was soon disclosed. The prospect of being ruled by the Jewish tycoon Moshe Shaarim, the true hidden identity of Mikhail Vorotavich, was projected as the most evil disaster that could possibly befall the Ukrainian nation.

This was an official PR stunt. Dirty, and openly published in the media for all to see. Unofficially, my opponents were far less subtle. They clearly played into the fear that a zhid like me wanted to overtake Christian Ukraine. This was taken straight out of the Protocols of the Elders of Zion, the hoaxed Jewish plan for global domination.

They claimed that I would ban pork fat and borsch as they weren't kosher. Although I was Jewish, these were two of my favourite dishes. Some extremists, I was sure, went further and alleged that at night I was eating the flesh of tender Christian children and used their blood in Jewish rituals. Simpletons, as many of the voters were, bought this bullshit.

The campaign cost a fortune. I spent millions from my own pocket, as well as millions that were contributed by my largest supporters. All this huge investment was threatened because of this anti-Semitic nonsense.

The elections took place on 31st March 2002. The good news was that I won my seat, along with seven of my people at the local constituencies. The bad news was that at the national level we didn't even pass the threshold barrier.

I aspired to gain the balancing power for a coalition. In Ukraine the parliament was made of many parties, and the ruling parties generally needed to form a coalition to have a majority vote. So even with a small number of seats I was hoping to be able to have a small sphere of influence at a national level. However, the election results were such that my eight seats weren't needed for the coalition's votes. My success was minor, in particular compared to the huge monetary investment.

I had failed, and failure tasted bitter.

***

When I was young my father taught me the basics of Judaism and the Hebrew language. The Ten Commandments in Exodus, the first book in the Torah, had a big impact on me.

While I was at the Institute of Higher Education in Kiev, we watched the 1956 movie 'The Ten Commandments' with Charlton Heston playing Moses. Moshe, my chosen first name in Israel, meant Moses in Hebrew. I would never forget the scene when God gave Moses the Ten Commandments.

"Thou shalt not kill.

Thou shalt not commit adultery.

Thou shalt not steal.

Thou shalt not give false testimony against your neighbour. Thou shalt not covet your neighbour's house. Thou shalt not covet your neighbour's wife, or his ox or donkey, or anything that belongs to your neighbour."

The Ten Commandments were beyond religion. They were the fundamental principles of ethics. Follow them and you are a good person. Don't follow them and you are an evil son of a bitch. Black and white.

I had murdered. I had committed adultery. I had stolen. I had given false testimony. I had coveted my neighbour belongings and sometimes his wife. If he had a donkey I would've coveted it as well.

I was a real son of a bitch without any morality. Forgive me father, for I have sinned.

Sometimes I woke up at nights and couldn't fall back asleep. My mind raced, thinking about all the immoral sins that I had committed. Yes, I made millions and I was richer than I ever dreamed possible. But still, was I better than any of those crooked, corrupted thieves who stole from the weak, undefended poor? Was I the evil in all the books that I read growing up? What good had I ever done to anybody? I was a lowlife scum. I was a piece of shit.

And pieces of shit are always punished in all the stories.

***

One of the guiding principles throughout my career had been to keep a low profile. Fly below the radar and you wouldn't get shot down. My brief venture into politics breached this principle. I exposed myself to the world. This was a mistake and you pay for your mistakes. The consequences were unpleasant.

On a fine early summers day in June 2002 I met the recently appointed First Deputy of the Minister of Defence of Ukraine for a business lunch at a highly recommended Georgian restaurant in the centre of Kiev. Arthur and David, our group's military experts accompanied me. John came along as well, as I thought the meeting would be an opportunity to integrate him more into the Ukrainian way of doing business.

The meeting was very informal - more a 'get to know you' courtesy to the new First Deputy, so nothing of importance was discussed. After a light lunch and a round of toasts, the First Deputy excused himself and left for yet another meeting. The four of us stayed behind to drink coffee and enjoy some Georgian sweets, while discussing our conclusions of the newly-appointed official.

We left the restaurant, and my driver, Nukri, a cousin of late Gigo, jumped out the driver's seat and rushed around the vehicle to open the doors for us.

As we approached the car, enjoying the summer sun gently warming our faces, a black Mercedes pulled away from the kerb about twenty metres away and started moving slowly towards us. As the car passed by, two barrels of automatic machine guns appeared from its front and rear windows and started spraying us.

Before I had time to react, Arthur instinctively jumped on me and took me down to the ground. He almost broke my rib cage as I landed face down, with Arthur's muscular frame on my back.

David, who was walking slightly behind us, also dropped to the ground drawing his gun as he fell, his military training kicking in instinctively.

John, on the other hand, just stood there like a deer in the headlights.

Nukri, who was standing with his back to the road, holding the car's door open, was shot five times in the back. He was thrown a few metres in the air and fell on his face, landing next to me, dead before he hit the ground. Before we could return fire, the Mercedes sped away.

Arthur jumped to his feet with his gun drawn, but it was too late to fire back at the disappearing Merc. The whole incident lasted less than five seconds.

John continued to just stand there, his eyes bulging and his body frozen with fear. The poor guy was in shock and nobody could blame him.

"Goddamnit," was all he kept saying.

I was in shock as well. Without a doubt, this was an assassination attempt on my life. I was lucky to have Arthur with me and Nukri as a human shield. Poor Nukri had stepped right into the line of fire as he rushed to open the car door for me, taking the brunt of the majority of the bullets.

Immediately, my brain went into overdrive, trying to work out who had the audacity to try such a thing. If someone tried to kill me in broad daylight, in the centre of Kiev, just after meeting the First Deputy of the Minister of Defence of Ukraine, nothing would stop them from finishing the job.

I wondered whether the Deputy Minister was involved or someone from my own inner circle. Obviously, the assassins knew about the lunch as they knew where and when to find me. Our security routine ruled out the possibility of being followed without my security noticing it, so this wasn't an opportunistic attempt at my life.

Two days later, and before the dust settled, I suffered another huge blow. Anton Lozinski perished in a car accident. His Mercedes hit a truck that crossed the Kiev-Odessa highway at an accident black spot and hit Anton head-on. As Anton was speeding close to two hundred kilometres per hour the collision was spectacular. They had to collect together his remains, which were splattered all over the road. I didn't believe the bullshit that it was an accident; it had a clear stamp and stench of old KGB techniques that were used to get rid of unwanted people.

We were hunted now. I was being punished for the sin of pride. I should've stayed behind the scenes and not exposed myself in the political arena. I felt ashamed, in particular in front of Boris, who had known Anton for years.

Somebody had to pay immediately. It had to be Vladimir Tischenko, who clearly lied to me about how promising my campaign was; like the wild exaggeration that we had 7% in the polls. All his projections proved to be complete crap.

His direct fees were over three million dollars. Naturally, he deserved no payment out of the promised ten million bonus, which was conditional on success. I felt that I needed to punish him. I was a novice in politics and he, supposedly, was a veteran. He should've warned me that the anti-Semitic card that was played against me was a trump.

I instructed Arthur accordingly. Surprisingly enough, Vladimir probably had good intuition, as he disappeared even before all the ballots had been counted. I was furious. By running away, Vladimir signed his own death warrant.

Three years later his body was transported to Ukraine from Paraguay for burial as cargo 200. If late Carlos were alive, he would surely have used such a brilliant opportunity to smuggle in a few kilos of coke into the country inside the coffin. Apparently, Vladimir had been suffering and died from a strange long-lasting disease, incurable by the local medicine in Latin America. He got what he deserved.

**

Because of the recent elections the governing elite changed. While under the previous government I had a strong backing, under the new one some of my business rivals enjoyed equal backing. The balance of power had shifted away from me slightly, so perhaps my rivals felt that this was the opportunity to get me out of the way for good, before I re-established my connections with the new government. By entering parliament I gained immunity from prosecution, but not from bullets or car bombs. I felt that my enemies were closing in on me. I had to get away.

I was never the bravest. I always found a lot of wisdom in the saying 'there are old pilots and there are bold pilots, but there are no old bold pilots.' This was the reason that flying below radars always appealed to me. It was time to fly low. It was time to go to stealth mode.

I felt like I had turned full circle. However, this time instead of leaving the country broke and heading to Israel, I was leaving the country rich and going to Switzerland.

Switzerland seemed like a good location to get away from Ukraine because I would be not too far away, and could continue managing the Group. Ukrainian government officials enjoyed visiting Switzerland, in particular when all their expenses were paid so they could come to visit me for business meetings. It was also convenient for them to personally deposit their cash payments at their Swiss banks while visiting.

The weather wasn't bad. The food wasn't bad. And it sometimes seemed that there were more Russian speakers in Geneva than French or German, as Switzerland was one of the favourite destinations for Russians and Ukrainians for private banking or keeping a low profile.

I rented a suite in a five-star hotel in Geneva, packed my bags and moved there, along with Masha, who was now a permanent fixture in my life. After couple of weeks I bought a house that she wanted, although it was less to my liking. But if she wanted it, why should I argue. What were a few millions compared to the happiness of your future wife? Happy wife means a happy life. I managed the group from Switzerland, leaving Boris and David as my people on the ground in Kiev.

Only after Boris arranged for me to meet some of the new faces in the new government, and Arthur used his connections to investigate who was behind my failed assassination, did I dare show my face in Kiev again.

Arthur didn't find any real leads, but this was an encouraging sign as it meant that most likely it wasn't one of the big sharks. Nevertheless, Arthur arranged for body guards to watch me 24/7. This was the price I paid for sticking my head over the parapet.

To alleviate my fears, Arthur arranged a meeting with one of the Ukrainian SBU's deputies. The meeting was arranged and held in Warsaw, Poland, a neutral territory. The deputy tried to convince me that the assassination attempt on my life was just a warning.

"If you were wanted dead, you'd be dead," he said, smiling reassuringly, but with a firm non-blinking stare, using usual KGB exaggerated intimidation tactics.

"Next time you decide to go to politics and to sell some silly ideas to the masses, make sure right people know and agree about it in advance. Democracy or not, if politicians want long, healthy career they need to clear their agendas with us. Otherwise, how can we guarantee their safety? In your case, no matter what documents you forge, we treat you as foreigner. You should know your place," he concluded abruptly, leaving no room for arguing.

I wondered whether this guy, who was now smiling at me slyly, was the one behind the shooting episode. He had no comment at all about Anton's fate, just ignoring my questions on this matter. His silence and attitude spoke loudly, confirming my conclusion that Anton's death wasn't accidental.

He then added, "Your friend Colonel Ivanenko sends his regards. He's no longer with the service. He left after he wasn't promoted to the position of deputy director."

I assumed that the colonel didn't get the promotion since he failed to subordinate my defence business. Leaving the SBU likely meant that he was *retired*. People at high ranks didn't just leave the SBU. I was sure that the colonel wasn't happy to lose his job and might've blamed me. I didn't need the colonel's acrimonious feelings towards me and I decided that I would sweeten his retirement in a generous fashion.

The unspoken message of the SBU deputy was clear. We were out of the service, and if we wanted a favourable attitude from the SBU, we needed to put our money on the new horses.

The meeting wasn't great, but Arthur counselled that the immediate danger had subsided. I had my doubts about whether Ukraine was the country in which I wanted to live and it definitely wasn't the country where I wanted to die. I also had my doubts whether it wasn't the time to clean up my image and become an honourable businessman, not that that would help me to avoid possible future assassination attempts. I didn't want to spend the rest of my life looking over my shoulder all the time. I didn't want to live in a constant state of paranoia.

It was time to diversify out of Ukraine and to go legit.

21 Going Legit

Geneva, 2003

How do you go legit? How can you change from being associated with criminal enterprises to someone who is an acceptable legitimate businessman and politician within the global business community? How do you convert from being a son of a bitch to a son of a nun? Can a leopard change its spots?

First, I had to go through everything we were involved in and get a clear idea of what had to be changed into a more plausible framework. On closer studying, I was surprised to discover that except for some illicit protection still charged by some of late Gigo's associates and the domestic animal vaccination operation, almost all the other businesses looked perfectly normal on paper.

Who could claim that owning an energy company or a steel mill was illegal? Indeed, the process of purchasing them wasn't the purest, yet nothing extraordinary or too criminal could be attributed to it. I had used a few loopholes in the privatisation schemes, but so what? Could anyone prove that the auctions were rigged? Let them try. These were honourable industrial companies, employing hundreds of thousands of workers.

I discussed with John, David and Boris how we could restructure Neplokho Holdings in such a way that any connection between me and apparently dodgy businesses would be well concealed. This was a necessary step anyway, as being a member of parliament meant I was formally required to quit any private managerial jobs.

The first steps were to formalise all protection activities and distance myself from the vaccination operation. I didn't think anybody questioned the vaccine's efficiency anymore, but it was still a good idea to cut any ties to it.

Addressing Gigo's protection venture wasn't complicated. We couldn't just give up on this business since we had to retain our security personnel. Without a private armed force nobody would take us seriously.

I arranged for Sasha's wife, Yulia, to register a new company under her ownership: Anti-Mafia Security & Protection Limited. She appointed a retired police general whom I trusted, as the company's general manager. All of Gigo's colleagues were officially employed by the new company. They even got uniforms. All their clients and protégées were convinced, or coerced, if necessary, to have security service contracts with Anti-Mafia Limited. Now, it wasn't my company anymore, and it was a decent business.

I agreed with the Lugansk tax authority for a small kickback to retain the services of Anti-Mafia Limited to protect the authority's headquarters and to screen all visitors. A number of other state authorities followed, once Anti-Mafia's managerial board was reinforced by a few renowned boxing and wrestling Olympic medallists. We sent the Olympians to speak with the board members of our prospective corporate clientele. Was this business still illegal? I thought that even the goddess of justice herself would be proud of the company's work. We were helping society to fight crime.

Vaccination was next. The shares of Neplokho Pharmaceuticals were transferred to my school friend and real estate contractor, Seva, who then drafted a will to bequest his shares to Neplokho Holdings. He signed all the legal forms transferring the shares back to Neplokho Holdings, to be held by it in trust, so I could use them if necessary. No more vaccination under my name. Ciao cows, goats, farmers and agrarians.

As for tax planning, my tax evasion schemes were complicated to prove as they were hardly discernible from legal tax avoidance schemes. The Bookkeeper cooked the books - a real master chef.

The defence business was formally legal, but it didn't project a positive image. Therefore, it was distanced from Neplokho Holdings and from my name.

Money laundering was my biggest concern. I had to stop working through Latvian banks and dubious currency exchange chains. I had an idea of how to deal with it and would need an insurance company, so I asked David to arrange it. David incorporated Neplokho Insurance and soon we were celebrating the receipt of the broadest insurance license by our insurance company, encompassing both life insurance and general property insurance.

The main idea behind Neplokho Insurance was to achieve a steady cash income from customers who were buying insurance policies and paying premiums. The cash income was substantial enough to cover fake money injections from insiders and connected companies under the pretext of buying an insurance coverage. For example, Anti-Mafia Security & Protection Limited bought an insurance policy for its offices and car fleet from Neplokho Insurance.

I could then legalise or launder these cash injections as insurance payments to my entities for artificial or fake insured events. If ladies can fake orgasms, we could fake insured events, as long as my insurance company was playing along.

I couldn't fake an earthquake or a tsunami. However, Neplokho Insurance was eagerly covering a variety of disasters that suddenly befell the other Neplokho companies, their owners and managers. Loss of harvest due to weather conditions, irreparable damage to my imaginary Stradivari fiddle collection, false failure of machinery at Lugansk Steel, and demurrage of vessels in Odessa port. We were struck by a series of calamities, and the insurance damages were much higher than the premiums paid, so clean, legal money was created within the Neplokho network.

This was an efficient money laundering machine, and within the supposedly regulated insurance sector. All these were just preparations. Now, after cleaning my business affairs, I had to improve my personal reputation.

***

America seemed like a place for honest people. The United States of America. The land of the free and the home of the brave. The most righteous, politically correct and awesomest country in the world. It even says 'in god we trust' on the dollar bills. God bless America.

I decided to go to New York City to sample the culture, the food and the constant buzz. As a Jew I would fit right in to a city with such a large and prominent Jewish community and Masha was excited by the prospect of endless shopping right on her doorstep. The time difference with Kiev would be a nuisance, but I was sure that I could overcome it. We started looking at brochures for apartments overlooking Central Park, higher than the fiftieth floor.

This plan quickly fell apart when I was refused a visa to the United States. It was a new experience that state officials, like those in the US Customs and Border Protection department, didn't accept payments for providing special services. They just blindly followed the rules and didn't allow me into the United States because they suspected that my business was illegal. What a pile of crap? Me? Illegal businesses? Come on! I wonder what gave them this absolutely ludicrous impression.

This bothered me. It was a stain that had to be removed so I hired the most prominent lobbying firm in the US to right this wrong. I retained the most expensive Washington DC law firm, which my rabbi's friends from Kiev had recommended. I was sure that this little misunderstanding would soon be resolved. But it would take time, so I had to move to plan B.

Plan B was to move to London; the capital of the United Kingdom and the shining beacon of the British Empire, or what was left of it. The Brits were much more relaxed about allowing foreigners to settle in England. If you brought with you a few millions to invest in the country, they welcomed you with open arms. London was almost as good as New York and the time difference with Kiev was much better. Masha talked excitingly about shopping at Harrods and Selfridges and having four o'clock tea at the Ritz.

With my Israeli passport, entering the UK didn't require a visa, especially since I had been there already in the past for a business meeting with Carlos. Entering the second time was always easier than the first one. Getting a visa for a long time sojourn in the United Kingdom was a mere formality.

I bought a huge house in Hampstead, a rich neighbourhood in the North West of London, for twenty million pounds. The house had an indoor Olympic-size swimming pool, a cinema for fifteen people, a garden as big as a football pitch, and most importantly; a sauna. Boris would love visiting us as his favourite activity was drinking vodka in the sauna.

I decided to spend a third of my time in London, a third in Kiev and a third travelling, including to Israel where my mother was still living. As my legal consultants simplified it to me, the taxation rules of most countries envisaged that if I spent less than half a year in any given country, then I wasn't deemed a taxable resident. Perfect! I thought that once I had children I would eventually settle in Israel since I wanted them to grow up in the Jewish state. That was what my father would've wanted, and it had always been the long term goal.

Now it was time to start working on my public image. I hired the PR consultants who were retained by the British Labour party during its successful election campaign, as my personal public relations experts. They were professional spin doctors that could turn any negative to a positive. It was all in the PR and the positioning.

I considered floating Neplokho Energy - the proud owner of Azov Sea Oil & Gas Company - on the stock exchange through an Initial Public Offering

Now that Ukraine had shown me how hostile it could be, especially if the political elite changed, I needed some hedging for my most valuable assets. An IPO would result in the Western European public co-owning my enterprises. I was sure that the Ukrainian establishment, hostile or not, would think twice about attacking a company that was publicly traded on a European stock exchange.

In this instance, I didn't need the IPO for raising money. The primary objectives were sharing ownership with foreign public investors, hedging and reputational benefits. I needed transparent accountancy and reasonable revenue figures. Since by then my energy and steel businesses were already vertically integrated from supply of raw materials, through production to selling the produce to end-users, I could easily regulate the financial flows inside the structure. These were truly attractive businesses.

Public companies traded on the London Stock Exchange could be used as my springboard into global business. They could apply for government tenders abroad and acquire businesses that I fancied.

In addition to my new house in London, I refurbished our expensive villa in Geneva. My PR team organised for it to appear in a magazine on elegant homes. The photos of Masha standing next to a grand piano in our elegant living room, with Lake Geneva and the mountains looking glorious in the background, added an element of style. How can you be a nasty man if you have such a lovely house and such a lovely girlfriend?

I incorporated a charity with a mission of building farms in Africa. This would help with restructuring the war-torn countries and give incentives to the locals to stop destroying the forests and wildlife. Now that they could make a living from the farms, they didn't need to eat the wild animals. This one was in remembrance of Gigo, who had so looked forward to seeing the wild animals in Africa just before he was killed. I ensured the Angolan mission HQ had a small memorial to the late Mr Gigo Ninoshvili.

The charity was an opportunity to combine a few trips to Africa for the arms dealing business with unique PR photo opportunities. I was surrounded by smiling children in one photo and by jumping antelopes in the next. And honestly, this charity wasn't used for money laundering. I really wanted to save the wild animals.

I donated a collection of paintings to the British Museum and organised a huge PR event around it. It was a collection that had apparently been stolen by the Nazis from some poor Brits, who happened to be trapped in continental Europe during World War II. When Berlin was liberated it was stolen by the Soviets. Now it found its way back to its rightful home in England. I say rightful, but evidently the English stole it before everyone else from Egypt.

My PR experts managed to bring a prominent financial magazine reporter to Kiev to make a favourable article about Neplokho Energy and its modest and decent controlling shareholder. The story was about the outstanding, self-made industrialist and politician who humbly started from nothing in communist Kiev. He was now fighting for modernisation, westernisation, Ukraine joining the EU, the rule of law and the protection of social rights for his thousands of employees. And this wonderful guy was no one else but me.

Even I started to believe all this horseshit. The PR machine was working. It reminded me the Soviet propaganda machine.

I wanted to be an active member in Davos World Economic Forum, lecturing about global competitiveness in emerging Eastern Europe. Can you imagine me lecturing on competitiveness? As I mentioned before, bullshitting was one of my strengths.

The community in Davos was rather exclusive, so I needed John to work his magic in Washington DC. I called him into my office.

"Johnny, I have a job for you. I want you to fly back home to America tomorrow. I've spoken with the lobbying firm working for me. They would arrange for you to meet with a number of Democratic and Republican senators. Your task is to organise for me an invitation for Davos, as one of the mentors. I also want you to arrange for me personal meetings with at least one or two senators."

"Oh, Michael. You know that I'm afraid of flying. It's a real torture for me," John moaned.

"I don't give a hairy crack of a rat's ass how you get to America, but you have to be in Washington on Wednesday. If you know a way to get there by car, fine with me. Maybe you can swim across the Bering Strait between Kamchatka and

Alaska. Maybe they've built a bridge there. I don't give a fuck."

It actually worked. John did what he was asked to do and did it well. Obviously, he was a strong player on his home turf. He arranged my invitation to Davos where I met a few senators.

All my efforts soon paid off and people started to perceive me differently. While before I was an unknown, wealthy criminal, now I was a well-known, wealthy, supposedly legitimate businessman. It was all about the image. If people associate you with money and Russia, then you're seen as a criminal. If people associate you with money and style, then you're perceived as legit.

Being more well-known actually brought new business opportunities. I was invited to events and had the opportunity to mingle with the rich and famous. I didn't need so many introductions anymore before meeting politicians and other businessmen. Just being in the same events and circles together with them showed them that I was serious.

The leopard changed its spots. But with spots or stripes, a leopard remains a leopard.

22 Wild Boar Hunting

Kiev, 2003

After a rather turbulent time, I felt at peace with myself again. I had time to think over the previous events while in 'exile' and I reached some conclusions. My naivety was gone. All the bullshit about changing the world almost killed me. It was just a waste of time. I had re-evaluated my goals in life and decided to aspire to top the list of the wealthiest of Forbes magazine.

I experienced different kinds of businesses. I spent time with politicians. I tried to be a politician and change the world. I thought that I better understood how the world works. Time after time my life experiences taught me that money was the absolute mean. For many it was also an ultimate goal. I finally convinced myself that money was the only name of the game. When I realised it I decided to dedicate myself to reaching the number one place in it. If the game was money, the person who had the most was the winner and logically the most successful. Wars and football games weren't won with superior soldiers or players, but with more money than that of the opponents.

***

Now that I sorted out the debris of my political escapade, it was time to show everyone that I felt stronger than ever. And there was no better occasion for a show-off than my thirtieth birthday.

To pass a clear message to whoever thought that I was gone for good into English exile, I wanted to make Kiev the main arena for my grand return. Besides, Kiev was beautiful at the end of spring. All the chestnut trees blossomed, illustrating why this tree was chosen to be on Kiev's emblem in Soviet times.

I didn't have to be too creative with planning my birthday. I just let Boris make all the arrangements. He was a true champion of decadent-style partying. My three day rule was to be applied, as I considered it a perfect length to balance the desires of day and night. I wanted Yuri and our Israeli defence and real estate partners to come over this time. After all, he hadn't been in his home town for twelve years. He had to see how it had changed in that time.

The main event was scheduled for the first evening in a famous Ukrainian restaurant at Pechersk Hills. Two hours before the late May sunset, the view was spectacular. The part of the city situated on the river's left bank was entirely in view, separated from us by the mighty and broad Dnieper River. It was decorated by islands and sandy beaches, still crowded with the sunbathing community.

As I had many foreign guests, I wanted them to taste authentic Ukrainian cuisine and hospitality. Salo, pepper horilka or Ukrainian vodka, chicken kiev, borsch and other local delicacies were all on the menu. A Ukrainian live band, gipsies, and gorgeous hostesses, instructed to be receptive for courtship, made the atmosphere.

Later, so drunk that we could barely stand on our feet, we went out to the World War II museum - The National Museum of the History of the Great Patriotic War. It was a short walk from the restaurant. Boris had arranged for a private viewing of the museum so nobody bothered us. Its fleet of tanks, planes, rockets and artillery standing there in the open air were enough to form a complete army for any African country. Some guests, in particular those who didn't speak Russian, could've received the impression that this stock of arms was mine. I was taking them proudly as a host for a walk among all those military machines and vehicles.

The hostesses from the restaurant followed us to the museum. After my guided tour some of the guests were combining love and war. Making love within the war machines. As some used condoms were on the premises, it seemed that we weren't the first ones enjoying this pervert adventure.

***

The other two days of my birthday celebration were designed to be spent in the countryside at Koncha Zaspa, twenty five kilometres from Kiev, at Boris's dacha. For a layman it looked like a summer palace of one of the Roman emperors.

While most of the guests were indulging in the dacha, I asked Arthur to organise a boar hunt. I wanted it especially for Yuri, who was keen on hunting and fishing but was unable to enjoy such pleasures in Israel. Unfortunately, fishing wasn't as exciting as it was a decade ago. Fishing poachers had been using dynamite to kill fish by the ton and had depleted the fish populace, except for three-eyed mutated fish, affected by Chernobyl radiation. However, hunting was still an exciting activity.

Arthur's men were supposed to corner and guide wild boars toward a specific place in the forest, where I, Yuri, and Yair, an Israeli, who couldn't miss the adventure, were waiting. Everything went as planned and we were approaching the designated point, holding hunting rifles ready to shoot. Arthur's men should've been ready just a few hundred metres ahead.

As we approached the spot, I signalled to Yuri and Yair to keep quiet, duck and get ready to shoot. Taking us by surprise, we heard shots from our left. Yuri, who was ducking next to me, fell down. My face was covered with blood and skin. I dropped down next to Yuri. Yair was hiding behind a tree. The blood was tricking from where Yuri's ear used to be, torn off by a bullet, and I was covered by its remnants.

There were supposed to be no other hunters in the area. Being paranoid, as always, I didn't believe that this was a friendly fire.

Yuri held the place where his ear used to be with his hand. Blood poured through his fingers and down his wrist. He grimaced and moaned with pain.

"Hold on, Yuri. I'll get help," I tried to reassure him.

While continuing to lie down with my rifle ready to shoot, looking around for any attackers, I called Arthur's mobile phone. However, he arrived before he had a chance to answer. He had heard the premature shots from the unexpected direction and hurried to our position accompanied by two of his men, to find out who was shooting.

"Stay here and stay low," Arthur ordered.

His two companions stayed with us, kneeling on one knee, assault rifles in hand. Their rifles were meant for killing people, not for hunting animals like our hunting guns. Yair came out of hiding and we attended to Yuri's ear with a bandage that one of Arthur's men gave him. Arthur disappeared.

"Don't worry, Yuri," I was trying to use some sense of humour to cheer him up. "They do fantastic prosthetic ears. You can choose to look like Mr Spock or an elf."

Yuri just looked at me. He didn't smile and didn't say anything.

Soon, Arthur called me and reported back.

"We encountered a group of five hunters. They claim they saw a deer where you were. I didn't find anything suspicious about them. I verified each of their identities through Kiev's police chief."

Even if it was carelessness, they deserved to be punished, so I said to Arthur, "Beat them up proper. Try to see if they have more to tell. Anyway, they will learn for the next time they go hunting."

"No problem boss," Arthur replied.

I was sure that Arthur diligently performed the task.

They nearly killed my childhood friend, who luckily lost just his ear. After such incidents I didn't really need to wonder why I was developing paranoia. Even John wasn't around on that occasion, which shattered the theory that I'd started to develop that his bad luck was attracting violent mishaps like a magnet.

After properly treating Yuri's ear, we did hunt the boar the next day. But it wasn't that exciting as Arthur delegated ten people to guard us closely in the forest. As everybody was shooting at the poor animal it wasn't clear who could claim the honour of downing the boar. Yuri got its head as a souvenir.

☐

***

A few days later when I was back in Kiev, I was given an unexpected birthday present. Arthur and I ate lunch close to the office, and as we walked out of the restaurant I saw a familiar face with a distinctively lazy eye. Nazar. I never forget a face.

"That guy..." I said, pointing him out to Arthur, "get him quietly; I would like a private word with him."

Arthur nodded and slipped quietly away, walked up behind the unsuspecting Nazar and stuck a gun in his back. He whispered something in Nazar's ear. Nazar froze. I walked over to them and stood in front of Nazar, smiling broadly.

"Remember me, Nazar? Come, my friend; let's go for a ride in my car."

There was a look of bemusement on Nazar's face as he wracked his brain for some recognition of me. Arthur forced Nazar into our car and we drove to a quiet cul-de-sac nearby.

"I remember you," Nazar finally spoke. "I hardly recognise you; it has been so many years. I hope there aren't hard feelings between us."

I didn't say a word. When we arrived at the street I told Arthur, "Get him out."

We stood outside, with Arthur restraining Nazar, I faced my old foe.

"There are no hard feelings, of course. I haven't had any feelings for many years now."

Nazar seemed to relax slightly as I spoke.

"But because of you, I fled Kiev. Do you remember Gigo? Because of you, Gigo lost his finger. You know, Nazar, that in our business, feelings aside, there always has to be retribution. An eye for an eye, or more precisely in our case, a finger for a finger."

I paused to let him get my drift. Nazar stiffened as it dawned on him that there was more to it than just a chat.

"Arthur...chop off his finger," I ordered.

In the blink of an eye, Arthur punched Nazar on the chin. He fell, and Arthur, sleek as a cat, ended up holding his arm in some martial arts manoeuvre so that Nazar couldn't move without breaking his own arm. The knife was already in

Arthur's other hand and in a quick, smooth slice, Nazar's index finger was off. Blood started gushing out everywhere. Nazar started yelling with pain.

"Arthur! I didn't mean that one. Cut off the middle finger," I said.

Slice. Another finger was off, and this time it was the right one. I stood over the weeping figure of Nazar.

"One finger for Gigo. A second finger for messing with Mikhail Vorotavich," I spat.

"Anything else? Maybe his testicles?" Arthur asked.

"I think he understood my message. Come; let's go," I answered.

On the way back to the office Arthur knitted his brows.

"What's up, Arthur? What have I done wrong this time?"

"You should've killed him. Revenge should go all the way. Now you have a mortal enemy that we could've terminated. I think it's a mistake."

23 Arthur

Tel Aviv, 2013

Arthur Slotski had been working for Misha Vorotavich since 1997. Arthur was a simple man in a sense. He was a man of black and white; no middle-ground grey. Once Arthur identified to whom he was loyal, he just did as he was told. No philosophical bullshit about right or wrong. No conscience. No second thoughts. No looking left or right, just straight ahead like a horse with blinkers. That was the reason that Arthur was an excellent soldier. He followed orders without asking any questions.

When Misha was attacked outside the Georgian restaurant, Arthur didn't think twice. He instinctively jumped on Misha, willing to take a bullet to protect his boss' life. This was his job. No hesitating. No blinking. Just do your job.

Arthur had served in the special forces of the Soviet military, the Spetsnaz GRU - Special operations unit of the Military Intelligence. He joined the military when he was eighteen, and after serving in the paratroopers, he joined the Special Forces. He fought in the war in Afghanistan, the civil war in Tajikistan, the East Prigorodny conflict, and several other military operations that were kept secret from the general public.

Out of all the conflicts in which Arthur participated and out of all the adversaries that he fought, he thought that the Chechen rebels were the toughest and the cruellest. If there was one group of people with which you didn't want to mess, it was the Chechens.

If he had a conscience, he wouldn't have been proud of some of the things that he had to do. He had executed defenceless civilians, tortured prisoners to extract information and inflicted horrible physical harm. Under his capable hands everyone eventually gave up everything they knew. Only someone with Arthur's personality could've done all these atrocities and still slept like a baby at night.

Arthur now stood guard at a hospital in Tel Aviv. He was protecting his boss, Misha, who was the cousin of Tolik, who was like Arthur's brother when they served together in the paratroopers. The Chechens killed Tolik in 1996 when Islamist insurgents ambushed Tolik's convoy in a mountainous region. All the vehicles were blown to pieces so that no bodies were ever found. Arthur was devastated when he heard the news and regretted so much that their career paths parted after the paratroopers. If they were together, it would've been much more difficult to wipe them out.

Arthur rarely left Misha with other bodyguards for more than a few hours, so he wondered why Misha had sent him to Kremenchuk two days before the assassination attempt. He had been charged with training some bodyguards for one of Misha's friends, Denis Filatov, and Arthur had argued that there were qualified subordinates who were more than capable of carrying out the exercise. But Misha had insisted, saying that the friend deserved the very best help, and had personally asked for Arthur to oversee the training. Was the attempt on Misha's life coincidental? Arthur didn't believe in such things.

Arthur took the assassination as his personal failure. It was his job to keep Misha safe. He simply failed. There are successes and there are stories. This was a story. A sad story. There was no middle-ground as far as Arthur was concerned.

Misha was lying with a bullet in his head and the people who did it must pay. Arthur felt that it was his fault that he lost Tolik. He didn't want to lose Misha as well.

***

Arthur's mobile phone rang. It was Andrei Topolski on a scrambled line.

"Yes," Arthur said.

"Arthur? It's Andrei. Is this a good time to talk? We have several leads on the investigation and I wanted to report to you."

"Go ahead, Andrei," Arthur said.

"First, there's this Nazar guy, you know the one? You and Misha cut his fingers off ten years ago. Our people discovered that he's been asking around about Misha lately. He's a violent man and undoubtedly could try to kill the boss. Nazar is now associated with an influential organised crime leader from Odessa."

"That's interesting," Arthur mused. "I'll look into this character. What else?"

"What may be a hotter lead is Colonel Ivanenko. He lost his job at the SBU and blamed Misha for it. Our contacts report that he has been saying that he'll someday have his revenge on Misha. He still has ties with the SBU and these guys can easily pull together an operation with a sniper."

"That sounds more likely. Do you have anything that might link him with the shooting?"

"One thing that especially aroused my suspicions was that I've received two different mobile phone tracking reports. The first from the SBU deputy chief and the second from a former subordinate of Colonel Ivanenko who now heads a department in the Ministry of Communication. The two reports are synchronised with the time and place of the assassination attempt. Both reports refer to the same cellular antennas, but the second report misses out about twenty mobile phone numbers. I've started to think that the discrepancy isn't accidental."

"So the friend of our friend is withholding numbers. Very interesting."

"By the way," Andrei continued, "there is one other thing that bothers me. While most of our group's numbers on the tracking report have logical explanations, as they belong to Misha, his driver, David, and the bodyguards, there is one number that belongs to our network that I don't recognise. Maybe you know? It's 037-31077712."

"Hmm. Yes, I know the number," Arthur said.

"Are you going to tell me?" Andrei asked after a long pause on Arthur's end. Arthur obviously analysed what he just heard.

"It's Boris' spare number, which he gave to his girlfriend, Natalia. Listen. Sever any contact with anyone in Kiev's authorities. We cannot verify their allegiances. Put surveillance on Natalia and Colonel Ivanenko. Don't tell Boris or anyone anything yet. Find out what this Nazar is up to, although I doubt whether this operation is in his league."

"Sure, Arthur. Will do," Andrei replied. "Do you think that Boris might be involved?"

"No," Arthur countered. "I'm certain he isn't. I know all his movements for the last few years better than he does. But, if he finds out that his girlfriend's name came up, he might spook her unintentionally."

"As you wish. Also, I've located the apartment from where the shot must've been taken. It's overlooking Parus Business Centre's entrance and was rented for a short period a few days before the attack. But we're still working on trying to identify who rented it. The tracks are well covered and we couldn't find any leads yet. I have an entire team working on it."

"Fine," Arthur said. "Keep me up to date with any developments regarding the apartment. If we work backwards from there, and also find a possible starting point, then maybe the investigations will meet in the middle."

"Yes, of course. The third lead, as you suspected, Arthur, points to the Russians. Our people in Moscow said that Misha has a few enemies there because of his business ventures. And generally, there's something going on against Ukraine as it rejects joining a Russian-led custom union and stubbornly insists on signing an association agreement with the European Union. We need more time to investigate this, as well as the other two leads. Overall, there are a number of parties with a motive to kill Misha and the means to do so."

"Okay, Andrei. Continue with investigation on all leads. All sound like potential culprits. Also put an eye on Denis Filatov, our former employee and Misha's friend. Tap his lines. I want to know why he needed my services to train his security personnel in Kremenchuk precisely when I was needed in Kiev. It smells bad."

"Done."

"One more thing, Andrei," Arthur continued. "Investigate whether our Chechen partners have anything to do with it. We upset them when Misha took over that joint venture with the Ukrainians. Chechens never forget and they are capable of anything."

Arthur hung up. He didn't feel any more informed after the report from Andrei. They still didn't know shit.

24 The Invasion of Russia

The Chechen Republic is a federal subject of Russia, located in the North Caucasus, bordering Georgia. Chechnya, striving for independence, has had two wars with Russia, the first war between 1994 and 1996 and the second between 1999 and 2000, following which the country was in shambles.

Since the second war's end there had been a large-scale reconstruction and rebuilding process in place that required substantial quantities of metals and other raw materials.

Chechnya, 2005

Russia always attracted me as a very similar country to Ukraine but with much bigger opportunities. I first tried to break Russia in 1999 through the purchase of a small distressed bank there. The deal almost closed, when the Russians put a stop to it in rather mysterious circumstances and the bank went to some unannounced acquirers. In 2005 a new opportunity to pierce Russia's iron shield presented itself as a spin off from a hostile takeover. The plan was to penetrate mother Russia through its back-door. The point of entry would be from Chechnya.

The economic department of Chechnya formed a joint venture with Ukraine Metallum, one of Ukraine's largest metal producers. The JV produced and processed metals in Ukraine and sold them in Chechnya, therefore controlling the entire supply chain. Given the endless source of top-quality Ukrainian metals and the endless demand for metals in

Chechnya, I thought that the JV had a superb business model and therefore a lucrative investment. I decided to take it over.

The plan for seizing the JV spanned two stages. In the first stage, Neplokho Commodities assumed control over the Ukrainian holdings in the JV, belonging to Ukraine Metallum Corporation. Although the Ukrainian government sold it to some foreign investors, we used our legal raiders to claim the deal was rigged and nullify the sale. We then re-bought the stake at the convenient price on the new rigged privatisation tender.

Ukraine Metallum owned some profitable metal production facilities in Odessa, Mariupol and Nikolayev. They could be a perfect supplement to the capabilities of Lugansk Steel. Once we assumed control over the company, we had control over its share in the JV. That was easy.

Having the Ukrainian part, the second stage of seizing the JV was to tip the overall balance in the JV to my favour. We held 50% of the JV through our control of Ukraine Metallum, so we just needed to take a few percents from Chechnya to get over the 50% threshold for control of the JV.

When two shareholders own equal proportional amounts of shares in a corporation, then dead-lock situations are inevitable. So, we called for an extraordinary general meeting of shareholders with an agenda item proposing to stop metal supplies to Chechnya and redirect them to China. The demand for metals was huge in China as it was initiating a series of gigantic construction projects in preparation for the 2008 Beijing Summer Olympics, and China was paying much higher prices than those that we got in Chechnya.

At the EGM we put forward our intentions.

"We're a commercial entity, after all," we argued. "If the Chinese pay more, we should sell to them instead of the

Chechens. We earn more and share more profits, partners. This is business, nothing personal."

I knew that the Chechens would never agree. For me it wasn't even a bluff. By going against the Chechen partners and trying to take over their holdings in the JV, we risked losing some of the Chechen customers of the JV's produce. The Chinese prospect was a realistic alternative to the Chechens.

My humble deductive reasoning brought us the desired outcome. We reached a deadlock at the EGM, since as expected, our Chechen partners strongly opposed stoppage of supplies to Chechnya.

Although dead-lock situations and disputes under the JV agreement were to be referred to an international arbitration, it wasn't difficult to *convince* a local Ukrainian court to assume jurisdiction. Once that happened, I knew that I would achieve my goal.

Eventually, the court ruled that the dead-lock was to be resolved through my purchase of 25% of the shares from the Chechens at the court's expert evaluation price and the court's expert was instructed by my experts how much it should be.

Since I controlled the process, I could've gone for the entire 50% holding of the Chechens in the JV. However, I wanted to keep them in as partners. The big picture was that I still wanted a foothold in Russia, using Chechnya as a springboard, so I wanted to keep the Chechen business. I believed that after the initial resistance I would find a way to cooperate with my new partners and retain Chechnya as a customer.

I expected that Chechen bureaucrats wouldn't be much different from their Ukrainian colleagues. I didn't take over their private shares, only those of the Chechen autonomy. So it wasn't personal, right? I knew how to appease officials of any nation. I couldn't estimate, however, the blow that this takeover inflicted to their pride.

After the court ruling, I was walking down the broad stairs outside the courthouse. One of the Chechen directors approached me and whispered in my ear.

"You won today, Vorotavich. But winning the battle means losing the war for you. You wait, just wait. You'll experience the wrath of Chechnya."

Further legal appeals by my Chechen partners were quickly rejected by the superior courts. Political pressure from Russia on Chechnya's behalf was averted too. The JV was under our control.

The Chechen government didn't like it. It could've looked for recourse in international courts and tribunals, but the legal proceedings to potentially overrule the Ukrainian courts' decision would take years.

We had invaded Russia. In particular, we had successfully penetrated mother Russia in the winter. We succeeded where Napoleon and Hitler failed. Following the formation of a landing bridge, I opened and staffed a luxurious trade house in Moscow for the needs of both the JV and other branches of Neplokho. I hoped to improve my relations or more correctly to create relations with the Russian establishment. I was happy. However, I should've known that upsetting the Chechens wasn't the wisest move. I didn't realise it back then, but I had created a powerful adversary for myself.

Chechens are like elephants. They never forget.

25 Wedding Bells

Kiev, 2005

I bought my mother a nice apartment in a modern building on the Carmel Mountain in Haifa, Israel. Mama had been living in Haifa since she made Aliyah to Israel. She had some friends who spoke Russian and she settled down nicely. She enjoyed the Israeli weather and didn't want to move again, especially now that she was fifty years old.

Every time I came to Israel I visited her. All she wanted now was to see me get married and produce some grandchildren for her. Sasha had already delivered her first grandson in 1992. His wife was carrying their third child. Now it was my turn.

"What about you, Mishenka? When are you going to get married with a nice Jewish girl?" she asked. "I'm not getting any younger, you know. I want some naches from you. I want to see your children before I die."

"Mama, you're fifty years old. Nobody is going to die."

"You say so, Mishenka. But you don't know. I'm worried. Seeing you like that, lonely without a good Jewish woman to take care of you gets me closer to the grave every day."

No matter how old I was or how successful, she always treated me as her baby. Like every Jewish mother it was impossible to keep my mother satisfied for too long. First I had to become a lawyer to make her proud. Then I had to make lots of money. Now I had to get married to a Jewish woman. Next I had to bring her grandchildren. No wonder so many Jewish men have an Oedipus complex.

I had been dating Masha for almost eight years. That was a long time. She was everything that I wanted in a woman. She was pretty, smart, witty and funny. Pretty is an understatement; she was stunning. Most surprising of all, her mother was Jewish, which meant that she was Jewish as well. In Judaism the mother counts since who knows who the real father was. And in Masha's case she actually didn't know anything about her father.

Masha ticked all the boxes for being a trophy wife. But while it was easy for me to take business risks, risking millions without a robust due diligence, in my personal life I was risk averse, conducting a long and thorough due diligence before taking any risk. On the other hand, I was probably suffering from a youngest child syndrome - always looking for ways to please my mother. If mama wanted me to get married, getting married I had to do.

So, I proposed to Masha. Ukrainian and Russian men were expected to be chivalrous, so I took her to a romantic botanical garden on a hill overlooking the Dnieper's left bank during a beautiful sunset. I looked around to make sure nobody I knew could see me, dropped to one knee, pulled out a two carat diamond ring from my pocket, and looked into my beautiful girlfriend's eyes.

"Masha, you are the love of my life. My life is incomplete without you. I want to spend the rest of my life with you. Will you marry me?"

This was a rhetorical question. I knew she wouldn't have wasted her time with me unless she knew that I was eventually going to marry her. Masha put her hand to her mouth and gasped.

"It's so beautiful," she gushed. "Of course I will marry you," she added, as tears began to run softly down her cheeks.

I stood up, held Masha's hands in mine, and recited a poem by Alexander Pushkin.

> "A magic moment I remember:
> I raised my eyes and you were there.
> A fleeting vision, the quintessence
> Of all that's beautiful and rare.
> I pray to mute despair and anguish
> To vain pursuits the world esteems,
> Long did I hear your soothing accent,
> Long did your features haunt my dreams.
> Time passed – A rebel storm-blast scattered
> The reveries that once were mine
> And I forgot your soothing accents,
> Your features gracefully divine.
> In dark days of enforced retirement
> I gazed upon grey skies above
> With no ideals to inspire me,
> No one to cry for, live for, love.
> Then came a moment of renaissance,
> I looked up - you again are there,
> A fleeting vision, the quintessence
> Of all that's beautiful and rare."

Masha's jaw dropped with astonishment that I was reciting poetry. After she recovered from the shock, we sealed our love with a long, lingering kiss.

We were married in the spring. I was thirty two years old now, and it was time to settle down and start thinking about children. I needed someone to get all my money after I died or more likely, after I was killed.

I wanted a modest, private wedding. However, as every good man should do, I let Masha make all the decisions and plan everything. Women dream about their wedding from an early age. Men don't dream about their wedding, ever.

I told her: "You have an unlimited budget. All I want to do is to show up on the day and marry you."

"You may regret saying that," Masha teased. "I have very expensive tastes."

"I know that already, my love. You chose me, didn't you? Do what you want."

And that concluded my part of the wedding plans.

We got married in Israel in a beautiful location next to the beach, with five hundred guests in attendance. Since Masha organised the event, it was civilised, without any wild partying. Even my mother was pleased with everything. And that was a big achievement.

I stood with Masha under the chuppah and said the blessing.

"Behold, you are consecrated to me with this ring according to the Law of Moses and Israel."

I put a bride ring on her finger, and then I broke the glass.

A roaring *mazal tov* from the crowd signalled that Masha and I were a married couple. She made a respectable man out of me, and now I had to live up to her expectations.

26 Revolution

In 2004 the Orange Revolution reshuffled the Ukrainian political scenery. It was the second revolution in just over a decade if you view the USSR's big bang as the first, when Ukraine shifted from communism to democracy. Now, following the revolution, Ukraine's state of an autocratic democracy slipped into what looked like a perfect anarchy.

Kiev, 2008

The Orange Revolution put Ukraine under the world's spotlight for a few glorious moments. The new regime was portrayed as open-minded and pro-Western, meaning foreign investors licked their lips in anticipation of a huge score for those who got on board early.

Ukraine's poverty seemed to be replaced by a decadent, unbridled richness. In the aftermath of the Orange Revolution, once-grey Kiev gave way to flamboyant colours of expensive boutiques, cars and whatever the rich freak culture could offer. Walking in Kiev's central parts, one could get an impression of a wealthy country. The quantity of expensive cars dwarfed even that of Monaco's renowned luxury. Rolls Royces, Maybachs, Maseratis, Ferraris, Lamborghinis and Bentleys weren't exotic anymore. Kiev seemed more glamorous than Hollywood.

Material goods were supported by the corresponding capitalist ideology and ambitions. This new wave gave Kiev a fresher look and to the ladies a whole rainbow of teasing aspirations. I wasn't that distinguished anymore. Even my armoured Rolls Royce looked nothing special amongst the ocean of wealth.

A sense of euphoria was in the air, as if the tyrannical past was over and a bright future waited ahead.

Between 2004 and 2008 Ukraine experienced a boom in real estate prices, which somewhat disguised a lack of reform, corrupt government, small elite controlling the economy, weak judiciary system, absence of some of the basic citizens' liberties and rights and so on. The country basically lived off its massive metal industry and sheer speculations about its economic prospects.

One factor fuelling the property market was that all transactions in the primary housing market had been denominated in local hryvnia, but pegged to US dollars. Transactions in the secondary market had been quoted and paid in dollars. Therefore, purchasing Ukrainian real estate always required access to dollars.

The hryvnia exchange rate was pegged to the dollar too. Mortgage loans, once nonexistent in Ukraine, suddenly became available. Buyers borrowed relatively cheaply in dollars and bought Ukrainian real estate. This worked fine as long as the hryvnia either appreciated or didn't depreciate against the dollar.

The general euphoria revived not only the real estate market, but other markets as well. The approaching Beijing Olympics and China's economic growth spurt fuelled global demand for all commodities. This and the generally favourable economic conditions led to all Ukrainian steel exports to be sold at high prices almost a year in advance.

While Ukraine's economic growth accelerated, the hryvnia mildly appreciated against the dollar. Light-headed from constantly increasing prices, sales and figures nobody expected that the trends may reverse.

When the property boom started, I sold properties that I'd bought years before for silly prices, making 1000% to 2000% profits.

It was ridiculous. In 1999 I laughed at John when he was offered to buy a villa at Pechersk Hills for four million dollars. Back then, it was unheard of. Only eight years later, and this amount wouldn't even buy the cheapest mansion in the same district.

Because of the prime locations that I offered, buyers were outbidding each other as if I was handing out gold for free. This was an opportunity that I couldn't just pass over. Of course, single apartments were too small a business to waste my time on, but land plots and construction sites were sold for hundreds of millions of dollars to eager buyers.

Since my days of working at the construction company, I had kept in touch with Sergei, who used to be Sasha's boss and one of the deputies of the mayor of Kiev. Since Sergei took care of Sasha when he was a junior in the company, I had taken care of Sergei since then.

I told Sergei, "You've been a dear and trusted friend for many years. You helped Sasha a while ago and I didn't forget it, as you can see. I would like to ensure that you have enough money to never worry about retirement or the retirement of your children and grandchildren. The only thing that I ask is that you arrange for the city council to allocate to me lands in Kiev. Conveyer's rate would be lovely."

Sergei happily cooperated. I then sold the lands to foreigners for astronomical profits. For each deal I asked John to set up a Cypriot Special Purpose Vehicle, meaning the CSPV or its Ukrainian subsidiary would own or lease the land. This meant we sold shares and not land, avoiding paying any taxes. We set up so many SPVs that we overloaded the Cypriot company registrar, causing it to crash.

Within two years I had made billions in real estate only. It was funny that after so many years of being involved in a multitude of businesses, it was good old, reliable real estate that emerged as my most profitable business in Ukraine in those years. Nothing beats bricks and mortar.

In 2006 we floated Neplokho Real Estate on the London Stock Exchange at a value of fifteen billion pounds. I was a seriously rich man.

Like every bubble, the real estate boom would explode soon. The world was about to experience the worst financial crisis since the Great Depression of the thirties. This crisis was going to separate the men from the boys.

***

In September 2008, my man on the inside of the Central Bank of Ukraine called me and asked for a meeting, stressing that it was in my best interests to arrange a get together as soon as possible. We met at a restaurant in Kiev, and what he had to tell me was shocking.

"Misha," he said as I joined him at a table set back in a quiet corner of the room. "Thank you for agreeing to meet me so soon. You would owe me, when you hear this out."

"No problem, Georgi, and don't worry about that. When the Central Bank talks, it's good sense to listen," I replied with a smile, extending my hand in greeting. "So what's the fuss?"

"The Ukrainian economy is looking fragile, Misha. The bank will not be able to keep the hryvna pegged with the US dollar much longer. I'm very nervous about the economy and the direction towards which it's heading. I wouldn't be surprised if the hryvna collapsed."

Unpegging the currency would mean a sharp drop in the exchange rate, the consequence being a collapse in real estate's prices because of a breaking of the carry-trade strategy. If he said that he wouldn't be surprised then it was a done deal. I knew Georgi as a harbinger, not an analyst.

"And what do your experts see as the immediate repercussions of such an event?"

"It will be serious. GDP dropping, real estate prices dropping, everything would be fucking dropping, falling, plummeting. Imagine, nearly half the value of your house wiped out overnight!"

"Mamma mia, that's apocalyptic! Thanks for the warning, Georgi, I'll see you're compensated for your troubles. How long do I have?"

"A week at most. My apologies, but I have to leave now. Stash some dollars, Misha."

Georgi left, probably hurrying to sell his warning to another client, and I sat at the table thinking about the news he'd passed on. I called Boris, David and John and set up a meeting where we could work out how best to manage the looming crash.

Once the initial shock was overcome, the meeting with my closest comrades yielded a battle plan to limit any negative effects of the coming crisis. We immediately switched employee salaries from dollars to hryvna. I almost completely eliminated my exposure to Ukrainian real estate and converted all my hryvna to hard currencies.

Ten days after Georgi's warning the hryvna started its rapid decline, accomplished within a period of three months during which it depreciated by almost 100% against the dollar. The property and credit markets came to a standstill. No buyer was willing to purchase lands that were bought only a few months ago for tens of millions of dollars, even for one-tenth of the purchase price. There was no sense in developing these lands either, as all purchases of real estate stopped. The market was totally dead.

The banks' real estate collateral and property holdings suffered unheard of depreciation in just a short period of a few months. The banks had run out of the necessary reserves to be able to lend, even if they were interested to do so. With no buyers, no construction, and no credit the real estate market went into a cardiac arrest.

Those few who didn't panic during this crisis, kept a cool head and used the opportunities that it offered, would make a fortune. I enjoyed the luxury of time, since I wasn't a forced seller at ridiculously low prices in a completely illiquid market. I was able to be a buyer and sell liquidity to a dry market at elevated prices.

Many investors tried to freeze their purchases and developments of properties until the market stabilised again. However, no freeze was possible. The Ukrainian authorities, once well-nourished by the booming real estate, now demanded expensive unofficial maintenance fees just to restrain from reclaiming the properties. If poor and bleeding foreign investors dared to disagree, the supportive and investor-friendly authorities didn't hesitate to deprive them of their rights. They were worse than any local private raider.

***

Luckily, Georgi's tip-off about the crisis helped me avoid the massive losses that befell most of my competitors.

The shares of Neplokho Real Estate on the London Stock Exchange dropped in value, but I knew that the reserve of properties that they represented was still extremely valuable. As Warren Buffet said *price is what you pay, value is what you get.*

Many of my rich peers were highly exposed to the global stock markets. As the wealth of many of my competitors fell through the floor, on a relative basis my wealth increased tremendously. While everything around me was falling down, I stayed more or less where I was, but on a relative basis I was shooting upward through the roof.

In 2009 I entered the Forbes World's Rich list for the first time. It was the first time not because I wasn't a billionaire before, but because it was the first time some of my wealth could be measured and categorised.

Entering Forbes meant that I was accepted and legit. My long term plan had come to fruition - I was a legitimate, respectable businessman and now I had only a finite number of people ahead of me to surpass to reach the top of the list

Seventeen years had passed since I had been sleeping on the beach in Tel Aviv, homeless and penniless. Now, I was one of the richest people in the world. How do you comprehend such a thing? Wow! This was like a football club moving from a local junior league to the top of the Premier League.

27 Football

London, 2010
Football is the most popular sport in Ukraine, and Dynamo Kiev was a true source of pride under the Soviet control. The club was the most successful team ever in the history of the Soviet First Division. When I was seventeen the club won the Soviet championship, beating into second place the defending champions, FC Spartak Moscow.

My friends and I never hated the Russians, as most of us had friends and relatives in Russia. However, we hated Moscow, and the main reason for this hatred was football antagonism. Similarly to English football hooligans, Spartak and Dynamo's fans engaged in a fierce battle twice a year on the side lines as the teams played.

You can imagine the pride that we felt beating the Russians, or more precisely beating Moscow. What a glory. It was good to be Ukrainian the day we took the championship. The underdogs from Kiev beat the arrogant snobs from Moscow. David kicking Goliath's ass. It was one of a handful days in my life that I was truly proud of my country.

In the nineties through my connections with foreign businessmen, I helped sell Ukrainian football players to European clubs. I made a few hundred thousand dollars on each transaction. It wasn't much within the context of my global businesses, but it helped to motivate the players of my Lugansk club that if they were any good, I could promote them to better leagues. And it was fun. If I couldn't be a famous football player, at least I was able to get involved in the industry.

In the mid-2000s, football became a source for serious money laundering. The process was pretty simple.

I bought a small football club in England, called Watford United that had unexpectedly made it into England's Premier League. Nobody gave the club any chance of surviving for more than one season in the Premiership. I, on the other hand, had big plans for Watford United F.C.

I was already an experienced football team proprietor. UEFA rules didn't allow owning two clubs, but that wouldn't be a problem. With all my experience in making ownership chains untraceable, it wasn't hard to conceal the connection between Metallurg Lugansk and Watford United. If Misha Vorotavich and Moshe Shaarim were two different persons, then the single owner of the two clubs had nothing in common with himself.

I decided to take a risk and dared to bring a young Russian manager to the English Premier League. This was unheard of at the time. He wasn't much of a player in the past, but he seemed to be a smart guy, who managed just in two years to bring what was practically a village team in Russia to be the third best club nationally. He was hungry to prove himself, unlike some managers who sit on multi-million pound salaries and had lost their killer instinct.

Another angle for choosing a Russian manager was that it was a great publicity stunt. As it was unusual, it hit the front pages of all the English newspapers.

"The Russians are Coming," "Russian Mafia Buys Watford," "From Russia with Love to Watford," "Vorotavich Brings a Russian Nobody to Manage Watford." It was a news story that attracted serious attention. Suddenly my club was interesting.

The first thing that I did once I bought the club was to recapitalise it. The capital was raised partly by a loan to the club and partly by selling newly issued stocks on the London Stock Exchange. Because I was a somewhat well-known international figure my involvement meant that the club now had a strong financial backing.

The club was able to buy players and invest in their training. In football, like in many other areas in life, money was the number one factor in attaining success. Rich clubs did better than poor ones, which was just a fact of life. The correlation between money and the amount of silver in the club's trophy cabinet was evident for all to see. The value of my club, and its stock price, went up as I expected.

After issuing the new shares on the LSE, I retained the majority shareholding and the club repaid my loan from the money that it raised through the issuance of the new shares. I entered into negotiations through agents to buy players from a number of other clubs. My agent was a Cypriot corporation. The transactions included secret pay-back fees paid by the selling club to my agent. These pay-backs were incorporated into the price that I paid for the players.

My agent's commission was paid onward to a third party, which was another offshore entity that I controlled. The total commission was equal to my initial investment in the club. I now owned the majority shareholding in a high-value football club at no net cost to myself. I also laundered the original purchase price of the club. Simple.

The money-laundering machine didn't stop there. I used money from my less legitimate businesses to introduce large investments of new capital into the club. The club spent a few millions on improvements to its ground, including a brand new canteen, new training facilities and medical staff. Each of these improvements was provided by companies that

I controlled, and the prices of the improvements were massively inflated.

With its new players, new manager and positive publicity, the club gained a great momentum. We started to win games. Unbelievably, against all odds, not only did we manage to stay in the Premiership for another season, we finished in fourth place. This Russian coach was a genius. Even the newspapers applauded him. This meant that the next season we were going to play in the Champions League.

At that point football stopped being just another business or money-laundering machine. Football was once again a passion. Owning the club was a source of endless pride and joy. Bringing guests to my private box at my club's home stadium was worth all the hassles associated with owning a football club. I wanted my club to win titles, so I increased its financing each year. A big portion of the money laundered through the club was actually reinvested right back into it.

In Ukraine I knew that my small local club from Lugansk had a glass ceiling. In England, however, I hoped it could be different. On top of that, football club owners formed a certain informal league in itself. If you weren't a club owner, it seemed, you couldn't be counted as true oligarch.

This all coincided with my company, Neplokho Construction, being awarded contracts to build and renovate two stadiums for the European Championship that was to be jointly hosted by Poland and Ukraine in 2012. We didn't even need to rig a tender. All we needed was connections with the officials and to give them a nice kick-back for allocating the contracts to us. We completely inflated the budget and used cheap materials, therefore basically stealing an enormous piece of state budget and making a huge profit. We came out with over a billion overbilled from the state.

I felt sportive after Euro 2012. So sportive that I wouldn't need much time to prepare to participate in the 'building and stealing' discipline in the 2014 Winter Olympics at Sochi. Especially since my Chechen metal base was virtually just around the corner.

28 Johnny

Kiev, 2013

John Wiseman lay in his bed, wide awake in the middle of the night, staring at the ceiling. He couldn't get much sleep lately. He wondered how his life would've been different if he hadn't joined Michael in 1999. It seemed like a lifetime away.

He was twenty eight then and was about to get a promotion in Oldman Sucks, the most prestigious working place for MBA graduates back in 1999. But that vacation on the Maldives, to which David had invited him, changed his perspective. Conservative as he was, even he couldn't have ignored the pleasures offered generously to Michael's guests. After hearing Michael's offer to join him in Ukraine, he thought why waste his life on a slow progressing banking career, if some damn hole called Ukraine offered such a brilliant shortcut?

Had he stayed with Oldman he would've probably become a managing director and a millionaire by now. He would've been divorced, with two heart bypasses and alimony payments. Investment bankers at Oldman didn't have prospects for a solid family life and a long life expectancy. Their wives were called 'Oldman widows' since they rarely saw their husbands.

He would not have lived a life of utter morality as an investment banker. It was asking too much to strive to live a moral life and be an investment banker at the same time. However, there was no doubt that the level of morality as an

Oldman banker was much higher than that of an investment banker in Ukraine. You couldn't get much lower than that.

Putting aside almost getting shot at three different occasions, he still struggled to come to grips with what he had to do at work on almost a daily basis. He bribed state officials. Handing envelopes full of cash seemed awkward at first, but he got used to it. He intentionally inserted loopholes in contracts. He structured companies to knowingly evade taxes. He laundered money. He lost count of how many felonies he committed.

Nothing was implicit, it was all explicit. If he was ever accused at a court of law, he couldn't claim that he didn't know. He damn well knew about everything. Defence of ignorance wouldn't hold for him. At least his wrongdoings were of a white-collar nature, with which any businessman could probably put up with, he thought of possible self-justification for himself. He was actually a victim not a criminal, as some violent crimes were committed against him recurrently in Ukraine.

As for money, he indeed became richer than what he would've done even as an Oldman top banker. He had over fifty million dollars in cash stashed in offshore bank accounts, a magnificent flat overlooking Central Park in New York City, a huge flat in London's Knightsbridge and a private house on Pechersk Hills in the centre of Kiev. He bought a new house for his parents in Long Island's Great Neck. He had everything that he wanted that money could buy.

On a personal basis he couldn't complain. He married a beautiful Ukrainian girl in 2002. Admittedly, she was a shiksa, not Jewish, so his mother wasn't happy. However, they had two beautiful children. She treated him by far better than any JAP - Jewish American Princess, would have. And the sex with her was taken straight from a porn movie.

She didn't complain when he came home late from work. She didn't complain when he didn't help her with the children. She just didn't complain at all. The roles in their household were clear. He was the man and she was the woman. He made the money and she took care of the family, spent his money and fucked him. Simple, old-fashioned Ukrainian chauvinism. She was happy just because he wasn't much of a drinker as opposed to the majority of Ukrainians. He didn't beat her; another high prized bonus. John was a super-husband. He was both rich and treated her well.

When he came to visit his friends back in the United States, they were all envious of him. He was richer, he had stories about adventures - at least those he could tell them, and he had a gorgeous wife. On the face of it, John had it all. The American dream. Even better.

But while he had everything that he ever wished for, still he wasn't happy.

After long deliberations he came to the conclusion that the main source of his unhappiness was the strong dislike that he felt towards his boss. John and Michael didn't see eye to eye on many levels.

What irritated John the most was Michael's belittling attitude towards him. John didn't feel that Michael respected him. He felt that he deserved to be treated differently. After all, he was an MBA graduate from Harvard Business School.

On a professional level, and grotesquely as it may sound since many thought that Michael was a brilliant entrepreneur, John didn't have a high opinion of Michael as a businessman. There was no doubt that Michael was an excellent thief and a schemer. He also had cojones - balls of a bull. He wasn't afraid of taking risks, most of which paid off. He was super rich, but it was only due to taking the right risks in the crazy Ukrainian business environment. Despite

Michael's success, John thought that Michael was mediocre as a businessman.

There were so many decisions that could've been done so much better. Why use an insurance company only for money laundering, if insurance penetration was so low in Ukraine and the potential was huge? It could've been a profitable legitimate business. Why get rid of the hospital in Lugansk, if medicine in Ukraine was just the next Klondike Gold Rush? Michael could've added so many payable services to the basic medical service provided for free.

Michael knew how to grab easy prey, but he was incompetent in how to best operate his own assets. He didn't have a slightest idea how to use banks, leverage his business and accelerate the growth rate. As the demand for steel dropped considerably during the last few years, if Michael just took a loan to modernise his steel production, he would cut his costs by 50% and make his produce highly competitive. John tried to convince Michael to implement some of his ideas many times, but all in vain. Michael took John lightly in everything connected with Ukraine.

John was earning millions, but it hurt his ego that some Russian thief was so contemptuous to his advice. If John headed the Neplokho Group, it would be a real business, a real global success story! He knew it. But yet he had to obey some bear of a boss. He was definitely unhappy, although the bear had been in a comatose hibernation.

With Michael out of the way, it was John's opportunity to take over the business. Michael's two deputies, Boris and David, had some good skills, but surely they couldn't head the entire Group. This was the moment that John was waiting for. He needed to carefully plan his next moves.

"Don't ever wake up Michael," John thought to himself. "I should lead Neplokho."

29 Highway to Heaven

In 1991, Belarus emerged as an independent country during the Soviet Union's dissolution. Belarus remained the most Soviet of all the other republics as Soviet-era politics were maintained, including state ownership of the economy. Belarus was like a European Cuba, and while Cuba preserved the look and feel of the Caribbean in the fifties, as reflected in the old cars and the overall appearance, Belarus preserved the look of the Soviet Union in the eighties.

Tel Aviv, 2013

At the beginning of 2013, Belarus announced its intention to tender the construction of a fast highway between Minsk, the capital of Belarus, and Moscow. At a meeting at our group's HQ in Tel Aviv, David, Boris and I discussed our intention to bid for tender on the massive project.

"Okay. Do we know what's going on in Belarus?" I asked both Boris and David.

"The project has been approved, generalisimus," David answered. He always made up titles for me and this time he used one of the titles of Joseph Stalin. Even he, an Israeli-born, rarely called me Moshe.

"What are the final numbers?"

"The tender is scheduled to close in three months. Three bidders will remain; two are our companies and the third is the company of the president's nephew. Three other bidders will be removed due to technical reasons. Any legal proceedings after the tender will be handled by *Big Bird*."

Big Bird was the nickname for the Chief of Staff of the President of Belarus. We chose this nickname since his surname, Orlovich, was akin to an eagle - Oryol. We liked to use codenames from the animal kingdom as most phone conversations were tapped in Eastern European countries, so we commonly used nicknames instead of using the real names for men in sensitive positions.

"Our Ukrainian company, Neplokho Transportation will win the tender with a bid of 5.4 billion dollars for the project's total budget. The budget covers construction, materials, salaries, as well as planning and technology," continued David. "The tender committee will recommend that we'll take the nephew's company as a sub-contractor and we'll have to pay the nephew 15% of the budget, but his company won't take part in any construction. In other words, we pay the useless bastard eight hundred million dollars just because his uncle is the president."

Both Boris and I grimaced at the high figures.

"The highway project will be financed 100% from the budget," David went on. "However, we'll show that we also bring an investment, equalling 20% of the budget as our own funds. This will allow us to take a 50% ownership of the company that's going to operate and maintain the highway. After we bring our own funds, the down payment that they pay us is going to be 40% of the budget, made against a bank guarantee. We won't need to bring a real bank guarantee; our Ukrainian bank's guarantee letter will suffice. Our costs will be 3% for planning and 15% for constructing the road using winter-proof asphalt. This is about 18% together. We can assume an overhead deviation of up to 10% of the above, making it up to 20%. It all adds up to a cost of up to 1.9 billion US dollars, including the payment to the inept bastard and the excess 10% of costs. This is a profit of three and a half billion dollars. What do you think?"

I thought that overall the project made sense. One advantage was that with such a project, the Group would enter Belarus. Its development was lagging that of Ukraine by a decade, which meant that there were numerous opportunities to repeat some of the plays we'd made before.

There might be further similar projects as Belarus developed its infrastructure to get in line with neighbouring countries. Developing an appetite on the way, the Belarusians would likely want to build a highway to Kiev or Warsaw afterwards. We could help them reach the decision that they wanted such further extensions by making it worthwhile to the decision makers or their advisers.

Another advantage of the project was that the nephew would ensure that the senior government officials, including his uncle, the president, would get their share and I wouldn't need to deal with each one separately. The payment to the pathetic nephew was expensive, but the senior leadership would know where the money came from and would be interested to do more business with us in the future.

We would need to take care of the less senior officials, such as the Chairman of the State Committee on Tenders of Belarus and the officials at the Ministry of Transportation. Those on the Olympus wouldn't throw them any bones, so we would need to keep them happy. If they were content it would be easier for us to win tenders going forward.

While it all sounded sensible, I decided to play hard ball with David. It was Friday and I needed some entertainment.

"David, you know that I was born at night. But it wasn't last night. Are you kidding me? Tell me something, David. You say they pay 40% down payment, but in fact I'm going to pay a 20% down payment of the budget for the maintenance company upfront from my own pocket, right? And I'm giving them a bank guarantee. Do you think that that's worth nothing? Maybe the contract they'll award me will also be worth nothing and they won't have money to even pay back the down payment. That's a big fucking risk, don't you think?"

Before David had a chance to reply I carried on, "I'm going to pay this little shit incompetent bastard 15% of the budget just because his uncle happens to be Veniamin Selevich, the President of Belarus. This little piece of shit nephew does nothing. He's going to get eight hundred million dollars for doing nothing. Are you fucking kidding me? Are you out of your fucking mind? Once you knew how to negotiate. Now you get confused by big numbers. What has happened to you guys? Who has cut off your balls?"

David and Boris knew me, so they didn't seem too moved by my response. This time Boris answered.

"Listen, Misha. I met with the worthless nephew, and the little bastard has an uncle, and the uncle has friends, and they also know how to count. According to their calculations the profit on the deal is 3.2 billion dollars. They demand a slice of 25% of the profit. We should be thankful that we can get out with more profit than they think."

"And don't forget, generalisimus," added David, "that later on we'll be able to sell the 50% stake in the company that operates the highway to the government or to the Chinese for at least another two billion dollars."

"Belarus isn't Ukraine. Selling anything in Belarus, except for weapons, is difficult, so we'll probably have to sell it back to the Belarusian government. You need to agree on this beforehand, including price, bonuses and all the other shit. Nobody else will buy a company in Belarus. Today you own it, tomorrow the government nationalises your holdings. Nothing could stop them," I said.

Both Boris and David were silent. After a pause of a few seconds, I decided to conclude.

"Fine. Make sure that they understand that they aren't going to get a cent more than the 15% of the budget. Neither the bastard rubbish nephew nor his divine uncle. What's more important is that I also want to win the tender for the segment of the road in Russia. This is our chance to start doing business with the Ministry of Transport of Russia."

"Yes, but Misha..."

"I don't care," I said, raising my hand to interrupt Boris. "For the Russian part I'm willing to give them 25% of the budget - not just of the profit, including the share to the Russians. I don't care how they divide the cash between them. You can hint to him that I have my own contacts in Moscow. If I get the deal without his help, they're out of the picture. They won't see a dollar. Capish?"

"It will be difficult, but if that's the position you want to take..." David responded.

"And another thing; we need to set up a maintenance company for the highway. And I mean right now. We cannot wait until the tender is closed. I want everything to be in place. Make sure that most of the work won't be covered by our limited guarantee. Start training the First Deputy of the Ministry of Transport and the members of the committee responsible for supervision. I expect a nice income stream from the repairs that will be on par with that of the prostitution business in Minsk."

The prostitution business in Minsk was a high bar and nobody knew it better than Boris.

"Anything else, Boris? David? No? Good. The meeting is adjourned. Shabat shalom. See you tonight at my mama's birthday party. Remember to behave; we're in Israel, not Kiev."

"You insult us, Misha," Boris said, feigning insult. "Are we not civilised gentlemen?"

"Fuck off, Boris. This is my mama we're talking about. Behave!" I ordered, as David sniggered at the exchange.

Overall, I had high expectations for this project. It was time to step up a gear and progress to the major league: projects with turnovers of billions. On IPOs I actually had to share ownership interests with others. Here, I shared nothing, except for commissions agreed in advance. It was all mine, mine, mine!

The post-Soviet countries were becoming richer and their reserves were full of hard currencies. It was the right time to help them to spend or to wisely invest the wealth that they'd accumulated.

I felt an adrenaline rush in my body from the prospects of making billions. I felt alive. I felt that the top spot of the rich list was in sight.

30 Old Fart's Deliberations

Tel Aviv, 2013

That evening was a joint birthday party for me and my mother. It was a relatively modest gathering of around fifty people to celebrate my mother's sixty-fifth birthday at the same time as I was turning forty. This required modesty and limited exposure to the usual immoral behaviour that occurred at my previous birthday celebrations.

The event was very low-key, but I must admit the tame celebrations were a welcome change from the usual raucous affairs. Maybe it was an age thing. Forty is quite a symbolic age and years before I had set it as the target age to achieve all my goals. Despite my success and wealth, my main goal of becoming the richest came closer but remained yet unachieved.

The party was a success, in the sense that my mother loved everything about it, from the venue, the lavish spread of food that was a mix of Ukrainian and Israeli fare, to the beautiful diamond necklace I bought her jointly with Sasha. When she left just after midnight, I had assumed I would want to move on to a club and start the real celebrations. Instead, I was content to bid my guests goodnight and return to my penthouse in Tel Aviv. The next day I decided to take a rare day off from worrying about multi-million dollar deals, and just relax.

Masha and the children flew back to Kiev on the early flight, so I could spend the day relaxing for once and meditating over my achievements. The round dates in middle age were good to think about life, its purpose and my personal score.

After having three highballs of Scotch my thoughts meandered around the universal drivers. Money makes the world go round. The richer you are the easier and cheaper is life. The world makes it easy for the rich to get richer and hard for the poor to be better off. The classes are preserved. The aristocrats or upper class stay at the top. The agrarians or working class stay at the bottom. The middle class gets screwed from every direction.

Everything on the face of it is absurd. For example, the more prestigious your credit card, the less interest you pay on credit. You need to be rich to get a nice platinum or insignia credit card. Evidently, the poorer you are the less prestigious card you get and credit is more costly for you. So the rich get cheap credit that they don't need and the poor, who really need credit, cannot afford it. If in theory there should be market or state mechanisms redistributing the resources more equally, in practice the rich get richer and the poor poorer.

The more you fly or spend using credit cards, the more free flights you receive since you accumulate air miles. I really didn't need free flights, since I could afford to pay for virtually anything, and I had a private jet on top of that. Those who would appreciate free flights didn't receive any. But that is how the world is built - screw the poor suckers and lick the balls of the rich.

I liked comparing my own path with that of my western competitors, whom I wanted to leave behind. In the West many people got super-rich using the same methods of corruption and fraud, but the difference was that it happened one or two centuries ago. Probably on a lesser scale the same was happening even now. And there it was usually covered in Western European wrapping or American elegancy and subtlety. In Ukraine, in contrast, there was no room for sentiments. Everything was crude and in your face. Lacking the centuries of tradition or breeding, I had to undergo a rapid transition to change from barbarian with a strong criminal smell, stinking from money to a subtle European aristocrat - well, that was a bit of overstatement, welcomed in the most prestigious forums.

The gradual transformation of my colleagues from the sporty look of racketeers to that of royals was comical. First, they were keen to acquire the most expensive version of whichever item took their fancy. If they wanted a cell phone, then it had to be a Vertu. If they were happy to spend thousands on a phone, when it came to acquiring a new watch then the brand worth wearing was something like Vaucheron Constantin, with each one costing from thirty thousand dollars and up. The next trend was to buy the most expensive cars, such as Maybachs, together with the fanciest yachts and outstanding properties.

It was considered a bad taste to buy cheap. Some, lacking subtlety, even boasted loudly, "Take a look at this watch. It cost me two hundred grand," being sure that any ladies within earshot were having an orgasm just at the sight of their watch and men were biting their tongue from hopeless envy.

Football clubs slowly became a must-have too. Most club buyers used cash from money-laundering schemes, tax evasion operations or stolen through dodgy privatisations from the Ukrainian or Russian nation. I didn't know if it was true for Arab sheikhs, who often bought clubs, but it was certainly true for many of my rich 'friends' and 'colleagues.' Football fans worshiped generous club owners, however, only a small number of fans understood the real source of these investments.

It was amazing how people who grew up under communism in Russia and Ukraine now had a lifestyle of tsars. Imperial Russia was back, only this time its oligarchy wasn't made up of the few aristocrats but of the few self-made billionaires.

From a distorted point of view the capitalism in Ukraine was ideal and it certainly was more honest than that of the West. For example, leaders of labour unions were bribed and did as the employer wanted them to do. The working force, therefore, didn't have an organisation that truly represented the common goals of the workers and cared for their rights. If you believe that socialism gets in the way of capitalism then this was a purer version of capitalism.

We were able to focus on making money, whether through legitimate and competitive business ideas or through stealing the public's money via connections with the government. Anyone who was successful earned respect and fear just because he was rich. We didn't pay any taxes, abused the employees, passed rules and regulations that were convenient for us and contributed prolifically to governance deterioration.

This was pure money-making, without social responsibility, patriotism and other similar ideological nonsense that got in capitalism's way.

Many oligarchs hated the state. Their families lived in Monaco or Sardinia, their children were educated in London and their wealth was stashed in Switzerland. Ukraine was used only as a place where you make money and squeeze it of its last drop of juice. Impenetrable walls, fences, armoured cars, personal jets, bodyguards and private armies tightly separated them from their countrymen. And abroad all of them had what they called a *reserve landing field* - a comfortable and prepared hideout, ready for any contingency in case anything went wrong in Ukraine.

Was this line of thought a kind of self-loathing? Definitely. I hoped I was a bit different though.

I actually loved Ukraine and its people. Or maybe I was getting sentimental with age. Most of the Ukrainian people were honest, decent and cordial. However, these traits, especially in the Ukrainian reality, got you nowhere. Everybody treated such citizens as lokhs. But I couldn't help them all. I tried, but the people didn't vote for me when I was running for parliament. They had their opportunity to give me a chance, and they blew it. They didn't help me to help them.

At least I made sure that my inner circle and my close employees got reasonable salaries and were treated respectfully. This was something that was in my direct responsibility and I cared about it being observed properly.

I also eagerly supported Ukraine joining the European Union. I established my foundation named '29 - Ukraine', promoting Ukraine as the twenty-ninth member of the European Union. I strongly believed that this agenda played an important role for Ukraine's future. At least I was spending on something other than merely a flamboyant lifestyle, I thought to myself. A little bit of rounding the edges of the truth.

***

I moved to the balcony of my sixteenth floor penthouse in one of the new residential towers in Tel Aviv, with a fantastic view of the peaceful Mediterranean Sea just a few metres away. I loved the sea; it always had a relaxing effect on me.

I took another sip and resumed my reflections, using the same comparing pattern. The way it was in the West, if you strip the wrappings down, was rather similar. Western lobbying, for example, sounded much more decent than

Eastern bribery, but in my perception they were similar in essence.

In the West, employees were supposedly protected, the lower classes were supposedly getting benefits, and every governmental project was supposedly going through tenders. However, in practice, much of it was just a disguise.

My favourite character Michael Corleone in the Godfather III, when he explained that all his life he wanted to get legitimate, but discovered similar criminal routines everywhere, phrased perfectly how I felt: "The higher I go, the crookeder it becomes."

Very few tycoons really paid taxes in line with profits, as they knew about creative tax planning, choosing favourable tax domiciles, offshore banking, placing assets abroad and not reporting revenues outside the country. Hard working employees didn't have access to all these tricks.

Similar to Ukraine, the state's assets were allocated to people close to the government. It was supposed to increase competition, however, the most valuable assets ended up in the hands of a small number of tycoons and wealthy families who controlled the economy. When you control the economy you control the government. Isn't that oligarchy?

Sometimes the reciprocity between businessmen and politicians was uncovered (primarily by journalists, not the police), and then some corrupt politicians were prosecuted. Obviously, it was only the tip of the iceberg. And the iceberg was huge. Since I was part of it, I saw the arrangements that were hidden from the public. The lies that were sold weren't a secret to me, such as that the benefits that were given to entrepreneurs and tycoons were dripping down to the benefit of employees and contributed to the creation of jobs.

The American dream was sold to the general public. Anyone can become rich and it's something within everyone's reach. It was theoretically true, but the statistics gave it the same probability as that of winning the lottery. The number of winners, or those becoming sizably rich, was extremely negligible out of the entire population. The vast majority was doomed to work in miserable jobs, dreaming big, but being satisfied by at least having their own apartment with a mortgage to be repaid over the rest of their lives. If they had a decent pension, they should be satisfied. They were slaves to the system. They worked all their life and their children would need to work all their lives as well. There would be no real change for the working class.

The middle class was paying for everything, but they didn't order the music. The majority didn't rule, undermining the notion of democracy. Oligarchs in the East, just as magnates in the West, having disproportionate influence on governments and politicians, had lost any sense of social responsibility, succumbing only to greed.

The wave of mass protests and uprisings throughout the world was a precursor of that. In many instances, people couldn't even formulate their demands. However, deep inside they felt that they were being screwed. And indeed they were. I was glad I had chosen not to bow to this system and skipped the career of engineer or lawyer.

Most countries were just the same. Their basic motto was in quintessence, 'bring in your money, no matter what its source, and we will worship you and you won't have to pay any taxes for a very long time.' Some countries, like Cyprus, Australia and others even established official citizenship programmes for 'investors,' 'entrepreneurs' and 'businessmen,' applicable similarly to all kind of crooks, drug dealers, and the likes. The only criterion of these programmes was bringing into the country a sufficiently large amount of money.

How did I reconcile for myself these thoughts with abusing any weakness of any country, where I didn't care to litter? Well, I didn't. I knew myself all too well to fight my own instinct and nature. A snake is a snake. I was a natural born swindler. Being the first one to plunder valuable assets and exploit corrupt political systems, didn't mean that I thought that the states shouldn't prevent these things. But if I stopped first, then my competitors would prevail and I wouldn't reach my ultimate goal of conquering the summit of the billionaires' chart.

I was confident that the current policies in countries bowing to big capital represented a hazard to me and other billionaires. I was perfectly aware that most people hated and felt envious of the nouveau riches. In this modern era the information about benefits and other incentives was made known to the general public, and thus hatred and envy multiplied.

Take Ukrainians, who were probably one of the most inert nations on earth. Perhaps the vodka made them inactive. It took something big to move them. However, even they were all out on the streets, once they felt that they were blatantly deprived of their choice of the president during the Orange Revolution.

Their bellies were full with corruption going on around them and general despair. But they needed a momentum or very specific cause to take it out. Too bad for them that their high expectations of the new rulers that they brought to power on their own shoulders had disappointed them miserably. Nothing really changed for the better.

However, since those people felt once that their march mattered; they might do it again, if the circumstances called for it. Considering the strained and gloomy atmosphere in which Ukraine was submerged after the anarchy ended around 2010, my intuition told me that such a moment might well present itself in the not too distant future.

***

From higher matters I returned back to myself and switched to cognac. I was forty years old, a significant milestone. Just surviving in my business and reaching such a distinguished age was an achievement. Forty is the perfect time for a mid-life crisis. When you're young, in your twenties, you're full of hopes and aspirations. You have high expectations about the future and you're too naive and inexperienced to manage them. All your future lies ahead of you. The world belongs to the young and you're one of the owners.

Normally, when you reach forty you realise that you haven't achieved everything that you wanted and you're unlikely to achieve your targets. With age comes real life experience. It allows you to manage your expectations more realistically. Unfortunately, with age you also lose the energy of youth and start to reminisce on how good you were when you were young. As the saying goes, *as I get older, I was better.*

My mind focused on my current reality, which wasn't too bad. I looked out at the olive trees, the glass-like still waters of the Med, and the white sandy beach below me. *Not too shabby,* I reminded myself. I was smoking a Cohiba Esplendido cigar, which was considered by Che Guevara himself as a super-premium smoke, drinking XO Remy Martin cognac and casually thinking about the project in Belarus.

A meeting to move ahead on the project was scheduled for the next day in Zurich. A few more projects were in the pipeline and the prospects were promising. Life was good; I really shouldn't complain.

I wandered back to the living room and flopped onto the sofa. Absent-mindedly I flicked on the television, and ironically there was a soap opera playing that was set in the world of Russian oligarchs. The scenes were supposed to describe the reality that was part of my life, so it was amusing for me to watch how people like me were perceived by the outside world. It was so naive. The way Russian oligarchs and their connections with the mafia were portrayed was just ridiculous and far-fetched.

I switched the TV off and threw the remote control onto the table.

"*Fucking ridiculous*," I said to myself. "*Making out we're all gangsters and murderers.*"

As I lay there, bored out of my mind, I heard noises coming from the kitchen.

"Tanya?" I called out. "Is that you, my darling?"

"Yes, I have some shopping to put away, be with you in a minute."

I lay back with my hands behind my head. Tanya walked into the living room moments later and sat beside me.

"What a morning," she complained, exhaling animatedly. "So many people at the market and it's so hot today."

"Poor Tanyusha," I teased. "Why don't you grab another bottle of cognac and we can toast my birthday once more."

Tanya didn't need asking twice. She moved to the drinks cabinet and returned with a bottle of XO and another glass.

As she poured the fresh glasses, I played with a couple of strands of her long brown curls.

"So Tanyusha, is it time for my special birthday blow job?" I asked.

"I don't know. Have you been a good boss?" she whispered sultrily.

Tanya had been working for me for nearly five years, and was almost family. I liked to joke around with her and she usually answered back. Once in a while things went further than just joking.

I was generally faithful to Masha. Occasional slips, such as getting a blow-job from Tanya, weren't a sexual relationship. There was nothing romantic or emotional involved. If it worked for Bill Clinton, the President of the United States, when he got a blow job from Monica Lewinsky, then it should work for me.

Admittedly, it was a bit of self-deceit, but I honestly thought that this was only a minor misbehaviour. I would never have a romantic relationship with another woman and betray Masha's trust. I considered myself a modern man, unlike most of my Ukrainian and Russian colleagues, who weren't faithful to their wives. I expected total loyalty from Masha and my close men and I repaid their loyalty with mine.

"I'm always a good boss," I argued.

"Maybe another time, Romeo. Your bed is still warm from your wife's body."

"And now I've lost my libido. Thank you, Tanyusha."

"Anytime, horny boss," Tanya said, leaning over and gently squeezing my penis through my trousers.

"You're such a tease. Maybe next time I won't ask. I'll take you when you least expect it."

"Promises, promises," she said, laughing. "Anyway; I have more important things to do than playing with your cock."

And with that, Tanya stood up and returned to the kitchen to grab her bag, and then left the apartment. I sat there drinking for a couple more hours, and as the sun went down I stepped out onto the balcony and took up my position overlooking the beach, restaurants and bars as the night-time lights were turned on. Tel Aviv was such a peaceful city, right in the middle of the crazy Middle East. Another year had passed, and still I had one thing to conquer.

There was a Forbes' Rich List to top. This was my Mount Everest.

"Onwards and upwards," I said as a toast to myself, and drained the last of the amber liquid in my glass. It was time to go to sleep as I had a jet readied to make the early morning flight to Zurich to meet with our friends from Belarus.

31 The Road to Minsk

Zurich, 2013

The private jet landed in Zurich Airport just before noon. The project in Belarus was too important to be left for Boris and David, and although I trusted them both implicitly, I wanted to personally test the waters.

Through Boris' connections we were able to organise for the Chairman of the State Committee on Tenders of Belarus to meet me for a couple of hours. It goes without saying that we paid all his expenses, which included first class flights, a five star hotel, top-class entertainment while in town, and some cash to cover all his miscellaneous expenses, trouble and valuable time. I wanted to understand whether the tender was tightly rigged or surprises could be expected. I had a low tolerance for surprises.

We met for lunch at the two Michelin-starred restaurant at the Dolder Grand Hotel, where a private room had been specially arranged for the two of us. To clarify who was the boss, I waited outside the restaurant so I was ten minutes late. When I entered the room Kirill was already ordering his drink. I didn't know Kirill but recognised him immediately from his photos on the internet. Boris called Kirill 'The Consultant.' He was in his sixties, below average height, overweight and balding.

"Vorotavich... Mikhail Vorotavich," I introduced myself and extended my hand.

"Kirill Vishnevsky," he replied and firmly shook my hand. A handshake tells a lot about a man. I don't trust people with a weak handshake. Between ordering the food and its arrival I broached the subject of our meeting.

"Look, Kirill, I see Belarus as a major country in my global business network. Belarus and Ukraine are neighbours and it's our national responsibility to promote our economies. The reason that I asked our mutual friends to arrange this meeting was that we want to participate in your country's large-scale tenders. It's important for us to receive fair treatment and a fair chance of competing and winning tenders where we can offer competitive terms."

This was complete bullshit since I had put aside large amounts of money to pay the right people to ensure that the tenders would be anything but fair. However, I took a cautious approach. The recent case of two Israelis who were arrested for allegedly bribing the Georgian Minister of Justice was fresh in my mind.

"As you know, we have bid on the tender for the construction of the new highway between Moscow and Minsk for its Belarusian segment. This is a very important project for us," I continued. "What do you think about our chances of winning the tender?"

"Can we speak openly?" Kirill asked in a soft voice.

"Sure, of course. I wouldn't want it any other way," I answered.

"The final decision will be made by the president himself," Kirill explained. "I don't know whether he's yet to make up his mind or has already decided. At this stage we're instructed to reduce the number of bids from six to three. Any new bids will be rejected."

"I hope that we're part of the remaining three," I said, half-stating a fact and half asking a rhetorical question. "This is a strategic project for my group and a significant project for me personally."

"You're part of the remaining three. Otherwise, I wouldn't have come to meet you in Switzerland," Kirill reassured.

"It's good to hear that we're being appreciated by the Belarusian authorities. I understand that a company headed by the president's nephew is also one of the bidders. Have you received any instructions about his company?" I asked.

I knew that if the winner of the tender hadn't been known, a tender of that scale wouldn't have been published. I was certain that Kirill knew already who was going to win.

"No, we haven't received any such instructions. As per my experience we'll receive instructions only after the tender is closed," replied Kirill, like a practised actor.

I knew he was talking shit, and it was time for me to lay everything on the line.

"Look, Kirill, I know that you're a loyal man of the president. You won't do anything without getting his instructions and anything you do is in line with such instructions. I appreciate loyalty. We have a reasonable basis to assume that our bid is very good and very competitive. All I'm asking you is to keep me updated if at any stage in the process the wind blows not in our direction. Is that okay?" I said.

Without waiting for his response I added, "The country will remember its heroes, Kirill."

I used the sentence that everyone knew was the code for a payment for services. At the same time I removed a white note out of my pocket and wrote '1,000,000 US dollars' on it. After Kirill nodded, probably taking a second to count twice the number of zeros, I put the note back in my pocket.

One million dollars was an excessive amount by Belarusian standards. According to the background information that was collected for me, Kirill wasn't used to such amounts. I was sure that this sum was higher by at least one zero than any payments that he had received so far. However, I had a few reasons to spoil him.

Although not a youngster, Kirill was a rising star in Belarus and was in the president's close circle. The regime in Belarus was considered strong and I was certain that the Chairman of the State Committee on Tenders of Belarus wasn't the highest position that Kirill was going to reach before retiring. Paying him above his expectations was a long-term investment. I had no doubt that this was a worthwhile investment with high expected returns.

In addition, there were reasons to get Kirill on my side for this particular tender. This was a strategic tender for Neplokho and our first foot in the door of Belarus. If Kirill reported to the president on bribes, and he probably did, the payment to Kirill would put us in a positive standing with the big boss. We would come across as being generous. Even when it was said that the tender was closed, at the magnitude of this tender I couldn't be sure at any stage. The winning bidder could be thrown away if the president got upset.

"Thank you for meeting me, Kirill. It's been a pleasure. And please, the suite is at your disposal if you want to stay on a few days. Anything you want, just have a word at the front desk and it'll be added to my account. Also, my driver is available to you to take you anywhere you wish to go."

"That is very generous, Misha," he said with a smile.

I already knew he was booked on an early evening flight back to Minsk, and was to chair a special meeting the following morning. It pays to do your research and to have people on the inside.

"Kirill, let's stay in touch then. See you soon."

I left Zurich with a good feeling about the project in Belarus. I felt that we could work with Kirill and I didn't expect any nasty surprises.

32 From the Shadows

Kaliningrad, 2013

The armoured Mercedes left the centre of Kaliningrad and swept along the empty highway that led out of the city. The highway soon changed to a single lane, badly maintained road that was lined either side by a never-ending sea of weeping willows.

"How ironic," The Russian Minister of Defence thought to himself as he stared out of the blacked-out window. "This authentic German city of Konigsberg adjoined to Russia in the aftermath of World War II remained Russian, while Ukraine and Belarus broke away. That's some real nonsense. As always, the army has to amend what the silly politicians did in 1991."

The car sped through miles of open countryside, divided into antiquated farms where people still toiled by hand for a meagre living. The car continued south, where the meeting had been arranged at an old dacha that belonged to a mutual friend - a retired general who also served with the ministers in Afghanistan.

The eighty mile trip was more uncomfortable than anticipated, as the driver couldn't avoid every dip and pothole on the neglected roads, historically built by Germans. Thankfully, after two hours of torture, the Mercedes slowed down, and pulled into a side road that led away from the main route south. Several kilometres later, the obviously once-magnificent old dacha came into view.

"Thank god for that," the minister muttered in relief. "Any longer and my back will be playing up for weeks."

The driver pulled around the side of the house, and parked up out of plain sight, under the ubiquitous willow trees, and next to three almost identical Mercedes. The driver opened the rear door and helped the aged minister exit the vehicle.

"Thank you. Stay with the car," the minister ordered the young driver, as he headed to the side entrance to the dacha.

Without needing to knock, the door opened and a Russian officer met the visitor with: "I serve the Soviet Union," a formal army greeting used in the USSR, and showed him to the meeting room.

"Your colleagues are already here, comrade General," the officer informed the minister. "Please, go ahead."

The Russian minister nodded and the officer turned and walked away. Turning the old-fashioned catch, he took a deep breath and entered the room.

An unexpected blast of intense heat hit him immediately as the door opened. An open fire crackled away, covering the walls with a perverse light show. Standing by the fire, warming their old bones, stood the Ministers of Defence for Belarus and Ukraine, along with the man who had called this unexpected meeting.

"Stanislav, at last," The Belarusian minister exclaimed. "This weather is disagreeable, don't you say?"

"It reminds me of Afghanistan. That winter in the Hindu Kush. You remember?"

"You're just getting old, my friend."

"As we all are, I'm afraid," the Puppet Master interjected. "Now we're all here, let's get down to business. Please; be seated comrades."

Everyone took their seat and waited for the Puppet Master to begin.

"Winston Churchill once said that 'democracy is the worst form of government except all others that have been tried.' Comrades, I agree with the first half of this sentence. Democracy was perhaps good for the West, but in Eastern Europe people need a fist of steel to rule them. A return to the old ways is necessary if we are to remain strong. Together, our countries are unstoppable. If we remain apart, we'll disappear, swallowed by the European Union with nothing but photos and history books to remember our glorious past."

He stopped and looked at each minister in turn to ensure his message was clear.

"Comrades...we've accomplished quite a lot and I want to thank each one of you for your assistance and participation. In Russia and Belarus the prospective opposition is busy with trying to weather through an assortment of criminal investigations. Bogdan here," the Puppet Master nodded at the Belarusian minister, "framed a few of the most fervent anti-Russian leaders for a conspiracy plot against the regime. Very efficient decoy, I must admit. They will spend time in jail, no doubt about it."

The Puppet Master took a short look at the fire that cracked especially loud and continued. "In Ukraine the situation is still equivocal, but if you look at the list of those who were pushing into the European Union's direction, you would see that it's much shorter now. Taras with some help of my men is really cleaning up the Augean stables in his territory. We had to resort to some extreme measures there. Anyhow, stage two of the plan is now in effect. All precautions have been taken, and nothing points or leads back to us."

The ministers nodded in approval.

"Taras; any developments concerning stage one?" he turned to the Ukrainian minister.

"Nothing at all. I've taken care of that episode that we've discussed. The target's people searched all the avenues we expected them to, but there's nothing that ties their findings to us. Hell, I even told my man in Communications, Pilipchuk, to provide them promptly with a list of cell tower records as they asked, after I'd instructed which numbers to delete."

"Excellent. What about that judge Zinovyev?"

"Not with us anymore, comrades," the Ukrainian Defence Minister stated with a broad smile, crossing himself.

33 Disturbing Developments

Geneva, 2013

David and Boris were sat on the balcony of Neplokho's offices in Geneva, taking in the spectacular view over the lake. Swans were gliding lazily along while people were walking next to it with their children and dogs.

David was staring at nothing in particular. It was hard to believe that no more than ten days ago Misha had been shot in the head. Now he and Boris were sitting in those tranquil surroundings, while inside he felt turmoil and rage.

The next day, the results of the tender in Belarus were scheduled to be published, however they had been informed that the President of Belarus had announced that the results hadn't been finalised yet and that the publication was going to be delayed. This was the second time this had happened, and Boris and David were starting to doubt that their group would be successful with its bid.

The first delay had occurred a day after the assassination attempt on Misha, when the president's office informed everyone that they had to discuss the tender's details with experts from Venezuela. Since Belarus was diplomatically isolated, if not estranged from America and the West in general, there weren't too many options from where to bring in the experts. Apparently, they knew how to build highways in Venezuela.

"So, did you speak with the Consultant?" David asked Boris. The Consultant was the insider in the tender's proceedings. "Did he explain why they were postponing publishing the results of the tender again? Does it have anything to do with Misha's injury?"

"Yes, I've spoken with him," Boris replied. "However, he said that they were postponing the tender's closure not because of Misha but because of a technical matter. Apparently, the president decided to take half of the members of the tender committee with him on his visit to Kazakhstan."

"This is very odd. Why would he take them with him?"

"I don't know. It is unusual," Boris agreed.

"This is a real bullshit," said David. "How come he decided to postpone everything in such a critical time for us?"

"Are you afraid that the bastard nephew is going to win the tender?" asked Boris.

"Screw the fucking nephew. Something doesn't smell right here. How come they postpone the tender at the last minute for the second time? Misha even met the Consultant in Zurich and said it was a done deal. I'm concerned that if we aren't able to bring this deal home we're finished in Belarus. It'll be seen as a sign of weakness."

"I know that," Boris spat angrily. "I'm doing everything I can to fix this mess."

"I know," David said quietly. "I'm not attacking you or blaming you. But people may think that we're losing control without Misha. Boris, you need to continue pushing our people to get this tender closed asap."

"You know that I'm doing everything I can," reiterated Boris. "What can I do if half the fuckers decided to go on a school trip to Kazakhstan? Who takes the fucking tender committee with him? And of all the godforsaken places to go, it's Kazakhstan! Why don't *you* see if you can get this show moving any quicker?"

The stress in all the recent conversations between David and Boris was obvious. Both men knew that the Group was at a junction because of Misha's condition and the situation in Belarus.

Boris's mobile phone rang. He looked at the screen and raised his finger to his lips, signalling to David to keep his mouth shut. The entire conversation, or more accurately the monologue, took less than thirty seconds. Boris just listened, and his face, as expected, gave nothing away.

At the end Boris uttered, "Okay. I'll be there."

"Well?" David prompted, once Boris had returned the mobile to his inside pocket.

"Perfect fucking timing. The Consultant says that *Papa* wants to see me tomorrow in Minsk. Nothing to be discussed on the phone."

Boris paused, thinking for a second. He then continued.

"Papa likely means the president, as definitely neither my father nor the Pope wants to meet me in Minsk."

On top of the news about the tender, Andrei Topolski, the Group's chief security officer in Moscow, had reported back with his disturbing news. Andrei hadn't concluded his investigation into the attempted assassination on Misha, but, as Boris suspected, he had discovered that some signs led in Moscow's direction.

This was bad news. Dealing with rival competitors from Ukraine, Israel or the West was one thing. That could be handled. However, the Russians were a formidable foe with massive resources behind them. The Russian government and its secret services would do whatever was necessary to support Russia's business interests. Rarely anything could stop them, even the power of the United States.

It also made sense that the Russians were somehow behind the delays in the tender in Belarus. They didn't want a Ukrainian company to get involved in a project between Russia and Belarus as they wanted the business for themselves.

"Someone is delaying the results of the tender on purpose," David finally said after a long pause. "I wouldn't be surprised if this has something to do with the assassination attempt on Misha. If the Russians are behind it we may be in deep shit. Perhaps Misha hit a sensitive nerve with them."

Boris quietly nodded.

"To tell you the truth, I'm even afraid of going to Belarus tomorrow. Given the latest developments and the potential involvement of the Russians, it might all be a set up. I may be walking into a trap. If they took down Misha, why wouldn't they take me down as well? They wouldn't think twice."

"But you can't just refuse to meet with the *Papa*."

"I know. I have a bad feeling and I don't believe anything they say recently."

"Crap...what is happening to us? And this on top of what's going on in Odessa."

"Odessa?"

"Oh fuck. You don't know yet?" David said, shaking his head and puffing out his cheeks. "With all this going on I thought you were already informed."

"What the fuck is going on in Odessa that I don't know about?"

David poured two drinks and handed a glass to Boris.

"It's not good, Boris. We are under attack from all sides," he warned, before explaining the developing problems in the Black Sea.

***

The previous day, David had received a worrying phone call from the manager of Ukraine Metallum which owned a steel factory in Odessa. The subsidiary factory had received a court order against it that decreed that Metallum's holdings in the factory were to be transferred to a company that had been incorporated only a few days before the court order was served. Someone was initiating a hostile takeover of Neplokho's assets.

David had immediately tried to find out all the information about who was behind the move, but couldn't trace the identity because its shareholder was incorporated in the British Virgin Islands. BVI companies were always well shielded from such enquiries.

It was clear that the takeover was cleverly planned, so as to go unnoticed until the court decision came into force. It appeared that all the court summons were sent to a wrong address, so the court decision was given ex parte, without the defendant's representation or even knowledge that the process had been started. Boris listened closely, his stony face betraying nothing.

"If only Misha was awake," he finally said. "Just one call to the president of the supreme commercial court and the court decision would be suspended. What is his name? Evgeniy or Dmitriy Zinov? You remember; that's the guy who awarded some strategic plant to Europeans in their dispute with Russians a few months ago. It was all over the news."

"I don't remember," David answered honestly.

"Yes...it starts with 'Z' for sure."

While Boris's face contorted as he tried to force the name from deep inside his mind, David watched the expression suddenly change to one of consternation.

"Where is that Swiss newspaper in English that you were reading? Give it to me," Boris demanded.

"It's inside. You want it?"

"Yes, get it now," Boris snapped impatiently.

David ignored his friend's rudeness and headed inside, returning with the newspaper.

"That's the one. Pass it here."

Boris started to leaf through its pages. On the newspaper's eighth page, Boris saw the headline that he was looking for.

"Yes...I thought so. Look at this," Boris said, folding the paper and passing it back to David.

David took the newspaper and studied the headline.

"The mutilated body of the chairman of the Ukrainian supreme commercial court has been discovered in Mariinskiy Park, in the centre of Kiev."

"What the fuck!"

"Read on," Boris prompted.

"The chairman...Dmitriy Zinovyev was reported missing a week ago...by his family...colleagues didn't know...last seen by his secretary, suspected to be his mistress...was barely recognisable. His death may be attributed to recent scandalous suits processed by the court...etc. etc."

David looked at Boris.

"This is a disaster!" he said, placing the newspaper in front of him.

"If it's connected with the attempted assassination on Misha, we're talking about an extremely serious onslaught. This Dmitriy Zinovyev, is what? Probably in eighth or tenth place of the political hierarchy? Misha told me that in most serious legal cases, he was someone we could count on. They were so close that Misha could pass him a USB flash drive with whatever decision he needed and if the money was right, it was printed out as the official court ruling the next day."

"Fuck."

Instead of using force to take the factory, their rivals were using the umbrella of the court, the law and justice departments. They were taking out of the game both the owner and his judicial krysha. Boris and David were silent for a few minutes as the knowledge that unknown enemies were closing in on them made them shiver.

The situation in Odessa required immediate reaction. Boris called the director of Anti-Mafia Limited and briefed him on the situation.

"Be prepared for a physical takeover. I have no doubt that it's going to follow the court decision," Boris warned the director.

David called Misha's connections in Kiev and told them to send a few loyal members of parliament to Odessa to prevent the police from entering the factory. If the police were to intervene on behalf of the anonymous raiders to enforce the court's decision, they wouldn't dare inflict physical harm on MPs.

After both finished their phone calls, David said to Boris, "If you're going to fly to Minsk, I should go to Odessa to manage the crisis locally. I don't see any other choice. We must show that we control the situation."

"I agree it may be necessary. Be careful over there, David," Boris warned him. "I have no doubt that this is going to turn violent. I hope that you'll be back in one piece from Odessa and I'll be back in one piece from Minsk. And I don't mean one piece in a coffin."

"Let's drink to safe trips," David said as he poured another drink. "Na zdorovya, Boris."

"Na zdorovya, my friend," Boris answered as they both emptied their glasses. "Take care of yourself."

A passing cloud obscured the sun and Geneva turned dark for a moment. The darkness reflected well the moods of Boris and David. It felt like the end was coming.

The attempted assassination on Misha, the delay in the tender in Belarus, the slaughtered president of the Supreme Commercial court and the problems in Odessa couldn't be a pure coincidence. Nothing was random in Ukraine. It seemed that they were slipping downward on a slippery slope on all fronts. Someone powerful was behind everything. Someone was pulling the strings behind the scenes.

34 Hospitable Welcome

Minsk, 2013

"What is it? They don't even have a proper summer here? This is shit," cursed Boris as he exited the airport into the cold drizzle that welcomed him to Belarusian soil.

He had hardly slept the night before, with all recent events rattling around in his brain as he struggled to piece together the fragments of information at hand, hoping they would somehow point towards the mystery attackers. Until the small hours he was verifying through a conference call between him, the chief of Kiev's SBU and his colleague in Minsk, that at least the Belarus secret services hadn't planned anything offensive for him. Although senior officer's assurances weren't to be ignored, they weren't 100% reliable. If the Chief of Minsk Security Services received an order from his superiors, he would forget everything that was said a few hours earlier and eat Boris alive.

Boris didn't have a choice but to hope the Belarusians wouldn't kill him. Even so, he asked Arthur to arrange for him the best bodyguards they had in the area to meet him when he arrived in Minsk.

Kirill, the Consultant, didn't come to meet him in the airport's VIP zone. It was a bad omen. Boris wasn't important anymore.

Boris called Kirill.

"Kak dela, Kirill? Where are you?"

At least he answered. They scheduled to meet near Minsk at a dacha of a former deputy chairman of the Belarusian communist party, who had introduced them in the first place.

The usual hugs didn't mean that everything was fine. It was simply the tradition and could well be followed by a gunshot to the head a moment later.

"When do you take me to Papa?" Boris asked Kirill. Straight to business, without excessive pleasantries.

"There will be no Papa," answered Kirill, making Boris twitch as this coincided with his worst suspicions.

"But don't worry," Kirill added with a smile, seeing Boris's reaction. "I have all the powers from high above to hold this meeting and deliver a message. Sorry for using Papa as a pretext. For anything else I wasn't sure that you would come right away."

Boris didn't believe any of it. As if reading his mind, Kirill continued.

"I know you might not believe me, but the situation is as follows. I don't know exactly who, but the Russians are leaning very hard upon all of us, especially there," he said, pointing at the sky in order not to say *president* aloud.

"They want this tender to be cancelled for whatever reason and for one of the Russian metrostroys to win the successor tender. They don't offer us anything close to what we agreed with you. It's a blatant pressure on their part, but you know well that it's very hard to withstand such force, especially since we're so dependent on them. Anyhow, we managed to leave it in the air for now, but the Russians argue that we don't have a deal with anyone, as there's no Vorotavich anymore. And if there's no Mikhail, there's no deal to discuss."

Boris tried to think how to protest against this logic, but he knew that Kirill had a point. He wasn't even sure that he and David together could accumulate enough funds to wire the 20% down payment if awarded the tender. Misha's policy was to keep himself as a single signatory on fat accounts, and Boris and David had only limited powers on some of the corporate accounts. They could manage transferring a few tens of millions. Perhaps even a hundred million. But the down payment was around one billion dollars. That was punching well above their weight. Without Misha, getting the project in place seemed impossible.

"Now," continued Kirill not expecting any obstruction, "my bosses cannot endure the Russian pressure forever. But they do want to do the deal with you, not because of your beautiful eyes, but because you'll make them very rich."

"So where do we go from here?" Boris asked, surprised at the hint of a way out of the mess.

"What I'm empowered to offer is that you have a fortnight from today to organise a letter of credit, confirmed by a 'Triple A' bank, securing your payment, and payable against signed contract for the construction of the highway. Obviously, this demand isn't on the tender's official criteria. But this is a small adjustment that we have to make, given the circumstances. I hope that you can organise it, Boris, as we sincerely prefer working with you and not with the arrogant Russian cunts trying to get in our way."

"Thank you for your honesty. I'll pass on the instructions to the board," Boris lied.

The meeting was over, everything was crystal clear. Boris had two weeks to arrange for the down payment and Neplokho would win the tender. If he didn't arrange it in time, the Russians would take it.

Kirill cordially offered to take Boris to the airport, so this visit wasn't so inhospitable after all. However, the bottom line was that the project seemed lost. Only Misha could organise the letter of credit with only a few signatures on banking instruction forms.

Boris called John and instructed him to get all the papers prepared anyway and have them at the hospital in the hope that Misha would wake and provide his signature. While conceding that it was probably a futile gesture, Boris wasn't willing to give up just yet.

At least Boris was on his way back to Kiev alive, and for that he felt a sense of relief. He could've ended up as worm food in one of the forests of Belarus.

35 The Pearl of the Black Sea

Odessa, 2013

David stood outside the airport and let the sun warm his face. The old outdated terminal was packed with holidaymakers as Odessa's high season got into full swing and it was a full ten minutes before he spotted Maksym, the deputy director of the Odessa steel subsidiary.

David knew Odessa well, having spent many a summer weekend hanging out in Arcadia, the famous beach and recreation area. But this trip was purely business, and David was apprehensive of what he was going to discover.

Finally, he saw Maksym, who was looking around frantically, resembling a meerkat as his head swept left and right. With pleasantries quickly out of the way, they were soon in a car heading out of town to the industrial centre where the steel factory was located.

An hour later they entered the huge business park and turned towards the steel factory. The factory was approached by a long, fairly straight road so that the entrance was clearly in view from a few hundred metres away. As they neared the steelworks, David could make out a large group of young men hanging around the main gate, looking like they were ready to storm it.

"Damn, it looks like it is about to kick off," David exclaimed.

"It has been like this for a couple of days now; I'm surprised they haven't got inside yet," Maksym replied with a shake of the head.

"I don't fancy trying to get through that lot."

"Don't worry. The fools don't know we have a back entrance."

They were coming up to a small slip road. Maksym steered the car off the main road and drove slowly along what was nothing more than a track that led to the rear of the factory.

Once inside, David followed Maksym to the manager's office and was introduced to the factory chief, Arsen, a middle-aged nervous looking man.

"So we have a situation here. What's the latest news?" David asked.

"Well, all those characters outside are waiting for a court enforcement officer with a court writ. I spoke with Odessa's police chief, but he's not going to intervene. He says it's a commercial dispute not criminal, so whatever was the court's ruling he doesn't care. He warned me that if justice is obstructed though, he might hold me personally responsible for any tragic consequences."

"I assumed we had a good working relationship with the police chief."

"So did I. I've drank so much vodka with that guy, that if he says such things to me, it means he has very clear orders from Kiev and it's not in his deliberation anymore."

"How many men did you receive from the Anti-Mafia people?"

"Thirty," Arsen answered. "And two MPs are on site to hopefully prevent the hooligans from daring to smash down the gates."

"So we're clearly outnumbered," David thought to himself, mumbling it aloud. "And I fear the presence of MPs means nothing to the crowd outside."

The report was abruptly interrupted as somebody started to knock loudly on the main gate, which could be clearly heard from Arsen's office window.

"Fine. Let's see what's up there. Maybe the courier has brought our pizza order," David joked, hoping to raise morale. Nobody smiled. He, Arsen and the two members of parliament went to the gate.

Arsen opened a small metal window in the security booth and said, "We're closed. Not receiving scrap metal today," treating the visitors as metal thieves bringing stolen metal to trade as scrap for a few peanuts.

"Very funny," David heard a male voice answer from outside. "I'm state enforcement officer Ivan Grachyov and here is the beneficial owner of the factory and its director. Under court order #54/2013 you're hereby required to transfer all factory's assets, documents and territory to this man."

David had to see who the supposed new owner and director was, so he pushed Arsen aside for a second to take a glance. David coughed with laughter when he saw the 'new owner' standing nervously beside the enforcement officer. He was a young man, barely out of his teens wearing a badly fitting, shabby suit and tie and big unfashionable glasses. Clearly the kid was just somebody's dummy, and the real opponents preferred to remain incognito.

Next to the kid stood a rough-looking man with a lazy eye. Something stirred at the back of David's mind, but he couldn't quite bring it to the fore. The crowd started chanting and yelling threats, and when they began waving their arms around and punching the air, David noticed another identifying feature of the man. He was missing two fingers.

While he had never seen the man before, David had listened to Misha's stories about his humble beginnings in Kiev. He knew straight away that the man was Nazar.

Switching places with Arsen again, David let him continue the conversation with the official.

"It's nice to meet you, gentlemen, we were unaware that somebody bought our Odessa subsidiary of Ukraine Metallum. Let me see the papers."

Once the papers were passed through the window, Arsen started to read them, as if he hadn't had the same set of documents photocopied three days before at the court's archive. Arsen was buying time.

David took the chief security officer of the steelworks to one side and spoke quietly so only they could hear.

"You don't bring seventy-something bandits and keep them restless for hours just for the menace. They have a clear purpose, a job to be done. Start calling all correspondents, TV channels and anyone you know who could give us media exposure. Tell them to send TV cameras down here now. Tell them anything you want, just to make sure they come. You can tell them that foreign investors are being raided, women are being gang raped or that extra-terrestrial aliens have just landed here. It doesn't matter. Just get them to send a crew down here right away."

But it was too late. Before he'd finished relaying his orders, a tear gas grenade landed next to David. He instinctively rubbed his eyes, but he felt weak and numb. Another grenade was launched over the gate and David felt himself on the verge of fainting.

"*This is no ordinary tear gas,*" was the last thought that entered David's mind before the blackness shrouded him.

***

David woke with a fuzzy brain, feeling like he'd been on a week-long bender of booze and drugs. He shook his head to clear the muzziness, but it was to no avail. He squinted around the room, unsure where he was, but didn't recognise anything. He wasn't tied up, which was a good sign. As his senses cleared a little, he thought that his arm ached terribly. He lifted the offending limb and realised it was in a plaster cast.

"Ah, you're awake," someone said. David rubbed his eyes and squinted in the direction of the voice. It was Arsen.

"You missed all the action, pal."

"What happened? I remember the tear gas, but after that it's just a blur."

"I'm afraid you took most of the initial blast, and it wasn't ordinary tear gas."

"That makes sense...When I was in the Israeli Defence Force I probably inhaled more tear gas than you could imagine."

"I don't doubt that, David."

"So what happened after the gas?"

"They stormed the factory. A bulldozer smashed through the gates and the MPs fled out the back door."

"Did the TV cameras arrive in time?"

"I'm afraid not."

"Damn. I should've thought of it earlier. How did my arm break?"

"As they started to storm the gate we retreated and pulled you inside my office. You were unconscious. The guy who was carrying you probably inhaled the gas and fell on your arm as he collapsed."

"Fuck."

"The Anti-Mafia fighters fought back, and at one point it looked like the attack might be unsuccessful. But then another five trucks full of fighters entered the compound and

I ordered our men to stand down before there was a total bloodbath."

Arsen had made the right decision by stopping the fight. Further resistance was pointless and clearly would've resulted in casualties. The attackers occupied the factory, and took the documentation and corporate seal. The control, both legal and physical, was lost.

The battle was lost. Were they about to lose the war?

36 Friends

Kiev, 2013

Denis Filatov and I were sitting in a café in Kiev, smoking Cuban cigars and drinking single malt scotch whiskey. Just as Kirill the Consultant was a rising star in Belarus, Denis was a rising star in the Ukrainian business elite.

He was about my age. His hair was darker than coal. Obviously he was dyeing it to conceal grey hairs. For me men who dyed their hair were vain. They weren't aging gracefully, trying to deceive the world about their true vintage year. It was fine for women to do so, since they needed to look pretty and ageless. But for men?

Denis started his career working for me as the head of the transport and commodity department of Neplokho Commodities. I knew when and how much he stole in his dodgy deals with suppliers and customers. However, Denis, the crook knew how to bring money for the Group too, so I kept him as long as I could control him.

He left the Group when he saw an opportunity to take over a truck factory in Kremenchuk. However, we remained in an amicable relationship. He didn't betray my trust so there was no reason to punish him. He made sure to tell everyone that I was his business guru. It was good PR.

Denis lit a cigar that I offered him, finished his whiskey, waived his empty glass to the waiter to fetch him another one and complained,

"Misha, I don't believe this country has a future anymore. Now I've heard that the president's family wants to take over Ukraine's entire automotive industry. And you know how these things are done. You receive an offer to sell your holdings for one tenths of their value. If you don't it's a suicide since the police, SBU, tax, bandits and every fucking other authority are on you the minute the deadline for accepting the offer expires. I don't feel that comfortable here anymore. If they put an eye on my factory, I don't think that even you could help me."

"Well, I don't know, Denis. I can be in the same position myself. I hope it never comes to it. But if you need something, let me know. I'll see what I can do," I replied, already sensing that this was a theoretical preamble to a practical question that Denis was going to ask.

And indeed, I knew him well, as he jumped on my offer.

"Thanks a lot, Misha. I really don't know how you manage to make money in this country being such a kind person. There's one thing that you could help me with. I know that you retain the best possible security in this dangerous country. I'm beefing up my security personnel to regain a bit of confidence and I would really appreciate it if you could send Arthur for a few days to train them in Kremenchuk, once I have it ready."

"You can count on it," I replied, relieved that he didn't ask for more complicated favours.

I often asked Denis to bid in tenders in which I needed a dummy competitor. These favours weren't free. Denis knew how to leverage my political connections for his benefit when he needed something in return. While we had good relations and we often went out together, I couldn't call Denis a friend. I knew that he would sell me out without thinking twice if the situation made it worthwhile for him. He probably wouldn't think twice before selling his own sister if enough money was involved.

"*With friends like Denis, who needs enemies,*" I thought to myself.

37 The Investigation

Kiev, 2013

David, still recovering from his trip to Odessa, flew from Israel to Kiev to meet with Boris and Andrei to discuss how the investigation into Misha's shooting was progressing. As was becoming all too common recently, the meeting didn't go ahead as planned. Andrei decided to stay in Moscow to closely monitor what he described as a rapid unfolding of events there, so he suggested holding a conference call instead of a face-to-face meeting. Arthur, who was in Israel protecting Misha, was added to the call. When they all dialled in, overcoming the usual technical difficulties of hosting a call from three different countries, Boris gave Andrei the order to begin.

"I had someone look into our friend Denis, as Arthur requested."

"I knew that snake would be involved somehow," Boris spat. "And what did your man discover?"

"He discovered that Denis has been meeting with Zoltan Lazarev, a senior director at Russia Highways, which won the tender for the Russian segment of the new highway between Moscow and Minsk."

"That's very interesting, Andrei," Boris said.

"And why is that?" David asked, as he didn't see the connection.

"Denis worked for Neplokho Commodities, before he went on his own and bought a truck factory in Kremenchuk."

"Well, my man started following Denis around the clock. They saw Denis also meeting with Natalia Myasnikova," continued Andrei.

Boris hit the table with his fist.

"Blyad suka. The bitch! Were those intimate meetings?" he roared. Boris had been fucking Natalia for the past six months. From plain jealousy his mind jumped to a more sinister idea, "She has been working with Denis. She has been sleeping with me to try to get info," he screamed, shaking his head. "The fucking bitch!"

"Yes, this is our suspicion," Andrei continued. "I'm sorry, Boris. Have you told her anything about the project in Belarus?"

"Perhaps...general details? You know how it is. The bitches are impressed when you tell them about big deals and anyway the project isn't exactly a secret. How the hell could I know that the bitch was sent to spy on me? What is she, some kind of Mata Hari?"

There was silence for a few seconds as everyone contemplated the information that Andrei had shared with them so far. Boris broke the silence.

"You know what? I was supposed to meet the bitch after we had the meeting when Misha was shot. She knew when and where we were going to be. Maybe she worked with the assassins. Maybe she gave them the details so they could shoot Misha."

"I've consulted with some people in Israel. People whose opinion I trust. They said that Misha was shot by professionals based on precise intelligence. They knew when and where he was going to be. They were likely working with a mole inside our group. I bet Natalia gave them the info," David added.

"So," Andrei continued, "we suspect that Natalia was working with Denis to provide information about the project in Belarus to Zoltan. Zoltan and Russia Highways have a clear motive to get us out of the picture. One possible conclusion is that they chose to do so by taking out Misha. Another incriminating fact against Denis is that he had asked Misha to send Arthur to Kremenchuk just before the assassination attempt. It was convenient for the attackers to remove Arthur so our defences were weaker. However, we have no proof yet that connects them with the assassination attempt and I'm not sure whether we will. All we have is circumstantial evidence, not a direct link."

"Then keep looking," Boris said angrily.

"It gets more complicated than this. We tapped Zoltan's mobile after we suspected that he was involved. We intercepted a call made to Ruslan Sanayev, a former director in the JV between Ukraine Metallum and the economic department of Chechnya. As you remember, we took over the JV in 2005 and the Chechens got really upset. Apparently, Zoltan has been keeping Ruslan updated with the details of the tender for the highway. Ruslan asked Zoltan to speak with the *White Tiger* to *clear the ground for new players*, as he phrased it."

"Who the fuck is White Tiger?" demanded Boris.

"We don't know."

"Then find out. We must conclude that the Chechens are trying to get their bid into the tender, and this could be killing two birds with one stone for them: taking revenge on Misha for taking over the JV and taking over a major infrastructure project in Belarus, snatching it from us and the Russians."

"Wow, even the Chechens are in our way again. Can't be good," David conceded as he massaged his forehead.

He looked at Boris who now stared out of the window, deep in thought. Arthur was silent on the phone. Arthur was always silent, so it didn't mean anything.

Andrei carried on, "There are two other leads. Colonel Ivanenko blames Misha for losing his position with the SBU. We weren't able to make much progress, but the colonel has the means and motive to hurt Misha. He may work with the SBU, alone or, who knows, perhaps with the Russians or Chechens. Ivanenko could be involved, but for now I suggest that he should continue to receive his monthly pension so he won't have any suspicions yet."

"And what about Nazar," David asked, remembering the thug from Misha's past turning up in Odessa.

"Well, I put my men on him as soon as you called me the other day. It can't be a coincidence that he was involved in a raid on one of Misha's businesses. Nazar has a strong motive. In fact he has two: his fucking fingers."

"This sounds like a twisted Agatha Christie novel," David said. "We have twelve suspects in a room and probably the butler did it. I have a headache. My head is exploding."

Boris leaned forward and gestured to David that he was ready to speak.

"Good job so far, Andrei. But I want you to keep digging. Whatever you need, you call me."

"I will do that, Boris. I have one more thing. This is going to blow you away…"

BOOM!

David thought that his head exploded. His ears were ringing. He grabbed his head with both hands forgetting that one was broken. His ears were sensitive to loud noises after spending years in the military, enduring loud artillery barrages. After discovering that his head hadn't actually exploded, he understood that the blast was heard on the phone.

"What the fuck!" David cried, looking at Boris and wincing from the acute pain in his arm.

"Andrei? Arthur?"

"I'm here," Arthur's unmistakable growl replied.

"Shit...It's Andrei. Andrei! Andrei!" David screamed at the phone.

He exchanged a worried look with Boris. This was bad. Arthur's voice came through again, flat and emotionless.

"Try Andrei on his mobile phone."

Boris fished his mobile from his pocket and punched in Andrei's cell number.

"Not fucking available," he snarled.

Finally, after a number of attempts to reach someone in Moscow, one of Andrei's subordinates called Arthur to report that Andrei had been blown up by a car bomb set off next to his office. The bomb was large enough to bring down the whole building with multiple casualties. Within minutes the area was full of police cars, fire trucks, ambulances and secret service agents. There was no way to approach the debris at the moment.

David didn't know what the others felt, but he was in a panic. Even when participating in military operations in Lebanon as a soldier of the Israeli military and being under mortar fire from Hezbollah, he didn't feel such horror. Nothing was more terrifying than trying to fight an unseen enemy.

"Listen," said Boris. "As long as a few of us are still alive to hear this, you must know the following. I've spent the last two days with the Minister of Defence of Ukraine, working on him so he would appoint Neplokho Defence as the intermediary for selling naval systems. While most of the base in Crimea will remain leased to Russia until 2042, in 2017 parts of it will return to Ukraine, meaning there's the possibility of Ukraine becoming a big player in the sale of naval systems. This is going to be a huge project and we want in. Misha insisted I make this potential deal a priority."

After taking a deep breath, Boris continued, "I took Taras to my usual resort to indulge him with sauna, prostitutes and non-stop drinking. After he was completely drunk and exhausted from all the physical activity, he started to mumble about the Russians and Belarusians. I thought that he was speaking about the highway. However, he mumbled something along the lines of 'the soviet union will rise again,' 'the three true soviet republics will unite,' 'the traitors can go to NATO,' and so on. He was mostly talking to himself without really noticing that I was sitting there with him. Perhaps the steam and heat of the sauna, together with the vodka got him confused. He isn't a young man anymore and shagging two young whores in the heat, while drinking non-stop, took their toll."

Boris gave another dramatic pause before delivering the punch line.

"Then he said, once he realised that I was there with him, 'I didn't want your boss to end up like that. It was the Puppet Master who wanted him dead. All this nonsense about Ukraine joining the EU had to be terminated.' Then, on the verge of fainting, he mumbled 'the Puppet Master called your boss his son-in-law. Your boss isn't his son-in-law, is he?' He then lost consciousness. What do you think this means?" Boris asked.

It was a lot of information to take in.

"One more thing I should mention. Andrei located the apartment from where the shot must've been taken. It's overlooking Parus Business Centre's entrance and was rented for a short period a few days before the attack. But we're still working on trying to identify who rented it. The tracks are well covered and we couldn't find any leads yet. I have an entire team working on it."

David was the first to respond.

"So it's Nazar, Colonel Ivanenko and the SBU, the Russians, the Chechens or this mysterious Puppet Master. Who the fuck is the Puppet Master? White Tiger, Puppet

Master. This sounds like a fucking fairy tale. What next, a talking lion and a dwarf with big feet? We have no fucking clue who did it, do we?"

Boris shook his head.

"And what is with this son-in-law business?" David carried on breathlessly. "Misha is the son-in-law of the Puppet Master. Are you fucking kidding me? What is this, Darth Vader tells Luke Skywalker that he's his fucking father? Am I crazy or does everyone else think that none of this makes any sense? It all sounds like a melodramatic Latin soap opera. We must call Masha to find out if this son-in-law thing means anything."

Then Arthur finally added his thoughts to the conversation.

"I know Puppet Master. He was head of KGB before the end of Soviet Union. He was my instructor in officers' academy for short while on strategic operational planning. He's no longer with KGB, of that I'm sure. If he's behind this, and judging from the multiple targets dealt with precisely and simultaneously he may well be, then officially nobody is behind this. If he's involved, then he's the prime adversary. All others play secondary roles."

David and Boris were in shock.

"What a big fucking pile of shit," concluded Boris wisely, pouring himself a large vodka. "That what happens when you climb the rich tree. Too many people want to see you fall down; those that you stepped over on your way up and those who are still above you."

38 The Work of the Righteous is Done by Others

Tel Aviv, 2013

David was asleep at his flat in the centre of Kiev. Unusually, he had gone to bed at ten o'clock, feeling drained after a stressful couple of weeks of flying back and forth between Tel Aviv and Kiev. As he lay in bed, tired but struggling to fall asleep as the recent events played over and over in his mind, his mobile phone started ringing on the table beside his bed.

"Hello. Who is it?" David said drowsily.

"David. This is Shimon. We have information for you. Can you talk?"

It was agent Shimon of the Israeli Mossad.

"Is your end secure?"

"Of course. Listen to me. A Chechen man called Xava Zelimkhanov is going to board a flight from Grozny to Tel Aviv, via Moscow, tomorrow morning. Ruslan Sanayev has sent him. We suspect that Xava is going after Vorotavich. We don't want to get officially involved, but the information is verified. We leave it to you. Once you extract information from Xava, we expect you to report back. Understood?"

"Understood," said David. "Thanks, Shimon. I appreciate it."

David swung his legs awkwardly out of bed and nursed his painful, still broken arm. After padding uneasily to the kitchen and grabbing a bottle of water from the fridge, he called Arthur.

"Arthur," he said once the connection was made. "I have something for you. A man called Xava Zelimkhanov is going to land at Ben Gurion tomorrow on a flight from Grozny coming through Moscow. He might travel under a false identity, so be aware of that. My connections tell me he's coming for Misha. Get him and squeeze every bit of information from him. Don't kill him before he talks, we need to start connecting some dots."

"Da," Arthur answered, and killed the connection.

***

Arthur waited at Ben Gurion arrivals area. Accessing the Russian security services' archives was a matter of connections and money. Arthur had both. His contacts had located Xava's file in the archives and emailed the picture that morning, so Arthur was ready to intercept his prey. The secret services had a thick file on Xava as he had fought against the Russian Army in the second war in Chechnya. Arthur flicked through the file with interest. Xava was a professional.

The plane landed on schedule, and Arthur shadowed the target as he walked to the taxi rank.

Xava stopped momentarily as he looked around, and Arthur bumped into him, quickly injecting a strong tranquilizer into Xava's thigh. It took less than two seconds for Xava to almost collapse into Arthur's arms. Arthur held on, smiling and patting Xava's back.

"Oh, my friend. You drink too much on the flight, yes?" Arthur said as he easily manhandled Xava away. There was nothing suspicious in two men hugging each other and one helping the other to walk to their car. To a casual observer it was just another drunk Russian visitor needing a helping hand.

A white BMW pulled up alongside Arthur, and the driver, Uri, who was a former IDF and Israeli SEAL, jumped out and helped Arthur get Xava into the back seat. They exited Ben Gurion and headed east to pick up Highway 6, which would take them to Qalqilya, a Palestinian city in the West Bank. Around forty five minutes later they arrived at a small garage on the city's outskirts, where they had an arrangement with the garage owner to ensure their privacy.

Arthur blindfolded Xava and tied him naked to a chair in the middle of the empty garage. They waited another forty five minutes to let the tranquiliser leave his system, before splashing cold water on his face. After a bit of slapping, Xava came around.

"Good morning, sunshine. You're going to tell me why you're here, who sent you and who shot Mikhail Vorotavich. You can do it quickly and we'll kill you quickly. You can do it slowly and we'll kill you slowly. Your choice. We have all the time in the world. You're going to tell us everything anyway."

Arthur removed Xava's blindfold to let him have a quick peek at his captors. The traditional torturer's tools of the trade were spread out on a small table next to Arthur. As ironing the flesh was one of Arthur's favourite methods, a brand new steam iron was puffing away and making friendly noises, signalling that it was ready for use. Uri's preferred style was more surgical. A scalpel, ten long, thin nails and a small hammer.

After twenty minutes, Xava couldn't take anymore.

Xava cried out in pain as Arthur ironed the inner thigh, creeping slowly towards the groin area.

"Stop! Stop! Infidel dogs! Just stop. I'll tell you everything."

"Good, now that wasn't so hard, was it? Start talking."

"I came to kill Vorotavich. Ruslan Sanayev sent me. I heard that Ruslan wants Vorotavich out of some tender so his boss can take it instead."

"So the Chechens tried to kill Misha?"

"No. No, they had nothing to do with the assassination attempt on Vorotavich. I swear. If they did, then I would know. The work was done by others. That's all I know."

"Bullshit!" Uri shouted, and smashed a hammer into Xava's fingers. Xava screamed in agony.

"It hurts, no? Don't worry, I'll stop the pain," Uri said softly as he picked up the scalpel and started slowly slicing off two of the shattered digits.

"Stop, please stop. I don't know who tried to kill Vorotavich. I swear to Allah."

"Is there anyone else working with you?" asked Arthur.

"Yes, yes. There was another guy on the plane with me," Xava said. "We never work alone. Sultan Alidarkhanov is probably slicing the throat of your fucking pig boss right now."

"Thank you," Arthur said, and shot Xava in the head.

"Bloody hell!" Uri shrieked. "He must know more."

"No, he told us everything. We can't hang around here; this Sultan may be at hospital already. Quickly go tell owner to get rid of this scum. We need to move."

Uri rushed off to settle up with the garage owner, while Arthur made an urgent call to his people at the medical facility.

"Is boss okay?" He asked, once the call was answered.

"No change in his situation," the guard reported.

"Don't leave his sight. I want one of you in room with him and second one at his door. We believe Chechen guy is on way to hospital to kill boss."

"No problem."

"I'm in West Bank now, so I'll be there in about an hour, okay?"

Arthur hung up before the man could answer, and speed-dialled David to report what had just happened. Uri reappeared and together they sped off back towards Tel Aviv.

"Is sorted?" Arthur asked Uri.

"No problem."

"Good. Now get a move on."

It took over an hour to get through the heavy traffic and reach the hospital. Arthur rushed to the private room where the guards reported that nothing untoward had happened. Arthur did a search of the hospital, but there was no sign of Sultan or anyone else that shouldn't have been there.

This was puzzling. Arthur knew when a tortured man was lying, and Xava had been telling the truth.

The Chechens sent men to kill Misha this time, but it wasn't them who shot him. While the Chechens were the worst foes that Arthur had fought, there was only one who was even worse: the Puppet Master.

***

Agent Shimon flashed his credentials to the guard, who signalled to his partner for the barrier to be raised. The SUV with blacked out windows headed to a distant hanger which, although it looked abandoned, was actually a cover for the entrance to the underground holding area. The SUV pulled into the hanger and disappeared from sight.

Agent Avner jumped out and opened the rear door. Taking the prisoner roughly by his restraints, he pulled the hooded man from the vehicle, where he crumpled in a heap at Agent Avner's feet.

"Get up, Sultan," Avner sneered. "We're going to have a little chat about what you're doing here in my country. Do not think you can withhold anything. I promise you that if you refuse to answer our questions, we have many ways of persuading you otherwise. Everybody talks before the end."

Sultan Alidarkhanov rose to his knees with his head bowed. Avner looked at Agent Shimon, who smirked back at him. Years of experience told them both that the prisoner was going to comply with little or no pressure.

Shimon joined his partner and, taking an arm each, they lifted Sultan to his feet and frogmarched him to the entrance of Mossad's Interrogation Centre.

"I wonder if the other guy will be an easy nut to crack?" Agent Shimon speculated.

"David has some tough Russian friends. We shall see when we compare notes with him."

39 Another Day at the Office

Kiev, 2013

The clock reached four a.m. and the man opened his eyes. He had trained himself to wake up when he needed to, always before any alarm clock went off. Iron discipline. Rely on nothing and no one but yourself.

He had executed more than twenty five people in the past five years, and to those in the know, he was considered the most reliable, slick assassin in Russia. His operators knew that he got the job done, no matter who the target was. No discrimination based on age, gender or race. He was an intense man, who killed people for a living. No wonder that people who knew his profession, weren't comfortable around him. He liked the mix of fear and respect that he evoked in others. His codename was the *White Tiger*. It was appropriate. The tiger sits at the top of the food chain, subordinate to no one.

After taking a cold shower, he ate breakfast, dressed in his normal plain dark-grey clothes, checked that his equipment was ready, closed the suitcase, and left his apartment. Just another day at the office.

The key was under the rug as requested. He entered quickly and locked the door behind him. The apartment was empty, except for one chair and a kitchen table. He moved the table next to the window. He placed the suitcase on the floor, opened it and assembled the Dragunov sniper rifle. He attached a bipod to the rifle, placed it on the table, loaded it and scanned the area through the optical sight. His target was to emerge near the high rise business centre, approximately three hundred metres away. The perfect distance for the shot.

Three cars pulled up in front of the Parus Business Centre and parked one behind the other. He zoomed in on the number plates and smiled when the numbers matched the ones he'd memorised. A driver got out and lit a cigarette, and leant casually against the black Rolls Royce. The shooter looked at his watch: 3:37 p.m. Good. He was ready.

Following the driver's example he pulled out a pack of red Marlboro cigarettes and lit one. He had some time to kill before he killed a man. Nothing moved inside his soul. He drank some water that he'd brought with him and performed a few simple stretching exercises to prepare his muscles for a long, motionless wait. He assumed the position, looking through the rifle's scope, and waited.

After a while a blonde woman approached the driver, said something and stayed nearby. It was the target's wife. She dialled her mobile phone and spoke for a few seconds. It would be soon.

Less than five minutes later the target emerged from the building accompanied by two other men. The blonde walked towards him and the target stopped, kissed her on the cheek, put his arm around her shoulder and walked with her to the awaiting car. It was the perfect moment.

The White Tiger smoothly squeezed the trigger, aiming just above the target's right eye. He envied that man. Not everyone died kissing an attractive blonde.

40 The Assassination

Kiev, 2013
Kiev was beautiful in the summer. The weather was hot and the sky was cloudless blue. Boris, David and I went to a meeting in the Parus Business Centre in the centre of Kiev.

The meeting was at the office of Dogma Financial Services, a boutique investment bank that we hired to represent us for securing credit facilities in the final stages of the tender for the construction of the highway between Moscow and Minsk.

Project Highway to Heaven was complex and we required extra discretion. Unusually, we came to the bank's office and didn't have the meeting at our office. I was planning to meet Masha after the meeting to take her for lunch and shopping. Boris also had a planned rendezvous with his lady friend, Natalia.

At the meeting with Dogma, as small talk we were chatting about wealthy Jewish bankers and the Rothschild family in particular. My thoughts were wandering. I thought that it would be interesting to find out more about the dynasty of the Rothschilds. Was it the richest dynasty of the nineteenth century? What about that of Rockefeller? I thought that he was the first official dollar billionaire.

Masha was waiting for me at the building's entrance, next to our bulletproof Rolls Royce. I turned around and said my goodbyes to David and Boris. I turned to face Masha and gave her a kiss on the cheek. She smelled so good. Still thinking about the Rockefellers and Rothschilds, I put my arm around Masha's shoulder, walked together with her to the car, heard an unusual hiss followed by blackness.

Then, I woke up and opened my eyes.

41 Good Morning

Tel Aviv, 2013

Misha Vorotavich woke up and opened his eyes.

He looked around confused at the unusual surroundings. A second ago he was kissing Masha in front of the Parus Business Centre in Kiev. Now he was lying in a bed in what seemed to be a hospital room. His muscles felt stiff. It was hard to move. His mouth was dry and his head was aching.

The nurse saw that he was awake and dropped a syringe in surprise. She and the medical staff were under strict instructions to tell only Masha and Arthur if there was any change in Mr Vorotavich's condition.

"Nurse...nurse," Misha tried to say, but his throat rasped, and the words came out sounding more like a gurgle.

"Good morning, Mr Vorotavich. You're finally awake!"

Misha tried to speak again, but still made no sense.

"Here; drink some water. You're at a hospital in Israel. I'll go tell the doctors and your wife you're back with us, okay?"

The nurse held the glass to Misha's cracked, dry lips, and he drank greedily, spilling it everywhere.

"Okay...slow down," the nurse urged. "Now let me go and get a doctor, I'll be back shortly."

Misha lay back in the bed and tried to work out what was going on. The nurse left the room, and seconds later

Arthur burst through the door. To say that Arthur was happy would be an overstatement, but he seemed somewhat excited. This was untypical for him. Even though Misha wasn't 100% aware of what was going on, he was still surprised by Arthur's exuberant demeanour.

"You're awake, boss. Good morning. How do you feel?"

"I'm fine, Arthur. What has happened? Where am I? Where's Masha?"

Not asking *who am I?* Or *who are you?* was a good sign, thought Arthur. At least Misha hadn't suffered amnesia or brain damage.

Arthur quickly updated Misha with a condensed version of recent occurrences, including the discussion that he'd had with Andrei, Boris and David, the situation in Odessa, the purported involvement of the shadowy Puppet Master, Nazar, the car bomb that had taken Andrei's life and the recent unwelcome guest from Chechnya.

Misha had a concerned expression on his face. He touched the scar on his forehead. He put together the mosaic in his head and broadly got the picture. He understood that he was in a great danger. There was a war going on around him and he was no Suvorov, the legendary Russian general who never lost a battle. He was just a businessman.

The persons suspected of being involved were just too bizarre and terrifying to digest. The former chief of the KGB who used to be known as the Puppet Master? How the hell did their paths cross? And why the fuck did he tell people that he was Misha's father-in-law?

Colonel Ivanenko and the SBU? The Russians? The Belarusians? The Chechens? Denis? Even Nazar back from the dead? Half the world was after him.

He drank some more water. Slowly.

He thought that the brave die once, while the cowards die every day from fear. If that was the opposition, the chances of winning the war were slim. But there was no one to whom he could really surrender.

"Don't tell anyone that I'm awake, except Masha and David. Tell David that he can tell Boris. Nobody else," Misha commanded.

He needed some time to think. With Arthur around he felt that he was safe, although even Arthur might not be able to protect him, given the possible enemies that were out to get him.

Arthur left Misha alone to digest the barrage of information he'd been given. Five minutes later he returned with a document folder in his hand.

The last thought that he had before what now seemed to be a dream came into his head. "Arthur, give me your smartphone for a sec," Misha said.

He needed internet access. He Googled 'rothschild' and found it on Wikipedia.

"Fuck. Here it is. The total wealth of the Rothschild family was estimated in 2012 at 1.7 trillion US dollars. Although none of the contemporary family members hold over a billion." He said it to Arthur, who didn't seem to give a toss.

Now, 'rockefeller.' "Fuck me. Forbes magazine considers Rockefeller as the richest person in history evaluating his wealth at 318 billion dollars in 2007 equivalent."

Arthur still didn't seem the least interested in what Misha was saying.

Misha felt deceived, his purpose of being the richest in the world now seemed much more distant than it was. But then, Misha thought, technically, if now the individual Rothschild family members didn't have more than a billion each and Rockefeller's wealth was recalculated in today's value with indexing to inflation, then these all were only calculations. The actual number that mattered in the modern world was today's total net worth. Not theoretical gobbledegook. The thought was amusing. He still hoped to climb the summit of the billionaires' pyramid. Not all was lost.

"I'm sorry, boss. These are some papers left by Boris. He said they're very important and you need to sign them immediately you wake up," Arthur interjected.

Misha took the documents, which had a note inside the front cover that explained everything.

Misha read the instructions twice, then closed the folder and placed it on the bedside table. The documents were to execute a letter of credit to pay the down payment and the project in Belarus was his. He shut his eyes and let the facts roll around his brain. His signature on the official papers was worth three and a half billion dollars. But this wasn't only about money any more. This wasn't only about taking him out of the project in Belarus; it was tied up somehow with a secret plan to unite Russia, Belarus and Ukraine to create a new Soviet Union.

"A few signatures here and I'm one step closer to being the richest," he mumbled aloud.

While Misha didn't fully comprehend all the details of the events that led to his attempted assassination, he understood that there was some kind of conspiracy concerning Ukraine and Russia aimed at some sort of a new union. He and maybe others were seen as an obstacle as they steered Ukraine in the direction of the EU. Misha had the money, connections and political clout to be a threat.

Connected or not, his involvement in Belarus pissed off a bunch of powerful figures. He needed to make a decision between pursuing more money and trying to stop this conspiracy. Did he care enough to intervene? Would he just accept the way it was?

Boris' note explained the delicacy of the situation in Belarus. This was nothing new, but this time the opponents were formidable. He had to make a decision fast.

Two doctors appeared and carried out a series of tests that all confirmed that most signs were back to normal. Exhausted, Misha slept for an hour. When he awoke, his next move was clear. He opened his eyes and saw that Arthur was sat in the room, waiting for him to come around.

"Arthur, get me out of here. Tell the pilot to prepare the plane for take-off in two hours with full tanks. Tell Masha to meet me at the airport in an hour and a half and bring the children. You're coming with us."

"You have bullet in your head, boss. You slept for nearly three weeks. Should you leave so soon?" Arthur asked, the concern in his voice an emotion Misha had rarely heard before.

"It's not a matter of *should*, it's a matter of *must*. We're in immediate danger. We must regroup and strike back. There's no time to lose."

"Okay boss. What's the flight plan?"

"Don't worry about that for now. There may be people monitoring our jet, best to leave it till the last moment when we're all on-board."

"Got it. David and Boris are aware of your recovery; do you want me to inform them?"

"No. I'll call them when we're clear."

***

The jet flew to the Cayman Islands, which is conveniently far away from Ukraine, Europe and Israel. Misha needed time to think about his next move.

A couple of days later the jet took off again, and this time the destination was New York City, where David had used his connections to somehow arrange for a visa for Misha and the family. Those same connections managed to set up a meeting between Misha and the CIA. Misha didn't count on the US too much, as with its current leadership it was no more dominant than Luxembourg. But trying to have a powerful clandestine agency at his side wasn't a bad move.

What Misha didn't know was that it was Mossad that arranged with the CIA to grant him a visa to the United States. David had called his friends at Mossad and told them everything he'd learned about the conspiracy. After comparing details, it became clear that there was a plot involving hardliners from the Soviet era to unite Russia, Belarus and Ukraine. They suspected that military officers and former members of the KGB were involved, although intelligence reported that the presidents and the secret services of the three countries seemed oblivious to the plan. David's information was highly praised.

Shimon even poked him jokingly for the first time, "You're a candidate for a medal, David. Of course nobody can know you received one and if they did we must kill them, but still."

The new Soviet Union would have a significant impact on the global balance of power. It would affect the position of the United States and China as the two leading superpowers. It would affect the balance of power in the Middle East, tilting it towards Russia and its allies, such as Iran. It would tip the dynamics of the global economy as the Soviets would control the global energy market, covering their own resources and influencing the Middle East's oil. The United States, Israel and others should be concerned about the looming implications of such a dark union.

***

The man who was once known as the Puppet Master called his friend in Ukraine. After hearing the report he seemed satisfied. He thought through the entire combination of moves like a Grand Chess Master. Ukraine wouldn't sign any association agreement with the European Union. Instead it would be brought back to Russia's embrace, this time for good.

The naive Europeans had made preparations for a summit in Vilnius to sign the association with the Ukrainian Leadership and to begin negotiating for Ukraine to become a full member of the European Union.

"Let them be entertained," the Puppet Master thought. "Soon we'll announce our little surprise. First we take Crimea, then we take Kiev. If everything goes smoothly, I might initiate a reconsideration of Alaska's sale to the US in the nineteenth century. Two cents per acre paid by the Americans doesn't sound right to me."

The only annoying development was the sudden recovery of Mikhail Vorotavich. He had done too much harm to Russian interests and was a fervent advocate of Ukraine joining the EU. He had too much money, and too much influence. He should've been out of the picture by now. Lazarev's people hadn't accomplished the task.

Vorotavich wasn't a major obstacle to the plan, but the Puppet Master didn't want to have any unfinished business.

While the first assassination attempt on Vorotavich hadn't finished him, it wasn't too complicated to arrange an auxiliary measure. He picked up his mobile phone and pressed a series of numbers.

"It's me. That thing we talk about. Do it. And this time do it right."

***

Now back in the Cayman Islands, Misha watched the sunset over the Caribbean Sea. He was drinking vodka and smoking a Cuban cigar, two of his favourite activities. The private doctor had finished his latest series of checks, so Misha could relax for the evening. How he had survived the assassination attempt was baffling to say the least, but the fact that the bullet had lodged in an area where it could remain without further damage was surely a miracle. He would forever buzz at security scans at airports, but that was a small price to pay.

He was reading the newspaper. One article that caught his eyes was about the Rothschild family. It was revealed that the family had a hidden fortune, previously unknown to the general public, concentrated in the hands of just a few descendants of the dynasty. Its value wasn't revealed, but the article claimed that it was by far the biggest estate that ever been in private hands. Misha's dream of reaching the number one spot in Forbes World's rich list was unachievable. Or was it only postponed?

Misha firmly believed that there was one winner. All the rest were losers. Nobody remembers who got the second place. There was no point going for the second spot on the list. Perhaps he needed a different goal for his life.

He flicked on the TV and found a summary of the latest round of games in the European Champions League. Watford United, his baby, won 2-1 in the group stage game with AC Milan at the San Siro Stadium. What a glorious result, only the second English club to win in Milan against either of that city's two massively successful teams.

Misha's mobile phone rang. He answered it, thinking it would be someone congratulating him on his club's historic victory.

"Hello?" Misha spoke cheerily.

"Misha. It's Sasha. They got…"

The line went silent.

"What the fuck!"

Then a different voice spoke menacingly.

"Vorotavich. We hold your brother. If you want to see him again we'll be waiting for you at Red Square in forty eight hours. Come alone."

Misha knew exactly who it was. He called Arthur.

"Arthur, they have made their move. It is time."

"As you suspected they would. Good…let's finish this."

"Everything is in place?"

"Of course."

"Then it is time to retire these old bastards."

"*This bit I won't sleep through,*" Misha said to himself. "*It's going to be too good to miss.*"

Epilogue

Kiev, 2014

Ukraine was burning. It was hitting the global news headlines as brothers fought brothers in Maidan Nezalezhnosti, the Independence Square, in the heart of Kiev. The country was on the verge of a civil war.

Just over twenty years ago, the same square was full of people happily celebrating Ukraine's independence. About ten years ago, the same square was full again during the Orange Revolution that righted the wrongs of rigged presidential elections. Back then there was no human loss. Now, however, they were killing each other.

But nothing is left to chance. Nothing happens without a reason.

The man who was once known as the Puppet Master opened the door of his office at the Kremlin's underground facility, approached his computer and filled the authorisation forms for the operation *Kievan Rus*.

It was time to take back Crimea. Crimea first, the east of Ukraine second and then Kiev. It was back to the USSR.

Ukraine was burning. The country was bleeding. He was watching with satisfaction as his plan was unfolding before his eyes. The East would rise again.

About the authors

The authors are Ukrainian-born Nik Krasno and Israeli-born Carlito Sofer. Nik grew up in Kiev and was engaged for years in the business and legal sectors in Ukraine. He immigrated to Israel and studied law together with Carlito, who later moved to London. Both are in their forties and this is their first work of fiction.

Acknowledgements

We want to thank David Thurlow for editing the book and Ilanit Galam for designing the cover.

Oligarch Series:

RISE OF AN OLIGARCH, The Way It Is: Book 1

MORTAL SHOWDOWN, Oligarch series: Book 1½

BE FIRST OR BE DEAD, Oligarch series: Book 2½

In the next book:

Misha needs to turn himself in or deal immediately with abduction of his brother, while he realizes that he's in the thick of a multilayered attack on him and his business empire. Making things even worse - among his numerous adversaries is one of Russia's most influential strongmen. From rich and powerful, Mikhail very quickly becomes a fugitive, struggling for survival. Counting on his wits and a handful of loyal associates, he searches for a way to even the score with each of his adversaries and to save his country from the Russian bear's grasp. In order to have the slightest chance in a face-off with his prime nemesis, Mikhail needs to attack head on, undertaking the greatest risk of his entire life. Unfortunately, the dangerous mission goes wrong from the very beginning...